hex

OTHER BOOKS BY MAGGIE ESTEP

Diary of an Emotional Idiot: A Novel (1997)

Soft Maniacs: Stories (1999)

hex

A RUBY MURPHY MYSTERY

MAGGIE ESTEP

THREE RIVERS PRESS
NEW YORK

Copyright © 2003 by Maggie Estep

Excerpt from *The Love Dance of the Mechanical Animals* by Maggie Estep. Copyright © 2003 by Maggie Estep. Reprinted by permission of Three Rivers Press, a division of Random House, Inc.

Published by Three Rivers Press, New York, New York. Member of the Crown Publishing Group, a division of Random House, Inc.

www.randomhouse.com

THREE RIVERS PRESS and the Tugboat design are registered trademarks of Random House, Inc.

Printed in the United States of America

Design by Lynne Amft

Library of Congress Cataloging-in-Publication Data
Estep, Maggie.
Hex : a Ruby Murphy mystery / Maggie Estep.
1. Women detectives—Fiction.   2. Horse racing—Fiction.   I. Title.
PS3555.S754 H49 2003
813'.54—dc 21   2002151269

ISBN 1-4000-4837-0

10 9 8 7 6 5 4 3 2 1

First Edition

To Mark Ashwill, my racing partner, gone into the ether.

To Neil Christner, for insisting this book be written.

To my mother, Nancy Murray, for putting me on horseback
     before I was one week old.

Acknowledgments

THANKS TO Annie Yohe and Kelly Sue DeConnick, for research assistance; John "The Phoenix" Parisella, for letting me lurk at his stable; Cornealius Cleary and Dalton, for a welcome mat at the Federation of Black Cowboys; my editor and friend, Shaye Areheart, for her critical eye and the keys to Zena Road; my agent, Rosalie Siegel, for tenacity, kindness, and gardening tips; Yaddo and all its inhabitants during the summers of 2000 and 2001; The Virginia Center for the Creative Arts; and Tom Gilcoyne at the National Racing Museum.

Thanks to my family, biological and non: Jenny, Stew, Shahram, Jon, Chris, Maman, Neil, Ellen, Lion, and, most of all, John, object of my affections.

Contents

hex

Ruby Murphy

1 / A Scarred Blonde

I'm eyeing a willowy blond woman's red wallet when the F train stops abruptly, causing two large Russian ladies sitting across from me to lose control of their grocery bags. As the Russian women make loud guttural exclamations, frozen pierogies spill out of one of the bags and all over the mottled floor. The larger of the ladies grunts, laboriously bends forward, picks up the stray dough pouches, then passes these over to her compatriot. The smaller woman produces a hankie from the folds of her formless dress, carefully wipes the pierogies off, then puts them back inside the bag.

Meanwhile, the willowy blonde has gotten a better handle on her wallet. She's closed the top of the tote bag it was peering out of. Not that I would have filched it anyway. I'm not that kind of girl. Anymore.

"We are being detained due to an incident at Smith–Ninth Street," the conductor announces ominously. "We hope to be moving shortly. We apologize for the inconvenience."

A nice enough sentiment, only it's piping through the subway car's speakers so gratingly distorted it sounds like a chicken being slaughtered. A sound I recognize because my neighbor, Ramirez, who, I believe, is a Santeria practitioner, does strange things to chickens. Not that I've witnessed this. But unfortunately, I've heard it. And the death cry of poultry sounds a great deal like this F train's speaker.

I cup my hands over my ears. I look back over at the Russian women to see how they and their pierogies are faring. The ladies look profoundly pissed off. Which is evidently a requirement. To be

2 / MAGGIE ESTEP

a Russian living in Brighton Beach, you've got to cultivate a kind of permanent sour puss, like your borscht is revisiting you after three hours of digestion. According to my friend Shapiro, all the Russians in Brighton are in the mob. These ladies look upstanding enough, but for all I know, they're cold-blooded panty-hose-clad killers.

There are few other passengers on the train. Coney Island, where I live, is either the end or the beginning of the line, depending on the direction you're traveling. For two stops after I got on, there were just four of us—a young Dominican girl, her kid, and an old black guy with a bucket full of crabs he probably caught off the pier at Tenth Street. All heading away from Coney Island and its environs.

At Neptune Avenue the Russian ladies got on. The blonde with the red wallet joined us at Avenue U. She floated in, sat down, and immediately focused her attention out the window like she was being paid to study Brooklyn's bawdy exterior and report its particulars to some newly founded Commission for the Preservation of Mundane Details. She looked out of place here in the hinterlands of Brooklyn. She had a graceful long neck topped by a small head, making her resemble a vase with a tiny flower bud popping out of its top. Her lone blemish was a sizable scar beginning at the right corner of her mouth and running along her jawline toward her ear. Her blunt haircut appeared designed to cover the scar, but each time she moved, the hair moved also, revealing the face's secret. In spite of this, the woman radiated a sort of poised and subtly sexy thing that I resent. I am neither poised nor subtle.

I look out at the endless tombstones of Washington Cemetery, standing up like teeth packed tightly in a tiny mouth. The scarred blonde also seems fascinated by the cemetery. Her intense focus is making her right cheek twitch a bit, like there's a glitch in her nearly flawless programming. Eventually, she glances around the subway car. Since I'm probably the only person on the train who doesn't look like a threat to her, she rests her eyes on me and smiles faintly. As if indicating that, in case of emergency, she and I will pair off. I return the faint smile even though, in a pinch, I'd probably team up with the Russian ladies, the crab guy, or even the Dominican girl and her addled tot before I'd want this woman watching my back.

"Running late?" the blond woman asks.

Although she's got her head turned toward me, she's not really looking at me, and at first I think she's talking to herself.

"Me?" I say after a beat.

She nods, arching one of her delicately plucked tan eyebrows.

I shrug. "Yeah, I guess."

"I'm quite late myself but I don't care," she volunteers, looking at me, her eyes like big blue saucers.

I grunt noncommittally and stare out the window.

After a second, I check my watch and start stewing over the fact that I'm going to be late for my piano lesson. Though I'm sure Ramirez—my only neighbor apart from the furniture store on the ground floor—would be grateful if the Juilliard School of Music blew up, taking with it my piano teacher and me, and any possibility of my ever practicing again.

I'm a horrible pianist, but I don't care. Two years ago, when I moved back to Brooklyn after living in Houston, Texas, I decided, at age thirty-one, to take up classical piano. There was no reason for this. I don't come from any sort of piano-oriented background. My mother is a Brooklyn-born former CPA turned dog breeder now living in Scranton, Pennsylvania. My father was a furniture mover until he was struck by lightning and died ten years ago. I grew up in Sunset Park until my folks got divorced when I was eleven. My sister stayed with our mother in Brooklyn. I went to live with my father. He and I roamed the country. He couldn't find a town to be happy in, and we moved nine times in the six years I lived with him. At eighteen I went off on my own to Tampa, Florida, where I met and moved in with an Englishman named Tony who was fifteen years my senior. Tony and I stayed together through four stormy years and five increasingly horrible apartments, the last of which was in a deranged little neighborhood out at the very end of Queens, New York. The house was built on stilts perched over a bay that, in a drunken spat, I shoved Tony into. He'd never learned to swim. I nearly let him drown before finally jumping in and saving him. We called it quits after that.

I moved to Colorado and got a job as a home health care aide taking care of old people. I took up Buddhism. And I drank. By the time I was twenty-seven, I was a seriously accident-prone drunk with a limp so bad I got fired from my low end go-go dancing job. I started hitting detoxes and rehabs. The last one, in Houston, took. I have no idea how I got to Houston. But I woke up there in a detox one day. Among my fellow patients was a pianist named Tom. He'd been a child prodigy and had gotten into pills to calm himself before piano competitions. He was not yet twenty-two by the time he landed in rehab, but was firmly addicted to Valium, Nembutal, and a few other choice pharmaceuticals. He spent much of his confinement there at the rehab playing the crummy Kawai upright in the day room. He was not a very communicative man but didn't seem to mind when I hunkered down in the corner and listened to his exquisite Bach. Where most people would have been happy to simply fall in love with Bach, I had to learn to play Bach. After spending two years in Houston, sharing a tiny studio with my friend Stacy—a beautiful, extremely pierced gay boy I'd also met in rehab—I finally saved some money, moved back to Brooklyn, got a job, bought a 1914 Steinway upright, and started taking piano lessons.

The minutes are ticking by and the train is still motionless. I get tired of staring out the window and I look around. The scarred blonde catches my eye. She smiles, then moves closer to the two seater I'm occupying.

"Do you think we'll ever get out of here?" she asks, using one of her long arms to motion at our surroundings.

"Sure. Eventually." I shrug.

"I shouldn't be in a hurry," she says, "I shouldn't ever hurry again."

"Yeah. Hurrying is overrated," I agree.

She laughs. A tinkly sound like a fingernail flicking at a champagne glass. "I'm late for an appointment. I never should have come out here this morning. But I couldn't help myself," she says.

"Oh?"

"I had to visit my father," she says sternly, frowning a little, making her scar frown too.

"That's nice," I say.

"Not really." The woman frowns harder. "He was a demanding and unkind man. Thankfully, he's dead. I went to visit his grave." She motions out the window, toward the expanse of Washington Cemetery, then turns back to scrutinizing me. "What is it you do for a living?" she asks in a peculiar non sequitur.

I don't like the question. And I take a moment to mull over a good answer. I drop my voice to a whisper and lean closer to her. "Don't look now, but you know those Russian ladies in the three seater across from us?"

The blond woman nods.

"I'm a private investigator. I've been hired to see what they're up to. And let me tell you," I say, "it isn't what you'd expect."

In truth, the only job I have these days is sitting behind the counter at the Coney Island Museum, a sorry but quaint little place nestled atop the building that houses the sideshow. Not many people pass through Coney in the off-season. The only things going year-round are the carousel—with its cantankerous boil-addled keeper—and one rusty bunch of bumper cars. Few souls venture upstairs to the museum to gawk at the lonesome baubles we have in there. Once in a while some eccentric comes in desperately needing a copy of *Sodom by the Sea* or *Good Ol' Coney Island*, the out-of-print books chock-full of old Coney history. Occasionally, a pack of kids will come stake the place out. But there's nothing of value in the museum to anyone who's not a Coney Island freak. The thugs inevitably lose interest and usually end up back out on Surf Avenue. Sometimes they badger the bumper car lady who sits in her glass booth, year-round, as the endless loop of the taped barker intones, "Bump bump bump your ass off."

My little lie has caused the blonde's blue eyes to grow to the size of dinner plates. She steals a quick glance at the Russian women then looks back at me. I see another question forming in her mind, but just then the train lurches forward.

"About motherfuckin' time," the Dominican girl says to no one in particular.

The Russian women both grunt and rustle their shopping bags. Crab Man picks up his crab bucket and puts it on the seat next to him. The train pulls into the next stop.

Three Chinese ladies get on.

The train passes the Smith–Ninth Street stop uneventfully. There's no trace of whatever incident kept us moored in the wilds of Brooklyn for so long.

I've got ten minutes before I'm supposed to meet my teacher, Mark Baxter—an eccentric and highly temperamental Juilliard student—in that fine institution's lobby. I hate being late. I hate giving anyone or anything a reason to be irritated with me. Even as a raging drunk I was punctual.

It's nearly rush hour now and each stop brings a fresh wave of irate citizens. By the time we get to West Fourth in Manhattan, the car is crammed and I have to struggle to make my way out onto the platform, shoving through a pack of maniacal kids being haphazardly herded by a tiny Spanish woman.

I rush up the stairs to change to the A train but an extremely wide man is laboring in front of me, climbing one millimeter at a time, grunting with each step. I try darting around him but can't. I'm barely containing my raging impatience when I feel someone tapping my back. I wheel around, ready to punch them out.

"I'm sorry," the scarred blonde says, "I need to have another word with you." She says it in an intimate tone, as if we've been having a long-term relationship and we need to work through some problems.

"I'm late," I say.

"I'll pay for your time," she says.

"I'm late for an important meeting," I say.

"Then let me accompany you," the blond woman says, her delicate, scarred face hopeful, her voice reasonable.

I envision her hunkered down in the corner of Mark Baxter's practice room at Juilliard, listening as I botch Bach and slaughter Bartók.

"I don't think that would work," I tell her. "What is it you need?" I plaster myself to the side of the staircase so as not to get jostled by the masses.

"I'd like to hire you," the blonde says, completely oblivious to the frustrated people trying to push past her.

"Come again?"

"You're a private investigator, right?"

"Uh . . . well . . . uh, yeah, I'm not licensed or anything. People just kind of give me little odds-and-ends-type jobs," I say, appalled that she's calling me on my crafty little lie. "But listen, I really have to go," I add, as I move out of the way of a pack of angry businessmen.

"I'd like to hire you," she repeats, firmly and loudly, putting a hand on my forearm and causing two teenage girls to stop and look from the blonde to me and back.

"Uh . . ." I stutter. "Why don't you call me and we'll talk about it," I say, deciding I'll be passive aggressive about the whole thing and just give her a fake phone number.

As I forage for pencil and paper in my bag, she adds: "I feel certain you would be the perfect person for this job."

The abject ridiculousness of the situation starts appealing to me. I sigh and write down my actual phone number and hand it to her.

"Call me, but I really have to go now." I turn away, but now my curiosity is piqued.

"What is it you want me to do anyway?" I ask, flipping back around.

The woman's face tightens. Her scar throbs.

It's a man, of course.

"He may not be doing anything at all," she tells me. "He always says I'm paranoid, and he's probably right. I am a nervous person," she says, wringing her long thin hands to illustrate, "but when you told me that you're an investigator, well, a bell went off in my head. I knew what I had to do." She sets her mouth as she says this, looking like a sort of tall, blond rendition of Joan of Arc.

A passing lawyer type ogles her. A short white girl in red plastic pants bumps into me and shoots me a filthy look. The temperature in the West Fourth station is approximately 350 degrees.

"I would like you to follow him around and tell me what it is he does when he's not with me," she says so softly that I almost don't hear her over the blare of the station speaker system.

"Why? What do you think he's doing?" I ask her.

"Having an affair."

"So leave him," I say impatiently.

"I love him."

"Oh, please."

"What do you mean?" Her eyes open wider.

"If you're suspicious of the guy, something's wrong." I start up the stairs again, and she follows me to the top.

"I'm suspicious of everything. There's a hex on all the women in my family."

"Excuse me?"

"Yes. Passed down from my Sicilian grandmother. She put a hex on my mother for having a child—me—with a man she didn't approve of. My mother died young. Now the bad luck has come to me."

"Ah," I say.

The woman looks about as Sicilian as iceberg lettuce. And equally as likely to believe in a hex.

"But that's of no importance," she says. "What matters is that you do this for me." She puts her hand on my forearm again.

"So call me," I say, feeling embarrassed because she looks so relieved. I'm sure she's got more problems than I or any one individual could ever handle, but my life's been a bit pathetic ever since my boyfriend moved out some months ago. Maybe worrying about someone else's disenfranchised love life will help me.

An A train comes romping into the station. I turn and board the train, waving at her through the smeared window. She just stares.

The car is packed and grim. I feel badly for lying to the blond woman. I've never been much good at lying or pulling off scams. It just makes me feel guilty. I decide that when she calls, I'll admit the whole thing was just a story I made up to keep myself entertained. I'll tell her if she really needs help stalking her boyfriend, she ought to try the yellow pages.

Mark Baxter

2 / Her Royal Stubby Fingeredness

I'm just stuffing down some sandwich when I notice that the clock atop the piano reads seven minutes past four. The alarm is evidently malfunctioning. The thing was supposed to go off at 3:45 to warn that my appointment with the Wench is imminent. Though, sadly, I hadn't lost track of time due to being hard at work on the partita, as I had hoped might happen. No. I was merely stuffing myself. With egg salad, no less. And I loathe eggs.

I put the sandwich back in its wax paper wrapping then set it on the corner of the piano so I will remember to eat it later.

I walk down the hall, passing Ian the Idiot, as I like to think of him. Ian is bumbling in front of his locker—no doubt having forgotten the combination again.

"Hello," I threaten.

He quivers, turns around, and looks up from under puffy white eyelids, "Mark." He cowers. "Hi."

"Forget your combination?" I say.

"Uh . . . yes."

I laugh. Bassoon players can't be trusted to remember their own names.

My ladyfriend, Wanda, calls me evil for mocking ninety percent of my fellow Juilliard students. But it can't be helped.

"You're so judgmental," she'll coo in a mock harsh whisper whenever I go on a tirade about the vast ineptitude of the average musician—a pastime I am often prone to right after Wanda's had her way with me, perhaps wearing her red corset, perhaps wearing nothing at all.

"That, dear Wanda, is patently untrue. I'm very fair. If someone is competent, I am the first to acknowledge it. For example, you, beautiful woman, are gifted."

And she'll laugh, throwing back her mane of brown curls.

I never tire of her. The many gifts of her body. Her easy laugh. Her rapt appreciation of music. And I love to sometimes meet her on a job and watch her work, performing complicated electrical procedures like a beautiful surgeon of voltage. I marvel at her lovely hips cinched by her tool belt, implements protruding from the pockets of her work pants or, better yet, from her exquisitely puffy mouth. There is nothing more glorious than Wanda with a screwdriver sticking out of her mouth. And then, when she's done with the day's electrical work, I accompany her home and watch her peel off her tired work clothes, stripping down to a T-shirt and thong, having her way with me and then leaving me to lie dreamy on her futon while I watch her paint. She paints murals on the walls of her apartment as she gets new ideas for her magnificently strange paintings of mythical creatures. Wanda herself is a mythical creature.

And, to some degree, so is the Wench. Her Royal Stubby Fingeredness. Ruby Murphy. My adult student. My lovely walking disaster of a fledgling pianist who never practices her scales and short-circuits at the mere mention of the Circle of Fifths. She came to me through Benjamin, my piano tuner, a lopsided soul who, in addition to tuning, travels throughout fair Gotham buying up broken-down pianos and restoring them. Ruby bought a piano from Benjamin, and, eventually, when Benjamin grew frustrated trying to teach her what little he knows about music, he sent her to me.

She arrived for her first lesson one gray afternoon in October. I'd told her to meet me in the Juilliard lobby. We're allowed to give lessons in the practice studios, and I certainly wasn't going to go carting some unknown new student to my home up at the northernmost corner of Manhattan. Ruby had told me to look for a dark-haired girl in a bright red coat, but it didn't matter, I'd have picked her out of the little crowd without these markers. She was pretty and half wild and just didn't seem at all like a Juilliard student.

I walked by her, then stood a few inches away, examining her from head to toe. She looked a bit alarmed then said, "You're Mark? Benjamin's friend?"

"That I am," I agreed, taking one of her stubby little hands in mine and examining the chewed-down nails. "What terrible things you do to your hands," I said.

She withdrew her hand, scowled, and looked capable of kicking me. Then she laughed. A laugh as easy as Wanda's, and for a moment I wondered if I'd have to court her. Thankfully, her boyfriend had recently moved out and she was nursing heartache. Besides, with Wanda, I really didn't need another wench. And Her Majestic Stubby Fingeredness was certainly a Wench. She'd probably been a gorgeous scullery maid courted by kings in medieval times. Or a court acrobat. Though certainly *not* a court musician. That, I found out the moment I'd ushered her up to my practice room, placed her chewed-up little hands on the keyboard, and ordered her to show me her stuff.

She was a disaster.

And furthermore, she played Satie. I wanted to find the nearest machete and chop her hands off.

"No!" I screamed. "That man lived in a rooming house and urinated in jars. You shall not play his ditties."

The Wench scowled. "What?" she said.

"None of that fussy weird Frenchman, please. And there will be no Debussy either. If you must touch that particular époque and country, you shall go with Ravel."

To her credit, she didn't get up and storm out. She considered me through narrowed eyes then carefully said, "Have you anything against Bach?"

Now it was my turn to throw back my head and laugh. "Okay, go ahead, make poor Johann Sebastian turn over in his grave."

She sniffed, and then, from memory, carefully picked out the first page of a lovely little prelude.

When she finished, I grunted, not giving her approval, though in truth I was heartened. She had a good feel, her hand position wasn't abominable, and she clearly worshiped Johann Sebastian Bach. It was a starting point. I could work with this wench even if she was thirty-three years old and stubby-fingered.

Six months had now passed and she was progressing. She was still awful, mind you, and those fingers certainly hadn't magically elongated, but there was a glimmer of hope that she'd one day do justice to a few of JSB's inventions and perhaps haul herself through some of Herr Beethoven's simpler sonatas.

I get off the elevator and emerge into the Juilliard lobby, but the

Wench is nowhere to be found. I frown at my naked right wrist. Wanda had given me several watches since our dalliance began, hoping I would not keep her waiting when she'd spent the afternoon shopping for a particularly fetching new sex garment.

I scan the lobby again, but no Wench. Just a gaggle of string players, all scattered around one couch, gibbering like small senseless birds. I loathe birds. But strings are, alas, necessary.

I don't want to sit, as those couches have served as cushioning to more rear ends than I care to dwell on. I pace.

Julia, a lanky blond cellist who often eyes me in a lascivious manner, takes the opportunity of my lingering to eye me in a lascivious manner. I turn and deliberately make a face at her, but she does not laugh. I've never been sure why I loathe her, but I do.

Growing impatient, I go outside to the steps, where many nefarious smokers are lingering. Among them is Maria, a lovely cocoa-colored soprano who never gives me the time of day and whom I therefore loathe on principle, her exquisite pipes notwithstanding.

I furiously pace in front of the Juilliard music store, repeatedly staring at my wrist, each time expecting a watch to have somehow appeared.

I am about to give up, go to a phone, and leave the Wench a scathing message on her phone machine when I see her come scurrying toward me. Her long hair is in disarray and her eyes look anxious. She is puffing on a cigarette.

"Put that out now, you'll stink up my practice room," I tell her. "Pianos loathe smoke, and I have food in there too."

"Nice to see you, Mark," she says. "I'm sorry I'm so late. There was an event on the F train."

Though I want to upbraid her a while longer, I'm so pleased at the way she says *event* on the F train that I can't stay annoyed.

"Well, I don't know why you insist on living out there on that island," I say impatiently.

"It's not an island. Hasn't been for a century or two."

I sigh, knowing she is about to launch into one of her lopsided oral histories. I usher her into the lobby, but that doesn't quiet her.

"When the first settlers moved to Coney, it was an actual island," she presses on. "They were a bunch of disgruntled religious zealots who got kicked out of Boston in 1680 or so. Headed by one Lady Moody. They went out there, to the end of Brooklyn, and built a little village. At that point, Coney Island Creek ran all the way around Coney so it really was an island. But the water level or something changed, or maybe it's just full of garbage, I don't know, but the water doesn't fully encircle it anymore. It's not an island now. Though I'd like to live on an island someday," she says, a little wistfully.

"You're so tardy that this will have to be a brief lesson," I inform her haughtily as the elevator lifts us up several stories.

She shrugs. "I figured. Actually, I thought you wouldn't give me a lesson at all. Maybe flog me a little and send me packing."

"Not today," I say, "although on other occasions it could be pre-arranged."

I lead the way through the labyrinthine halls to my practice room.

"Nice sandwich," she says, gesturing at my befouled egg salad on the piano. The wax paper has come loose and the filling is oozing out from its casing of white bread.

"Do not mock my food," I advise.

I order her to play scales. Which she does haltingly. I yell at her about the necessity of practicing her scales, particularly at her age. She makes faces and grunts but then pleases me with her Schumann. It's just a little ditty from *Album fur die Jugend*. I'd learned it when I was five. But she is playing it well, considering I only gave it to her the previous week.

"Well," I say when she finishes, "that was adequate."

I then regale her with the story of Schumann's fourth finger. This was one of the pleasures of teaching the Wench. She delights in anecdotes about the composers. She grows pale when I explain how Herr Schumann, tiring of his fourth finger's inadequacy and lack of flexibility, devised a sort of harness for it. This he attached to a wire suspended from the ceiling. As he slept or idled about the house, he kept the finger in this contraption, being pulled on in order to stretch it. In the end he crippled his finger and his career as a pianist. He then, thankfully for us, switched over to composing. This went well for a while. Until he started unraveling. Possibly syphilis, though such things weren't discussed at the time. In his forties, he tried to drown himself and was then institutionalized. A few years later he died, in the laughing academy, of an unspecific "mental malady."

Ruby looks aghast.

"Don't worry, I won't make you do that," I tell her.

She rolls her eyes, pays me my full fee, and leaves. No doubt getting lost in the halls on her way out since I refuse to show her to the elevator. Perhaps Ian the Idiot will still be bumbling at his locker and offer to help her. Of course, stubby-fingered and inept as she is, I adore the Wench. I wouldn't wish an idiot on her.

When I am sure she is gone and won't come back, I put the sandwich in the trash and cover it with a few sheets of crumbled paper so I won't have to see it again. I check the alarm clock. It is now five. I will fight with the partita for an hour and then, at six, walk the seventy-three blocks down to the loft in Tribeca where Wanda is busy installing lighting in some temperamental painter's new loft. I don't know how Wanda deals with these awful ornery artists. I suppose she's just gifted.

Ruby Murphy

3 / Broken Voices

As the F train grinds to a halt I notice a gamy smell wafting out of my bag. I shut the bag tighter to keep the meat odor contained. Although I'm a vegetarian, my two cats, Stinky and Lulu, live on raw meat. Specifically, organic ground turkey. According to the various natural cat books, raw food is the answer for virtually anything that ails any cat. And my cats are both plagued by ailments. Stinky, a black and white cat who resembles a raccoon, is obese, while Lulu, a small nervous calico who came in my window one day and refused to leave, was apparently abused in her youth and hisses if anyone other than me comes near her.

The raw meat diet hasn't rendered Stinky slender or Lulu sedate, but both cats look better and have greatly improved breath. However, organic ground turkey is hard to come by at Coney. Which is why I usually pick some up from the overpriced upscale food store near Juilliard. Only the stuff doesn't travel well. Even though I have a special dry ice pack in my backpack for the occasion, the stuff is getting malodorous. My lone fellow passenger, an old black woman with the dignified dark-clad look of a Jehovah's Witness, is glancing at me sideways, and I'm very relieved when the train doors open. The lady and I both shuffle onto the elevated platform. There's a nice view of Coney—a bright sight in the middle of summer, when Astroland is alive and churning, but somewhat ominous late at night this time of year, when the place hasn't quite woken from its long winter sleep.

As the woman forges ahead down the stairs, I stop to look

around. Even though I've lived out here for two years, I never get tired of gawking at the place.

The wind is howling, whipping through the shut-down rides that look like dark metal birds, their wings taped to their sides. Off in the shadows, where the old Thunderbolt rollercoaster used to stand, is a big vacant lot. To its right the new baseball park, home of the Brooklyn Cyclones.

Straight ahead, toward the boardwalk, a lone light glows from Guillotine's trailer. Guillotine is a French expatriate who, as the story goes, was a famous clown in his youth but had tremendous socialization problems. He finally ended up at Coney, running one of the kiddie parks. In winter Guillotine hibernates in his trailer with his five pitbulls. He's not the friendliest guy in the world, but that's usually the case with both clowns and kiddie park operators. Guillotine never expresses much warmth to me, but I sense that he watches my back.

As I linger on the platform, taking in the view, I light a cigarette—my first in several hours. Though I've never succeeded in controlling anything in my life, I've recently started trying to control my smoking. As a result, I'm constantly thinking about cigarettes. It takes my mind off sex, at least. Which is pretty much all I've thought about since Sam moved out.

I stub out my cigarette and then descend the endless stairs into the crumbling station. There's a small stream coursing down one of the old tiled walls. Yellowed water streaks over the ancient Stillwell Avenue sign. The whole station is undergoing a sorely needed renovation. All the same, I'll miss the dingy glory of the place and I'll never get over the loss of Pete's candy store, the candy-apple-serving institution with its grimed old windows looking off into the station's bowels.

I pass through the turnstile and wave at Mikey, the token booth man. He nods at me with his chin.

There's not much life on Surf Avenue, just one knot of kids hovering around the pay phones near Nathan's. They eyeball me as I pass by. Not many white people live right around here. There's me. My boss, Bob, who lives in back of the museum. Half a dozen white crack whores who room at the SRO on Eighteenth Street. Mostly, though, it's Spanish and black people and, a few blocks north, Russians.

I turn right on Stillwell and cross over to my building. The furniture store I live above is closed—though there's no telling if they bothered opening at all. The two old Russian cranks that run it are extremely moody. Often they're too irritated to open the store long enough to discourage whatever shoppers happen to straggle in.

x

MY NEIGHBOR Ramirez has his door open as usual. He's sitting at the kitchen table, eating something that looks frighteningly like feet. Maybe chicken feet. Maybe Ramirez makes double use of his Santeria chickens.

"Hey there, Miss Ruby," he says, glancing up.

"Ramirez," I say cordially. We smile at each other for two moments, then I turn to my door and open it.

Stinky tries to trip me and Lulu takes a running leap at my leg. I set my bag down and, for a minute, just stand there, relieved to be home, away from the world and all its debilitating extravagances. I like my apartment. It has odd touches. A strange rounded wooden step leading from the narrow living room to the bedroom. To the right of the step, a wooden door to the bathroom—which has an avocado-colored toilet and sink.

Lulu weaves between my legs and Stinky lets out a wailing hunger cry then follows me as I walk into the small kitchen that some macabre previous tenant painted bright green. I wash my hands then pull the packet of meat from my bag. Lulu leaps onto the counter and starts pawing at the package. Stinky, who's much too large to leap, sits staring up at me, periodically letting loose with a low howl as I mix vitamins and baby food vegetables into the meat, put it into bowls, and set these on the floor.

I open the fridge and stare at the wilted items inside. Brown lettuce, congealed rice, and old carrots assume various poses of desperation. I sniff at some lentil soup I made two weeks ago, the last time I had the energy to cook. Ever since Sam moved out I've been a bit nauseated. He drove me insane and had the communication skills of a hammer, but I loved him. And was vehemently opposed to his leaving. But he went anyway, taking my appetite with him.

I end up peeling a banana, putting it in the blender with some juice and protein powder, and calling it dinner.

I wander into the living room and notice the little white answering machine blinking fiercely. I stare at the thing, wondering if one of the messages is from Jane, my closest friend who's been neglecting me.

I press Play, but no Jane. Instead, I have a series of increasingly fevered messages from the scarred blonde. None of which includes her actual name. She's left me her many phone numbers and various elaborate instructions as to how and when to reach her. Just as I'm pondering exactly how to tell her I'm just some woman who works in an amusement park museum, the phone rings.

"Oh hello, I'm so glad you're there," comes the voice.

"Ah, you," I say to my would-be employer.

"I hope this isn't a bad time," she says, "but I just can't stand it anymore. I couldn't say all of this to you today, but he's gone all night sometimes. When I say something about it, when I express any doubts at all as to the veracity of what he tells me, he calls me paranoid."

I sigh. "You never told me your name," I say.

"I'm sorry. Ariel. Ariel DiCello."

"Ariel DiCello, I say your boyfriend is having an affair and you should dump him."

Silence. Then: "You may be right, but humor me. I'll pay you well. Find out for me."

I sigh again. "Look, I'm really not a private investigator. I made it up. I do that sometimes. Someone asks what I do and I get defensive and make stuff up. I should have told you right off it was a joke. I never thought it would go this far."

Another long silence.

"Really?" she says after a while.

"Really," I assure her.

"Oh."

"So listen, I hope it works out for you, but there's not much I can do."

"I don't know about that."

"What?"

"I think you could help."

"No, I swear, I'm useless. I work at the Coney Island Museum. I've never followed anyone in my life."

"You could do it, though. You have that kind of verve."

"I have what?"

"Verve."

"I thought you said that."

Verve happens to be one of my favorite words. Chances are, had Ariel not said *verve*, I never would have agreed to come by her apartment and meet with her. But she said it.

I tell her I'll come by the next day.

"What time?" She presses.

"I dunno. Afternoon. I got stuff to do in the morning."

"Work?"

"No, I only work Friday through Sunday. Just stuff."

"Oh," she says in a lost soul voice.

"Okay," I relent. "Late morning." I jot down her address on West Twenty-third Street, including her apartment number.

Ariel DiCello thanks me profusely and hangs up.

x

THE CATS are staring at me. The apartment is cold. Jane still hasn't called. It's been three days since we've spoken. She's probably sitting somewhere in a yoga-induced trance and has long forgotten I exist, never mind need attention. I hear a strange thudding sound coming from next door and take a moment to ponder exactly what Ramirez might be doing in there. Then I put on a Lucinda Williams CD and lie in the middle of the living room floor, staring at the ceiling and listening to Miss Williams's beautiful broken voice.

Pietro Ramirez

4 / Crazy Shit with Animals

There's some kind of meat smell pouring into my kitchen, and I'm not even cooking any meat. Maybe it's from that health food meat shit Ruby brings those cats of hers. Girl's out of her mind. Going all over the ends of the earth looking for health food meat for a couple of cats. And I know she thinks I'm the one does crazy shit with animals. One time, I had my door closed and I heard her whispering in the hall, telling one of her friends I sacrifice chickens for some kind of Santeria shit. All because my girlfriend Elsie brought over a couple of chickens one night, wanted 'em fresh and, being as she grew up in some little town in Puerto Rico, knows exactly how you kill a chicken. One of those things her Mami Esposito taught her from the time she was in pigtails. That's just how it was, and Elsie, even though she came over from Puerto Rico more than fifteen years ago, she likes to keep up her traditions. Part of why I love the girl so much. She earns her living as an exotic dancer, letting other men look at her stuff, but she still knows how to kill and cook a chicken.

Ain't no other lady kept me as happy as long as she has. And I've had a lot of them. My mother was a white lady and even went to college, and my pops came over from the Dominican Republic and worked as a mechanic all his life. They raised me and my two brothers in Brownsville, Brooklyn, on a street that was mostly black people. As a result, I don't have a type as far as color goes. I try 'em all. Spanish, white, black, even had a Vietnamese lady I brought back with me from 'Nam. May Ling. Found me next to dead after I'd been lying in a ditch for close to a week, and dragged me into some bunker her and her sisters were hiding in. I don't really remember exactly what all they did to me. I know they put leaves and mud and some kind of animal shit inside my wounds and it made me heal. I fell in love with May Ling and married her right there. Three weeks out of the ditch.

Got my honorable discharge and came back here with her, but she didn't adjust so good. She was always running off to Chinatown and hanging around in the back of some dirty kitchen in a restaurant where some Vietnamese people she had met worked. We never even went to bed once after leaving Vietnam, and when one day she told me she was divorcing me to hook up with a dishwasher at the restaurant, I didn't put up much fight. Easy come, easy go. There were dozens more after her, only I could never stay happy with any of them. Even had a California blonde once. Jessica. Girl was getting a Ph.D. in psychology from Columbia University. I'd met her answering some ad for Vietnam vets. They'd pay us fifty dollars to get interviewed and tested. Psychological tests. Jessica was the one interviewed me. She was gorgeous. Out of my league. But she liked me. I lived with her on Central Park West for a good year before a saucy little Dominican girl I used to see roller-skating in Central Park got to me. I don't even remember her name, but Jessica would. Wherever she is.

The health food meat smell starts to really bother me, so I light up some candles to try to burn the smell out. I go back to sit at my kitchen table and think. The thing is, I've got a problem. My Elsie's not doing so good. Two weeks back, for her thirty-fifth birthday, I got her some new breasts. For a long time she'd been saying she was pretty sure the dancing place where she works was gonna fire her. Thirty-five is old for a dancer, even one whose stuff is as bouncy and nice as it was when I met her five years ago. She keeps thinking they're going to let her go and then she'll have to dance at some low rent joint in Queens where all the girls have faces like rhinos and tits hanging down to their belly buttons.

Elsie's a smart girl, and for a while I've been on her to think about doing something else to make money, but she always tells me ain't no other way for her to make close to two hundred dollars a night, and she has a point. During the season, she helps me with Inferno, the spook house I run over in Astroland, but that doesn't bring in much cash. So, not wanting my lady to be unhappy, I dug around a little and found a doctor to do her operation pretty cheap. Told her about it early so she had the surgery the day before her birthday, and then, presto, at age thirty-five she had some very large and rounded breasts and she was pretty sure they'd keep her on at the job because of it. Only now they're infected. And we can't get hold of the doctor. Dominican guy I know from some people in the old neighborhood. They'd all told me he was a good doctor, only doing it so cheap in light of my being from Brownsville. But now none of them knows where to find the guy either. And my girl is sick. Currently down visiting her sister in New Jersey.

I put my head in my hands to think and then I start to get angry. I try not to because it's no good. When I get angry, I go back to 'Nam. I can't stop it. I throw the chair I'm sitting in against the wall. Then the other chair. I feel like a jackass when I'm doing it but I'm still doing it. A couple pictures come clattering down and their frames smash. My body is shaking and now I don't know what to do. Then there's a knock at the door. It's the neighbor girl. Ruby.

I breathe a few times and then go to the door. "Yeah?" I say to the girl as I open it.

"You okay in here?" she wants to know.

"Yeah," I tell her.

"Ramirez," she hisses at me through her teeth, knowing I'm not okay.

"I'm fine, girl."

"No you're not. Where's Elsie?"

"Ain't here."

"Ramirez," she hisses at me again.

"This isn't a good time, lady, okay? Come talk to me later," I say, and I slam the door in her face.

I feel bad about it. She's a nice girl. Used to be, we didn't really talk much at all. Once in a while I'd knock on the wall if she was playing her piano late at night. That was about it. Then one day her and Elsie got to talking in the hall and became friends, and then, before I knew it, Ruby was always coming over here or Elsie and me going over there. Ruby loves making us dinner. Damned awful health food shit that Elsie claims to like. Me, I just shovel the food around my plate a little, make it look like it's going somewhere.

The thing is, Ruby's interrupting me actually made me feel a little better. I guess it got my mind off my foul thoughts. I sit back down at the kitchen table and take the paper out and go over the sports scores like I actually give a shit about them. Eventually I pick up the phone to try calling Elsie out at her sister's. It rings and rings but no answer and no machine coming on to tell me anything. I put the phone back in its cradle and stare at the floor and suddenly remember this dog we had when I was a kid. Little gray mutt named Pepper. Dog used to make me laugh a lot, chasing its tail and whatnot. I wish I had a dog now. It might help.

Ruby Murphy

5 / Rite of Spring Man and the Scarred Blonde Again

After failing to find out what's bothering my kind but intensely strange neighbor, I retreat into my place and sit at the piano for a while. All I can think of is poor Schumann's finger though, and this depresses me. It's not very late yet but, since I plan to get up early, I decide to call it a day. I change into my long white nightgown, herd the cats over to the bed, and climb under the covers. Sleep comes quickly. It also leaves abruptly at eight A.M. when the alarm wakes me. I stumble into the kitchen, feed the cats, brew coffee, then go back to bed to ruminate and read, drink coffee, and smoke a somewhat foul-tasting early morning cigarette. It takes a lot to wake me up. My father was the same way. He was always in exceptional physical shape. Did manual labor most of his life and ran several miles every day. He ate pretty well and took vitamins. But he also chain-smoked and consumed endless pots of coffee. He couldn't face the day until he'd smoked a half a pack while lying in bed reading.

After he died, I started noticing that I'd taken on a lot of my father's habits. I became an obsessive vitamin consumer while continuing to smoke. I ran every morning until my knees started to wear down. Then I followed my friend Jane into the world of yoga, which I now practice each morning before leaving the house. But not until I've smoked a few cigarettes and had three cups of coffee.

I read twenty pages of *Anna Karenina* then finally get up, put on a bathing suit that doubles as a leotard, go into the living room and roll out my yoga mat.

An hour later I pop out of lotus and rub my sweat into myself.

The Yoga People call sweat "nectar" and insist that it not be wiped or showered away for at least a half hour after practice. I'm not sure why, but I go along with it. It's entertaining to go along with other people's peculiar customs.

After rubbing in my nectar, I put on sweatpants and two long-sleeve shirts, grab a towel, then head outside for a quick walk that will culminate in a dip in the sea, which I do from time to time, even in cold weather, to keep myself on my toes.

I cross Surf Avenue, walking briskly toward the boardwalk. As I pass the fence surrounding Guillotine's trailer, his pitbulls, loose in the little yard, greet me with low growls. No matter how many hundreds of times I pass by, the beasts refuse to view me as anything other than a potential threat to their kingdom of weeds, buckets, and trashed Tilt-a-Whirl seats.

I walk past all the sleeping rides and onto the wide tan beach. A few agitated seagulls are flapping above the flat gray sea, dive-bombing the detritus that's been spit onto the sand. I strip down to my bathing suit, put my clothes in a little pile, and jog ahead into the cold surf.

Vicious needles of ice shoot into me, and in a few seconds I go numb. I dip my head under, listen to the sea's wild roar for a few seconds, then emerge and race back to the beach. A man has suddenly materialized and is standing near my stuff, staring at me. This happens sometimes. I come out of the water and find a person or two on the beach looking at me with amazement. Russian ladies or fishermen or kids from the projects. This is a middle-age black guy, though, just gaping at me as he stands there.

"Did you just come out of that there water or do I need to change my medication?" he asks as I scoop up my towel and cover myself.

"I just came out of the water, yes."

The man has a boom box perched on his shoulder—though he doesn't really look like the boom box type. He has big eyes that are radiating madness and intelligence. He's wearing a worn-out over-coat and his shoe tongues are hanging out. His hair is clipped short and he looks clean-cut, yet somehow off his rocker.

"That's good for you?" he asks, squinting at me.

"I don't know." I shrug. "I think so."

"Huh," he says. "Well, God bless you, lady, and if He don't, I will." He turns his back to me and hits a button on his boom box.

Music comes blaring out, and I stare after the guy because, incongruously enough, the music is Stravinsky's *Rite of Spring*, one of my favorite pieces of music. And not the kind of thing you gener-ally expect to hear blaring out of a boom box in Coney Island.

The guy evidently feels me staring at his back. He turns around, grins wildly, points at the boom box speaker and says, "Nice, huh?"

I nod emphatically. He keeps walking as the bassoon sings its song.

I stand there another few moments feeling happy. It's these tiny bits of unexpected kinship with total strangers that make life worth living.

The wind picks up, and I grab my clothes and break into a jog as I head back toward home. I reach my building, go up the stairs two at a time, peel off my half-frozen bathing suit and plunge into the shower. I stand there for quite a long time, humming *Rite of Spring* as the deliciously hot water pours down on me.

x

AN HOUR and a half later I emerge from the subway onto West Twenty-third Street. It's a bland street of utilitarian buildings hous-ing magazine publishers and toy-related businesses. As I cross Sixth Avenue the sky bunches up and I get caught in a sudden violent shower. I have an umbrella at home, though I've never actually used it. I prefer pretending that I'm at one with the weather and that I can dodge the drops. In a few steps I'm severely drenched.

All around me the thunderstorm is having its way with the city;

umbrellas start littering the streets like dead birds and water runs in big streams while humans run in all directions.

By the time I reach Seventh Avenue and look for the number of Ariel's building, the rain has soaked through the hood of my jacket and my head feels like a roll of wet toilet paper. I find 222 West Twenty-third and stand there, confused. It's the infamous Chelsea Hotel. Where Sid Vicious died. Where countless artistic denizens have lived, worked, and sometimes died. My friend Hal, a musicologist, lives here when he's in New York. It's a notorious gorgeous mess of a building with loopy balconies and an old neon sign throbbing out from a red brick facade. Not at all where I'd expect my fair-haired acquaintance to live.

I go into the lobby, a dimly lit high-ceilinged place decorated with paintings by various artists who have lived here. At the reception desk a surly-looking white woman is frowning into a magazine and a skinny Spanish guy is shouting into a telephone. Neither one of them pays any attention to me, so I walk over to the stairs and head up. As I wander the wide quiet halls, looking for number 297, a door opens and an extremely fat man peers out at me. I walk on, eventually coming to Ariel's place. There's a golden doorbell sticking out with a tiny golden nipple. I press it, and in a moment Ariel appears at the door.

"Ruby, hello," she says, looking at me with something like hunger as she gestures for me to come inside.

"How are you, Ariel?" I ask automatically.

She sighs. She looks on the verge of weeping but instead she shrugs.

Her apartment is completely filled with flowers and plants. It's nice in a sort of carpeted, civilized way that makes me feel like I'm going to leave stains and break anything I happen to touch. Including Ariel. She's so perfectly coiffed and manicured. She's wearing a lavender cashmere sweater and white wool pants. Her delicate feet are bare, the toenails varnished to match the lavender of her sweater. She looks like direct contact with another human would never be possible—never.

"Would you like a towel?" she asks as I veer toward the couch.

I realize I look and smell like a wet dog. "Yeah, thanks, where's the bathroom?"

"Just there." She indicates a door to the right. "But the towels are in here." She floats over to a place in the wall and presses her palm against one part of it, causing a door to pop open, revealing shelves of perfectly folded fluffy white towels. She hands me two and I retreat to the bathroom.

There's nothing in it but an elegant mauve toilet, a minimal sink, and a discreet showerhead sprouting from the far corner of the ceiling. The floor is made of tiny white tiles. Apparently, the entire room is one big shower stall. There are no doodads or gewgaws. It's all functional and elegant. Like Ariel herself.

I rub myself dry then check the towels to see if I've stained them. They're a little grayish but nothing drastic. I come out of the bathroom, hand Ariel my used towels, and watch her slip them into yet another magical door in one of the walls.

She indicates the severe white couch. I sit down. Nervously, spine erect.

"Can I get you a drink?" she asks.

"I don't drink, thanks."

"I meant water. Or juice. Or coffee. Or tea. I have several kinds of tea," she says, anxiously flitting over to the open kitchen area where various chrome appliances gleam. "I have Earl Grey, of course. Or chamomile, if you'd like something herbal. I have ginger too. Or peppermint. Oh, and I have gunpowder tea also."

"Water would be fine, thanks," I say.

"Sparkling or flat?"

"Flat is good."

She brings me water then immediately flits off again and comes back with a photograph. "That's Frank," she says.

The photo is of a square-jawed blond guy. High cheekbones, crew cut, broad shoulders. He's staring into the camera like he's trying to shatter it. Central casting's version of a handsome thug.

"Huh," I say.

"He's a good-looking man," Ariel says.

I shrug noncommittally. I'd have expected her taste to run to a more refined stick-up-the-ass, overbred kind of guy. "What's he do for a living?" I venture.

"Oh," she makes a gesture of despair, "he's a sort of handicapper."

"A who?"

"He handicaps horse races."

"Oh yeah?" I brighten. I love horses, and have, on occasional visits to the racetrack, done pretty well for myself in the gambling department. My little system of looking at the horses before the race and trying to gauge their moods has, to other people's astonishment, yielded good results.

"I was raised to stand by my man, no matter what," Ariel says now, for no apparent reason.

"Ah," I say.

"I mentioned to you that my mother lived with a hex on her head."

"You did say something about a hex."

"My grandmother hexed her. Her own daughter. My grandmother didn't approve of my father. He was rich. Handsome. But my grandmother mistrusted him. '*Faccia de miseria*,' she told my mother. My father had the face of misery. My grandmother swore he'd make my mother unhappy. Which he did. And yet, my mother stressed to me the importance of loyalty. Though my father was seldom at home and was cold when he was there, my mother said only kind things about him. When she grew ill and began wasting away, he rarely came to check on her, but still she didn't say an unkind word." Ariel is staring ahead, looking like an elegant blond zombie.

"My mother died when I was twelve. For a few months I was sent to live with my grandmother in Sicily. She tried to shape me into a proper Italian girl. Taught me to cook and, in particular, to grow things. Plants. Flowers." Ariel motions at the extravagant horticultural display around us. "Then she died too. My father sent for me. I was brought back to Westchester County and raised by a succession of governesses. My father was always a distant figure."

I'm starting to get the feeling Ariel needs a shrink more than she needs an investigator. I squirm in my seat a little, uncomfortable with these confidences from someone I barely know.

Ariel suddenly picks up the photo of Frank from the glass table she'd put it on. She looks at the photo wistfully.

"I've been with Frank close to ten months now. I love him. I don't want to say disparaging things about him. But, well, I'm afraid his employment isn't strictly on the up and up. When we first met, he told me he was a racing handicapper. Said he contributed regularly to various racing magazines. He does know a great deal about horse racing. But I've scoured the various racing forms for his byline and haven't found it. Still, that isn't what bothers me, Ruby."

Ariel leans closer, puts her hand on my forearm. She smells delicate and rosy.

"What I can't abide isn't even that I think he's running around on me," she says, "it's the lying about it. I'd like to just know the truth. And he isn't going to level with me." She sighs and looks on the verge of tears again, then gathers herself and hands me a sheet of paper.

"Here is his information. Date of birth. Full name. Cell phone number."

"You have an address? Where am I supposed to find him?"

She hangs her head. "I don't know it," she admits. "He lives in Midtown but I've never been to his place."

Clearly this guy is the catch of the century.

"He's supposed to come by tomorrow evening. He tends to simply appear when it suits him, but I would guess it would be around nine. I would like it if you could be nearby. Do you have a cell phone?" she asks.

"No, I don't," I say, refraining from going on my Luddite's anti-cell-phone rant.

"It's fine. I've got extra phones," Ariel says, and I immediately picture yet another cleverly disguised closet, this one chock-full of electronic gizmos. "I'll give you a phone and we'll install you in a room here in the Chelsea. When Frank comes, I'll make some excuse and ask him to leave without spending the night. You can follow him from here."

She pauses and thinks for a moment.

"I want you to know I really appreciate this, Ruby. I didn't want to go to a formal detective agency. That would make me uncomfortable. I had planned on simply ignoring the situation. But when I met you, I knew you could help. I don't like having troubles. It interferes with my work, which is quite important to me."

"Oh?" I picture her in some sort of high-tech lab, endeavoring to uncombine Recombinant DNA.

"I'm a flower designer. Weddings, funerals, and intermittent points in people's lives. I brighten these occasions with flowers. Do you like flowers?" Ariel rises now, gliding over to one of the long tall vases that resemble her.

"Sure," I say.

"What flowers do you like best?"

"I have a thing for really tiny orange roses."

Ariel smiles. "Of course," she says knowingly.

"What, is that gauche of me or something?"

"Oh no, not at all, Ruby, no, it just suits you is all."

I'm not sure how to interpret this so I leave it alone. Ariel and I get down to business. We agree to thirty bucks an hour, which is a lot cheaper than the going rate for this kind of thing but certainly more than I, humble museum worker, ever make.

"Look," I say then, "I really do think this whole thing is a bad idea. Your boyfriend sounds like he's up to no good, and you should dump him and call it a day. Or else follow him yourself. There's nothing I can do that you can't."

"Please calm down, Ruby, we can work this out."

And work it out she does.

By the time I get home to Coney there's a message from her on the cell phone she's just given me. It's all been arranged. I am to present myself tomorrow evening at the place of an acquaintance of hers in the Chelsea. I should just stay there, at her friend's, phone in hand, waiting for her to call and tell me when Frank leaves her apartment.

It's all a bit much and I need a nap. I herd the cats over to the bed and lie down face first on the comforter.

Next thing I know, I'm startled awake by the sound of rocks being thrown at my window.

Oliver Emmerick

6 / Saint Ludwig's Mood Swings

Some days it's so bad I can't move, other days it's the kind of bad where I *have* to move. I wasn't quite sure which this was gonna be but the sun was streaming in, blending with the bright yellow of the walls, hurting my eyes a little with its brilliance, and though I was nauseated and had pain traveling up and down my body, I threw back the covers, got up, and put on Ol' Dirty Bastard's first record, which I knew was the only thing that would get me moving.

Once the music was pumping loudly enough to knock a few weighty volumes off the bookshelf, I went into the kitchen and stared at my many boxes of tea. Ever since I got sick, everyone I've ever known has come by bringing me soothing and healthful items. I liked tea even before the cancer, though.

I select one particularly handsome square box of tea that I think had arrived courtesy of Isabelle, one of my more recent exes, an exquisitely intelligent woman who also happens to be a bit of a nympho. Isabelle, though blond, blue-eyed, and enviably young, manages to be loved by all people. All colors. All creeds. And so, though no one else I know gets a very good response from any of the shopkeepers in Chinatown when poking around the beautiful herb stores there, Isabelle is loved by even the notoriously surly Chinese herb store folks. She'd gotten them to make up a specific tea blend involving all sorts of exotic and horrible-smelling herbs that would ostensibly get in the way of my cancer.

I boiled water, then let the tea steep. Ol' Dirty Bastard was going off on a tirade about bitches and ho's, which was bound to disturb Mrs. Nauman next door. Of course, once I'd started noticeably losing weight and hair, Mrs. Nauman, a previously churlish neighbor, became a solicitous soul, and there hasn't been a peep of complaint out of her in six months. All the same, ODB was starting to get on even my nerves, so I changed over to Beethoven's Seventh. Which Mrs. Nauman would approve of, even if I wasn't sure I always did. The thing with old Ludwig is the mood swings. He'll do something so heartbreakingly exquisite, like the beginning of the second movement of the seventh, and then suddenly go bonkers adding highly unnecessary flourishes and drama. I used to state emphatically that I hated Beethoven, but then my beloved friend Ruby, crafty lass that she is, made me a mixed tape, sneaking some particularly gorgeous Beethoven excerpts onto it. And I was sold on Ruby's sainted Ludwig.

I sit down to start sipping at my tea, not sure if I'll be able to keep it down. The cancer is mostly in my esophagus. Doesn't make eating or drinking an easy proposition. Or living, for that matter.

The phone rings and I let the machine get it. Deedee. Another fairly recent ex. A fine woman. Dancer. Used to get me to perform with her sometimes. Hoisting her up over my head. Rolling around on the floor with her. Most of my friends have always made much of my physical abilities. As a kid I was on the swim team, and it shaped my body. Then, from the time I was twenty until a few months ago, I earned most of my living building things. Which made my body strong. Until now, that is. Now I'm a bag of bones.

The tea stays down and actually does a little something to me. I feel a slight bit better than a half hour ago, but I know if I keep sitting here I'll start to feel lethargic.

I get dressed. Pull my belt tight around the waist of my black pants. All my clothes are too big. I put on my smallest button-down white shirt with two layers of T-shirt underneath. I'm not sure where I'm going to go exactly, just know I have to go somewhere.

I look outside and see that the vivid ball of afternoon sun has suddenly hidden itself behind thick clouds. I grab my raincoat and head out the door.

I start walking down First Avenue, my body not feeling full of energy, but my lungs and mind glad for the change of scenery. Before I realize what I'm doing, I'm on the Brooklyn bound F train. It's empty this time of day. Just a few schizophrenic-looking individuals. Not that, as far as I know, schizophrenics have visible markings, just that I once heard a statistic that, of the small percentage of Caucasian cab drivers in New York City, ninety percent are schizophrenic. I believe a similar statistic could be applied to daytime F train riders.

We're far into the wilds of Brooklyn before I realize I'm going to Coney Island. Maybe I'll get on the Cyclone, shake up my gray matter. Make myself feel better. I stare out the window as the long dormant parachute drop becomes visible in the distance. I feel my heart dance a little, pleased at the prospect of beautiful desolate Coney. Maybe I'll even drop in on Ruby, unannounced, force her to entertain me awhile.

I get off the train at the second to last stop, and as I emerge onto Surf Avenue, I realize it's too silent. The Cyclone isn't running. I cross over to stare at its entrance anyway. A sign informs me the thing is only open on weekends until the season starts.

I stand looking around, taking in the raw beauty of the place. It's windy and the clouds are rolling through the sky, blowing out toward the sea.

I notice a pack of cute young girls standing near a pay phone, snapping their gum, throwing back their lovely heads. I love girls.

I consider going over to the Eldorado Arcade to waste a handful of quarters on Skee Ball. But I don't really feel like it. My body hurts. I walk south on Surf, heading toward Stillwell to go see if Ruby's around.

At her building I stare up at her windows and get seized with a tender feeling. We haven't had sex in a long time. The romance aspect of our liaison faded out years ago after a quick and failed attempt. But I'm crazy about the girl and, over the last few years, whenever bad moments have come to either of us, we've spent nights together, just holding onto each other for dear life. Haven't had one of those in a while, though. Ever since the verdict on my extremely terminal condition. I don't like to impose my mortality on people I love.

I crane my neck up but don't see any sign of activity in Ruby's windows other than one of the cats, the crazy one, crouched there, looking like some sort of tricolored gargoyle fending off bad spirits and birds. I scoop up a handful of pebbles from the street and start hurling them at the window the cat isn't guarding. I'm just about to give up when I see Ruby's face appear.

She opens the window and squints down at me. "Oliver?" She looks incredulous.

"Let's have dinner," I say, feeling suddenly lighthearted as hell.

"Dinner?" She squints.

"Yeah, food, dinner," I say.

"What are you doing here?" she says, not seeming upset at the interruption, just surprised.

"Came out to ride the Cyclone but the fucking thing isn't running."

"Weekends only until Memorial Day," she says.

"Yeah. I know that now. Come on. Let's go. Food," I say, all of a sudden feeling starved—which doesn't necessarily mean I'll be able to keep anything down.

She tells me she has to get dressed. Asks do I want to come up. I tell her no. I want to stand here. Breathing. Looking around at the big sky and the silent rides.

"Give me five minutes," she says, then closes the window and disappears, presumably to change fifty something times because, although she's not a prissy fashion victim or anything, she takes good care with her appearance and always emerges into the world looking like one of the most delectable women on the face of this fine earth.

Just as I'm standing, savoring the anticipation of ogling Ruby, another stroke of good luck befalls me and the pack of girls from near the Cyclone ambles over toward me. One of them is carrying a surfboard. Though what anyone would do with a surfboard in these docile waters, I don't know.

I accost the girls. "Hey, you guys surfing?"

They look at me with that "white men are disgusting maniacs" look that I love.

I grin. Tell them I used to surf a lot. One of them, a particularly lovely lass in blinding bright pink jeans, offers a tentative smile and explains about the surfboard. Some of the girls just came back from a trip to the Atlantic side of Puerto Rico. Did a little surfing. They're just transporting the board from one house to another right now.

As the girl speaks, her long silky ponytail sways in the wind, punctuating the rhythm of her speech pattern. I love it. I love her. And all her friends too.

Just then Ruby emerges. I see her squinting at me. I motion for her to come over. My girls start to look uneasy.

"Ruby, do you know these ladies?" I ask.

Ruby glances at the girls then shakes her head no.

"Ladies, this is my dear friend Ruby Murphy."

One of the girls, a funny-looking pudgy one, says she's seen Ruby in the Coney Island Museum. Ruby brightens at this, asks the girl if she's interested in Coney's history. The girl shrugs. Not really. Just wanted to see what was up there. Ruby smiles, and when I can see she's about to launch into some baroque anecdote about Coney's glorious past, I take her elbow and guide her toward Surf Avenue, bidding the lovely girls adieu. Beethoven's Seventh floats through my head. The beginning of the second movement. Before the mood swings.

Ruby Murphy

7 / Ball and Chain

"I love girls," Oliver states.

We watch the pack of Spanish girls he'd accosted amble off into the evening, a symphony of sashaying hips and bopping ponytails.

"I know." I roll my eyes at my friend.

"I want bad Italian food," he says.

"Ugh."

"I have cancer, you have to do what I want."

"That's pretty low."

"But effective," he says, grinning, squeezing my arm, then leading me over toward the subway station. Up ahead I see Guillotine threading his way down Surf Avenue, pitbull pack in tight formation before him, dogs and man forming one fluid mass of muscle as they walk, parting seas of lingering humans. I wave to Guillotine. He frowns. Nods with his chin.

Oliver and I go into the station. A light wind is singing through the entrails of the place and follows us up the stairs.

There's a D train waiting, doors open. We get on and sit down. Oliver rests his head on my shoulder.

"You're not losing your hair at least," I say, staring at the top of my friend's head.

"Yes, I am. Look." He rakes his fingers through his hair, producing loose strands.

"Oh. Well. It doesn't *look* like you're losing it," I say, wondering if I should express the gloom I feel. Gloom tempered by the fact that Oliver is one of the most resilient, indestructible people I know and has rebounded from things that would have felled most folks a thousand times over.

We get off the train and emerge onto Emmons Avenue. Oliver takes in a deep breath and looks pleased at the twinkly garish sight of Sheepshead Bay.

Moored powerboats bob in the water to the accompaniment of Frank Sinatra, whose crooning emanates from a waterfront restaurant's outdoor speakers. Old people and teenagers amble along, peering into the mostly empty restaurants.

"So? Which restaurant?" I ask Oliver.

"That one looks horrible enough." He motions at a big white building with breast-shaped stucco implants sprouting from its sides.

The shrubbery flanking the entrance is decorated in throbbing Christmas lights that keep time with the Frank Sinatra song.

Oliver and I walk inside the place—which isn't doing much business right now. We're greeted by a thickset man wearing black pants and a white shirt unbuttoned to reveal a carpet of chest hair.

"Two? Dinner?" he demands.

"Yes, please," I say brightly.

Chest Carpet escorts us to a table at the far side of the dining room. He tosses two huge laminated menus at us then lumbers away.

"He likes us," Oliver comments.

"Yeah, he especially likes you, of course," I say, referring to Oliver's service hex: Waiters, copy shop attendants, salespeople, all are invariably hostile to Oliver. For no apparent reason. He's a good-looking man. He's polite. But evidently he radiates retroactive traces of youthful insolence, and if there's neglect or abuse to be heaped on someone, Oliver will be the recipient—and weather it with masochistic pleasure.

By the time our waitress—a gum-snapping white-lipstick-wearing princess in pink platforms—neglects to bring Oliver's soda after three requests, Oliver lets loose on her.

"Do you hate me?" he asks as she stands pressing one lazy hip against the edge of our table.

"Huh?" she sneers, and snaps her gum.

"You refuse to bring me soda. I take it you have something against me. I've offended you in some way."

The girl stops in mid-chew and stares at him. "Soda?" she finally utters.

"I ordered a soda. Maybe you should sit down here and I'll go get it," he says, standing up, offering her his chair.

Our fellow diners start eyeing us.

The waitress looks from them to us. "All right. Okay. I'll get your soda," she says, teetering away.

A few moments later the waitress slams a glass of soda in front of Oliver and resentfully takes our order.

After an interminable wait we finally get our food and start digging into the doughy raviolis and greasy escarole. Oliver is inhaling the stuff. And though it's fairly disgusting, I shovel it down pretty quickly myself.

"Hey," I say to Oliver after we've both ingested most of our food, "I got a job."

My friend squints at me. "I thought you had a job."

I explain about Ariel and her unlikely decision to turn me into a private investigator.

"You're being paid to stalk someone," Oliver says with wonder, like it's what all sentient beings work for all their lives.

"I'm just following him."

"Life likes you," Oliver segues.

"What?"

"Good things happen to you. You go around minding your own business and strange women offer to pay you money. Why doesn't that happen to me?"

"But it does."

"Strange women, yeah, paying me money, no."

"Speaking of which, what happened to the married lady?" I ask him.

After Oliver and his long-term girlfriend Isabelle broke up, he started seeing a married woman. All I know about her is that she routinely turns up on his doorstep wearing a raincoat, fuck me pumps, and nothing else. Just as I attract strange and interesting life circumstances, Oliver attracts strange and interesting women.

"Nothing. I'm not seeing her. I have no sex drive. She visits me sometimes. Brings me presents. She tried to blow me the other day but my body wouldn't respond and it just freaked me out. You realize I might never have sex again?"

"Yes you will."

"Not if I die."

"You won't die."

"I'm supposed to."

"Not now. Not soon," I say. "You can't die before me. You'd miss the wedding."

We long ago vowed we'd marry each other when we'd given up our respective search-and-destroy missions of love. Both of us have a possibly stupid blind faith that eventually we'll either get it right and stay with someone—or else simultaneously discover that we actually want to be with each other.

"Yes, baby, I've gotta be your ball and chain." Oliver nods and his impish smile turns sad.

We continue eating.

We make it through dinner without being murdered by the waitress or the maître d'. Emerging from the restaurant, we start walking in the general direction of Coney, ambling down back streets lined with modest houses. We go slowly, savoring the ripe night.

"You'll spend the night with me?" I ask Oliver when we eventually reach Stillwell Avenue.

He raises his eyebrows at me. "Oh yes."

X

RAMIREZ'S DOOR is open and he's sitting at his kitchen table, chin resting in his palms as he stares ahead, dazed.

"Hey," I say softly.

"Ruby," Ramirez utters without enthusiasm.

"This is Oliver." I gesture at Oliver.

"Oh," Ramirez says.

"What's the matter?" I ask my neighbor.

He hesitates for a moment, then: "Elsie got medical problems. Come in," he adds, "both of you."

Oliver and I enter. There's a smell of cheap olive oil and *café con leche.*

I stare at my neighbor's ordinarily welcoming face. It's all bunched up now, black eyebrows knit tightly.

"Tell me," I say.

Ramirez scowls. "Sit down, Ruby. You too." He motions at Oliver, who obediently takes a seat.

"I fucked up," Ramirez sighs, looks down at his stubby hands. "I thought it'd be nice for her," he says. "I bought her some new breasts."

"You what?"

"New breasts. Titties," he says, putting his palms to his own flat chest. "You know, she make better money dancing that way. She said she wanted that. I found a doctor said he'd do it for two thousand dollars. Nice Dominican doctor."

"You mean breast implants?" Oliver asks.

"Yeah. That's what I mean," Ramirez concedes, "but this doctor, he talk nice but he don't cut so good. My lady's all messed up now. Her breasts are swollen and she don't feel good."

"When did she have the surgery?" I ask him.

"Two weeks ago."

"Maybe that's normal. For them to be swollen, I mean."

"I don't think so." Ramirez shakes his head sadly. "She's down at her sister's place now in New Brunswick. She called me; she's in a lot of pain."

"I bet she'll be fine," I tell him, but I can see he's not convinced.

"You go on to bed now," Ramirez says after a while, "I'll let you know what happens."

I feel so badly for him that I shock us both by actually hugging him. Ramirez and I definitely have affection for each other, but we've never gotten physical. Now we're both mildly embarrassed—but possibly pleased—by my gesture.

Oliver and I retreat into my place. He plunks down on my couch, stretching his legs and leaning his head back. Stinky and Lulu immediately materialize and climb all over him, both cats unfailing in their tendency to gravitate toward alleged cat haters.

"Can you please get these off me, I have cancer," Oliver says unconvincingly. I roll my eyes at him.

A few minutes later we get into bed. We spoon our bodies together. In seconds Oliver's breathing grows smooth and even with sleep.

The bedroom is cold and quiet. I prop up on one elbow to stare at Oliver. He looks about twelve; all the creases relaxed from his face, his mouth open a half inch. I want to touch him, run my finger over his lips, but I don't want to wake him. Maybe sleep will save him.

I get up and softly pad into the living room. I stare at the piano, needing to play but not wanting to wake Oliver. I walk to the window. Lulu jumps up into the windowsill and makes a chirping sound. I run my hands down her back as I stare across at the subway platform where a train is waiting, its digital window panel announcing its destination, its doors open like luminous jaws.

Lulu arches her back and chirps again.

After a long while I go back into the bedroom and climb in bed. I drape one arm over Oliver. Stinky is nesting at my friend's feet. Lulu jumps up and curls near my pillow.

My eyes close. Sleep comes.

Oliver Emmerick

8 / Bewitched by Beasts

I roll onto my side and collide with a body. Which scares the hell out of me. Until it all floods back. I'm at Ruby's place. There are cats all over the bed and Ruby is curled on her side, red nightgown jacked up around her ass, exposing her stuff. I gently tug the nightgown down, feeling a little indecent ogling her goods—which are certainly ogleworthy but which, at this stage, I can't do much with.

The large cat regards me with wide green eyes, then in slow

motion opens his mouth and emits a moaning sound. I frown at him. He appears to frown back.

I get up and go into the bathroom to wash my face. I don't feel that bad today, although I don't look all that great. My face is gaunt as hell, crevices like ravines etched into it. I wash it again. The crevices remain.

I put my pants on and go into Ruby's weird green kitchen to see about some tea. Had I known I'd end up here, shacking up for the night, I'd have brought some of my vast tea resources with me. This girl clearly doesn't think too highly of tea. There's coffee up the wazoo but only one pathetic little box of Lipton's.

I boil water and stare out the window at the train platform across the street. Business as usual over there. The trains like long silver snakes, coming and going.

I'm just pouring myself a cup of dreaded Lipton's when Ruby stumbles into the kitchen. She's thrown a puffy white robe on over her red nightie, and the cats are at her heels, both of them meowing and weaving between her legs.

"You sleep okay?" she wants to know, and I nod, then watch her pull a package of raw meat out of the fridge.

"Don't get me wrong," I say. "I like a girl with meat on her hands, but what the hell are you doing?"

"Feeding the cats. They eat raw food. It's supposed to help them feel more like cats. I mean, more like cats in the wild. Catching their own food or whatever."

"Ah," I say.

The phone starts ringing but Ruby steadfastly ignores it.

A woman's voice speaks into the machine: "Please, Ruby, I know you're there, please pick up."

I watch Ruby screw up her forehead and scowl at the phone.

"Who is that?" I ask her.

"Ariel DiCello, my new employer."

"Shouldn't you talk to her?"

"I don't want to."

I guess it's a bit obnoxious of me but I'm dying of curiosity. I pick up the phone. A breathless woman asks for Ruby. I hand the phone to the dear girl, earning another scowl from her.

Ruby talks to the woman for quite a while. And doesn't look so happy when she hangs up. The woman apparently wants Ruby to start her stakeout of the nefarious boyfriend *now*.

"She's got some friend there at the Chelsea. I'm supposed to go hang out at this friend's place, wait there for Ariel to call me."

"Let's do it," I say, suddenly feeling completely enthralled with this whole harebrained thing. Leave it to Ruby to find herself ensnared in some bizarre but highly interesting mess.

She seems cheered by the idea that I'll actually come with her. With me urging her to hurry, she rinses the meat off her hands, gets dressed, and about half an hour later we're heading into Manhattan.

I haven't set foot inside the Chelsea Hotel in years. Last time was for a tryst with one of my married ladies. I attract married ladies like no one you've ever met. Even now. When I'm a walking skeleton. It's incredible.

There's a pack of giggling Japanese girls in the lobby, looking at the paintings there, most of these handed over in lieu of rent from the various artists who live in the place. Some of the works are good, in particular a huge horse face that sort of looks like a sexy woman.

Ruby and I go past the reception desk where two big guys look at us but don't say a word. We catch the elevator up to the fifth floor and get lost a few times before finding 501, the room we're supposed to go to.

We ring the bell marked F. LIVINGSTON. The door cracks open and a man's face looks out. "Ruby Murphy?" he asks, looking at her, then at me.

"Frederick Livingston?" she says. The guy nods and opens the door. He's a small, handsome guy with bright eyes and short hair. He looks at me with interest.

"This is my friend Oliver," Ruby says, introducing me, and the way the guy continues to look at me, I get an indication as to what his sexual preference might be. I feel sort of flattered by his apparent approval of my countenance. I mean, I am, after all, not at my best right now.

Ruby and I follow Frederick inside the room, which turns out to be several rooms and much more sumptuous than I'd have expected. There's a lush red carpet and big fluffy furnishings. In the corner stands a magnificent grand piano. I hear Ruby asking the guy if he plays, and the guy looks a little ruffled. He peers from me to her and back and then explains that he's a concert pianist. A rather well-known concert pianist.

Ruby and I both make apologetic noises for not knowing that the guy's famous. I'm sure he thinks we're Philistines.

"Can I get you anything?" Frederick asks us, and both Ruby and I, wanting to be polite after failing to know the guy's a big deal, claim we don't need anything—even though, in truth, I'm parched.

Thankfully, Frederick is an intuitive host and insists on refreshing us. He disappears into some sort of kitchen area, reemerging with a bottle of Pellegrino and two glasses. I gratefully gulp mine down as Ruby sips genteelly, propped at the end of one of the blood-colored couches.

There's an awkward silence, and I can hear Ruby swallowing a sip of her water. The girl has something weird going on in that throat of hers, can't seem to drink quietly. Maybe left over from her days as a drunk.

Eventually, Frederick starts talking about how glad he is that Ruby's going to help Ariel. "It's quite touching how you two met," he says, and Ruby does a little double take, like "touching" might not have been how she'd describe it.

"I'm really not sure I'm gonna be of help at all," Ruby says then, "but I'll try, I guess."

Frederick gives us a thumbnail sketch of the situation, how he himself is sure that the nefarious boyfriend is up to no good and he hopes that Ruby will prove as much conclusively. Force Ariel to move on. Ruby looks worried. And then changes the subject by blurting out that she's a fledgling pianist.

"Really?" Frederick looks totally delighted. "Who's your teacher?"

"A Juilliard student. Mark Baxter. He's sort of impossible but I like him."

"You must play," Frederick tells her, springing up from his chair and going over to grab Ruby by the hands, trying to force her to the piano.

She won't budge, though. "Oh no, I can't. I can barely play in front of Mark. No." She's flushed bright red. Which I find impossibly sexy. If only I could get my body to work, maybe we could renegotiate the sexual aspect of our liaison.

Frederick and I both try to convince Ruby to play, but even though she shoots lustful looks at the piano, she won't. Instead, she gets Frederick to serenade us. At first he demurs, saying he's already played for three hours this morning, but Ruby makes a beseeching face which no one could possibly resist and Frederick finally agrees. He even asks for requests, though when I mutter something about Prokofiev, he looks peeved.

"There's nothing wrong with Prokofiev, but the piano music isn't my favorite. Bach?" he offers.

Ruby and I both agree that Bach would be swell.

We settle next to each other on the couch and watch Frederick at the piano. He sits surprisingly far from the keyboard and his small arms suddenly look long. His back is straight as a rod, eyes at half-mast as he sort of bows his head to the instrument then brings his small well-made hands over the keys.

I don't know what he's playing, other than it's definitely Bach and it's definitely beautiful. A few minutes in he's interrupted by a ringing phone. Frederick doesn't seem to miss a note, but both Ruby and I look around, trying to locate the offensively ringing instrument. It takes a couple of moments for Ruby to realize it's the damned cell phone Ariel gave her. She starts to furiously forage in her bag, grabbing for the thing like it's a grenade then springing up from the couch and walking into the kitchen area to talk.

I just lie there, eyes closed, letting the music wash through my body in a pleasing manner. After a while I feel Ruby come back to sit on the couch. I open one eye to look at her, and with the way the music is going through my body, taking away all the discomfort, I feel glad to be alive.

Frederick finishes playing and I hear Ruby telling him the phone call was from Ariel, summoning her to arms. Before I've had time to transition back into the brutal reality of things, Ruby is pulling me up from the couch. I'm tempted to tell her to go easy, I have cancer, but I figure the ghoulish humor is possibly getting to her by now so I keep my mouth shut, letting her pull me to my feet. In a moment we're saying good-bye to Frederick, who insists we must come back when we have more time. He gives me one last appreciative glance, and then Ruby and I are out the door and into the hall.

"We've got to look for a blond guy in a motorcycle jacket," Ruby informs me as we race down the stairs, not trusting the ancient elevator to get us down in time.

We reach the lobby and rush into the street, where we do in fact see a man with white-blond hair lighting a cigarette. The guy takes a pull on his smoke then fishes an electronic organizer from his pocket and furiously types into it. He turns his head slightly, and Ruby informs me this is indeed our man, the nefarious boyfriend Frank.

I feel a little snake of excitement in my stomach as we follow the guy across Twenty-third Street. I study the way the guy moves. Like an athlete, light on his feet, a controlled sort of bouncing stride.

He heads north on Seventh Avenue, and we follow until, just past Thirty-first Street, he ducks into the stairs leading to the belly of Penn Station.

"Where's he going?" I rhetorically ask Ruby, who grabs my hand, urging me forward so we won't lose Frank in the swell of humans.

Frank makes a right, into the Long Island Railroad terminal. We rush down the escalator after him as he strides directly over to one of the platforms, right onto a waiting train.

"Now what?" Ruby looks at me.

"We take a train ride," I tell her, and we get on just as the doors whoosh shut.

Out of the corner of my eye I see Frank sitting in the first row of seats, his big blond head bent forward. Ruby and I walk past him, taking seats two rows back just as the train groans into the tunnel leading out of Penn Station's entrails. Pretty soon the conductor's voice comes onto the P.A., telling us we're on the Belmont Special, making station stops at Jamaica and Belmont Racetrack.

"We're going to the track?" I ask Ruby.

"I guess so. Makes sense. Ariel said the guy claims to be a race handicapper."

"Yeah? We're gonna play the ponies?" I ask Ruby.

"Sure. If he does. He told Ariel he writes a racing column. Only she can't seem to find his byline anywhere and I've never heard of him. He's probably just a compulsive gambler trying to delude himself. And her."

"Shhh." I put a finger over her lips as she's saying "compulsive gambler" a bit louder than she ought to. A hunchbacked guy sitting to our right is scowling at us. We are in fact *surrounded* by compulsive gambler guys—and a few gals—their faces long and hollow, like the flesh has been eaten away from the inside.

The conductor comes by collecting tickets, and we get saddled with a two-dollar penalty for not buying our tickets ahead of time. I can't say that I care, though. What money I had I've given to friends, since I don't have any health insurance and the hospitals would just take it all, leaving nothing for my sister. My sister and I aren't close, but our parents are both dead and she lives dirt poor in Wisconsin. If I've got to die, I'd rather give whatever cash I've got left to her than to hospitals and doctors—who've given me less than stellar treatment, and in fact misdiagnosed me for a long time, attributing my symptoms to ulcers, leaving the cancer to run rampant.

As the train races forward and out into the bright day at the edges of Queens, I lean my head on Ruby's shoulder and close my eyes, feeling her run her fingers through my thinning hair. Only when the big, gorgeous Belmont oval looms into view do I sit up to gawk at it.

I love the track. I first came here with a former ladyfriend named Amanda. She was a femme fatale and a racing fanatic. She would put on a skintight red dress and spike heels and drag me out to the track no matter what the weather or what caliber of horses were running. She'd just stare gape-mouthed at the beasts, marveling at them—and maybe at the jockeys too. She took up with an exercise rider after giving me my walking papers. After things unraveled with her, I found racing had gotten into my blood. Ruby was intrigued by it since she had spent time around horses while living in Florida. She can actually look at a horse and tell if he's moving funny and maybe has something wrong with his legs. We started coming out here together, catching some of the big races.

The train slows down and groans to a halt, and both Ruby and I pop out of our seats, excited by the sight of the track, as if this were just another one of our expeditions. But, of course, it's not. We press our way through our fellow passengers, keeping close behind Frank, whose pale blond head is thankfully easy to pick out in the small crowd.

We pass through the turnstiles leading into the cavernous grandstand, and I just want to buy a program, go ogle the horses, and put down a few bets. Ruby urges me forward, though, not letting me stop to look at the tote board. We follow Frank as he heads past the program sellers, then through a series of glass doors and into the inner sanctum of the clubhouse.

At the clubhouse gate Frank flashes some sort of ID to the attendant and breezes through. Ruby and I pay an additional two dollars for admission into the nearly empty clubhouse. We tail the blond man down some stairs and outside to the spectator area of the saddling paddock. Frank walks to the frontmost tier of the viewing area and leans against the railing there, apparently scanning the horses and humans gathered around the saddling stalls.

Grooms and assistant trainers are leading horses into numbered stalls as gamblers, owners, and track employees look on. In two seconds flat I think both Ruby and I have forgotten all about Frank and his activities. We're raptly watching the horses, bewitched at the sight of the beautiful beasts. We're lost in equine reverie until Frank starts having a shouting match with some short guy standing there inside the saddling paddock.

Sebastian Ives

9 / Girl of Fire

The horse has a bad look in his eye so I get Macy, the mostly useless hotwalker, to hold Truehaft's head firmly as I tighten the girth. Macy being Macy, though, he doesn't have a good grip, and Truehaft almost manages to swing his head around and bite me. Thankfully, I've been around horses so long I know what they're going to do before they've even thought about it and I hop out of the way. I yell at Macy to keep a hold on the ornery colt, and then I take a breath before pulling the horse's legs out. Truehaft, feeling pleased with himself for almost getting his teeth in me, settles down now. He doesn't protest as I get hold of each forearm, lift, and pull it out slightly so as to avoid his belly getting pinched by the girth.

I'm just giving the gray colt a final once-over before leading him out into the walking ring when I notice that my employer, Arnie Gaines, has gotten into a shouting match with someone out there and is causing a ruckus. I tell Macy to keep Truehaft in the saddling stall and I go to see what's what and try to control Gaines's temper before he gets fined again.

Gaines is standing next to the big Secretariat statue, and now I see he's yelling at Frank, the groom, another ne'er do well in our organization, who often tops Macy in unreliability. Though at least Frank knows what's what with the horses. He was even Gaines's assistant trainer at one point a few years back until he got on the wrong side of the law and got locked up for twenty-eight months.

"Arn," I say, coming up to Gaines's side and taking his elbow. "Keep it down," I urge my short, fat, and very white employer. Not that I care so much if he makes an ass of himself, but if he gets cited too many times for violating etiquette, he's gonna have his license suspended and I'll be out of a job.

By now Frank has dipped under the railing from the spectator area and, infuriating the paddock judge by crossing the horse path, comes to stand in front of Gaines. "You told me not to come in this morning," Frank is saying in his tightest voice. His big shoulders are tensed up around his ears and he's got his chin sticking way out like it's gonna lead him somewhere.

"I told you not to come in *yesterday*, Frank. What the hell is wrong with you?"

Bob McCutchen, the paddock judge, comes over, looking none

too pleased. He starts waving his finger at Gaines, telling him this is the last warning. If he starts a scene in the paddock one more time, that's it, thirty days suspension.

Gaines is furious, trying to hold it in, looking like his little head's gonna come popping right off his neck stem.

McCutchen turns to Frank then, telling him he's getting fined for crossing the horse path. Frank's shoulders get even tenser, but he keeps his mouth shut. McCutchen, apparently satisfied, walks off.

I leave Gaines and Frank to stare each other down as I go retrieve Truehaft from Macy. I lead the colt onto the path just as McCutchen calls "Riders up." Truehaft's rider, Edgar Jimenez approaches. He's not a friendly man but he's got good hands and horses like him— even if I don't. His light brown skin looks dark against the pink and white silks he's wearing, the whole effect making his big old hook nose look even longer than usual, to the point where I wonder how he can see past that thing.

Gaines suddenly appears at my side and nudges me out of the way, sending me to stand on the other side of the horse while he himself gives the jock a leg up. As Jimenez puts his feet in the stirrups, Truehaft bolts to the left a little, knocking into Gaines—no doubt putting the bossman in an even fouler mood.

I lead Truehaft around the walking ring. Jimenez says not a word to me as the heathens in the stands catcall at the jocks—though no one has anything to say to Jimenez or Truehaft, who are going off at 30–1. I talk to Truehaft a little, letting him know I'd appreciate a win out of him someday soon. I watch as Jimenez pilots the colt into the tunnel leading to the track. I loop Truehaft's halter over my shoulder, then walk into the grandstand, over to the rail where I watch Jimenez steer Truehaft over to Asha Yashpinsky, the best-looking exercise rider working at Belmont. Asha and her trusted pony horse, Gumball, work some afternoons ponying for Gaines and a few other trainers. Truehaft affectionately nuzzles at Gumball as they make their way into the procession leading to the starting gate.

Frank and Macy are standing near me at the rail, looking like a pair of useless individuals if ever I saw some. I keep a few feet away from the two, not wanting to be disturbed in my contemplation of Asha Yashpinsky's thighs, so lovely against the brown leather of her western saddle.

Normally, I don't like white girls. I'm dark-skinned myself and usually like my ladies as dark or darker than me—no high yellow for me and definitely no white. But this is one exceptional white girl. She's got a very nicely made hind end that would do justice to any black woman. And she's got style. She wears pink pompoms on her crash helmet and always looks fresh and well kept—except for her red-blond hair, which, the moment she takes her helmet off, spills all over her shoulders like curls of fire.

Right now, though, with Truehaft and Jimenez at Gumball's side, my view of Asha's thighs is impaired. All I can see is part of her upper body—which is nothing to shrug at, but it's her thighs that send me over the edge. In fact, I've even been thinking I might ask her out. Been more than a year since I've had a ladyfriend—the last one Yvette, a tall well-made Jamaican girl, worked as an accountant. Yvette was outstanding in the lovemaking department but there wasn't much to talk about afterward. Girl couldn't understand why a man would spend his life around horses the way I do. Thought it was some kind of perversion, working for such low pay. She was upset with me when she found out I used to be a schoolteacher but gave it up for horses. I wouldn't have that kind of problem with Asha. Girl was born on a horse. Don't know how she feels about black men, though. And, just as I'm speculating as to what Asha Yashpinsky's color preferences might be, I see Truehaft acting up, trying to bolt. Jimenez gets thrown off balance and looks like he might come off as the colt ducks out again, but Asha and Gumball are on the case. The lovely girl gets a better hold on Truehaft, and Gumball pins his ears at the colt, issuing some sort of equine threat that Truehaft chooses to take seriously. They manage to make it to the starting gate and load into the number five slot without further incident.

I watch Asha join the other pony riders and canter off the track. The bell goes off and the nine three-year-old colts spring out of the gate. Truehaft breaks okay and gets a spot in mid-pack, running straight, looking like he might mean business. One of Will Lott's horses is in the lead, with two others right at his neck. Truehaft is a strong fourth and stays that way down the backstretch and around the bend. Jimenez steers the gray colt closer to the rail at the turn, manages to save a little ground. He's looking for an opening between Lott's horse and Cash Curse, a little bay I've always liked. The Lott horse switches leads and gets a length on Cash Curse, leaving an opening at the rail, which Jimenez shoots Truehaft through. The move puts Truehaft into second place until, out of nowhere, the eight horse, some 45–1 long shot from Maryland, suddenly hits the gas like nobody's business, coming on like a comet on the outside, sailing past Truehaft and Lott's horse too. Truehaft crosses the finish line third, which is certainly better than last but won't exactly amount to a large cash bonus in my pay envelope. I sigh. And catch sight of Frank, loitering there at the rail, smoking a cigarette. All of a sudden I'm sure it's all this wipe-ass's fault. Him not showing up threw everything off this morning.

I tell him as much. "You gotta get your shit together, Frank," I say, and just as I do, I notice a little white girl standing nearby, apparently staring at Frank. She's with a white guy with a skinny face and they notice me looking at them and both quickly look away. Weird.

I give Frank a few more pieces of my mind until Gaines's new assistant trainer, Ned Ward—a quiet white guy who came out of nowhere but seems to know his way around horses pretty well—materializes at my side, hands me Truehaft's cooler and, in his quiet way, suggests I get my ass over to the horse and lead him off the track. I shoot Frank one last dirty look and go collect the colt.

Jimenez steers the gray over toward me, hops down, wipes some mud from his cheek, scowls at me, and strides off to the jocks' room to change his silks.

I scan around trying to see where Asha and Gumball might be standing, waiting for the next race. I don't see her, though, so I guess any activity in that area will have to keep.

I have a word with Truehaft as I lead him back toward the backstretch. I compliment him on a valiant effort. But my heart's not really in it. I got a woman on the brain.

Ruby Murphy

10 / The Nefarious Boyfriend

We didn't have time to put money on the race but both Oliver and I are such horse fanatics that just watching the gorgeous creatures do their thing is enough to get us extremely stimulated. I was cheering for the 45–1 long shot who came out of nowhere, overtaking the favorite in the last few strides. My throat actually hurts from yelling so loudly and I feel like a bit of an imbecile. Though Oliver was yelling too. Now, the payout prices are lighting up the tote board and the long shot is in the winner's circle, having his picture taken and receiving accolades. Meanwhile, Frank is standing just a few feet away, smoking, which makes me want to smoke but I refuse to do in front of Oliver. It's not like he has lung cancer or like he even smoked that much, it just seems rude to flaunt voluntary self-destruction in front of someone whose days are probably numbered.

Oliver and I are both eyeballing Frank, while trying to look like we're not. Right now he appears to be getting a tongue-lashing from a skinny black man who seems to work for the same trainer as Frank. Frank isn't taking it well and he looks pretty relieved when a third guy comes over, hands the skinny black guy the horse's blanket and says a few words to Frank.

Frank stands there radiating hostility for a few more moments then abruptly strides off.

"Let's get him," Oliver says with a crazy smile, like we're gonna go up and tackle the guy.

We follow Frank back outside, through a crowd of people throwing away their betting slips, and over to the security gate leading to the track's backstretch.

After Frank flashes ID to the guard, we nonchalantly stride up to the gate and try walking through.

"Can I help you?" the guard asks in a distinctly unhelpful tone.

"I lost my pass," I venture.

"Sorry. You'll have to get a new one."

"I will, but I've got to have a word with that groom that just came through," I say, motioning ahead at Frank's receding form.

"No can do, lady." The guard frowns, impassive.

I smile at him. He does not return the favor.

Oliver and I turn away.

"Is there some other way back there?" Oliver asks.

"Probably not. I don't know what to do," I say, feeling useless and a little forlorn. I've always wanted to amble freely around the backstretch. "I guess I should call Ariel."

"Screw that. Let's gamble!" Oliver says brightly.

"Let me call Ariel first."

"Then we gamble?"

"Sure," I say, and to appease my friend, I walk with him over to one of the booths selling the *Daily Racing Form*. A bony woman with large ears sells us a *Form* and two little green Belmont pencils.

I leave Oliver on a bench, hunched over his *Form* as I go looking for a quiet place to make my phone call. Eventually I enter the cavernous ladies' room. There aren't many ladies at the track on a day like this, and the rest room is one of the quietest spots in the place. The attendant, a squat Spanish lady in a pink smock, eyes me warily as I turn the phone on and punch in Ariel's number.

"Ruby," Ariel breathlessly answers on the first ring.

I give her an update on her boyfriend's whereabouts. "But I can't follow him onto the backstretch," I explain.

"That's probably where *she* is," Ariel says.

"Where who is?"

"The other woman," she says darkly.

"I don't know about that," I say, "but it's safe to venture that Frank works there, Ariel. On the backstretch. I don't think he's a handicapper or anything. More like a groom. Or an assistant groom. But if he's got another girlfriend, I haven't seen any sign of her so far."

Silence at the other end.

"You there?" I query.

"I'm thinking."

"Oh." I wait.

"All right. Let me see what I can do about getting you a pass for the backstretch. I'll call you in a half hour."

Of course, when the phone rings twenty odd minutes later, making its ominous sick cricket sound in my raincoat pocket, it's about a half mile into the fourth race and both Oliver and I have money on a little bay filly who is, right now, running in third place.

"Yes," I say, clicking the Talk switch.

"What's the matter?" comes Ariel's voice. "Is he doing something?"

"What?"

The filly is falling back to fourth place now.

"Ruby? Are you watching Frank?"

I barely hear the poor woman because the truth is I'm watching our filly pull on her inner reserves, switch leads, and hit the accelerator, fighting back into third then cruising past the chestnut in second. She valiantly scrambles to catch up with the leader but misses the jackpot by a nose as they cross the finish line.

"Son of a bitch," I say.

"What? What has he done?" comes Ariel's choked voice.

"Sorry," I tell her, "I was watching a race. My horse ran second."

"Ruby, you're not being paid to watch horse races," Ariel snaps. I offer her a few seconds of stony silence.

"I'm sorry," she counters, "I didn't mean to get angry."

"Yeah," I say flatly. I turn my back to Oliver so he won't see the look on my face. I don't do well with authority. It's why I live the life I do. I would never make it in an official business environment or in any kind of traditional hierarchical arrangement. The reverse is also true: I can't stand telling people what to do, even if their whole lives have been devoted to following orders.

"I'm not going to be able to arrange any credentials for you today," Ariel says in a softened voice. "I'm afraid we're going to have to start from scratch again tomorrow."

"Yeah," I say, still flat and cold.

"I'm sorry I was testy, Ruby, please understand," she says.

"Yeah, don't worry about it. I'm sorry too. I get carried away when I'm near horses."

"Oh?"

"Yeah. I like horses."

"Perhaps you could pass yourself off as an exercise rider," she says. Of course I think she's joking, but when I realize she isn't, I tell her it would take a bit of doing for me to stay on one of these horses for five minutes—let alone steer one around a racetrack while looking like I know what I'm doing.

"Maybe you can try getting me credentials as a journalist," I tell her, feeling a nice thrill at the prospect of potentially ambling around the track with an "all access" pass. "I'll wait around out here anyway," I add, "see if Frank maybe catches the gambler train back to the city after the last race."

"The what?"

"The racetrack special. Frank took the gambler train this morning. Maybe he'll take it back into the city this afternoon. I'll wait and see."

Ariel thanks me profusely, clearly contrite. I click the End switch and stick the phone in my pocket.

"So," Oliver says, "I got some betting to do. Can we go to the paddock and look at the horses? I want to see what kind of mood they're in."

"Yeah, maybe Frank will surface again too."

"To hell with Frank. I've got money to make," Oliver says cheerfully as we head out to the paddock. On the way, he stops at a betting window to cash in his ticket for the last race—since he prudently bet the little bay filly to place, he collects a tidy twenty-two bucks on his three dollar bet.

We spend the rest of the afternoon losing ourselves in the sight of glistening horseflesh, tiny brightly clad men, wild, toothless degenerates, and unbelievable blue skies. I keep an eye out for Frank, the swarthy trainer, and the skinny groom. From my program notes I learn that the trainer's name is Arnold Gaines. But he doesn't have any more entries today. And I gratefully give up trying to spot him or his iniquitous employee Frank.

The last race of the day is about to go off but neither Oliver nor I have found much to be inspired by in the twelve entries; 14K claimers with spotty past performances.

The sky darkens, and around us gloom starts to prevail as hopes of hitting the jackpot wane. Oliver collects his modest winnings—I'm down twenty bucks—and we head toward the train. We plant ourselves in a spot near the grandstand exit and watch for Frank, who fails to materialize. As the last stragglers climb onto the train, Oliver and I get on and collapse into a three seater. Oliver rests his head on my shoulder and the train pulls ahead.

"You feel all right?" I ask, looking down at the top of his head, wanting to cradle it, instill health in it.

"I feel great," he sighs. "I got chemo tomorrow, though. After chemo, I'll be sick for days. Don't worry, baby," he adds, looking up at me. "I don't care about petty vagaries of the flesh, I'm rich!" He yanks a wad of cash from his pocket and waves it in front of my face.

In a seat across from us a lumpy older guy glowers at us, clearly having not fared as well.

A half hour later the train pulls into Penn Station. Where this morning's cargo was full of inflated hopes and swapped tips, now the mood is dour. Surly guys jab by, hurtling themselves to the nearest bar. Raspy older women set their mouths tight and disappear into the glaring burlesque of rush hour Penn Station.

Oliver and I say our good-byes. He kisses me on each cheek then turns away, waving like a shy, young boy. I watch his ghostly thin frame as he threads through the rush of people.

I turn and head down into the subway. I feel a little sick to my stomach.

Mark Baxter

11 / A Tenderness Between Us

Wanda is up to no good. Clad only in a paint-smeared antique black lace nightie, she is painting some sort of mythological she-creature on her wall. The creature has an exquisite head adorned with horns. The body is that of a hyena with eight frightening breasts. Sometimes it is alarming to consider what must be lurking in my lady's subconscious.

As Wanda reaches up high to add a touch of red to one of the creature's horns, her nightie travels up her thighs, revealing her delightful bottom. She is wearing conservative cotton panties but they're a bit loose, and now, as she bends forward, I am tortured by the beauty that lies between her legs. I am not permitted to touch her while she's working.

During the opening weeks of our liaison, she would often throw me out of her house the moment I had sated her considerable sexual appetites.

"You've inspired me and I thank you, now I must work," she would say, and, still naked or clad only in one of her lovely sex garments, she would literally shove me out the door. In time, I coerced her into letting me stay to watch her work. While she does this, I practice piano in my head. These practices are particularly fruitful, inspired as they are by the sight of Wanda.

When she bent forward moments ago, I had just been working on a difficult passage of the Schoenberg that I'll be playing in the Havemeyer Competition a few days from now. I'd been making good progress until Wanda bent forward.

Now I am in pain.

I quietly get up from the futon. I am wearing only my boxer shorts, which are tenting gloriously at the front. I walk up behind Wanda and put my nose an inch from her wondrous hair. She smells of sex and paint thinner. She suddenly reaches behind her and jabs at me with a paintbrush, managing to streak my stomach and boxer shorts.

"These were exorbitantly expensive," I say, motioning at the boxers as she turns around to scowl at me.

"You know the rules, Mark. You stay in your spot and leave me be or you are out."

"But look at me," I protest, indicating the streaks of paint on my stomach.

"Now look at you," she says, suddenly sweeping her paintbrush up my arm, coating it too in blue paint.

Were she anyone else, I would be extremely angry. But she is Wanda. Though she is eight years my senior, she is an impetuous, horrible child, albeit an intelligent, radiant one. And I love her.

She stands, measuring me with her honey-colored eyes; her mouth is in a half laugh. I look at her sternly.

"It's impossible to look severe with a hard-on like that," she says, reaching down into my boxers. "You're now going to pay for disturbing my work," she threatens, pulling the boxers to my knees and putting her mouth on me. But I want more than her mouth. I pull her up by the shoulders and turn her around, yanking down the ungainly cotton panties and entering her.

That keeps her busy for a while.

But then it's the same old story. After she comes three times, she kicks me out. I'm still naked and half blue, but she shoves me toward the door.

I'm not amused anymore. I break away from her, and, no longer feeling good-natured about her fractiousness, go over to the futon to start putting my clothes on. She's turned back to her painting after hastily pulling her nightgown back on.

Once I dress, I collect the scores I brought—I had planned to read through these as we lay side by side on the futon. In this romantic fantasy, Wanda would read *Demonology*, a book of short stories she was completely enraptured by, while I absorbed myself in JSB's piano concertos in D minor and occasionally nibbled at Wanda's exposed body parts.

I stuff the scores into my satchel, suddenly feeling angry. I loathe feeling angry. I walk to the door. I hear Wanda come bounding behind me.

"Mark," she yells, "what are you doing?"

"Going," I say, not turning around.

She quickly inserts herself between me and the door. Gives me a show of rounded eyes and breasts spilling out of nightgown. It makes my heart hurt.

"Don't be angry. I'm sorry," she says, leaving her lips parted a fraction of an inch.

"Don't worry," I say, opening the door and passing through.

I can feel her astonishment. I'd never before reacted badly to her irreverent treatment of me. I stride down the hall and down the wide marble steps of her tenement. Just then, I loathe Wanda.

There are malingerers on her stoop. Hippie-type young white girls who are sitting dreamy-eyed, doing nothing at all.

"Excuse me," I threaten as I weave my way through them.

"Sorry," one of them beams up at me. She's glassy-eyed. Probably too much pot. Or perhaps she's another victim of yoga. Like the Wench.

Thinking of the Wench brings a wave of warmth. I hadn't dwelled on our most recent lesson just yet. The many horrors of it. Well, there really hadn't been that many. She had apparently practiced a bit. No doubt after doing her infernal yoga. The Wench is always trying to get me to go to a yoga class, claiming it will help me reduce stress before competitions. I once made the mistake of wearing a short-sleeve shirt, and Her Royal Stubby Fingeredness saw my rash.

"What's the matter with your arm?" she asked blatantly.

I told her it was none of her business, but this seemed to wound her, so eventually I confessed that it was just a bad case of dermatitis brought on by stress. Then, of course, she wanted to know what was stressing me, and I had to explain about the piano competitions. It was imperative for my career that I win one before turning twenty-one.

The Wench had instantly jumped up from the piano bench to demonstrate something called sun salutations. It was quite a spectacle, although I can't say I was opposed to the lovely Wench crawling around on the floor of my practice room at Juilliard. It did give me something to savor later. Nonetheless, the Wench still hasn't succeeded in getting me into yoga.

As I walk north, thinking I'll eventually hop on a subway, I picture Wanda as I'd first seen her, wearing an absurd white plastic coat with a fake fur collar. She'd been gawking at a small Rembrandt at the Met. I go there regularly to visit the Caravaggios. I find that I can amuse myself for long stretches of time by observing the masses as they amble through that particular gallery. Almost everyone is drawn to the Caravaggios. It is deeply enjoyable to see the pull that strange, long dead little man's work has on people whose lives he would be hard pressed to fathom.

On that particular day, having an hour to kill before crossing the park to get to my next class, I took my time, going to look at paintings other than my beloveds. Though I loathe Vermeer, find Goya abhorrent, and have little use for Titian, I am fond of Rembrandt. I went to take a look at one of my favorites, a nice little dark depiction of Saint Peter in his dotage. I found that a lass was hoarding the painting, standing just a few inches in front of it and effectively blocking if from anyone else's view. I was so horrified by her white plastic coat that I refused to look at the face that belonged to it. Until she turned around. When she turned around, I was lost.

"Don't mind me, I like to pretend it's mine," she said, gesturing over her shoulder at the Rembrandt.

"Of course," I said, understanding perfectly. "Don't let me interfere." My initial annoyance was melted by the radiance of her grin. It made me feel generous and tolerant.

"Come," she said, reaching for my arm and gently pulling me to stand at her side. "It's so tragic," she said, indicating poor little withered Saint Peter. "When I'm sad I come see it and the sadness leaves."

We stood together, blocking the Rembrandt from all interlopers. Many minutes passed.

"I must go," I said eventually.

She looked up at me, smiled, and then, shockingly, rose onto her tiptoes and kissed me full on the mouth.

I stood swaying a little.

"Go on, then," she said, laughing. "You said you had to go."

"But—" I protested.

"But I will see you back here at the same time on Friday," she said.

I was there a half hour early on Friday. I parked myself on the bench nearest the Rembrandt. For three days I had been weak-kneed remembering the strange encounter. It had taken monumental feats of concentration to practice properly. I was exhausted by it all. I sat on the bench, waiting for the lovely woman who loved Rembrandt.

When she arrived, wearing a purple coat this time, I instantly took her arm and led her to my Caravaggios.

"Oh yes, I guessed that you loved them too," she said.

Then she kissed me again. At first I resisted. I was afraid my legs would embarrass me by giving in. But she demanded that I succumb and I did. Until a security guard archly recommended a motel room.

I was blind and addled as she led me out of the museum and onto a downtown bus. The bus was filled with people, none of whom had a clue that this attractive woman was torturing me. She wasn't looking at me or touching me but I was burning alive from fever. Eventually the bus ride ended. She led me up to the top flight of a five-story tenement, into an apartment reeking of paint and cigarette smoke.

After locking the door, she removed my coat and dropped it on the floor. I didn't protest although it was a black cashmere coat given me by my godmother, Dot, who also pays my Juilliard tuition. She removed her own coat and stood before me, her body an inch from mine. She arched her face toward me, her honey-colored eyes looking earnestly into me.

I asked her name. Wanda wasn't necessarily the answer I'd hoped for, but I've come to like it.

She unbuttoned my white cotton shirt and ran her hands over my chest. "You're very young," she said.

"So are you," I said, already sensing that, though she was older than me, she was just an overgrown impetuous child.

She smiled at this. She was about to do God knows what to me when I took control of the situation, surprising her by ripping the little row of buttons fastening her green pants and hiking the pants down over her hips. She stood grinning at me, pleased at what I'd done. I turned her around, removed her sweater, and kissed her lower back, my lips trailing down to her ripe bottom. I bit each luscious cheek. She tried to turn back around but I gently pushed her onto the floor. I covered her with my body and bit her neck. She let out a small yelp. She struggled underneath me, apparently unaccustomed to not being in charge. I let her up. She looked crazed. She ripped at my pants, breaking the zipper as she tore them off me. She put her mouth on what was, until then, the most painful erection of my life. I didn't want to come that way. I pushed her back and told her I wanted to be inside her now. I watched her hunt around for condoms. She was wearing bright pink lace panties and a translucent pink tank top. She was exquisite.

Eventually she located a condom and put it on me. I entered her, finally.

I didn't let myself come. I didn't trust her.

For two weeks I would visit her each night but never let myself come.

I can't say the same for her.

I'd had my share of sexual encounters before Wanda, and they'd all left me wishing I hadn't taken the time. These encounters had been with nervous girls who were gifted musicians or dancers. None of them understood their own bodies, never mind mine. Now, all that was changed. However, Wanda didn't give me much of herself when we weren't in bed. Just little bits here and there. She was estranged from her parents and had put herself through two years of art school by doing electrical work. Eventually she had tired of school. She now worked thirty-odd hours a week with electricity, the rest with paint— and with me. She soaked me up. She was avidly curious about music and knew nothing. I taught her.

When the Wench started taking lessons from me, I saw the first sign of jealousy in Wanda.

"Who is this woman you're teaching?" she'd wanted to know when I came to her place after giving the Wench her first lesson. Ordinarily I only taught children. But I thought an adult would be challenging. And I was right.

"Just some woman. She's a little odd. Took up piano a year ago and she's not young. There isn't much hope for her but she's intelligent and she pays me."

"Is she beautiful?"

"Not exactly."

"But she's very attractive."

"Maybe," I conceded.

"Tell me," Wanda said, turning the jealousy into a fierce sexual encounter, making me tell her, as I entered her, what I imagined Ruby looked like unclothed.

I felt slightly odd the next time I gave the Wench a lesson. But I wasn't truly interested in the Wench. She was more than ten years my senior, she was stubborn, and most likely not attracted to me.

Now I find myself thinking of the Wench wistfully. Wanda was difficult. The other women who pursued me were like birds. Flighty and insubstantial. But the Wench probably isn't the answer. All the same, I decide to call her. We have to set the time of our next lesson anyway.

I take my cell phone out and ask it to call. I have her in my phone book under *Wench*. The phone rings four times and a machine comes on, asking that I leave only really good messages.

"A tall order, your highness," I tell the infernal machine. "This is your piano teacher. I wonder when it is you would next care to show me what you've been doing to JSB. Do call me."

Referring to Bach as JSB had formed a tender bond between us. I had always thought of him that way, and during our second lesson, Ruby called him this, which is when I'd known with certainty that I could teach her.

I put the phone back in my pocket and keep walking uptown.

I feel sad.

Ruby Murphy

12 / Hotwalker

I get home to Coney and find Ramirez's door open. My neighbor is in his customary position at the kitchen table. Chin resting in hands. Skin dark against his white wife beater and the bright yellow of the kitchen. Elsie, his girlfriend, is standing near him, leaning her hip on the edge of the kitchen table. She's wearing nothing but a pair of panties and one of Ramirez's T-shirts, the front of it distended by her enormous, surgically enhanced breasts.

"Ruby!" She beams.

"Elsie, hello," I say, endeavoring not to stare at her minimal getup.

"We were just feeling my chest," she says, putting her small pudgy hands to her enormous breasts. "They hurt like a motherfucker. Feel this," she says, grabbing my hand and placing it on one of her gargantuan glands.

Her face is eager for my reaction as my fingers play over the hard lump. "Oh God, Elsie, that's horrible." I pull my hand back.

"Feels nasty, right?" Ramirez asks.

I nod. "Are you gonna be okay?" I look at Elsie, trying not to stare at her chest.

She shrugs. "I guess so. The thing that makes me mad is I can't work now. Ain't nobody gonna give me a job with fucked-up titties."

"Come on," I protest, "there's got to be something you can do."

"Pfffh. I used to think about law school. But not now. Not at my age," she says.

"Why not?" I smile, picturing her kitted up in a business suit, sexy and bossy in bitch red nails and a navy mid-calf skirt.

"I'm old," says the woman one year my senior. "And I'm tired," she adds, cupping her breasts again to show me exactly what has tired her so profoundly.

I roll my eyes at her. Then, to take her mind off her troubles, I tell her about my own new job following Frank. Neither she nor Ramirez looks particularly approving.

"That doesn't sound safe, lady." Ramirez frowns and shakes his big head.

"It's fine, for now," I tell my neighbor.

At which point Stinky, who's heard my voice through the door, starts wailing out his hunger cry. I excuse myself, leaving Elsie and Ramirez to their own devices.

There is chaos in my apartment. Stinky has evidently gotten in under the sink and pulled the trash bag out of the can. There are eggshells, coffee grounds, and other malodorous items strewn across the light green linoleum floor. Lulu has jumped up onto the shelves and knocked all the spice jars down. Anytime I'm gone more than a few hours, the cats express their disgust in this way.

I notice that the answering machine is blinking wildly. I begrudgingly hit Play and listen to two messages from Ariel and one from my

insane piano teacher, Mark Baxter. He sounds sort of down. I contemplate calling him back but my fiercely anxious cats are weaving
between my calves, demanding dinner.

No sooner have I put the beasts' meat in their bowls than the cell
phone chirps. I pull it out of my pocket and hit the Talk button.

"You're very fond of horses, aren't you, Ruby?" Ariel says by way
of greeting.

"Sure," I tell her. "Why?" I add, suspicious.

"I'd like it if you put in a little cameo appearance as a hotwalker."

"What?"

"Hotwalkers are the people who walk the horses off after morning exercise."

"Yeah, I realize that. . . ." She's beginning to annoy me.

"I'd like for you to go work as one for a short time. With Arnold
Gaines, the trainer that Frank works for. If you present yourself at
Belmont tomorrow, Gaines's assistant, a man by the name of Ned
Ward, will hire you."

"How on earth did you work that out?"

"That's of no importance," she says tersely.

"But I don't want another job," I protest.

"It's not a job job, Ruby. It will enable you to keep an eye on
Frank. You needn't do it for very long. A week should surely suffice.
Maybe less. You'll be paid. By me and by them. Though what they'll
pay you isn't much. Five dollars a head, I believe."

"Five dollars a head?"

"Each horse you walk off."

"Christ. You know how long it takes to cool a horse down?"

"I have no idea."

"A long time."

"Oh. Does this mean you'd rather not do it?"

"No."

"No?"

"No, I don't mind. I guess."

"Oh, Ruby . . ." she says.

"Yes?"

"Thank you."

"Right," I say.

"Oh, there is one thing. . . ."

"What's that?"

"You need to present yourself at the Belmont security gate at five A.M."

"*Five* A.M.?"

"Oh my. I was afraid of this. Are you not a morning person?"

"Being at Belmont at five A.M. requires something above and beyond a morning person. Do you know what time I'll have to get up?"

"Oh. Well . . ."

"Well I guess I'm getting up in a few hours."

"I truly appreciate this, Ruby."

"One would hope, Ariel."

I click the phone off and stare from my piano to my cats to my red shoes, which are sitting in the middle of the living room floor. I feel obscenely lonely.

I try calling Mark Baxter back. Not that he's likely to cheer me, but as insane as he is, there's something deeply sexy about him, and really, the only thing that's kept me from pouncing is a previous experience with a twenty-one-year-old. In conversation I discovered that his mother was only six years older than me. This was too weird. I don't need to revisit such feelings. All the same, it is pleasing to talk to insane sexy men. Mark's machine comes on, his clipped voice carefully enunciating the number I have reached. I hang up.

I walk over to the piano and forage for my Handel piece in the stack of sheet music. Lulu perches on top of the ancient Steinway and watches as I attempt different voicings of the opening chord. About a half hour into my Handel session, the phone rings. I jump up from the piano bench, glad for the distraction, and get it on the third ring.

It's Jane, my closest female friend. Jane the yoga addict who has all but abandoned me this last year as she's forged further and further into the world of yoga.

After chastising her for not calling in many days, I ask how she is.

"I held a ninety degree headstand for twenty breaths today," she announces.

I sigh. Listening to exacting reports on the details of Jane's yoga practice is my penance for boring her with the particulars of my currently nonexistent sex life.

I dutifully ask questions about the ninety degree headstand, and even have mild pangs of jealousy since I can only hold it for a few seconds before I come clomping down, not so much from lack of balance or strength as from an overwhelming fear that I'm going to fall forward, crunch my neck, break my spine, and spend the rest of my life incontinent and paralyzed.

After Jane has pattered on a good while, I casually mention my new career as a private investigator and hotwalker.

"What?" Her voice climbs two octaves.

"I'm being paid to follow this woman's boyfriend. And now I have to get up at three in the morning and go work at Belmont."

"What?" Jane's voice stays in the high registers.

I run it by her again.

I have, hands down, won the "*bet you can't top this*" contest that is one of the tender rituals of our friendship. I then tell her what's what with Oliver. Though she doesn't know him well, Jane adores Oliver. And, like me, she can't quite come to terms with someone so full of life being diagnosed with terminal cancer.

"I can't believe you dragged him to a racetrack," Jane chides.

"He was so happy, though. You should have seen him. Radiant." Jane sighs.

"I should go now," I say eventually. "I have to go see a man about a horse in four hours. Or see a horse about a man. Something. In four hours."

"And do I ever get to see you again, actually have dinner with you or something?" Jane asks.

"Yes. I have no idea when, though, now that I'm the girl with three jobs."

Jane bids me sweet dreams and we hang up. I feel a little bit better.

I round up my cats and put them onto the bed. Before I've even gotten under the covers, they both jump down and shoot me withering glances for trying to impose affection on them.

I pull the blanket over my head and fall into a deep, dreamless sleep.

x

SEEMINGLY MOMENTS later, the alarm goes off. I stare in disbelief at the clock's face telling me it's three A.M. With a wave of horror I remember that I not only have to get up, but I must travel all the way to the far reaches of Queens to partake of physical labor.

I feed the cats, slug back two cups of coffee, get in three pages of *Anna Karenina*, and then do ten perfunctory sun salutations. I throw on some clothes, stuff a hairbrush and a raincoat in my backpack and head out.

Ramirez's door is, for once, closed. One of the mysteries of Ramirez is that the man never sleeps. No matter what time of day or night I come in, if he's home, he's awake with the door open. Ramirez works as an independent contractor for the city in the winter, doing clean-up jobs; in summer he operates the Inferno ride in Astroland. It's not like he doesn't need sleep. Either of these jobs is fairly taxing. But I think he's like the guy in the Tom Waits song:

He came home from the war with a party in his head
And an idea for a fireworks display . . .

There are things inside Ramirez's head that keep him up most nights.

I emerge into the predawn darkness and walk to the subway station, climbing up the many stairs to the deserted platform. A train waits with open doors, its innards brightly lit. I take a seat and stare ahead.

In theory I like the idea of what I'm about to do. Pretending to be someone I'm not. Spending time around horses. In practice, though, it's already turning out to be a logistical nightmare. I've got to get all the way to Jamaica, Queens, and switch over to the Long Island Railroad. Then walk a ways from the train station to the track. And then what? Are they just going to laugh at me when I present myself? And will Frank catch on to the fact that I'm watching him?

I worry over all this as the doors whoosh shut and the train begins making its way through the darkened hinterlands of Brooklyn.

At Avenue U, the ill-fated stop where Ariel got on forty-eight very long hours ago, yet another willowy misplaced-looking blonde gets on. This one, thankfully, minds her own business.

I switch over to the Long Island Railroad in Jamaica. It's still too early for most commuters. There's one lanky gray-haired guy who looks like he washes his face with Ajax, and across from him there's a crazy woman with a bunch of suitcases. She smells strongly of lilacs.

x

TWENTY MINUTES later I'm walking along the highway to the racetrack's backstretch entrance. It's chilly out but I'm so busy worrying that I'm sweating by the time I reach the Belmont security booth.

A brassy blonde in a brown rent-a-cop uniform sneers out a "Can I help you?"

"I'm here to see Ned Ward, in Arnold Gaines's barn," I say pleasantly.

"And you are?" She appraises me with vicious little button eyes.

I never look like I fit in. No matter where I go. Even if, like right now, I'm trying to look the part. I'm wearing old black jeans, a loose black sweater, and worn-out combat boots. I have my hair knotted at the back of my head. I figure I look like someone who's ready to walk a bunch of persnickety thoroughbreds. But obviously, to the security guard, I look out of place. I give her my name. She picks up a phone and dials.

"Yeah," she drawls into the receiver, "there's a Ruby here." She listens a moment. Frowns. "Yeah, asked for you, Mr. Ward." She fastens her tiny button eyes on me. "He don't know what you want," she says, pleased to tell me I'm not wanted.

"May I speak with him?" I reach for the phone.

"Tsk." She furiously swats my hand away.

"Tell him I'm supposed to come hotwalk for Arnold Gaines."

Security Bitch practically spits on me now that my true identity as a lowly hotwalker is revealed.

"Yeah, says she's here to walk hots," the brawny matron says into the phone. "He'll come get you," she says, hanging up the receiver. "You can stand outside." She motions to the door.

"Have a nice day," I say, smiling menacingly as I pull the door shut behind me.

I stand to the side of the security booth, under one of the enormous old trees flanking the main entrance to the backstretch. It's a misty morning, fog deadening the sound of cars and trucks as they pull in. Security Bitch looks on eagle-eyed from her glass booth, checking each vehicle for its ID sticker.

After waiting ten minutes, I start to feel like a complete jerk. I should just give it all up, go back to Coney, and put in my shift at the museum. Ariel DiCello can solve her romantic problems without me and I can go back where I'm actually needed—lording over the ancient baubles that are all that's left of Coney's bawdy history and entertaining the various disturbos who come into the place.

Just as I'm thinking this, a guy walks up to me and introduces himself as Ned Ward, assistant trainer. He's lanky and has a pair of beautiful green eyes behind wire-rimmed glasses. The sight of him promptly dampens any notions about going anywhere but here.

Ned Ward

13 / My Hotwalker-to-Be

I'm in Joe's stall going over the bay colt's hind legs when Sebastian hollers at me that there's a phone call. It's a little early in the day for the cretinous owners to be bothering me with their various *issues*.

"Who the hell is it?" I yell at Sebastian, keeping my hands on Joe's fetlocks.

"Marla up at Security," Sebastian hollers back.

I mutter under my breath, stand up, pat the colt on the neck and walk out of his stall. I go down the aisle to the office. Sebastian's already disappeared somewhere.

"Yeah?" I say, picking up the phone's receiver.

Marla, the unpleasant lass who mans the front gate security booth, informs me there's a girl to see me about walking hots. I grumble at Marla that I'll be over to get the girl. I'd forgotten all about it.

Arnie called me at home last night, disturbing me from the unwholesome task of flushing out the wounds on a kitten that had gotten kicked by a horse and that I'd taken home to look after. Arnie told me I was hiring a new hotwalker the next morning. Came recommended through a friend of his, which is no keen recommendation. Arnie's an adequate trainer but a lousy judge of character. The people he calls friends are a scabrous lot of inept misanthropes, and I can't say much better about the owners he attracts or the help he hires. His head groom, Sebastian, is the only good egg in the bunch, and it's a fluke Arnie ever hired him to begin with.

I'd told Arnie I'd do as he asked and hire the hotwalker and then I hung up before he started going off about any number of the things that get his goat. I went back to looking after the kitten. A little black and orange splotch of a thing that had never had any sense around the horses and that I'd have to find a home for soon since I'm almost always at the track. I'd been having Lena, the tarted-up Russian émigré next door, come in to tend to the kitten twice a day. But I didn't feel good about that. Lena wanted to get down my pants, and I was sure she was going through my drawers, probably fondling my socks and reading my junk mail.

Eventually I'd finished tending to the kitten, gotten a whopping four hours of shut-eye, then headed back to the track. The kitten hadn't eaten much this morning, so between worrying about her and trying to figure out why Joe, the bay colt, wasn't amounting to much as a race horse, I had my head full and had completely forgotten about the hotwalker.

I take the shitty blue bike out of the office and hop on, riding it down the main road that weaves between the endless rows of green barns. Would have taken me fifteen minutes to walk all the way up to the main gate to retrieve the new hotwalker. The bike, crappy as it is, will get me there in three. I get the thing going at a pretty good clip and have a hell of a time stopping when a loose horse suddenly appears right in front of me. I slam on the backpedal breaks, which makes the front wheel skid, and I come off, landing on my ass and nearly getting trampled by the loose horse.

A frantic-looking groom is circling the horse, holding a bucket of feed, trying to corner the colt. I leave the bike and get on the other side of the horse, helping the groom out. He finally gets to the horse's head, grabs hold of the halter and gets a lead shank on. After all that, the guy doesn't even thank me, just shoots me a filthy look like it was my fault the horse got away from him in the first place.

I hop back on the bike and the rest of the short trip is uneventful.

Waiting outside the security booth, looking extremely uncertain about everything, is a good-looking woman. I probably do a double take. And then decide she's waiting for somebody else. I walk right past her, into the security booth, where Marla turns her little eyes to me.

"That's her out there," she says, motioning at the babe. "The hotwalker."

"Oh. Thanks, Marla," I say. She chortles and grunts and turns back to her *People* magazine.

I go back outside the booth. The babe has her back to me now. Good ass. I walk around to face her.

"You're the hotwalker?"

"Yeah," she says, still looking deeply uncertain. "I mean, I haven't done it before, not racehorses, but I've been around horses." She speaks quickly and looks like she's expecting me to tell her to take a hike.

I don't really need another useless hotwalker but at least she looks good. She has a lot of dark hair tied up at the back of her head. She's wearing fairly shapeless clothing, but I can tell by the way she holds herself that she has something nice going on under there. As for her face, it's a great thing. Huge gray eyes and a very inviting full red mouth. The nose is elegant and small.

I guess I get a little absorbed because I'm startled when she speaks.

"So what do I do now?" she asks.

"Oh," I say, staring at her. "Work, I guess. We'll try you, at least."

"Yeah?" she says, and some life comes into her eyes, making her that much more tantalizing.

"Let's go," I say, a little gruffly because she's unsettling me. Not the way Lena the émigré does. No. That's just annoyance and tart tactics. This hotwalker girl is understated. Makes you want to pull her clothes off her. Just what I don't need in my life. A distraction on the backside.

I push the crummy blue bike at my side and walk briskly, noticing that the girl, being substantially shorter than I am, has to half jog to keep up with me. Then, the minute we start walking between the rows of barns, the girl goes goofy on me. She comes to a dead stop and just gawks ahead.

"What's the matter?" I ask impatiently.

"Horses," she says, rapt and breathless, like a lunatic or a visionary.

"Yeah, you see a lot of that around here," I say, shaking my head and walking on.

She takes a deep breath, inhaling slowly and smiling. "I'm Ruby, by the way," she says, scrambling again to keep up with me.

"So you are," I tell her.

We reach Arnie's shedrow and I lean the bike against the outside office wall, knowing someone else will need it soon. I poke my head in the office to see if Arnie's come in yet, but he hasn't.

Sebastian is just leading Joe, the bay colt, out of his stall.

"There." I indicate the colt to Ruby. "Walk him around the shedrow once."

She looks startled, stares at me for a second, then gathers herself and goes over to where Sebastian and Joe are standing.

"Sebastian, this is Ruby, we're gonna try her out walking hots," I say.

Sebastian grunts at Ruby then hands her the colt's lead shank. I watch. At least she knows to get on the left side of the horse. Once she has a firm grip on the shank, she goes and stands by his left eye, letting him get a look at her. She pats him firmly on the neck. Joe puts his ears forward, seeming to approve.

"That's Raging Machete," I tell her, "but we call him Joe. Nice enough individual. Won't kill ya. Walk him around the shedrow once then put him up on the wall."

The girl blinks at me. "On the wall?"

"You'll see a bungee cord on the wall of the horse's stall. You tie him to that. Okay?"

She nods then turns her attention back to Joe. She seems far more taken with the horse than with me. Maybe she'll turn out to be a decent worker after all.

I follow her with my eyes until she and the colt disappear around the bend of the shedrow. No doubt when she gets to the other side, where Christopher Murray keeps his string of claimers, she'll get catcalled by Pepe and the rest of the sleepy-eyed louts Murray has working for him. Murray and his brother Jonathan are decent trainers, but they don't exactly rake in the big bucks, and this means they have to feed off the bottom of the barrel helpwise. Pepe and the others are lazy and lecherous as all get-out. The bunch of them almost had a heart attack the time Lena the émigré came by to stand around on her wobbly spike heels and exclaim "Ooohh, pretty horsey" until I made her leave. But girls like her live for that kind of attention. Ruby, I guess, does not.

I put the hotwalker out of my head for a few minutes and go into the office to check Arnie's notes for which horses are working this morning. While I'm in there the phone rings again. This time it's Lena, wanting to know what time she should go check on the kitten.

"You use your judgment, Lena," I say, and when she doesn't seem to understand, I tell her to just go check on the cat at noon and I hang up. Arnie arrives, looking like a man who's slept badly and owes a lot of money. My employer is not a pretty man, but right now he's unprettier than usual. He's about five-seven, but he's at least as wide as he is tall. He doesn't have much hair and does unusual things with what is there. His nose is bulbous and his lips are fat.

"Morning, Arnold," I say.

"Yeah, what's good about it?" he demands. He has an unlit cigar stub planted in his mouth. I want to rip it out of his face. I've only been working for the man for six or so weeks but I've already grown tired of him. Unfortunately, I need the job. So I just grin at him, like his foul mood is a quaint thing I'm honored to be privy to.

I give him a quick report on how all the horses look this morning. He grunts at me then tells me to get things going, take the first set up to the track to work.

"Oh yeah, and Ruby showed up," I tell him.

"Who?" he says.

"Ruby, the hotwalker you told me to hire. She seems all right."

For a moment he looks puzzled, then he seems to remember. He grunts once more.

I leave the office, go down the aisle and into Lotus Cat's stall to start tacking him up. Lotus Cat nods at me vigorously as I pat his neck.

Most of the time, I prefer the company of horses to that of humans.

About ten minutes later I have three horses ready to take up to the track. As Lotus Cat is a fairly reasonable young colt, I've given him to Ruby to lead, while Sebastian has Cipullo's Honor, and Macy is trying to contain Miss Seattle, a feisty bay filly who hasn't raced yet but, we all suspect, will be worth her weight in gold once she starts.

Gaines has disappeared without offering me a ride up to the track. I consider riding the bike up but then opt for walking along next to Sebastian and Cipullo's Honor, a decent allowance horse who runs good but is fidgety as hell around the barn.

Sebastian isn't in a talkative mood. After exchanging a few

thoughts on some of the new exercise riders—he's very enthusiastic about one particular redheaded lass named Asha Yashpinsky, whom I happened to notice him ogling a few mornings in a row—we fall silent.

X

THERE'S FOG hanging over the track, giving the whole place a ghostly look, what with horses and humans suddenly materializing out of nowhere.

I go over to where I see Ruby standing with Lotus Cat. Both horse and woman are attentively staring at the track. As I go to tighten the colt's girth, I'm gratified to find that Ruby knows to hold the horse's head tightly so he can't take a nip at either of us. I like this girl.

Which is more than I can say for Little Molly Pedersen, apprentice jockey and our main exercise rider, who has just appeared at my side.

"Morning, Molly." I offer a half smile.

The girl grunts at me, looks at Lotus Cat, and fusses with the strap on her crash helmet.

She'd be a real looker if it weren't for her personality. She's a small blond woman with bright blue eyes and a pretty mouth that unfortunately is almost always pursed in disgust. She comes from a long line of horse people, each one more unpleasant than the last. Her uncle is head groom for Will Lott, one of the nicest, wisest trainers going. Why a guy like Lott would hire such a surly individual no one knows, though rumor has it that it all started with Fakir, the great champion Will Lott had back in the nineties. Fakir supposedly loved Jimmy John Mancuso, Molly's uncle. And Lott has kept him on ever since. As for Molly, she's as grouchy as her uncle, but it all goes away the second you put her on a horse. Maybe it's why we keep hiring her. For the fun of watching her transform from rabid bitch on wheels to purring kitten the second you give her a leg up.

And now, as I prepare to do just that, she turns her sneering little visage to me.

"He gonna fuck with me today?" She indicates Lotus Cat with her chin.

"Hope not," I tell her.

"Where's Arnie?" she asks as I throw her up into the saddle.

"He's coming," I tell her just as a Mercedes SUV noses up to the rail of the track and my employer, the charming Arnold Gaines, emerges right on cue.

"You stay on that colt today, will you?" Gaines barks at the blond woman.

Molly rolls her eyes at him and then launches into a tirade about how Arnie might consider getting his horses out of their stalls a little more often so they might not attempt to murder anyone who gets on their backs.

Arnie doesn't like this and issues a few barbs about Molly's talents. "You think it's an accident you're still an apprentice?" he quips, at which point the small woman's eyes pop with rage.

She promptly hops down off Lotus Cat's back, hands the reins to poor Ruby, who's standing by with her mouth hanging open, and storms away.

Sebastian, Ruby, and Macy all feign deep interest in their shoes as Gaines stands there, looking like a cartoon character with steam coming out of his ears.

"Who are you?" he suddenly barks at Ruby.

"Ruby," she tells him.

"You ride?"

"A little."

"You got a license?" he asks her.

"She's the new hotwalker," I intervene, before he tries putting the poor girl up on the colt's back. "I'll go retrieve Molly."

After asking a few grooms if they noticed where she went, I

encounter none other than Asha Yashpinsky, her eyes twinkling with amusement as she tells me Molly has gone into the clockers' shed.

I climb the steps and find the unpleasant Miss Pedersen giving the poor clockers a piece of her mind. The two old guys, helplessly clutching their stopwatches and binoculars, are trying to keep their eyes on the horses they're timing as Molly rants about Gaines like it's got anything to do with them.

"I'm sick of that fat piece of shit," she says, turning her wrath on me.

"We all are, Molly, but could you please just go out there and get on the horse? I don't want to have to hire Asha Yashpinsky."

This, as I suspected it would, gets her goat. Though Asha is too tall to be a jockey, and until recently was only a pony rider, lately she's proving to be a fine exercise rider. And she's likable. Molly looks furious at the suggestion and promptly follows me out of the clockers' shed and back over to where Arnie and the rest of the group are standing and waiting.

Ruby and Lotus Cat both appear to be lost in some daydream. Horse and hotwalker are staring out at the track longingly. I startle Ruby by putting a hand on her shoulder.

"I'll take him," I tell her, reaching for the chestnut's lead shank and bringing him over to Molly.

Molly spits on the ground once then fits her tiny foot into my palm, letting me throw her up into the saddle once more. Lotus Cat dances and chews on his bit. I watch Molly take a strong hold of him as Herbie, one of the pony riders we use, steers his bay gelding over to Lotus Cat's side. Lotus Cat, who adores Herbie's horse, buries his nose in the bay's neck and keeps it there as the bay leads the way onto the track.

The sun, struggling out from the cloud bed, is starting to burn the fog off the track, and the geese that live in the pond at the center of the track's green oval are flapping their wings and honking. I remember one time, during a race, some geese were resting on the track and, as the horses came around the bend, a goose attempted to fly away but didn't get enough lift and smacked one of the horses between the eyes, stopping the colt's momentum. All wagers on the horse were refunded, even though he managed to finish seventh. The goose died.

I focus my binoculars and pick Lotus Cat and Molly out from the pack.

Sure enough, the little witch is transformed, face split open by a grin—an uninhibited, beautiful grin. She presses the colt into a strong gallop and the pair hit full speed as they pass the five-eighths pole. I get a little pang of envy, like I do sometimes. I ride okay but I'm much too big for exercising. Once in a while I pony one of our horses in the morning, but I've never gotten to go full speed. I envy her.

As the two fly past the wire, Molly stands up in the stirrups, pulling the big red colt down to a slow gallop and eventually a trot. I go back to the rail, where I see Ruby standing, looking rapt and dreamy. I get a very keen urge to just fold her in my arms, maybe pick her up, carry her over into the grandstand and make out with her for several hours, as if we were high school kids.

Instead, I go stand at her side. I say not a word as we wait for Molly to bring Lotus Cat off the track.

Ruby Murphy

14 / Two Ornery Blond People

I'm at the rail, stupefied at the sight of so much gorgeous horse-flesh. The way I feel right now, I'd gladly spend the rest of my life standing right here. But no sooner have I formulated this particular thought than it's time to make the doughnuts. Molly, the foul-tempered apprentice, is steering Lotus Cat back toward where I'm standing. Though my first impression of Molly wasn't good, the moment she got on the colt, she stopped spitting expletives and turned gorgeous. And still looks that way now. Until she catches sight of Gaines.

She's frowning horribly as she hops down, hands the reins to Ned, and strides off without another word.

Ned passes the colt's reins to me. "Take him back to the barn, cool him out. Hold him while Sebastian bathes him," he tells me, then pulls a little memo pad from his pocket and scrawls something in there.

I stare at him, feeling overwhelmed. He looks up.

"Lose something over here?"

"No," I say, feeling like a dolt.

I try to look composed as I take the colt's lead shank and steer him toward the muddy road back to the barn area. Lotus Cat is tired. His neck is black with sweat and the veins are sticking out. His eyes are bulging a little, like they've just glimpsed something unfathomable.

As we make our way back toward the rows of dark green barns, other hotwalkers and grooms look at me like I'm dessert. There aren't exactly a lot of women around here, and from what I've gathered, most of the workers live on the track and don't get out much. I think the only women they ever see are owners—who probably aren't exactly approachable—and the occasional female trainer or backstretch worker, none of them renowned for their beauty. Though I'm not exactly the Sex Goddess of the World, my stock is evidently running pretty high here on the Belmont backside.

I find Sebastian outside the barn, bathing Miss Seattle, the bay filly who just had a schooling session with the dreaded starting gate—the metal contraption the horses have to learn to pop out of, going from zero to forty in fractions of seconds.

Macy is holding the filly, talking to her as Sebastian dunks her tail in a bucket of suds. I start walking Lotus Cat in little circles, not sure if I'm supposed to bathe him myself or what. I keep hoping Macy will look up and volunteer his help. He does not.

"Uh, am I supposed to bathe this colt?" I ask tentatively.

Macy and Sebastian both stop what they're doing and stare at me. They make an abruptly contrasting pair, Macy big and very white, Sebastian thin and black, with most of his narrow face obscured by the brim of a maroon-colored Jockey Club Gold Cup baseball cap.

I offer a tentative smile.

"Hotwalkers don't bathe," Sebastian says curtly.

"Ah," I say. I walk the colt around in a circle.

Sebastian suddenly wheels around to look at me again. "Get the tack off that horse." He frowns. "Then unwrap him," he adds, motioning to the wrappings on the colt's legs.

I peel off the exercise saddle and padding. Lotus Cat stands still as a saint as I crouch down and unwrap the bandages from his hind legs.

A few minutes later I hold the colt as Sebastian starts bathing him. Lotus Cat isn't very pleased about this and dances and tugs on the lead shank.

"Stop dancing," I tell him, tugging back. He flicks one ear forward, like he's considering my request. He stops dancing.

Sebastian actually grins up at me from under the brim of his cap. I guess I haven't ever seen him smile. His whole face is transformed, the narrow severity broken up by a wide grin full of even teeth.

Sebastian soaks the colt's red coat with warm water, carefully rubbing between the ears, under the forelock, and down between the eyes. The colt starts snorting and blowing snot on me, then suddenly leans into me and rubs his huge heavy head against my chest, nearly knocking me backward.

I laugh, push his head away and, as Sebastian crouches down at the colt's hind legs, put my nose up to Lotus Cat's and nuzzle with him. I feel like an idiot when I notice Ned Ward standing a few feet to my left, staring.

I look down at my soaking wet shirt then back at Ned. I grin. He frowns a little and walks away. I wonder if I've failed some sort of test.

Over the next few hours, the sun climbs high and beams down over steaming horses and frantic workers. I go about my business trying to pick up the details of my new job while keeping an eye out for Frank, who still hasn't appeared.

After the last set of horses has worked, I'm given my final charge of the morning. The bay colt with the white blaze. Raging Machete, aka Joe.

Joe's feeling a little droopy, having just put in a five-furlong work in 58.4. It's the fastest time on the track this morning, which, according to Ned, doesn't mean he's actually going to win a race anytime soon. The colt has a habit of putting in blistering works then forgetting how to run when he's in an actual race. Though Joe is well-bred and cost over $100K as a yearling, he's not proving to be much of a racehorse. He won his first ever start by ten lengths wire-to-wire but hasn't run in the money since. And no one can find anything wrong with him. Gaines apparently even sent Joe to some people in New Jersey who specialize in bringing the gold out of late bloomers. They had him swimming every day, gave him acupuncture and massage and even hired an animal psychologist. But no one could find a reason why Joe runs poorly in races. And Gaines, I gather, is sick of him. In fact, everyone seems sick of him, and I think the horse knows it. I swear, he seems sad.

He's standing with one hoof tucked under, head hanging low, slouching as I drape the sweat sheet over his back. He stares ahead blankly as I run the lead shank over his nose and through the back of his halter.

I lightly tug on the shank, asking him to walk.

He lets out a low groan, sighing like an old man with digestive distress. He's acting more like a thirty-year-old gelding than a three-year-old stallion. He seems so depressed that I drape my arm over the top of his neck.

"Come on, it's not that bad," I tell him. Joe sighs again.

I get him walking, and as I talk to him in an insanely cheerful voice, I imagine taking him away from here, keeping him in my backyard and growing old together. I have a recurring fantasy of living somewhere with a few acres and a couple of horses in the yard. I probably wouldn't even ride them. Just have them around for company. Let them poke their noses in the kitchen window in the morning when I'm making coffee. Groom them now and then, pick out their hooves and whatnot, but basically just let them be.

Of course, I don't even have a backyard.

A few minutes later, as I bring Joe to chomp at the grass on a little embankment, I finally come face-to-face with Frank, who apparently showed up while we were all up at the track with the second set of horses.

The sullen blond man is grazing a gray filly named Liz's Tizzy, a lovely allowance mare Ned introduced me to earlier, showing me how she's an angel as long as you don't touch her ears, one of which is malformed from when she got into a wasps' nest as a yearling.

Frank doesn't look at me or at anything other than the filly he's grazing. I try to think of hotwalker small talk, but before I can come up with anything, he turns toward me and scowls.

"Hi. I'm Ruby," I say.

"Oh yeah?" he drawls, not keenly interested.

"You like working here?" I say, trying to sound cheerful, friendly.

Frank looks at me like I'm a sick jerk, then says, "Maybe."

He tugs on his horse's lead shank and walks away.

What a guy.

I let Joe graze another five minutes before bringing him back to his stall. I take his halter off and watch him turn around twice before burying his nose in a flake of hay. I latch his stall door shut and drape his halter over a hook outside.

Ned is in the aisle, wrapping a bay filly's hind legs. He's down on his knees, trying to keep away from the filly's hooves, which she keeps lifting and aiming at his head. His hair is falling over his eyes and his glasses are perched at the end of his nose. He looks up at me. The glasses slide back where they're supposed to be.

"Who's that?" I indicate the filly.

"Sunrunner," he says, running a proprietary hand up her leg. "Another one by the late Seattle Slew. Well-bred little thing. Not so friendly, though."

Demonstrating precisely how unfriendly she is, the filly pins back her ears and shakes her head at me. This isn't a flattering look for her. She has a very small head that makes her eyes seem particularly large and flylike.

"She's got a weird face," I comment.

"Yup. That's her daddy. Most of them come out like that. But they can run. This one too," Ned says, finishing the wrap then slowly standing up. He keeps one hand on the filly's neck as he looks at me.

"So how are you doing there, Ruby Murphy?" he asks, much more solicitous than he's been so far.

"Good. Fine." I nod. "I like Joe."

"Joe." Ned sighs. "You wanna ask him what his problem is?"

"Huh?"

"Ask that horse why he doesn't want to win any races," Ned says, in apparent seriousness.

"Oh." I nod. "Okay."

Ned frowns at me. "You know, you won't get anywhere falling in love with horses like Joe."

"Get anywhere? Where am I going?"

"I assume that an intelligent woman isn't looking to spend the rest of her life walking hots or even rubbing. My theory is you've got your eye on my job."

For a minute I just stare at him, not sure if he's joking.

"Yes?" Ned says.

"Yes?"

"Is my theory on target?"

"Uh . . . I hadn't thought about it." I shrug. "I just needed a change from what I normally do. And I love horses. I thought it'd be a kick to do this awhile."

He looks at me like I'm completely insane. Yanks the sleeves of his sweatshirt up over his elbows then folds his arms over his chest. "Nothing to do with horses is a 'kick,' unless you mean that in the literal sense," he says. "It's backbreaking work. No money. No sleep. Beats your body up."

"Oh. So why do you do it?"

"Can't help it." He shrugs and looks down, as if admitting to a twenty-year dope habit.

He suddenly ducks into the tackroom and grabs a box of Vetwrap—the green elastic bandage material sometimes used on the horses' legs.

"What's the deal with that exercise rider girl, the blonde?" I ask quickly.

"Who, you mean Molly?" He turns back around to face me.

"Yeah."

"What about her?" He looks a little suspicious.

"What's she so angry about?"

"Dunno." He shrugs, then smiles a little. "They're all like that. The whole family. Wait till you meet her uncle. Guy's so surly he makes Molly seem like a cheerleader."

Ned stares at the box of Vetwrap like it's perplexing him. "The girl can ride but she can't keep her mouth shut. Comes from a long line of 'em. Her mother rubbed for Shug McGaughey until she got nasty arthritis. Now her uncle's head groom for Will Lott. Whole family of nasty horse people that would just as soon kill you as look at you. But horses like 'em. Molly's a good rider. She's an apprentice, you know. A bug girl. That's why Gaines uses her. She gets a very healthy weight allowance."

"Oh?" I say, just as Frank suddenly materializes, leading the gray filly to her stall. Ned calls him over and introduces us.

"Yeah, we met," Frank says, uninterested.

"You can call it a day," Ned tells him.

Though I know Gaines has two horses running in the afternoon's races, evidently Frank doesn't rate enough to be needed. And he certainly doesn't seem to care. Or maybe it's just that he has the personality of a cardboard box. He leads the gray to her stall, puts her away, then walks off without another word.

"And you can go home too," Ned tells me.

"I can?" I say, worried, figuring this means I'm fired.

"Yeah. You did good," he says, shucking me on the shoulder in a weird playful manner. "See you at five A.M.?" he asks, arching his eyebrows.

"Yeah, I'll be here." I nod vigorously.

Ned smiles, looks like he's on the verge of saying something more, then abruptly turns back to Sunrunner.

I stare at his back for a second, then grab my bag out of the tack room and quickly try to catch up with Frank. He's vanished, though. Swallowed up by the maze of barns and dirt roads.

A passing groom hey babies me and I nod, then walk toward the rest room trailer to clean up before starting the long journey home to Coney.

There are few women working on the backstretch, and the ladies' rest room is fairly pristine—though it does stink of faux citrus air freshener. I run warm water in the sink and dunk my dirty face in. As

I straighten up and dab myself with a paper towel, Molly comes in and stands at the sink next to mine. She gives me a perfunctory smile then turns to studying herself in the mirror. She's very pretty but all in miniature, like a painting of an Elizabethan child queen, the subject clearly a child but rendered in adult proportions.

"You're Little Molly?" I venture.

The girl turns and scowls at me. "Who the hell are you?" she spits, with a pronounced Brooklyn accent that's incongruous with her tiny Elizabethan frame.

"Nobody." I shrug and smile. "I just saw you riding today."

"Don't call me Little Molly."

"I'm sorry. I thought that's what they called you."

"Who the fuck is they?"

"I dunno, just people at the track, I guess," I say, horrified.

"I don't know who you are but I think you need to mind your own business," she says.

She looks at herself in the mirror one last time then turns and heads to the door.

"Hey," I call after her.

"What?" She wheels around, hissing.

"You don't have to be so rude."

"Oh I don't, huh? Says who?"

"You just don't," I say.

"Who the fuck are you?" She sneers.

"I'm Ruby."

"What's that supposed to mean?"

"That's my name. Ruby. I'm a hotwalker."

"You're a goddamned *hotwalker*?"

"So?"

"I'm a rider, okay? I put my life on the line every fucking day several fucking times a day. I don't need no shit from some fucking *hotwalker*."

Molly's eyes are about to pop out of her small head. Thankfully, at that moment a well-heeled older lady walks into the bathroom and I watch a phenomenal event take place on Little Molly's face as she tries to control her fit of pique—for the benefit of the well-heeled lady, who looks very concerned.

"Molly? Is everything all right?" The lady's gray eyebrows knit together like small sweaters of worry.

"Oh yes, Mrs. Levy, yes, everything's just fine," Molly says, stretching her tight mouth into something resembling a smile.

"Molly and I were just having a tête-a-tête about proper names," I tell the lady.

"Oh? Is that so? Well, don't let me keep you girls," Mrs. Levy says, daintily walking into one of the bathroom stalls.

Molly glowers at me then turns and goes out the door. I follow her out, fantasizing about tackling her from behind and rubbing her face in the dirt. Then my cell phone rings. I click the Talk switch and say "Hello, Ariel" into the phone as I watch Molly storm away.

"I remembered your cell phone number," comes Oliver's exuberant voice.

"Where are you?"

"At Sloan-Kettering. Getting chemo."

"Oh," I say dejectedly.

"I'm toxic right now. Where are you?"

"Belmont."

"Again?"

"I work here now," I say.

"You're working at the racetrack?" My friend sounds completely astonished.

"Yeah," I say, launching into a jumbled breakneck explanation of all that's happened since we parted yesterday.

"My God, that's beautiful," Oliver says when I stop for breath. "Why don't you get us a horse?"

"What?"

"Become a trainer and get us a horse, one of those cheap ones from the claiming races. Make us some money."

"I think most of these people don't make any money. They just like horses. Or they're immigrants and can't get any other jobs."

"Oh yeah?" Oliver is enthralled and immediately starts pumping me for details.

I give him a brief synopsis of my day on the backstretch. He in turn horrifies me with details of his afternoon of injections and vomiting.

"I don't want to make you stand around talking on a cell phone all day, I just wanted to say hello, and I had fun yesterday."

"Yeah, me too," I tell him softly.

I put the phone away and stand there, feeling sad and useless. The sky is streaked with gray, like it's empathizing with me.

I start walking to the main gate, going slowly, my body tired and sore. I'm just passing Barn 27 when I see Frank emerging from a tack room with none other than Little Molly at his side. The two seem to be exchanging vehement words, arguing as they walk up toward the track.

I want to go home. Lie on the floor. Listen to Bach. Instead, I tail Frank and Molly at a safe distance, wondering what Frank has done to incur the tiny blond woman's wrath. I follow the pair through the long tunnel leading from the backstretch to the saddling paddock. Ahead, a groom is walking a horse. The sound of hooves echoes off the tunnel's cement sides.

As Frank and Molly emerge from the tunnel, I see Molly gesticulating wildly. Frank hangs his head then suddenly turns on his heels and walks away from her, back toward me. He's so preoccupied he doesn't notice me. I follow him as he heads straight past the security gate and out in the direction of the train station.

Frank is evidently mulling over his troubles and doesn't notice as

I get on the train and take a seat two rows back from him. At Jamaica, I have to stay on the train rather than switching over to the Brooklyn bound subway.

At Penn Station, I follow Frank up the escalator and out onto Eighth Avenue.

It's early afternoon. Office workers are milling about in the half gray day, clutching newspapers and Starbucks cups. Frank pauses for a moment, fishes an electronic organizer from his pocket and fiddles with it. After a few minutes of this, he starts purposefully heading down Eighth Avenue.

I'm relieved when he makes a left on Twenty-third Street, evidently heading to the Chelsea. Once I've watched him enter the place, I call Ariel to tell her she's about to get a visit from her boyfriend.

"Oh . . ." she says in a plucked, tight little voice.

And right on cue I hear her doorbell ring. "There's Frank," I say into the phone. "I'll call you when I get home. Or call me later."

"All right," she says, though I can tell she wants to ask me eight hundred questions.

I hear the doorbell ring once more before she clicks off.

I put the phone away and look around me.

I need to buy cat meat and I'm in the middle of Chelsea, a neighborhood I don't know well. One given over to wealthy gay men and dot com people, who, come to think of it, are probably prime candidates for organic meat consumption.

Sure enough, I hit the jackpot at the first gourmet health food store I stumble into.

I fight my way through narrow aisles packed with expensive girls and arrogant guys, all of them looking disaffected, even as they shop for produce. As I make my way to the meat counter, I feel alienated and gnomish. I don't know if it's Manhattan or the world at large that's gotten like this: wealthy, pathologically self-involved. Shiny in a glassy, organized religion kind of way. One minute New York was a juicy boil of lust, crime, and possibility, the next it was just another innocuous American city. Thankfully, a lot of Brooklyn and all of Coney are intact. Lonesome and soulful in their faded neon grunginess.

A vicious-looking brunette in a red raincoat blatantly cuts in front of me in the meat line. I growl at her back. Her cell phone rings.

"Brent, hi! How are you?" she gushes into her minuscule phone.

When she finishes her conversation, I tap her on the shoulder. "You cut in front of me," I say.

"What?"

"You cut in line. Get behind me please."

"Ohhh." She forces out a faux smile and comes to stand behind me.

I order my organic ground turkey and get the hell out of there, scurrying for the Brooklyn bound subway, back to a safe corner in a world that baffles me.

Pietro Ramirez

15 / My Girl, Dancing

I'm running my hand up Elsie's smooth coffee leg, thinking that this is what it all boils down to: being next to someone, touching someone you know wants to be touched by you. For a few good moments I think about this and nothing else, but then Elsie, feeling my hand on her leg, wakes up from her little nap and turns over. She's got her breasts covered with a T-shirt, but I know what's under there and how it looks and that just isn't good.

"Hi baby," she says, opening her eyes and putting her hand to my cheek.

I kiss her hand. "Go back to sleep, my lady," I tell her, pulling the sheet over her.

She makes a little moaning sound and then says no, she's slept enough. She sits up in bed. Looks down at her chest. I wince. She shrugs.

"I gotta pee," she says.

I sit up in the bed, holding my head and feeling horrible as Elsie trots off into the bathroom.

The fact is, I ought to be down at the Inferno. We're opening up in three weeks, and Indio, the fire-eater from the sideshow, is down there supervising an ungodly bunch who are repainting my Inferno as well as designing a couple new mummies and a coffin or two. Indio's a good kid, but he smokes too much weed, and I imagine is right now passed out in a coffin somewhere while his crew runs amok.

Elsie comes out of the bathroom and she seems to feel good now. She leaps onto the bed and climbs on top of me.

I shake my head, knowing she's going to be wanting another round of intimate activity and she's already worn me out this morning.

"Aw, come on, baby," she says, tugging at my boxers.

Sure enough, my lower body is coming to life there, even though I know going another round will probably do me in.

I pull my boxers back up. I get out of the bed and scold my lady then pull her to her feet, telling her to get dressed, we've got to go see what Indio's up to out there.

She pouts a little but then gets excited at the thought of going down to the Inferno and bossing some nice-looking teenage boys around.

It takes my lady a while to put on her war paint. Girl would be good-looking no matter what you did to her but she won't leave the house without two pounds of mascara, a glossy lipstick, and red platform shoes.

Finally she's ready and we go on outside, where we run right into Guillotine, who's out airing his pitbulls.

"Ramirez," Guillotine greets me.

"Hello, Bertrand." Elsie grins at the old French guy. Elsie is the only person who uses Guillotine's first name. She's also the only person who can get away with it.

Guillotine nods at Elsie but won't really look at her. Once he told me a story about some lady breaking his heart twenty years back and how he hasn't gone near a woman since—can't bear even looking at pretty girls.

Now, he grumbles into his beard, tugs his dogs' leash, wanting to get away from me and the pretty girl with me.

"That's a new one," Elsie says, stopping him by indicating a new dog. This one's not a pitbull but a very appealing looking dog with bluish speckled fur.

"That's Lenny. Australian cattle dog. Some creeps had him locked in their yard for a few months, and a friend of mine, knowing how I am about neglected dogs, told me about it. I went and took him." Guillotine reaches down and fondly pats Lenny's head. The dog seems to be smiling. "Dog just needed someone to be attached to. Plus, the pits get out of control, Lenny herds 'em."

Elsie oohs and aahs over Lenny a little while longer as Guillotine smiles on happily.

Finally, I tug at my lady's elbow, reminding her we've got some work to do.

As we head over to the Inferno, Elsie babbles on about Lenny and what a good-looking dog he is, and I can see that any minute I'll be having to get a speckled blue dog.

The Inferno's facade is looking a little weather-beaten. The paint is chipped on the ten-foot head of a spitting Satan that hangs down from the roof, and the zombie mural isn't looking very scary anymore.

The left-hand door to the Inferno is wide open; any creep who wanted to could walk in. I get a little angry to see it.

Elsie and I go inside and find the kids all sitting down in the ride's carts, eating and smoking.

"No smoking in here," I say gruffly.

A kid with a fat face gives me a look and asks who I am.

"I own this place, boy."

The kid's eyes get angry at my calling him "boy." He pouts but he starts putting his cigarette out.

"Where's Indio at?" I ask the smoker.

The kid just shrugs at me. A different kid tells me Indio had to go home for a minute. I feel myself getting very angry.

"All of y'all out of here," I say, at which four pairs of confused eyes look at me. "I got business in here," I tell them.

Not one of them says anything as they all slowly get up and file out.

The moment they're gone, Elsie puts her fists on her hips and asks me what I think I'm doing.

"Kids ain't no good."

"They were taking a break, Pietro."

"They been taking a break for a few days," I say, motioning around us where, clearly, not much has been done.

Elsie surveys the inside of our Inferno and, I guess, decides I'm right. All the monsters are a mess. The witch's face has caved in and Vomit Man is lying on the floor, not looking too happy. I go over to pick the poor guy up. He's a life-size dummy that looks like a bum. Indio rigs him up outside the Inferno where, as Vomit Man, he continuously pukes into a big barrel. Only now his hair has fallen off and he's naked.

Elsie comes over and wraps her arms around me from behind. "Don't worry, Pietro, it'll all get done. Indio's gonna do the right thing."

Though I sincerely doubt that, my lady has managed to get me seriously excited, and I turn around to grab her, careful not to ram myself into her poor swollen titties.

Elsie pulls me back behind the dirty black curtain that covers up the storage area full of broken mannequins and carts. Before I know what's what, she's making me sit in one of the carts and she's got her skirt hiked up and is climbing on top of me. As I try to hold perfectly still, not interfering with her getting hers, I think about how having the breast problems kind of seems to be making my lady extra horny. And again I think about how she's probably gonna kill me with this amount of activity. I been with Elsie a few years now, and she's always had some big appetites, but this is getting to be a bit much.

Not two minutes later she's throwing her head back and letting out a cry that sounds a lot like some of the stuff we've got on the Inferno's soundtrack.

And not a moment too soon. Elsie's barely gotten over herself and I haven't yet gotten mine when we hear a voice calling out "Hello" and I'm hiking my pants back up and Elsie's trying to organize her panties and skirt.

"Yeah, be right there," I call out, and Elsie and I brush each other off and emerge from behind the curtain. We find Indio, looking at us with a laugh in his eyes. Indio actually almost always has a smile on his face. Between that and his crazy Don King style hair and his gold tooth, the ladies go crazy for him. And that smile all the time is part of why I like the kid too. It ain't doing much for me right now, though.

"Ramirez, how's it goin'?" the kid says.

"It's not," I say, frowning at him. "That was a nasty ass crew you had in here. Didn't do shit either."

"Oh." Indio shrugs. "Sorry, my man, I tried." He smiles some more. "But look what I did," he adds, then darts out front for a second and comes in toting a damn awful looking female mannequin.

"I give you Vomit Woman!" Indio says proudly, standing the hideous creature up at his side like she's his date. "No more lonely nights for Vomit Man."

She's a real sight, this Vomit Woman, thin and horribly white, with Band-Aid-colored hair hanging in ugly flat wings. Indio has done a great job making oozing sores all over her arms and face. I gotta hand it to him, the kid is not only the best fire-eater Coney's seen in a damned long time, he's got a way with ghouls.

I'm so impressed by Vomit Woman that I do partially forgive Indio for the useless crew of kids.

"That's gorgeous, baby," Elsie purrs at the boy.

He grins widely. "Yeah, she's a good one."

"Okay, Indio, how 'bout this," I say. "How 'bout you get rid of them no good motherfuckers and just do the paint job yourself."

The kid's face falls. He loves making the special effects stuff but plain old painting doesn't do it for him.

"Me and Elsie will help you out some and maybe we can get Ruby to put in a few hours," I say, throwing Ruby into the mix since I know what kind of reaction she gets out of the kid.

"Ruby? Yeah?" he says, looking very interested. "She's got a boyfriend these days?"

"I don't know, Indio."

I laugh at him a little. He smiles again.

"We'll leave you to it and come back in a couple hours," I tell him, and he shrugs, looks sadly at the gallons of paint and then offers one last smile.

My lady and I go outside, where the day seems awful bright after being in the dark awhile. Elsie looks very beautiful, the sun shining down on her, making her face look like it's dancing.

"You want an ice cream, baby?" I ask her as we come to Denny's Soft Ice Cream, where Luba, the little half Russian girl, is standing behind the counter, looking eager to sell some cones.

Elsie tells me yes, she wants a cone, and this eases my mind some, makes me think maybe she's feeling better.

We're standing there, licking two cones of bright green pista-chio, shooting the shit with Luba, when a white guy comes over and orders a chocolate cone. While Luba's fixing his cone, he looks over at me and says hello.

It takes me a minute to realize it's Ruby's friend, Oliver, the guy who's sick. "How ya doin'?" I ask him.

"Came looking for Ruby but she's not home," Oliver says, then takes a lick of his cone.

"This is my girlfriend Elsie," I say, introducing my lady.

She smiles at the guy and starts asking him questions about how long he's known Ruby and all that. The two seem to be hitting it off a little too well for my comfort, and so finally I suggest to Elsie that we head on back home.

"Come with us. You can wait for Ruby at our place," my lady says.

Not exactly what I had in mind, but what the hell, he seems okay.

We all head back to my place, and as soon as we're inside, Elsie turns into a hostess the way she likes, offering the Oliver guy *café con leche*. Oliver says no, the coffee doesn't agree with him so well right now. He goes explaining about his cancer, and Elsie gets all worked up talking to him about special herbs and teas and deciding to brew him some kind of crazy ass tea she's got there in a little tin in the kitchen.

I just sit there, sipping my *café con leche* and letting those two go at it, gabbing away, until finally Ruby comes up the stairs.

"Pretty lady, you're home," I call out to her. "Look who we found on the street." I point to her friend.

The girl looks pretty surprised. Frowns some. Stares from me to Oliver and back.

Oliver smiles at her: "Right after I called you I got the idea that I ought to try riding the Cyclone again. I feel so fucking horrible, it's the only thing that makes sense. I got off the subway and it wasn't open again. Then I ran into these guys." He motions at me and my lady. "I've been regaling them with cancer stories."

"He's been through a lot," Elsie says. "Took my mind off my troubles."

Ruby takes my lady's troubles off her mind a little more by telling us some insane story about going off and working at the racetrack all day.

"Baby, you're crazy," Elsie says eventually.

"I am?"

"Nobody would do that. Go running around like that working at a racetrack."

Ruby shrugs. "You know me. I love horses. What the hell. But what about you?" she asks my lady. "Did you call that doctor of yours?"

"Doctor?" Elsie says. "We're talking lawyer, girl. That doctor wouldn't see me. I went to another doctor, brother-in-law of a girl I used to dance with. Up on Ditmas Avenue. Doctor takes one look at my tatas and tells me I want to get myself a lawyer. He got me taking these," she says, showing Ruby a huge jar of pills. "Antibiotics. Maybe I got to go in the hospital a few nights if the swelling don't go down."

"You got bad implants?" Oliver asks her now.

"Yeah," Elsie sighs.

"Can I see?" Oliver asks.

At which I start to feel more than a little upset. "Elsie," I say to her, but she just laughs and pulls her powder blue T-shirt up over her head.

I can't handle this, so I get up and go into the bedroom, closing the door behind me and lying on the bed.

A few minutes pass and eventually I hear Oliver and Ruby leaving.

Elsie comes in. "I'm sorry, baby," she says.

I don't say anything.

"Pietro," she says, making me look up at her.

And then my girl starts dancing for me. Moving her pretty little ass and smiling.

I feel better.

Oliver Emmerick

16 / Hybrid Women

Though the chemo is coursing through my body and I feel profoundly ill, I figured the combination of forcing ice cream down my gullet and seeing Ruby would make me forget about it some. And it has. As has my little visit with Ruby's neighbors, the nice-looking Spanish girl with the bum implants, and Ramirez, the guy, kind of inscrutable but an okay guy.

I finish drinking the awful smelling tea that Elsie has made me, and then Ruby and I bid the neighbors a good afternoon and go across the hall to Ruby's place. My lovely friend starts babbling madly about her day at the track, telling me about all the characters and getting particularly flushed and excited talking about some horse named Joe.

"He's such a sweetie," she coos, her eyes milking over like she's just consumed an inordinate amount of opiates.

I just look at the girl and smile, pleased to see her so enthusiastic about something, particularly in light of how gloomy she's been these last months, ever since her breakup with the surly live-in boyfriend who I never liked.

Ruby finally stops babbling about the horses and notices the mess her awful felines have made in her absence. The living room is festooned with ripped white garlands, and the guilty parties are both roosting on the couch, looking at Ruby with accusatory eyes.

"Ah, those awful cats," I say, feigning disgust as I sit on the couch and pet the beasts. They lose interest in me when Ruby goes into the kitchen to play with the raw meat.

I get up off the couch and follow them all into the kitchen. I stand next to my lovely, watching the felines eat their meat.

"Do you feel horrible?" Ruby asks me.

"Marginally horrible. I puked twice. But then I had ice cream and kept it down. And now I want a doughnut."

"*A doughnut?*" Ruby says, aghast. She has, after all, known me to thrive on downing hunks of raw tofu.

I shrug. "My body wants a doughnut."

She shrugs back. "Well then, your body shall have a doughnut," she says.

I give her time to wash her face and put on clean clothes—including a fetching tight-fitting black skirt—and we go back out into the glories of Coney Island, heading for Dunkin' Donuts.

The sun is leaving the sky, trailing streaks of orange and pink as it goes. Gulls are pecking at the sidewalk near Nathan's. Packs of kids and old people are roaming around.

We find the Dunkin' Donuts closed, and the way my emotions are haywire from chemicals, I have a hard time not weeping over this misfortune. Ruby promptly suggests fries from Nathan's, though, and we cross over to that faded establishment.

The place is empty other than a pair of chunky cops eating hot dogs and Koko the Killer Klown, a dwarf who works at the sideshow. Koko is sitting at one of the tables, ripping up a napkin and staring balefully at a paper plate of fried oysters. Ruby nods at the guy but he just stares right through her.

We walk up to the counter, where a very wide teenage girl resentfully takes our order for two large fries. I smile and try to flirt with her, but this has absolutely no effect other than to make her frown and look even more foul than before.

We sit down, two tables away from Koko—who is apparently having some kind of psychotic episode and is now frantically pulling napkins out of a dispenser and shredding them all. His plate of fried oysters lies neglected to the side.

I eat about six fries before my stomach starts issuing warnings. I sit perfectly still for a minute, breathing into my belly, trying to get things to settle in there. One good thing is that Ruby got me into yoga a year ago, and it's taught me a lot about keeping all my body parts happy. Of course, none of my body parts are happy about chemo but at least I know how to try and appease them.

"What are you doing?" Ruby says, noticing that I'm looking a little green at the gills.

"Breathing. Stomach not happy about fries," I say, pushing my mostly uneaten container over to her side of the table. "Seltzer," I manage to say, and Ruby jumps to her feet and rushes over to the counter, coming back a moment later with a large cup of seltzer. I sip the stuff gingerly and send encouraging thoughts to my stomach. Which seems to grow calmer.

Ruby and I sit there a few more minutes, waiting for everything to settle in me so I don't go vomiting all over the place.

As we get up to leave, Ruby tries once more to say hello to Koko, but again he fails to respond. We go back outside.

The air smells good now. There's a nice breeze blowing in from the water as we walk down Surf Avenue, past the bumper cars that, as ever, are open for business. Ruby and I stop and press our faces to the dark glass of the window and gaze in at a thick throng of kids inside the bumper car building. Ol' Dirty Bastard's cover of Rick James's "Cold Blooded" is blaring through the speaker system. A strobe light pulses over various scary looking black kids, some standing in packs against the wall, others in bumper cars, sometimes four shoved into one car. The ubiquitous taped barker's eternal invocation to "Bump bump bump your ass off" mixes in with the din of the ODB song.

We stand with our faces glued to the glass for quite a long time, until my stomach starts emitting some rather ominous gurglings and Ruby and I, looking at each other and laughing, turn away and start heading back toward her house.

As the bumper car sounds recede, I hear a snatch of classical music in the air and I start looking around because it almost sounds like it's pumping down from the heavens.

"Look," Ruby says, indicating a black guy walking toward us. "It's Rite of Spring Man."

I don't know what she's talking about, but now the guy is just a foot away from us and I see that the classical music is coming out of a boom box perched on his shoulder. He sees Ruby and smiles at her.

"Going swimming?" he asks her.

She gives a return smile and tells him, "Not tonight."

The guy nods and walks on past us.

"Who's that?" I ask Ruby.

"Rite of Spring Man," she tells me again, and leaves it at that. I don't ask any more questions.

We get back to Ruby's. The cats, appeased by their raw meat, are off sleeping somewhere. I'm about to collapse onto the couch but Ruby takes my hand and leads me into the bathroom, closes the toilet lid and sits me down, then starts running steaming hot water in the tub. Apparently, after spending the day helping bathe a bunch of horses, she now wants to bathe *me*. And I can't say I mind.

I sit watching the water run as Ruby busies herself, bringing a shitload of candles, ripping open the bathroom cabinets and pulling out all sorts of strange bathing unguents.

The tub's almost full now, and I'm about to point this out to Ruby but she flits off again, and next thing I know, there's music piping in from the living room. Very lovely piano music. My diabolically possessed hostess returns again to the bathroom, which is now so thick with steam that I can barely see her. Ruby makes me stand up. She starts peeling my clothing off. I apologize for my thinness and she grins a rueful grin, saying, "You look pretty damned good to me."

"Forgive the sci-fi appendage," I say, indicating the feeding tube, an eight inch stretch of clear plastic tubing that I have to feed myself through when I'm too nauseous to eat. It sort of looks like a hard-on, actually. A long plastic hard-on. Thinking this makes me laugh a little, and Ruby, not sure what I'm laughing at, frowns up at me and orders me into the tub.

I do as I'm told. And watch as my lovely friend takes her own clothes off, shimmying out of her tight skirt in a way that would give ninety-nine percent of the population a heart attack and is actually giving me some stirrings in the groin area.

She gets in the tub behind me, wedging her legs around mine, her stomach and breasts pressing into my back. I would really like to fuck her. In theory. And then she starts bathing me. Rubbing unguent into me and sponging me down with a huge sponge that in fact looks like it could be used for horses, though I wouldn't guess she'd be stealing stuff from work her first day on the job.

A lot of time passes. Periodically, Ruby adds some hot water or dashes out of the bathroom and into the living room to put on a different CD. Eventually, when we've both long turned to prunes, she tells me to get out of the tub.

She wraps me in a soft white towel and dries me. Tenderly.

We go into the bedroom and get under the covers. I wrap my arms around her.

The phone rings.

"Phone," I say in her ear.

"The machine will get it."

A moment later, the voice of Ruby's friend Jane comes floating out of the answering machine. "I'm sad. Speak to me," the voice implores.

"Talk to her," I command my lovely friend.

Ruby moans a little then dutifully throws off the covers and trots into the living room. I hear her pick up the phone and ask her friend what the matter is.

I close my eyes and envision Jane naked. Though she keeps her black hair cropped short and wears modest, loose yogi clothes, Jane has a pronounced natural beauty and radiates understated eroticism. I've often imagined yanking down those loose yoga pants and giving her a little spanking.

Thinking about this doesn't get me anywhere, though. I empty my mind and just breathe, trying to feel as calm as possible.

Eventually, Ruby comes back in, gets under the covers, and sighs heavily.

"Something wrong with Jane?"

"No no, she's fine. Just the usual. Her husband's upset because she's proposing to go to India for three months to study with Guruji, live on shaved fruit, and shit into a hole in the ground. But they'll work it out. The problem is Ariel. She called while I was on with Jane."

"Oh?" I prop up on my elbow and look at Ruby. "Anything good?"

"No. Frank came over to her place and she said he seemed agitated. She didn't know about what, though. Then she made me give her exacting details about that Little Molly person. Ariel wasn't very happy about that. She wants me to stay at the track, find out whatever I can. Then she went on this long tirade about hybrid orchids."

"Who?" I say.

"She breeds orchids or something and is in the middle of developing some new rare orchid. She talked about this fucking flower for ten minutes, telling me she'd invested most of the money her father left her in this orchid and how soon she'd be rich. Then she'll pay me to follow Frank for the rest of our natural lives."

"Oh," I say. "Well, you'll be rich."

"I doubt that very deeply."

"You'll buy us a horse."

"Yeah. Joe. Who hates racing. I'll put him in the yard."

"You don't have a yard."

"I know. I'll get one."

"Okay. And now can we sleep?"

Ruby agrees to this. She flicks off the light and spoons behind me. Sleep comes.

Ruby Murphy

17 / Ever Still

I feel something wet and raspy on my face and wake up fully to find Lulu licking my forehead. I look over at the alarm clock and see it's nearly time to get up. I remove Lulu from my head then get up slowly so as not to disturb Oliver—who's sleeping on his back, mouth open, snoring a little.

I pad into the living room, turning on the light and finding Stinky curled on the couch, blinking. It's so early he doesn't have an appetite yet. I tromp into the kitchen, make coffee, slap meat into the cats' dishes, stuff a banana down my throat, then go back in the bedroom to quietly forage for clothes. I'm naked, about to slip into some durable unsexy cotton panties, when I hear whistling behind me. I turn to find Oliver staring at my nude ass.

"Go back to sleep," I tell him. "I'm leaving keys for you on the dresser. Lock up behind you. Or you can stay if you want. You want to?" I say, suddenly insecure, like he's a new boyfriend I'm asking to move in. Naked.

"Can I? I swear I won't puke everywhere," he says.

"If I'm not back by six, will you feed the cats? You saw the whole routine last night, right? The meat? You just add a scoop of vitamins and maybe shred up some vegetables. It's very easy. If you get stuck, go get Ramirez, he'll make a big stink about it and tell you how much he hates cats but he'll help."

Oliver stares at me like I'm a lunatic. Then smiles his small mischievous smile. He throws off the covers and follows me into the living room. I put on a heavy sweater and combat boots and stuff some things in my bag.

Oliver kisses me good-bye. I go out into the hall and down the stairs two at a time, hauling my fatigued ass over to the subway.

X

BY MID-MORNING I'm soaked with sweat. We're having the first hot day of the year, and horses, hotwalkers, grooms, and trainers alike are all wilting like exhausted flowers. Even the numerous cats and goats—who serve as barn mascots and sometimes friends to the horses—are lying low.

I'm draping horse laundry on the clotheslines in front of the barn, bandages and rub rags that are drying almost the moment I put them out. My back hurts a little and I'm tired but I don't feel horrible and I'm just contemplating sneaking off for a cigarette when Sebastian accosts me. "Give Joe a walk around the shedrow please," he says, motioning at Joe's stall.

"Oh yeah?" I say, surprised. Joe will be racing this afternoon, and I figure there's some very serious prerace protocol that I, as the new hotwalker, wouldn't be ready to handle.

"What's the matter?" Sebastian frowns at me.

"Nothing, nothing at all, I like Joe," I say, like an idiot.

"I heard." Sebastian rolls his eyes then favors me with a small smile. Then, disgusted with himself for smiling, he says, "Don't just stand there, get the horse. Walk him ten minutes then take him back to his stall."

I nod emphatically then go over to the bay colt's stall, where I stand for a minute, peering in at him. Joe nickers at me and I feel wildly pleased. I go in and put my face close to his nose. He blows on me then nuzzles my forehead, licking the salt from my sweat. I put his halter on, loop the shank over his nose, and lead him out into the aisle.

The shedrow is very quiet and peaceful right now. One of the barn cats, Aloisius, a delicate orange beast that most of the horses seem to love, is asleep on top of a trunk. Joe very gently puts his nose down to sniff the cat, who opens his eyes, stretches, and stares at the colt.

After visiting with Aloisius, Joe tries to stop in front of a gray mare's stall, but I encourage him to keep walking as the mare pins her ears back and throws her head in the air, clearly not pleased at Joe's attentions. Two roosters dart in our path, but Joe, who seems to know he's racing today, is in a very focused frame of mind and just snorts perfunctorily, not letting it get to him.

As we come to the other side of the shedrow, where the Murray brothers keep their string of claimers, a very small man wheeling a very large wheelbarrow full of manure asks me if I'd like to have his children.

"No thanks," I tell the guy.

"What's the matter, baby, you got something against Latin men?" he says.

"No, just ugly men," I say, immediately regretting it.

The guy seems to like this, though. He laughs, then picks his wheelbarrow up and wheels it away.

I bring Joe back to his stall. The colt goes in, turns around twice, then buries his nose in the ground, where his flake of hay should be. He truffles for a minute, and then, when he can't seem to make any hay materialize, picks his head up and looks at me.

"Sorry. You can't go racing on a full stomach." I shrug.

Joe looks at me a moment longer then turns his hind end to me. I pick a piece of straw out of his tail and pat him on the rump. As I walk out of the stall, I notice Frank, emerging from a stall down the aisle. The blond man strides away purposefully. I look around, making sure no one's watching, then follow him.

He walks to the far reaches of the backstretch where a pair of abandoned barns stand. He disappears behind one of the empty barns. I walk closer to the empty barn then carefully peer around the corner. Frank is standing just a few feet in front of me, talking to Little Molly. The woman has her back to me, and Frank is staring down at her so intently he doesn't notice me. I turn and go back to the front of the shambled barn, trying to figure out a way to eavesdrop.

Most of the stall doors have fallen off or been ripped down. I walk into one of the ghostly stalls, reach in my pocket to turn the cell phone off, then put my ear to the wall. ". . . someone's been following me, Frank," Little Molly is saying.

I glue my ear to the half-rotten planks, surprised to be overhearing something this dramatic.

"I doubt that, Molly," Frank is telling her.

"You doubt that? What are you implying? I'm an idiot? You're mixed up in a big fucking mess, Frank, and now you're dragging me into it by default. I'm not a fucking idiot."

Now I'm really surprised. And slightly worried.

"I'm getting out. I told you," Frank is saying, "it's going to take a little time. I wish you wouldn't get so irrational."

"*Irrational?*" she screams. "You want to see *irrational*?"

Stone silence. Apparently Frank does not care to see *irrational.*

"Say something, Frank," Molly urges after a few moments.

"There's nothing to say. If you're not happy, then that's that."

Silence.

"Christ, it's almost one," Molly says. I imagine her looking at her watch. "I gotta ride a fucking maiden filly in the third race."

Frank says nothing.

"Can we talk about this?" Molly seems contrite now. "Will you meet me back here right after the eighth race?"

There's a grunting sound out of Frank. Then: "Okay."

The two then evidently walk away from their rendezvous spot. I wait a few minutes before emerging from the stall and turn my phone back on. I don't know what the hell I'm going to tell Ariel. I head back to Gaines's barn.

I'm so distracted over the Frank and Molly drama that I walk straight into Ned. "Where are you going?" he says, catching me by the shoulders.

I look up and blink.

"What's the matter?" he asks, keeping his hands on my shoulders.

"Matter? Nothing. Why?"

He squints at me. Inspects me head to toe like I'm some well-built but difficult filly he's got to figure out how to train. "Can you stick around this afternoon?" he asks after a moment. "We need extra help. Got horses racing. You mind?"

"Oh. Sure," I say, flattered, but also disappointed since I'm already exhausted.

"Thanks. You're doing a good job." Ned grins at me. "Take a coffee break now if you want."

He pats me on the shoulder, grins again, then suddenly looks awkward and walks away. I stare after him.

I jump when the phone chirps in my pocket. I take it out, flick the Talk switch, and greet Ariel.

"Well, you're right," I say, cutting to the chase. "I think Frank is carrying on with that vicious apprentice jockey."

"What? What do you mean?" she asks, sounding very much like a woman on the edge.

I relay Frank and Little Molly's conversation.

Ariel is quiet for a long time, and as I stand there allowing her this prolonged moment of silence, Arnold Gaines materializes and frowns at me. His radar has apparently picked up on the fact that one of his lowly workers is making phone calls on his time.

"What are you doing?" he demands. "If you're going to work for me, you're going to have to pull your weight." His chubby face is bunched up, making his small eyes disappear into pockets of fat.

"I have to go," I say into the phone.

"Ruby, no!"

"I'm going to get fired," I say, and click off.

I shove the phone in my pocket and look at Gaines.

He is not an attractive man. There's a light sheen of grease over his thin, mousy hair. His eyebrows are bushy and threatening. "You think we hired you to fuck around?" he snarls.

"I'm sorry," I say as genuinely as possible, even though I am rarely sorry for anything and every cell of my being wants to tell Gaines to fuck himself twice. I try to look humble and apologetic. Evidently with some success. He grunts—presumably accepting my apology—then skulks away.

I stand there for a second, deliberating about calling Ariel back, until Sebastian appears, takes me by the elbow and leads me into the tack room. The skinny man tells me to run a sponge over Joe's racing bridle then come hold Joe while he wraps his legs. I do as I'm told, carefully going over the bridle. I'm still inspecting it, making sure it's perfect, when Sebastian hollers for me to get out there.

"You gotta move faster around here, lady," he tells me as he foists Joe's lead shank at me.

I talk to the colt, trying to keep him happy as Sebastian crouches down near Joe's hind legs and starts meticulously pulling thin bandages around the legs. When he's done with the bandaging, Sebastian stands up and pats the colt's neck.

"All right, Joe." He stares into the colt's right eye. "Be a racehorse for once, show us your stuff. You got it in ya."

Joe flicks his ears and shakes his head, as if agreeing.

Ned and Gaines materialize and come over to inspect the colt. Gaines has a cigar stub propped in his mouth as he runs his hands over the colt's wraps, double-checking Sebastian's work. I watch Sebastian's face tighten. Gaines straightens up, shoots a filthy look at the bunch of us and says, "Let's go."

In the distance the track announcer calls the fifth race as we make a tense, hopeful procession up to the saddling paddock. I walk behind Sebastian and Joe. Gaines is behind me, barking at someone on his cell phone.

We reach the paddock, where a dozen or so owners are standing around the statue of Secretariat, chatting idly, talking at their jockeys and trainers. A bony man in a dark suit detaches from this group and approaches Gaines.

Ned leans close and, indicating the bony man, tells me his name is Duncan Munchinson, one of Joe's owners—the only vocal one.

"Total Jerk," Ned says as we lead Joe into stall number seven and proceed with the prerace protocol.

I stare with fascination and horror as Sebastian ties the colt's tongue down—to prevent his swallowing it. I watch Ned put Joe's saddle on and tighten the girth. Joe pins his ears back, nips at the air in front of him, and kicks once, just for show, not actually aiming at any of us humans.

Sebastian leads Joe out of the stall and around the ring once, with the other horses. Then, as the paddock judge calls "Riders up," Ned gives Joe's jockey a leg up. The jockey, Louis Jimenez, is a prickly, self-assured man with crazy blue eyes. He gathers the reins and settles his diminutive rear end in the saddle.

A few spectators are yelling out unwelcome suggestions to some of the riders. The only comment addressed to Jimenez and Raging Machete is an encouraging, "You gonna wake that nag up, Jimenez?" from a middle-age fat woman in a baby blue sweat suit.

I head inside, to the grandstand, weaving my way through packs of dissolute-looking individuals. I go to a betting window and smile at the clerk as I put twenty to win on Joe.

"Good luck, kid," he tells me.

I tuck my betting slip in my pocket then head over to the rail where Sebastian is standing, Joe's halter looped over his shoulder.

"I put money on him," I tell Sebastian.

"I didn't," Sebastian says grimly.

It's a short race—six furlongs—and the starting gate is on the far side of the track, difficult to see from where we're standing. I tell Sebastian I'm going inside to watch on the video screen. He grunts noncommittally, not seeming to care if I fall through a hole in the earth.

I plant myself among the other spectators, craning my neck up to the immense screen, staring transfixed at the horses loading into the gate. Though one chestnut colt is making a big fuss, Joe is completely poised, amiably letting one of the assistant starters lead him into chute number seven.

A moment later the announcer calls, *"They're off!"* and two breaths later: "And in the early lead it's Raging Machete by a head, with Salamander Sam coming up on the rail."

I start to panic. A horse going right to the lead does not necessarily bode well, even in a sprint, and I distinctly heard Gaines telling Jimenez not to get involved in an early speed duel with Salamander Sam, one of trainer Nick Zito's horses, who likes to set a blistering pace. But evidently Jimenez and Raging Machete have other plans. I watch Joe's bay nose struggling to keep ahead of Salamander Sam's. They go the quarter mile in less than twenty-one seconds, a nearly obscene pace. In a few more strides Joe manages to grab a length over Salamander Sam, but suddenly, Baron Ron, the chestnut that was acting up going in the gate, starts challenging, pulling within a nose of Raging Machete. The whole pack of them is practically neck and neck at the half-mile pole, just an indistinguishable mess of hooves, pinned ears, and bright silks. And then Joe starts to fade. The pack passes him. All the other horses have their ears pinned back, are intensely focused, but Joe's ears are flopping forward and he even turns his neck at one point and looks into the grandstand. And then it's over. The rest of the horses have already passed the finish line, Baron Ron winning by two lengths. Joe sloppily hand-gallops across, looking happy as can be at having lost another race.

I feel demoralized. Joe just doesn't seem to understand the concept of getting to the finish line first. His owner will probably read Gaines the riot act. Gaines will in turn spread the discontent to his employees.

It takes me a few moments to snap out of my misery and realize I ought to find Sebastian and see what's needed of me.

I catch up to him as he and Ned lead Joe through the passageway back toward the backstretch.

"Where the hell were you?" the skinny man barks.

"Watching the race on the video screen like I told you," I protest, looking over to Ned, hoping he'll come to my defense. He does not.

"This horse is hot," Sebastian says, snatching the cooler from my arms and throwing it over Joe, who still has his ears forward, looking around good-naturedly, as if expecting accolades.

Ten minutes later we're all back at the barn. Sebastian has taken Joe's tack off and I'm leading the colt around the shedrow, leaving slack in the lead rope, talking to him. As we come around to the other side of the barn, a pair of grooms from the neighboring stable eyeball me but don't say hello. News of our loss has probably reached these guys, and they're afraid the bad luck will spread to them.

Once Joe's cool enough, I take him over to a grassy embankment and watch him bury his nose in the ground. I start thinking about Frank, Little Molly, and the conversation I overheard. I've kept my phone turned off, although I'm sure Ariel is trying to call. I just can't deal with her quite yet.

I'm frowning, my eyes focused on Joe's neck, when I feel someone standing behind me. I turn around and find Ned there, arms folded over his chest.

"What the hell is wrong with you?" Ned asks.

"What? What did I do?" I ask, startled.

"I was talking to the horse," Ned says, planting himself in front of Joe, scowling at the bay colt. "He's got it in him. He *can* win races, he just doesn't." Ned shakes his head and looks sad.

"Maybe he just doesn't want to," I say, great horse psychologist that I am.

"His owners—or at least Munchinson, the only one we ever hear from—he's not happy," Ned says, looking deeply sad himself.

"What's that mean? What's he gonna do?" I say, alarmed, flashing on horror stories I've heard of racehorses sold off per pound to the butcher.

"Drop him down to claiming," Ned says ominously.

"Oh no."

Running a horse in a claiming race not only means dropping him down in class but also that the owner is willing to risk having him claimed by anyone with an owner's license and a few thousand dollars. It's the crown of dishonor for a colt of Joe's potential.

Ned leans over and runs his hands down Joe's elegant bay legs, feeling for any heat that might indicate an injury.

"Warm?" I ask, half hoping the colt hurt himself and has a solid excuse for his poor showing.

"Cool as a coffin. Colt is totally sound. I don't know what his problem is."

Ned and I are both quiet for a spell as Joe unabashedly munches grass and generally looks pleased with himself.

"You want to get a drink later?" Ned asks out of the blue.

"A drink?" I say, startled.

"Yeah, you know, rum and Coke, beer, bourbon. Drink."

"I don't drink, actually," I say, trying to gather myself.

"Oh." Ned looks confused. "You mean you don't drink alcohol? Or you're married, or otherwise engaged?"

"The former, I guess."

"You guess? Who should I ask?" he says, smiling but looking a little rattled.

"I don't drink alcohol. But no, I'm not married. At all." I look up at him, into those strange green eyes. "The thing is, I can't really have even a metaphoric drink today."

"Oh?" He frowns, then: "Should I ask you another day or not?"

"It'd be nice if you did."

"Yeah?" He looks relaxed again.

"Yeah," I reiterate.

We stare at each other like stone idiots.

"Call it a day when you've put Joe away," he says eventually, "and I'll see you tomorrow?" He doesn't seem too sure.

"Yeah, of course." I nod. There's another prolonged stare. I break eye contact, turn to bring Joe back to his stall.

I take the colt's halter off and watch him perform his ritual of turning around twice. I latch his door shut. Walk to the tack room to retrieve my bag. I feel disjointed. The thing with Ned startled me. And the prospect of going to eavesdrop on Little Molly and Frank isn't doing much to calm me.

I walk over to the ladies' room to wash some of the grime off my hands and face. A pair of grooms zip past me on clunky bicycles. They stare at me then say stuff to each other in Spanish. I feel like maybe I should go over to the cafeteria and just hang out and let all the employees of Belmont inspect me head to toe. Get it over with.

Instead, I go in the bathroom and inspect myself. I don't look so good. These last few days have been a whole lot more action-packed than I'm equipped to deal with. I'm not a slovenly physical specimen, since my yoga practice alone is pretty grueling, and I also swim and bike and generally keep my body busy. But this horse work is more business than I can handle. I'm tired all over.

I come out of the bathroom and nearly trip over a black and white cat. The cat looks up at me and blinks its green eyes. I apologize aloud, then head toward the deserted barns. There's a light wind having its way with one of the half unhinged stall doors. The door creaks and groans, an appropriate soundtrack to my little stakeout. I go into the stall I eavesdropped from earlier, waiting for Frank and Little Molly. I squat down on my haunches, cup my face in my hands and try to breathe evenly.

About ten minutes later I hear a rustling sound on the other side of the stall wall. I peer out between the loose planks and see Frank, just a few inches from me there on the other side. He looks down at his watch, cranes his neck left and right.

I wait. Frank waits.

For fifteen interminable minutes we wait, and then, abruptly, Frank storms off. I quickly race around to the front of the barn in time to see him stride away. I follow.

He stalks over to Gaines's barn and looks around. I plant myself under the awning of the facing barn and watch. Frank hesitates for a moment then ducks into the tack room. He's in there a few short minutes then emerges wild-eyed. He leans forward as if to vomit. He dry heaves. At that moment Gaines appears.

I see Frank pointing to the tack room. Gaines goes in and emerges seconds later. He pulls a cell phone from his pocket and frantically punches some numbers in as Frank stands staring ahead.

This can't be good.

I get a very queasy feeling in my stomach. I walk around the outside of the barn next to Gaines's barn. I stop to peer into a stall where there's a goat standing next to a chestnut horse. Both creatures look at me for a moment then simultaneously put their heads down to a flake of hay on the ground.

I eventually come back to the front of Gaines's barn.

In the three minutes my little promenade has taken, a lot has happened. Two security guards are standing in the door of the Gaines tack room. Gaines himself is on the phone. Some grooms have materialized, and as I step a little closer I hear one of them say, "It's Molly Pedersen. She's dead. Looks like a heart attack."

Another groom is muttering, "Damn speed freak."

My whole body turns to ice as I stand there, rooted to my spot.

In a few more moments the place is swarming with security guards and cops. Fat cops. Skinny cops. One female brunette cop with an impressive chest, which she puffs out as she stalks back and forth in front of the tack room where Molly's body lies. Not that I've seen the body yet. I've just been minding my business, rooted to my spot, queasy.

I feel someone standing behind me. I flip around to find myself face-to-face with Ned. He's scowling and his glasses are down at the very tip of his nose.

"This is horrible," I say, shaking my head.

"What is?" he asks, pushing his glasses back up.

"Molly."

He frowns. "What'd she do now?"

"You . . . you . . . uh . . . she's dead," I say, barely more than a whisper.

"What?" Ned gasps. His glasses slide down his nose. He catches them.

"Dead." I point at the tack room.

"Fuck," he says, which strikes me as strange, because he almost doesn't seem that shocked about it. Just angry. He goes over to where the chesty cop is standing. I watch her listening to Ned and motioning to a plainclothes cop. The lot of them go into Gaines's office.

Eventually, three paramedics carry Little Molly's body out of the tack room on a stretcher. From where I'm standing I can't see anything wrong with her, yet I can tell she's dead. There's a horrible stillness to her tiny body. Near me, a pair of weather-worn grooms are speculating about what might cause a nineteen-year-old to have a heart attack.

The paramedics wheel the stretcher over to an ambulance that has pulled up between barns. As they lift the stretcher, Molly's head lolls to one side. She looks angry. I would be too.

My stomach twists up.

I slip off to call Ariel. I get her voice mail and leave a message. Telling her to call me. Soon.

I look around me. Ned and Sebastian are still inside the office, talking to the brunette cop.

I feel a little weird just wandering off into the sunset, yet that's exactly what I do. Picturing dead Little Molly's face as I make my way to the LIRR station.

I'm waiting for my train when Ariel calls. "I heard what happened," she announces. "Frank called me."

"Ah. What'd he tell you?"

"That one of his coworkers had a heart attack. That he found the body. I asked him point-blank if he was sleeping with the girl. He denied it, of course. But something is not right."

"Yes. Something isn't right. A woman is dead. However, I guess this is the end of my Belmont career."

"What makes you say that?"

"The source of your suspicions is dead."

"I still want to know what's going on. I have a bad feeling," Ariel snaps.

She doesn't seem to have a bad feeling about Molly being dead. Just about what the girl's body may have been up to before all life left it.

"Well, Ariel," I say, irritated, "I can pretty much assure you there was something going on between those two, but I can't see that hanging around the track would garner much more information about it."

"I want to know if Frank did it."

"Frank did what?"

"Murdered her."

"Murdered? I heard it was a heart attack, and if not, then I think that sort of thing is best left to the police."

"I'm not asking you to put yourself in danger."

"You're not?"

"Of course not," she says tersely.

"I'm not sure what you want me to do, then."

"Put in another day at the track. See what you can learn."

I'm not crazy about this idea.

"Please?" she says in a small voice.

Ariel is the antithesis of a *please* kind of girl. Hearing her say it sways me. "Okay," I say.

She thanks me.

I fall asleep on the train, waking to find I drooled on myself.

Sebastian Ives

18 / The Hole

I sit in a corner of Gaines's office, trying to keep out of the way of the police, who are everywhere. Even though I know plenty of retired cops—fellow members of the Federation of Black Cowboys out there in East New York, where I keep Prince, my quarter horse—those are old black cops, and knowing them doesn't mean I'm all that comfortable around a bunch of young white cops. Particularly this here lady cop with her big chest sticking out. She's already asked me a bunch of questions I didn't know answers to and some that I did. Like the last time I saw Molly alive. Which wasn't more than an hour ago. Incredible, if you think about it. One hour ago that little girl was riding in a horse race, now she's been taken to the morgue. Makes you wonder.

Gaines is on his phone and Frank is sitting in a chair right near him, looking green as the lady cop asks him questions. Frank's not a good egg but it doesn't mean he deserved to find the body. Plus, he'd been carrying on with the girl for a while. I know he's got some serious ladyfriend, but he had it bad for Molly, which is bound to make the cops and the *federales* interested in him big-time. Whatever. So long as they don't try pinning it on me. There's always funny shit going on in the backstretch. Trainers trying to sneak new, undetectable drugs in, accusing grooms of feeding the horses poppy seed bagels if the equines turn up positive for opiates. In my time, I been questioned by the *federales* and the local cops, and they've given me a hard time a few times too, always looking to blame a black groom before they go pinning something on a nice white trainer. But I never done anything funny to a horse in my life. And not to a human either.

It's too damned crowded in this office that ain't meant to fit more than three people to start with, so I make my way over to the door, thinking I'll check on the horses.

"Where you going?" the lady cop wants to know. I tell her I'm going to see about the horses and she tells me not to go far. I assure her I will not.

I go stand in front of Liz's Tizzy's stall, petting the little gray's nose and mulling things over in my head for a minute until it occurs to me that Ruby's not around anymore, and I get a tiny strange feeling about it, about her, how she turned up on the backside here out of nowhere, clearly not knowing her way around a racetrack and now all of a sudden there's a dead person. But then I put this thought out of my mind. The horses like the girl. And I trust that.

As I'm standing there, I see that Little Molly's uncle, Jimmy John Mancuso, has suddenly turned up, and I count my blessings that I'm not standing in that office right now. With the kind of temper that guy's got, it's very possible that objects and people are gonna start flying. The man loses his cool over little things, and I just don't want to know what he's gonna do over the death of his pretty, young niece.

To get as far away as possible from the office, I go all the way down to Ballistic's stall and go in to stand next to the horse. Ballistic isn't the friendliest individual in Gaines's string and he doesn't seem all that interested in my little visit, but I do need to check on his feet—looked like he might be getting a touch of thrush this morning. Though I'd yell at anyone else for such negligence, I don't bother tying the colt to the wall and just ask him to lift each foot for me, risking him reaching down and biting me on the ass. The horse seems to know what's good for him, and I inspect all four feet without interference. No thrush either. Guess I was being paranoid.

I look the colt over for a minute. Nice-looking chestnut, though not much of a racehorse. I look at my watch and see it's five now. Dinnertime. I wonder if the police will give me a hard time if I feed the horses and head on home. As I stand there debating it, a lovely person materializes there outside Ballistic's stall.

"Hi, Sebastian," she says, and I look at Asha Yashpinsky and am very glad I'm not a white man because right now I'd be blushing to the roots of my being.

"Asha, hello," I say.

"Little Molly is *dead*?" she says, her pretty face pinched up with worry.

I nod at her and we both cast our eyes down for a moment.

Asha asks how much I know, and I tell her not much. Apparently a heart attack. Maybe some kind of amphetamine overdose. We both fall silent again until all the horses, knowing it's dinnertime, start getting anxious, some turning around in their stalls, almost all poking their noses over their stall guards and looking out with the devil in their eyes.

"I gotta feed," I say, then immediately wish I hadn't for fear it's going to make Asha disappear.

"You want a hand?" she asks.

"That'd be great," I say, smiling at the gorgeous girl. "Everybody else's still talking to the police."

Several horses shake their heads vigorously, apparently approving of Asha's offer.

A few minutes later we're down to brass tacks, feeding. And we're just finishing up when the short white lady officer comes over. I barely contain a need to moan out loud.

"Ives," she says, walking up to me and getting a little closer than I like, "I need your home number. We're done with you now but Agent Osterberg of the FBI may need to get in touch with you tonight."

"Sure, officer," I say, giving her my number, glad to know that I won't be reachable, as I'm heading straight to the Hole to ride Prince until nightfall.

"You got a cell number, Ives?"

"No, ma'am, I'm afraid not," I say.

The little lady doesn't look like she believes me, but what can I do? She turns and walks back over toward the office, and I turn back to Miss Yashpinsky.

"You interested in riding on the beach at Jamaica Bay?" I ask her all of a sudden, not even realizing I'm about to ask her.

"The beach?" Asha frowns a little, seeming confused.

"I got my horse out at a place called the Hole, out on the border between Brooklyn and Queens, not too far from JFK and Aqueduct out there. I ride him on the beach at Jamaica Bay most nights. It's a nice ride. There are a few horses out there you could ride."

"Yeah?" Asha tilts her head.

"It's nice out there," I tell her. "It's where the Federation of Black Cowboys hang."

"Oh yeah, those guys." She nods. "But I'm not black, Sebastian," she says, laughing.

"That's okay, you can be an honorary black cowgirl," I tell her, and the fire-headed woman lights up at this prospect.

I finish up with evening chores, then Asha comes with me as I pop my head in the office. Gaines and Ned are still surrounded by cops and the both of them are looking strained.

Gaines glances up at me and shrugs. "Yeah, go on home, Sebastian," he says, and I'm not about to protest.

Asha and I walk over to where I've got the Buick parked. I open the passenger door for her, which seems to surprise her a little. I go around to the driver's side and get in, noticing how good Asha looks with her red hair against the tan insides of the car.

A half hour later, after a peaceful drive—where we've both managed to talk about most everything under the sun while steering clear of what happened at Belmont today—we're approaching the Hole.

I show Asha the *Dip* sign that stands at the main road down into the Hole. I drive through the dip slowly and then nose the Buick ahead, past a half-dozen little stable areas and off to the left, where I keep Prince in a tiny but clean stable run by my friend Neil, a big Jamaican fellow I've known since he was a youngster.

Asha is wide-eyed, staring all around, reacting the way most people do seeing stables surrounded by projects and highways. It ain't exactly horse country.

I disarm Nunu, Neil's rottweiler, letting the dog know that Asha's okay as I unlock the padlock securing the big gates.

"Heavy security, huh?" Asha grins, looking from the gate to Nunu, who, now that I've let her know Asha's all right, has put her fangs away and is licking the woman's pale freckled hands.

"Yup," I concur. "We don't take chances around here." I motion toward the projects, which I know well, considering I grew up in one of the stumpy run-down tenements that was a precursor to the tall bleak buildings.

I lead the way into the little four-stall barn and throw open the back door, letting light pour in over the four horses living in here.

Prince whinnies at me and shakes his big white head, as does Dalton, Neil's horse, who almost looks like Prince's twin, what with being almost all white but for one pale splotch of yellow on his neck.

"This is Prince," I say, introducing Asha to my horse, who, proving his good taste, shows instant approval of Asha by licking her on the forehead—a thing he normally doesn't do until he's known someone a bunch of months.

"And this is Dalton," I say, rubbing the horse under the chin. "You can ride him, or you can take Ellen, the little Arabian mare there. My friend Neil just bought her off some kid who couldn't handle her. She' s a little wild but a nice ride."

"I'm up for a quiet ride. I'll take Dalton," Asha says. "And who's this?" she asks, going to stand in front of the fourth stall, looking fondly at the huge retired carriage horse.

"That's Hanover. He used to pull a carriage in Central Park. He's almost thirty now. Neil puts his nephew on the horse's back once in a while but that's it. Old guy's had a full life. Deserves a little peace and quiet."

Asha spends a long while scratching Hanover's face, obviously smitten with the huge horse.

"He'd probably appreciate a little walk and some brushing, if you want," I tell her, and the girl looks delighted, like I've just offered her a bucket of diamonds.

"I'd love to," she purrs.

As I get to work tacking up Prince and Dalton, Asha takes Hanover out of his stall and starts fussing with him, clacking her tongue with disgust over the layer of dust on the big chestnut's coat.

"He ain't neglected," I advise her. "Old guy likes to roll. Even at his age. Can't keep him clean five minutes before he goes getting into something."

It takes a while for Asha to feel satisfied with her handiwork on Hanover. Only after I've promised her she can give Hanover a nice long walk when we get back does she finally lead Dalton outside and get up in the saddle.

I haven't ridden Prince in three days and he's letting me know it, acting like a damned thoroughbred, looking around at everything, snorting at Nunu like he's never seen a dog before. I talk to the gelding and hold him with my legs, keeping only light contact with his sensitive mouth as we head out toward Linden Boulevard.

Asha looks less than thrilled at the prospect of crossing Linden Boulevard on horseback but I assure her both Dalton and Prince do it almost every day. I'm surprised to see her nervous. Exercise riders aren't exactly prone to such things, but neither are they used to riding across highways.

Asha relaxes once we've reached the other side of the road and are cutting through quiet back streets, heading out toward the bay. By the time we've got the two geldings onto the beach, Asha is radiant, her pale eyes bluer than usual, the setting sun adding red to her hair.

We keep the horses at a walk for a while and talk some more. Miss Yashpinsky tells me about her childhood growing up in Queens with her parents, who ran a ballet school.

"How'd you end up on a horse, then?" I ask her.

"Yoga," she says.

"Yoga?"

"I started taking it to help with flexibility—a dancer's hips get tight. There was a guy used to come to my yoga class who was an exercise rider at the track. I'd ridden when I was a tiny kid, when my folks' school was doing good business, but then things got lean and no more riding lessons for me. I dunno. I got to talking to Jim, the exercise rider from yoga, and one thing led to another and I came out to Belmont one day. Guess I rode enough as a kid to have some good basics. And I just loved the track. The horses. I never turned back."

I tell her my own horse history, how, growing up in East New York long before the Black Cowboys started building stables in the Hole, the only horses I ever saw were occasional cop horses, but I always was drawn to 'em. Then I went off to college down South on a scholarship and there were horses everywhere. I rode whenever I could and would spend hours around stables. Graduated and went back to Queens to teach high school English for ten years. By then the federation had its stable set up not far from where I lived. Pretty soon I was going by there every day. Helping out. Then that wasn't enough. The pull of horses got so strong I hung it up with teaching and went out to the track to walk hots. Worked my way up and probably could have been assistant trainer to any number of fellows I'd worked for but I didn't want the pressure and dealing with owners. I like being a groom.

"I'm forty-seven, you know," I tell Asha after I've finished with my story.

"Yeah?" she says, not seeming to fall off her horse in shock at my advanced age. "I'll be thirty-six next month," she tells me.

"*Thirty-six?*" I say.

She laughs. "I know, it's the baby fat on my cheeks," she tells me, reaching up to pinch one of her lovely, slightly plump cheeks. "Makes me look not a day over twelve, right?"

"Well, twenty-five, maybe," I say, feeling relieved because ever since I'd started noticing Asha, I'd been a little upset with myself; not only was she a white girl, but I figured she was a couple decades my junior. Thirty-six ain't so bad.

"You wanna lope?" Asha says then, and I agree that yes, Prince could probably use it, and the two geldings break into a soft canter without any urging, both of them with their ears forward, Prince throwing a little buck of appreciation.

We go quite a ways before I feel Prince tiring and I pull him back to a trot and then a walk. We turn around, heading back toward the Hole at a leisurely pace.

"Stop a second," Asha says.

I do as she asks, bringing Prince to a halt.

She steers Dalton so close to Prince that mine and Asha's knees are touching. She looks at me. She's smiling a little.

"You ever kiss a white girl?" she says.

"Nope," I say, although this isn't entirely true. I did kiss a white girl once when I was nineteen, but that was it, just a kiss.

"It's not all bad," she says, leaning over, putting her pretty pink mouth to mine.

And she's right. It's not bad at all. Kind of makes the world slip away entirely. And it's not until many hours later, after I've given Asha a ride back to her place in Queens and am finally home, that I come down from the pull of that kiss and remember about poor Little Molly. I feel pretty shitty about it, but that kiss was the kind of kiss to soften any blow.

Ruby Murphy

19 / A Black Wish

When I get back to Stillwell Avenue, it's close to seven and Coney is in full bloom. Most of the ride operators have come slinking out of hibernation, the lights are on and pulsing, the rollercoasters are chinking up their tracks, the night carries sounds of shrieking girls and barking game touters.

I put my key in the front door, then climb up the stairs. Ramirez's door is closed—which I hope means he and Elsie have gone out to dinner, as opposed to something ominous having happened with Elsie's chest.

Entering my apartment, I step into a strange clean world. I'm not a completely reprehensible slob but I don't keep the place spick-and-span. Oliver, it seems, has taken exception to my housekeeping skills. The place is sparkling.

"Oliver?" I call out, but there's no sign of him.

No sign of the cats either. Which means Oliver must have fed the beasts. I put my bag down, sit on the couch and rest my head in my hands, trying to block out the images of Little Molly's body that keep flashing before my eyes.

And I'm still sitting like this, struggling through these mental images, when Oliver comes in.

"You're home!" he says, putting down an armful of groceries.

"I am," I concede.

"Look," Oliver says, reaching into his grocery bag and proudly proffering a container of tofu, "and look at these," he adds, wielding bumpy pale vegetables I've never seen before. I don't know where he found tofu in Coney Island. It's not like the locals are soybean-consuming types. "I thought I'd cook up a feast. Turn Ramirez and Elsie on to tofu. What do you think?"

"I think Ramirez is out. He and Elsie go out to dinner most Saturdays. And how the hell do you have all this energy, Oliver?"

He frowns at me like it's an asinine question, a question that he ignores: "I'll cook for us, then."

I've never known Oliver to cook anything, and the idea of him trying here and now isn't a soothing one.

"How about we go ride the Cyclone? I need it. I saw a dead person today," I say, not necessarily trying to be dramatic, just wanting to get it out without fuss.

"What?" Oliver squints at me.

"Dead person. An apprentice jockey. She was nineteen. Had a heart attack."

My friend's jaw drops.

I tell him the whole story.

He frowns harder and harder as I go on. Then, when I've reached the end of the tale: "I think you'd better stop doing what you're doing."

"Why?"

"Why? Someone *died*, Ruby, don't be stupid. This could be life and death. It's not a joke." Oliver's brown eyes go black and his mouth turns down at the edges.

"I'll figure it out," I say softly. I let a few moments pass. "On a more frivolous note," I say, "the Cyclone's open. Can we go ride it?"

Oliver badgers me a little more about my dangerous pursuits but finally agrees that yes, if I'll eat his cooking, he'll ride the Cyclone with me.

I go pour myself a bath and soak in it, leaving him to his dubious kitchen practices. Again I run through the bank of images from this afternoon.

Eventually, I get out of the tub. I dry off, put sweatpants and a T-shirt on, and in spite of being exhausted, roll my yoga mat out in the living room to do ten sun salutations and a few standing poses to help me face Oliver's culinary debacle.

Strange smells are wafting in from the kitchen, and as I stand on one leg, holding my other leg before me in the air, Oliver comes in, sees me wavering on the one leg, and comes to assist me, putting his hand under my airborne foot, helping me get the leg so high it practically smashes me in the nose.

"Enough circus tricks," he says, dropping the leg. "Time to eat."

I'm frightened at this prospect but I'm starved. I roll my mat back up, then go into the kitchen, where I'm stunned to see he's lit candles on the tiny table and has steaming plates of food waiting for us.

I'm even more stunned to find the food is actually delicious.

"Unsuspected talents, huh?" He grins after watching me shovel many forkfuls into myself.

I nod enthusiastically.

After cleaning up and giving ourselves time to digest, we venture out onto Surf Avenue to go ride our beloved Cyclone.

x

A ROUND-FACED older guy I've never seen before is taking tickets at the rollercoaster. Though I'd heard that the former ticket taker, a man named Gary, died in January, it somehow hadn't hit home until now. I give my ticket to this new guy, who doesn't even look up. Gary would always wish me a nice ride. Nothing more. Never a "How are you today?" just the simple wish for a nice ride. From the first time I ever got on the monstrous wooden contraption at age twelve, right up to last October when, on closing day, I came over and rode eight times in a row.

"We've gotta wait for the front car," I tell Oliver, parking us behind two girls who are staking out the spot on the platform where the front car will pull up.

"Yes," Oliver agrees as we fasten our eyes on the two girls. They're tough-looking hefty girls with sizable asses packed into thin stretchy blue jeans.

One of the girls flips her hair back and turns to glower at me and Oliver. He smiles at the girl and she melts. They all do.

The coaster comes clanging up to the platform and stops. Oliver and I wait, watching the girls squeeze into the front car and, as a slum-bum-looking Spanish kid endeavors to close the security bar over their immense laps, girl number one looks up at Oliver and waves coyly.

Oliver smiles.

The white-haired rollercoaster hand is an immense man who once told me he hadn't been able to fit on the Cyclone for seventeen years. But he runs it just fine. He now shoves his wooden control lever forward, setting the train on its course.

The wood and steel structure groans and thrashes. Its victims scream into the bright evening. After two minutes the little wooden train pulls up in front of us once more. We see that the hefty babes are still in there, paying a reduced fee to ride again, but they graciously move back to the second car, freeing the front for me and Oliver.

"We didn't wanna be pigs about the front car," girl number one says, offering Oliver a tiny smile that's at odds with her huge, tough countenance.

"You couldn't if you tried," Oliver says, winking at the girl.

We settle into the front car and the white-haired man pulls his lever, sending the train chugging up the imposing first hill. The train stops and careens, holding its breath before diving down the perilously long first drop. Oliver lets out a scream as we plummet wildly, the track rushing toward our faces. My stomach drops. And then the train climbs the second hill. I feel my mouth spreading into a huge grin. I can hear the hefty babes behind us, squealing. And then, before I've had time to completely bask in the horrifying deliciousness of it all, the ride is over and Oliver and I are handing over another three bucks each to ride again.

After four more rides, we get off and wobble through the turnstile back to the street. It's getting close to ten now, and though I wouldn't mind a few games of Skee Ball, I have to get up and go back to the track in six hours. Though he claims to feel fine, Oliver looks a little pale, and I suggest we go on back home.

We're heading back toward my place when someone behind me calls my name. I turn around and find myself face-to-face with my boss, Bob, from the museum.

He's wearing an orange T-shirt and Kelly green pants. His long gray hair is shooting out of his head in angry kinks.

"Bob," I say, "you remember my friend Oliver?"

The two nod at each other.

"No time to work but time enough to party, huh?" my boss says—even though he didn't seem to mind when I told him I'd need a bit of time off from the museum to pursue my unlikely new job.

"Come on. Be nice. I put in something like fourteen hours of physical labor today and I saw a dead body."

"Body?" Bob says, tilting his head, interested.

"Body of a dead jockey. Little tiny mean blond girl."

"Oh my," Bob says.

I give him some of the details, and though he's intrigued, he doesn't seem alarmed at the idea of my involvement. He asks when I think I'll be back to work, and when I tell him soon, he shrugs, wishes me and Oliver a pleasant evening, and wanders ahead into the night.

Oliver and I make our way back to my place and within twenty minutes are spooned under the covers.

Next thing I know, the alarm is going off, and in no time at all I'm back at Belmont.

X

SECURITY BITCH turns her button-eyed gaze to me but neither nods nor grunts any sort of greeting. I make my way toward the barns and stand completely still for a few seconds, soaking in the smell of hay and horses before proceeding on down the muddy little road leading to Gaines's barn. I find no signs of the fact that a woman dropped dead here just thirteen hours ago. It's business as usual—apparently.

Gaines is in his office, hunched over some papers at his desk.

"Morning," I say, sticking my head in the door.

He looks startled, covers something with his arms. "Who are you?" He frowns at me.

"Uh . . . Ruby? The new hotwalker?"

"Oh. Right. Get to work, it's late, first set's already working," he says.

I don't know what he's doing in his office if his first set of horses is at the track galloping. But I don't have much time to dwell on it before Sebastian sees me.

"I need you working extra today," the skinny man tells me. "Frank can't make it in. Got shook up, what with finding the body."

"Oh yeah?" I say, not expressing anything, wondering if Sebastian will volunteer what he thinks of all this.

He does not. Just sends me up to the training track to collect a colt. And the day begins.

By the time the sun is all the way up, my back muscles are seizing. And no sooner have I handed what I think is my last charge of the morning over to Sebastian for grooming than Ned appears, barely nodding hello before shoving another colt's lead shank at me. A bay colt by the name of Permanent Midnight who is so cantankerous no one's bothered to give him a nickname. He's a two-year-old, bred to the teeth and pissed off at the world. Which he demonstrates by stepping on me, taking a nip from my shoulder, and banging me into a stall. For no reason at all.

"Ruby, you're being too nice to that beast," Ned's voice says behind me.

I turn around, giving the colt an opportunity to lurch forward in a valiant attempt to pull my shoulder from its socket.

"See?" Ned says.

He comes over, takes Permanent Midnight's lead shank from me, gives it a brusque pull and speaks to the colt in a sharp voice. The bay pins his ears back as Ned gives me a lecture about how horses, particularly these extremely high-strung thoroughbreds, have to be taken strongly in hand.

I nod my head dutifully. I know this already. It's just that I can't quite bring myself to do it. "I'll be mean, I promise," I tell Ned.

He gives me a half smile and slowly nods his head. Looks at me over the top of his glasses then looks away. Stands there, seeming to hesitate.

"So, uh, what's going on?" I venture casually, keeping one eye on Permanent Midnight's mouth, the other on Ned's face.

Ned frowns. "What do you mean?"

"I mean, with, uh . . . Molly."

Ned frowns harder. "I don't know," he says, narrowing his eyes at me. "What's it to you?"

I shrug and quickly change the subject, telling him I'm going to put Permanent Midnight away.

"Yeah." Ned nods, not really registering what I've said. "Good."

I take the ornery colt back to his stall and pat him on the neck to try to make him feel guilty for being such a shit. He pins his ears and shows me his teeth. As I come out of the stall I see a gray-haired man come striding over to the shedrow. He looks up and down the aisle, then bangs on Gaines's office door.

"He's not in there," I call out to the guy.

The man scowls at me like he'd just as soon smash my head into a wall as look at me. Thankfully, Ned emerges from Liz's Tizzy's stall and intervenes.

"Mr. Mancuso," Ned says in a placating voice. "Hello."

"Where's Gaines at?" the man barks.

"He's up at the track," Ned tells him.

"I gotta talk to him about that fucking Frank. Now," the guy says. Ned takes the guy inside Gaines's office, presumably to calm him down.

I turn around and find myself face-to-face with Sebastian.

"That's not a happy man," Sebastian says.

"Who is that?"

"Little Molly's uncle."

"Oh . . ."

"Cops talk to you?" he asks me.

"No. Why, were they going to?"

"I dunno. Thought they were talking to everybody. Sure wasted plenty of my time."

"Oh yeah? What'd they want?"

"Just asking about Frank mostly. Told 'em I don't know much. I reckon Gaines gave 'em an earful. You know the story, right?"

"What story?"

"Frank used to be Gaines's assistant trainer."

"He did?"

Sebastian nods. "Got into trouble, though. Drugs and some breaking and entering. Went off, did a little time. Came back eventually, but now all Gaines lets him do is walk hots."

"Oh yeah?" I say, surprised at Sebastian's sudden talkativeness. "So, what, maybe Frank's pissed off being demoted to hotwalker?"

"I'd reckon, yeah. But I don't mean he had something to do with Molly dying. I wasn't implying that," Sebastian says, looking worried. "Why you wanna know anyway?" he asks, suddenly suspicious, seeming to forget he brought the whole topic up in the first place.

"I don't really, I was just . . . uh, I dunno."

"What you doin' working here anyhow?" he asks me. This seems to be a lot of people's favorite question.

"I needed a change. I like horses."

"Yeah? You ride?"

"When I can. Not much. You?"

"Yeah."

"You have a horse?"

"Yup."

"Here?"

"Here? Thoroughbreds? Nah. I got a quarter horse. I'm with the Federation of Black Cowboys."

"The who?"

"Black Cowboys. We put on rodeos. Parades. Ride around the projects letting kids see the horses. Got a stable out on the edge of East New York. The Hole."

"The Hole?"

"That's what we call it. That's where I first met Frank. When he was about yay high," Sebastian says, holding his hand three feet off the ground. "Had to be the only white kid growing up in East New York at that time. Quiet kid. Used to come nosing around the stable. We put him to work. He did good. I'm the one brought him to work for Gaines six years ago. Started out walking hots, and then, like I said, got all the way up to assistant trainer before he got his nose in too much trouble."

My interest is seriously piqued and I want to ask some questions, but at that moment Molly's uncle and Ned emerge from the tack room. The uncle storms off. Ned looks over at me and Sebastian.

"I'm gonna go rub Cipullo," Sebastian tells no one in particular, then turns and walks toward the colt's stall.

Ned looks at me and frowns, like he's about to chide me about something. "You wanna have dinner?" he asks abruptly.

I stare at him. I nod. "But I'm done for the day and you're still working," I point out.

He contemplates this. His little glasses slide down his nose. He pushes them back. "Where do you live?"

"At the end of Brooklyn."

"The end?"

"The end. Coney Island."

"You live at Coney Island?"

"Yeah. And you?"

"Queens."

"Yeah?"

"Born and raised," he says, shoving hands into pockets.

I suggest meeting at a Russian place I know in Brighton Beach. Ned seems to like the idea. Pulls his little memo pad from his pocket, jots down the details.

He starts walking away then turns back. "Eight good for you?"

"Very," I say gravely.

I watch his ass as he walks away. I get a slight pang of guilt over enjoying another man's ass when, in effect, I'm shacking up with Oliver. Even though he'd be the first to tell me to go for it.

I mull this over as I retrieve my bag from the tack room then head to the ladies' room to clean up. I'm running a brush through my hair when the phone chirps in my pocket. I put it to my ear.

"Have you found anything, Ruby?" Ariel asks breathlessly.

"No. Not yet. I had to do my hotwalker work first. Now I'm gonna poke around."

"Poke around?" she says, sounding irate.

I tell her about Jimmy John Mancuso, uncle of the deceased apprentice.

She cuts in: "You're not wasting my time, Ruby, are you?"

I have a strong urge to reach through the telephone and rip her head off. "Ariel," I say, restraining myself, "this was your idea. I didn't want to come back here. Remember?"

"I remember. But don't think I'm made of money."

"Okay. I'm not thinking that."

"Are you being flip with me, Ruby? This is not a joke."

I say nothing. I don't know what the hell to think. Ariel DiCello is sounding distinctly unhinged.

"I'm encountering some difficulties," she says eventually.

"Oh?"

"Perhaps this is enough," she says.

"Enough?"

"Enough from you. I can't spend any more time thinking about all this. I must organize myself."

"Okay," I say softly, "you're terminating me, then?"

She mulls this over. Then: "No. Keep doing what you're doing. For the moment."

"Ah. Okay," I say, half expecting her to change her mind again. She doesn't, though.

"Tell me everything, Ruby, everything you learn."

After vowing to keep her posted, I turn the phone off. I finish brushing my hair as I ponder Ariel's psychological well-being. Or lack of it.

Emerging from the ladies' room, I make my way over toward Will Lott's barn, hoping to find Little Molly's uncle.

The shedrow is quiet and mostly empty. Horses' heads poke out over stall guards. Horse laundry dries on a makeshift clotheslines. A tiny black guy dozes in a lawn chair. Down the aisle, I see a Spanish kid, raking. When I ask him if Jimmy John Mancuso is around, he squints at me.

"What you need him for?"

"Just wanted to ask him a question."

"Oh yeah? You wanna ask me instead?" The kid leers.

"Thanks, but no. You know where Jimmy John is?"

"Captain Cash's stall. Gray colt. Other side of the shedrow." The kid motions.

I make my way around the barn and find a man leading a gray colt to a stall. The colt is a handsome beast, well-made head, kind eyes. The man tending to him is the one I saw earlier, banging on Gaines's office door. He's stocky, with salt and pepper hair, and bears no physical resemblance to Molly other than a similar sour facial expression. He puts the colt up on the wall and starts currying him.

"Mr. Mancuso?"

"What," he says flatly, without looking up.

"My name's Ruby Murphy. I was sorry to hear about your niece."

"You knew Molly?" He squints at me.

"No, not really."

"So what do you want?"

"I just wanted to ask you some questions about Molly."

"Why?"

"For a friend."

"What the hell are you talking about?" He scowls, holding the currycomb like it's a weapon.

"Was your niece involved with Frank, the hotwalker who works for Arnold Gaines?"

Next thing I know, Mancuso comes popping out of the stall and shoves me, throwing me down and pinning me to the ground. As I yelp out in pain, he puts his mouth to my ear.

"Don't ever make suggestions like that about my niece."

My heart's beating fast and I feel myself breaking into a cold sweat. I must look scared out of my mind because, as I stare up helplessly at Jimmy John Mancuso, his frown relaxes and he loosens his grip on my hands.

I don't trust his sudden benevolence so I just hold still.

"You can get up," he says, and then, begrudgingly, adds, "Sorry, I'm a little uptight."

I stand up slowly, wobbly.

Jimmy John Mancuso looks pretty contrite now. He glances in at the gray colt. Like the horse is gonna open his mouth and pronounce judgment on Mancuso's untoward behavior.

"Look, I'm sorry," Mancuso says, "but that's my niece you're talking about. I'd like it if you'd just leave now."

The way he apologizes, it's clear he's not accustomed to doing it.

"I just wanted to ask a couple questions."

"You're a cop?" He sneers.

"No. I'm just friends with a lady who's a friend of Frank's."

"That piece of shit was stalking my niece, and you have the nerve to come over here asking me questions? I'll give you some answers," Mancuso threatens, angry all over again.

He grabs the front of my shirt. The abrupt movement spooks the gray colt, who skitters and bangs his shoulder against the wall. Mancuso lets go of me and soothes the horse.

I step back.

The horse calms down and Mancuso turns back to me. "If I were you I'd get the hell out of my sight right now," he says.

"Right. Well, thank you, sir," I say, turning and hurrying away from Molly's insane uncle.

I bump smack into the young hotwalker who initially directed me to Mancuso. "I think you're right," the kid says to me.

"Huh?" I gape at him.

He's probably about sixteen, but it's hard to tell because he's on the small side anyway. He has close-cropped black hair and a fine-boned face.

"I overheard what you were asking Jimmy John."

"Oh yeah? And what am I right about?"

"How 'bout I tell you over a drink." He grins.

"How about I don't drink but I'd be happy if you told me something?"

"How about coffee?"

"I don't have time for coffee right now," I say, watching his face cloud over.

The kid sighs, rolls his eyes, then says, "That Frank guy. He was up to something. And Molly knew about it. Only she was hot for him so she kept her mouth shut. I seen those two together—if you know what I mean. And that Frank, he's a black wish."

"He's a what?"

"He's a curse. A black wish. Nobody on the backside will hire that guy. Except Gaines."

"So what are you saying? What do you think?"

"I can't tell you that. How come you wanna know, anyway?"

"I'm friends with a lady who goes out with Frank."

"Why?"

"Why what?"

"Why she goes out with Frank?"

"I have no idea. But she does."

"You sure you don't want a drink?"

"I don't want a drink and neither do you."

"That's true." He drops his head. "I hate drinking," he admits. He pauses. Scrutinizes me a little. "How come you working for Gaines?"

"I needed a job."

"There are other trainers."

"What's wrong with Gaines?"

"A lot of bad shit happens around that guy," the kid says obliquely.

"Like what?"

"Why am I gonna tell you? You work for him."

"I'm not planning on working for him long."

The kid looks thoughtful. Then he peers around to see if anyone's within earshot. He lowers his voice to an intimate whisper: "You know a horse Gaines was training died two months ago, right?"

"No."

"Yeah. Dropped dead. Insurance company investigated and all. I guess they thought something was up. Expensive horse. Good bloodlines but he didn't run good."

"Oh yeah?"

"Yeah," he says. He scans around again, lowers his voice some more. "Frank always walked that horse."

"You told this to anyone? Cops?"

"Nah."

"Why not?" I say, highly unconvinced of the kid's allegations.

"Nothing to tell. I never actually seen anything bad happen. Just know things go wrong around that Frank guy." The kid shrugs. "You gonna have coffee with me tomorrow?" he asks.

"Maybe I will. What's your name?"

"Larry, but I didn't tell you none of this," he says, narrowing his brown eyes. "I'm serious, man."

"Okay. Sure, Larry. But you know anyone else I can ask about this?"

"No way," he says, shaking his head vigorously. "If something like this is really going on, folks get violent."

"Like Molly having a heart attack?"

The kid's eyes get round. "No way. She just had a heart attack. From the speed," he says. Then: "I gotta go. Don't tell nobody you talked to me. And you have coffee with me tomorrow, right?"

"Okay," I tell the kid.

He grins lecherously then turns and walks away.

I don't know what to think. So I head home.

x

AS I WAIT for the LIRR train, I dial Ariel.

"Hello?" her voice quavers.

"I've got some news. It's not so nice." I relay what the kid told me. "The kid's probably talking out his ass," I tell her, "but it bears looking into."

"So Molly's uncle thinks Frank was stalking her? In a sexual manner?" Ariel sounds like she's having trouble getting her breath.

"I don't know what kind of manner and I don't know if I can believe a word the kid said. But yeah. I guess that's what the uncle thinks," I reply calmly.

"Oh," she says weakly. I can barely hear her as my train clangs into the station.

"Train's here. I'll call you tomorrow?" I say, hanging up. I switch my phone off, with no intention of turning it back on until tomorrow morning.

The train doors swoosh open and I get on. Within a minute of sitting down I find myself turning the phone on again and dialing my tempestuous piano teacher's number. We haven't scheduled our next lesson and, with all this crap going on, I need one badly. The voice mail answers, haughtily telling me to state my purpose.

"Ruby here. Mark, I need a lesson badly. Please call." I click the phone off and stare out the window, trying not to think.

Mark Baxter

20 / Raving Beauties

Unfortunately, I've discovered that my interest in cheese has waned. My mother was raised in France and, accordingly, had pronounced tastes in cheeses. Tastes she passed on to me. Of course, my mother, Isabelle, is unwell and living in an institution now. It was perhaps these very tastes that drove her mad. Or rather, the difficulty of having developed keen tastes at a young age and then, later in life, being deprived of the things she'd learned to crave. Her parents were killed when she was seventeen. She married at eighteen, had me at nineteen, then was abandoned by my father. She was a beautiful, intelligent woman but she didn't know how to hack through the world's brutalities. She found a way to afford piano lessons for me and pressured me to work hard the moment she realized I had potential. Driving me to play Carnegie Hall—an event I feared might never happen—took the last of her inner resources. By the time I was twelve there wasn't much left of her. She managed to show up for her job at the glove counter at Bergdorf's, but she almost never spoke and streaks of white appeared in her wheat-colored hair. She was locked away when I was fourteen, and my godmother Dot raised me for the next four years. My mother remains under lock and key to this day. She has deteriorated but is still in many ways beautiful. It is for her that I work as I do. And I carry her refined tastes inside me. But now I find they are changing. Though I have a slab of perfectly ripe Brie here in my practice room, I'm finding it difficult to negotiate. I am nearly crippled with hunger, after working all day on the JSB partita. I have been relentless in my quest, and all this time the cheese has been ripening.

I walk over to where the plate of cheese is sitting, on a small table to the left of the piano. I pick up the plate and hold it to my nose. The odor is repellent.

I sit down cross-legged on the floor and rest my head in my hands. The head is very heavy right now despite being light from hunger. I have not heard from Wanda since walking out her door. The way she protested my abrupt departure, I thought surely she would call or, in her inimitable fashion, worm her way through Juilliard security and find her way to my practice room. Each time I've left the room to urinate or get coffee, I've expected to find her here upon my return. But she is not here. Not physically. Though apparently her absurd preferences have infected me. Wanda is a vegan and the very idea of cheese is appalling to her.

A sudden noise startles me. I lift my heavy head, crane my neck to the little window in the door and see a face. Though I will it to be Wanda's, it is not. It is the cellist. Whatever her name is. The willowy thing who looks at me with lust in her eyes. I stare up at her. She mouths something, probably a request to be let in. I slowly stand up and approach the door. The tiny window frames her face. I stare at it long moments before at last unlocking the door and opening it.

"Yes?" I say, letting her know my displeasure at the interruption.

"You've been in here all day," the blond woman says. "You must eat, Mark." I now see that she's proffering some sort of sandwich.

"Is that egg salad?" I demand.

"It is not. I'm aware of your loathing for eggs."

This startles me. I barely remember ever conversing with this woman. How would she know of my loathing for eggs?

"Grilled portabello mushrooms," the girl says. "I am a vegetarian and can't say I encourage the consumption of meat and dairy products."

Another one. My mother wouldn't approve. Such a limited palate these vegetarians have.

"Don't tell me, you do yoga too, don't you?"

"Don't be snide, Mark. You could benefit from such a thing. Look at you," she says, motioning at my body. "You're hunched and slumped and no doubt aching all over."

"I most certainly am not," I protest.

"I know you've forgotten my name. It's Julia. I am a cellist."

"I know."

"You know my name?"

"No no, the cello," I say irritably.

"Ah," she says.

I have to admit she is what most people would consider beautiful: slender, blond, ethereal, with eyes that actually show some intelligence. But I want my Wanda.

"What is it you need, Julia? I was working."

"It's what you need. You need to come out of that room at once. I am taking you outside and you will eat this sandwich."

The girl has audacity. She now grabs my arm and forcibly pulls me out of my room.

"I must lock," I say, motioning at my room's door.

"You have no need to lock. No one wants to go in there, they all think you're insane, Mark."

These events are taking a decidedly unpleasant turn. But the demented cellist has my arm in a viselike grip and is pulling me toward the elevators and, for some reason, I am letting her.

A few moments later, after startled looks from some of our fellow students, Julia has steered me outside and over to the cement steps facing the Juilliard entrance. There are smokers everywhere, and though I loathe smoke, it reminds me of Wanda so I say nothing.

Julia has unwrapped the sandwich from its wax paper and is shoving it toward my mouth. I grip her hand, extract the sandwich from it, and halt her unceremonious effort at feeding me.

"I can eat by myself, thank you," I say curtly.

She smiles at me, and this surprises me. Perhaps I've never seen her smile before. There's something in this smile, something that piques my interest.

I bite into the sandwich and find it to be rather good. I chew slowly. Julia's eyes are on me. As if much is riding on my approval of the sandwich.

"It's quite edible," I tell her before taking another bite.

Her smile becomes a gleeful grin. "Of course it is. I have remarkable tastes. You would know this if you ever gave me the time of day."

The girl really has some fight in her, perhaps due to my previous wholehearted dismissal of her. Whatever the cause, her sudden strong attentions are not displeasing.

I eat the entire sandwich as Julia strikes up a conversation with a nearby smoker, a nervous Asian man with terrible acne scars who, I believe, is a violinist. I see the effect Julia's attentions are having on him and fervently hope they'll never do such a thing to me. The man is putty.

When I've dispatched every last crumb of the sandwich, I tell Julia I must go back to my room.

"Your room can wait, there is life to be lived out here, Mark Baxter," she says, making a sweeping gesture that takes in the blue of the sky. I notice that this blue is the same as her not unlovely eyes.

"Be that as it may, I am returning."

"When will I see you again?" she brashly demands.

"I suppose there will be chance encounters in the halls of this fine institution," I say, standing.

"That's not acceptable," Julia says.

"You, fair miss, are out of control," I scold her.

"Entirely, yes. That's part of my charm."

"I will see you around," I say firmly, and then walk back to the revolving doors.

I flick my identification through the security scanner and hurry ahead to the elevators before that nuisance of a woman can catch up to me. In moments I am back at my room. I go in, lock the door, and quickly forage for something to put up over the little window to the hallway so Julia can't look in as I work. I tape a copy of a brusque Shostakovich piece I've been toying with up over the window. That ought to deter her.

As I turn back to the piano I catch sight of the ghastly Brie. I put it in the trash and cover it with tissues from the little tissue dispenser I recently purchased. I am about to turn my attention back to the piano when I think to check my phone for messages from Wanda.

The phone's screen informs me that I do indeed have a new message. With eager fingers I enter my code and the message is played for me. Alas, it is Her Royal Stubby Fingeredness, grown suddenly concerned about our next lesson. She sounds breathless and worried and is ranting about needing a lesson. She is a likable wench. Perhaps I'd do well to distract myself from Wanda by pursuing her—though it would doubtless be demoralizing. Eccentric and thirty-three, Wench is certainly set in her ways and would most likely require baroque methods of courtship that I probably don't have the strength for.

All the same, I call her back. The phone rings twice and a man answers.

"Who is this?" I demand, unsettled by the male voice. The Wench told me of the demise of her live-in boyfriend. Surely she couldn't have moved a new one in already.

"This is Oliver," the voice says evenly. "Who's this?"

"This is Mark Baxter. I am returning Ruby's call."

"She's not here. She'll probably be home soon, though."

"Who are you?" My voice sounds more suspicious and icy than I intended.

"What's that supposed to mean?"

"Are you Ruby's boyfriend?"

"Who the hell are you?"

"Her piano teacher."

"And you want to get down her pants?"

"Certainly not," I say vehemently, "I'm merely concerned about her. She needs to practice."

"Uh," the man named Oliver grunts at me. I do not like this man.

"Please tell her I returned her call," I say, then click off, very disheartened.

I briefly toy with the idea of calling Wanda, but suddenly I'm struck with the thought that this is all the handiwork of the gods. The perverse gods have taken my Wanda from me and have made some man answer the Wench's phone. The perverse gods are seeing to it that I give all my attention to JSB and the business of winning this competition and paving the way for myself. My mother has put them up to it. I look up to the scarred drop ceiling of my room, but there are no gods there. I put my hands on the instrument and play.

Ruby Murphy

21 / A Beautiful Night

The train pulls into the Stillwell Avenue stop and I slowly get up and walk out onto the platform. My body hurts and I'm tired and confused, but all the same, the sight of my beloved Coney makes me feel better.

The sun is slipping from the sky like a large red ball some kid forgot to take home. All along Surf Avenue the Russians have their little junk stores open, crap laid out on blankets in front. Anytime anyone tries to buy anything, though, these cantankerous keepers of mostly useless and unwanted items inevitably name some astronomical price—or simply refuse to speak to their would-be customers.

I veer right on Stillwell, away from the din and chaos and over to the relative sanctity of my building. I slowly climb the stairs and find Ramirez standing in the hallway, wearing only a pair of jockey shorts, holding a fly swatter and looking extremely distressed.

"What's up?" I motion at the fly swatter and avert my eyes from the stained jockey shorts.

"Flying cockroaches," Ramirez says.

"What?"

"Flying cockroaches," he scowls, "motherfuckers."

"Aren't flying cockroaches indigenous to like South America or something? I don't think they can survive in Brooklyn."

At which my neighbor lets off a stream of Spanish expletives and cranes his neck to look up at the hallway ceiling where, he's convinced, flying cockroaches are hiding.

"I hate to distract you, but how's Elsie?"

This startles Ramirez back to reality and he frowns and shakes his head. "My poor baby," he says sadly, "antibiotics is helping but she still got pain." He shrugs then asks me to come inside his place a moment.

I follow him into his bright yellow kitchen. On the table sits a thick sheaf of papers, what look like printouts of Internet articles. Ramirez picks these up and waves them in my face.

"My baby gonna have a lot to deal with," he says. "See this." He points at one of the sheets of paper, evidently a first-person testimonial from a girl whose botched implants gave her a life-threatening infection. "My niece got me all this off the computer."

Though I'm redolent of horse manure, and Stinky, who's heard my voice through the door, is loudly insisting that I get my butt home, I sit down with Ramirez and read through the botched implant stories. Grim tales of scarred and putrefied flesh, mood swings, headaches, hideous nipple discharge, and that's not the worst of it.

Ramirez is very worked up, which is probably part of what's got him thinking we've got an infestation of flying cockroaches. Suddenly, he looks at me, as if he's really seeing me for the first time tonight.

"How come you so dirty, girl?"

"I was working. At the track."

"What's up with that?"

"Oh, it's kind of incredible. Someone actually died out there. And it's possible that Ariel's boyfriend had something to do with it. There's even a chance someone is killing horses for the insurance money. And the boyfriend maybe had something to do with that too."

"Died?" Ramirez's eyes nearly pop out of his head.

"Yeah. Heart attack. Supposedly, anyway. Speed overdose is what I hear."

"Little girl, I don't like this. You stop this shit now," he says, banging the kitchen table for emphasis.

I try to explain that it's not as bad as it sounds, which my neighbor does not believe for a minute. He gives me a severe tongue-lashing. I hang my head and act contrite. At least I've distracted him from the psychosomatic flying cockroaches.

Changing the subject, I tell him I'm about to go on a date. The first I've been on in a while. But this doesn't seem to please him either.

"What about your friend? Oliver?"

"He's my friend. But we don't have sex. Haven't in years."

"That's a shame, Ruby."

I agree that it is a shame. But it is what it is.

I stand up, lean over and kiss Ramirez on the cheek and bid him a good evening. I cross the hall, knock to alert Oliver that I'm home, and then let myself in. Stinky hurls his entire body at my legs.

I call out Oliver's name but only the cats respond, chanting in famished unison. As both beasts weave between my legs, I hunt through the fridge and discover I'm out of cat meat. I forage in the cupboards, locating two cans of Pet Guard—one of the only Jane-sanctioned brands of canned cat food. Pet Guard doesn't use lugubrious by-products or preservatives, which is something I would not have thought about a mere two years ago. Since then, Jane started helping her yoga guru—an avowed cat fanatic—do research on all the hideous things that can fall under the categorization of *by-product.* Anything from diseased animal parts to fecal matter.

Stinky head-butts my leg. An annoying yet endearing habit that usually makes me feel cozy, but now for some reason gives me a wave of extreme melancholy. I feel like a fucking cat lady. I am going to die alone, serving cats and babbling at myself as I roll around in balls of cat fur. I'll store plastic bags in a knot at the side of the sink because you never know when you might suddenly need 573 plastic bags.

Gloom presses at my temples. I stand frozen for a few seconds until Stinky's loud wails force me to continue putting food in the dishes.

As the cats dig into their dinner I lower myself into the kitchen chair. I put my face on the table and close my eyes. There's no reason to feel this low. I have Oliver to keep me company. I have three jobs. Two cats. I'm solvent. But nothing helps. I think about my dead father. I miss him.

Tears begin to slide over my cheeks and onto the table surface. I think about everyone I know who has died or been wounded. I think about my ex-boyfriend Sam who moved out in the not so distant past. I usually don't let myself think about him. But now I get a sudden image of the last time we fucked. Me on my stomach. Him yanking down my favorite pink thong. Who knew it would be the last time?

I start to get angry. Like it just happened. I spend a few moments envisioning Sam having really bad sex with dim-witted girls and I start to feel better.

I get up from the kitchen table, take my clothes off, get in the shower, and scrub myself thoroughly. My off-white washcloth turns brown.

I dry off, lotion myself, and go stare at my closet. I want to look sexy but I don't feel like having an episode with my clothes so I just put on black cotton pants, a tight soft black sweater, and red shoes.

I go back into the living room and sit at the piano, launching into the Handel piece. I get lost in the music, and the next thing I know Oliver is fumbling with the locks as he lets himself in.

"I love Coney Island," he announces, coming through the door.

I look up and see that he's nearly naked. Wearing just a pair of boxer shorts, sneakers, and socks. In his hand are the rest of his clothes, balled up. His torso is bare, revealing the protruding feeding tube.

"What, have you been running naked in the street?" I ask, indignant.

I endeavor to maintain a low profile in the neighborhood. My beautiful emaciated friend parading around mostly naked isn't going to do much to further that particular cause.

"I went running," he says. "Had to do something to stop feeling so sick. I got overheated so I took a few things off."

"Oh," I say, not wanting to ask if it's a good idea that he exert himself like that.

And clearly it wasn't a good idea. Oliver is slightly gray and he barely makes it to the couch before collapsing. "Maybe I pushed a little too hard," he says.

I put my hand to his clammy forehead. "Oliver, could you please take care of yourself?" I say severely.

"Hush," he says, laying back on the couch and closing his eyes, "no reprimands."

Once his breathing gets even and his coloring improves, I tell him about my day.

"People usually don't kill racehorses for insurance money," he says. "That's a thing that happens with show jumpers and stuff. Usually not racehorses."

"How on earth do you know that?"

"I dated this girl a few years ago, Eliza, little blond girl that rode jumpers."

"Christ."

"What?"

"Is there *any* type of girl you haven't gone out with?"

"I don't know. But I'm open to the possibilities." Oliver beams, then his face turns serious again: "What you're doing is dangerous, Ruby."

"I can handle more than you think."

"You're not a cop." He pronounces *cop* the way only a person who's had run-ins with them can. "You're just a lovely and somewhat innocent woman," he says, shocking me completely because I don't think anyone has ever called me innocent.

"It's okay. I can take care of myself," I insist.

"Life is important."

I can't say anything to that. Life can't possibly be as important to me as it is to him right now.

We're silent for a few moments. Lulu comes and jumps up onto Oliver's chest. He grimaces from the weight of her.

"Oh," he says then, "some guy called for you, wanted to get down your pants."

"Ned?" I say hopefully.

"No, Mark something. Piano teacher."

"My piano teacher wants to get down my pants?" I say, incredulous.

"Apparently. He grilled me. Asked if I was your boyfriend. Guy sounded insane. And in love."

"I doubt that. He's a bit weird. But I don't think he wants me. He's just possessive of his students."

"No, he wants you," Oliver assures me.

"No he doesn't. He has a girlfriend. He's young. Twenty or something."

"Is he hot?"

"Hot?"

"Do you want him?"

"No. He's twenty. He's nice-looking but he's a weirdo. No. I don't want him. However, I am going to cheat on you tonight."

"What?"

"Ned, the assistant trainer guy, asked me out. I'm having dinner with him over in Brighton."

"You shouldn't be *dating* those horse people. What if he's killing horses? How would you feel fucking a horse assassin?"

"I don't think Ned is a horse assassin. I'm not going to fuck him, anyway."

"Such crass language," Oliver scolds.

"You started it."

We glower at each other for a minute and then Oliver laughs. "Well, you look nice. He's a lucky horse assassin."

"Is it okay that I'm abandoning you for the night?"

"No, of course not. But don't let that stop you. I realize you have needs."

We spar for a few more minutes, then I go to the bathroom and brush my hair one more time.

I kiss Oliver good-bye and head out.

It's a beautiful night.

Ned Ward

22 / She Is Exquisite

I've been home for all of two minutes and I'm just picking up the kitten to inspect her wound when there's a knock at my door. I sigh, knowing I'm in for a dose of Lena the émigré. I scratch the kitten's chin and stare at the door, trying to will the woman away. The knock comes again, louder. She knows I'm here, no doubt keeps a vigil at her window, waiting for me to get home so she can douse herself in violent perfume and throw herself at me.

"Yes, Lena," I call out.

She doesn't respond, so, begrudgingly, I tuck the kitten under one arm and open the door.

She's really outdone herself this time. Smells like the inhabitant of a bordello and looks like one too. Has on some sort of clinging low-cut red velvet top and a leopard print miniskirt. She's packed makeup all over her face and piled her Band-Aid-colored hair atop her head. Her red spike heels match her velvet top. She's probably someone's wet dream, just not mine.

"Ned," she coos, pressing herself in through the door and coming to stand about a millimeter away from me so that her considerable cleavage is touching my shirt. I have half a mind to shove this cumbersome bosom away but don't want to get that involved with it.

"Lena," I say, backing up several feet. "I just got home."

"Oh?" She rounds her eyes in mock surprise. "You must be tired," she says, "and hungry."

"Yup. Got a dinner date. Gotta get ready," I say, watching her for what I hope will be a quick retreat. But no. Nothing's ever so simple with a dim, single-minded girl. Her face falls several miles and, I believe, she manufactures some moisture in her eyes.

"You have date?" she says at length.

"Yes, Lena, a date. You have dates too, remember?" I say, trying to bring her back to the reality that she only gets hot on me between victims—most of whom are rather large men who are either extremely blond and Eastern European or deeply black and American.

"I don't want dates, I want you." She quivers her bottom lip and brings more moisture into her eyes.

"Lena, please, I'm very grateful that you're helping me with the kitten," I say, "but right now I have to clean up and get going."

"No!" she exclaims, stamping her foot. "This is not good, Ned," she says, and before I know what's what, she's lunged for me, making me drop the kitten, who thankfully is very much a kitten and lands on her feet, unharmed. Lena has grabbed my shoulders and is attempting to attach her mouth to mine. Suddenly she drops to her knees and starts unzipping my pants with alarming alacrity.

"Jesus, Lena, stop it," I say, pulling back, but she's on me like a hyena and already has my pants down over my hips and is yanking my boxers away, and before I can pull back from her she has her mouth on me and her long red fingernails digging into the skin of my hips, threatening to claw me if I move.

"Lena, *stop!*" I say, which just seems to get her more worked up. She's doing terrible things to my cock with that red mouth of hers, which, most unfortunately, has my mindless cock responding.

"You want me," she says, taking her mouth off me for a second and looking up at me with big pleading eyes. This gives me a chance to leap back several feet and hoist my pants up.

Lena's coming at me again but I'm ready for her this time and shove her a little harder than I'd intended, causing her to fall back on her ass.

She sits there, savage-looking, panting a little. "You want me," she says again, pointing at my crotch, which, thankfully, is slowly returning to a restful state now that the mouth is away.

"No, Lena. No. You're not my type," I say mercilessly, sick of it all.

"I am all man's type," she says, unceremoniously reaching her hand up her skirt and spreading her legs a little. "Look, I have beautiful pussy," she says, and at this point it's very difficult not to laugh because this is just fucking ridiculous.

Until today, I've gone a great many months without any action at all—ever since I stopped seeing Rebecca, a cute little federal marshal I met in my travels. Rebecca was a smart lady and very sexy, but took her job quite seriously and brought it home with her to bed. She couldn't get off if she didn't have me trussed up in handcuffs and a gag, which was interesting as an experiment but ultimately tiring as a preferred sexual routine. Rebecca and I parted ways and I vowed to be more careful before plunging into a relationship again, which isn't to say I haven't needed to get laid. I've needed it. Badly. And now, the night I finally have a goddamn date, I'm practically raped by the savage Russian psycho next door, who, ironically, does have a beautiful pussy, and it's not like I'm some martyr or something. As a rule, someone throws pussy at me, I don't tend to shove it away.

"Lena, you're a beautiful girl and most men would like nothing better than to make love to you. As it happens, though, I have a date and I also know that you will lose interest in me by next week. Okay?"

She's still sitting there, on the floor, leopard miniskirt jacked up, revealing her lack of panties. Her mouth is parted a little and she's still panting slightly. "You are homosexual," she finally spits out.

I shrug at her.

She stands up, pulls the skirt down, walks to the door, and slams it behind her. I hear her cursing in Russian as she walks down the hall, back to her place.

My first thought is to call a locksmith, but checking my watch, I see that I have all of forty minutes to clean up and get over to Brighton Beach to meet Ruby.

I take a few moments to feed the kitten, who looks as put out as Lena when I refuse to drop everything and play with her. I jump in the shower, throw soap on myself, taking care to rub the baroque bordello perfume stench off my cock, then dry off and put clothes on.

I take the time to rig up a contraption that will give Lena some problems should she choose to let herself in when I'm out. I lock the kitten in the bedroom, out of harm's way with a bowl of food and a litter box. Then, just in case Lena does make it past the booby traps and lies in wait for my return, I remove my Smith & Wesson from my dresser drawer, put it on under my light jacket, making sure it's well concealed. I'd prefer not to have to explain to Ruby why I'm armed for our dinner date—which would lead to explaining why I have a gun in the first place, which isn't something I can tell Ruby right now.

I don't plan to brandish this thing on Lena if she does make a return visit, I just want to make sure *she* doesn't have access to it. I go out and around the corner to the outdoor lot where I keep the fucked-up old Lincoln town car inherited from my dead uncle Jack who envisioned himself something of a pimp. I take a moment to muse that Jack would have loved Lena. The very thought of her would have kept the old guy alive another decade. But such is the timing of life.

I get in the car and drive.

It's hell finding a parking spot in Brighton Beach, and it also occurs to me that it's a strange irony to be meeting Ruby in a Russian neighborhood. It would be astonishingly awful if Lena, in her sorrow over her failure to blow me, happened to come trolling around to hang out with her fellow Russians.

I finally wedge the vehicle into a semilegal spot and quickly make my way to the designated restaurant, where I am instantly greeted by a hostess who bears an unfortunate resemblance to Lena. I explain I'm meeting someone. The hostess begrudgingly lets me look around for Ruby. Not finding her, I go back outside to wait for her there.

Directly above is an ancient elevated subway. A train grinds by. Neon signs throb out their urgencies in front of the many shops and restaurants lining the busy thoroughfare.

I consider lighting a cigarette then remember I quit five years ago. I lean against a wall, clearing my head of everything, wanting to savor the first moment I lay eyes on my hotwalker in this new context.

My mind is blissfully clear when Ruby comes striding down the street, lovely in a nicely fitting black outfit and a pair of red shoes with slight wedged heels.

She grins her crooked grin and asks if I've been waiting long. I assure her I have not. I'd sort of like to dispense with all the formalities, pull her into an alley and fuck her right now. But that might be awkward.

"Shall we?" I say, holding the restaurant door open for her.

The hostess shows us to a table. A great many Russian-looking individuals eye us as we take a seat.

"You Russian or something?" I ask Ruby as she settles in her chair and accepts the menu the hostess is offering.

"No. I'm not sure why I picked this place," she says, looking around and seeming to suddenly doubt her own decision. "I've only been here once and it was remarkably loud. I just couldn't think of anywhere else."

"It's nice," I lie.

She smiles—grateful for my indulgent fib—then looks down at her menu. I stare at her.

"What?" she says, looking up.

"Just looking," I say, "sorry. You're easy on the eyes."

I tend to be an idiot when I like a girl. And my idiocy seems to actually be making this particular girl blush. I can't believe it.

She ignores the comment, frowns at her menu. Taking it a step further, I reach over and softly try unfurrowing her brow with my finger.

She's startled and pulls back a little. Then laughs. "What are you doing? I'm not a horse."

"No. That's obvious."

She laughs again.

I have a perverse urge to tell her about Lena. I restrain myself, and feel any further inclinations toward idiocy leave me.

We fall into easy conversation. Pausing to let a chunky bleached blond waitress take our order.

We exchange biographical sketches. I tell her about growing up in Queens and walking hots at fourteen and falling in love with horses. I leave out a few things pertaining to one of my alternate careers—but nothing she needs to be concerned about right now.

She's got a very expressive face, and she frowns and grins and revels in certain aspects of her story as she tells me her own high-lights. She's a live one, all right. Quick-witted but sincere. Pretty but relatively unimpressed with herself. She tells me she used to work at some museum at Coney Island. Might go back to it if it doesn't work out for her with the horses.

"It'll work out. If you want it to," I assure her.

She smiles some more. "I've got to make a bit of serious money, though. I need a new piano."

"You're a pianist too?"

"A bad one. But it's my love," she says, and the way she says it, I don't doubt her at all. "I want a Steinway grand. An old one. From Hamburg. They're like forty something thousand dollars."

"That's not cheap."

"No," she says, looking a little despondent.

I want to run out and buy her one. Instead, I shovel in my food. She does the same, and forty minutes later we escape the unfortu-nate Russian restaurant and, by mutual unspoken agreement, head to the beach.

We're walking toward the water when I pull Ruby to me, put my hands at her waist and lean down to kiss her. She responds with an almost shocking amount of fire. I feel myself going a little blind. I pull back a bit and stare down at her. She stares back. I kiss her jaw-line. I hear myself growl a little. I want this girl.

I contain myself.

I feel her doing the same. She launches into some explanation about a houseguest. I refrain from explaining Lena the émigré and the possibility that she will be camped out at my house, jerking off in my boxers.

We walk. Back over to busy Brighton Beach Avenue, on into Sheepshead Bay. We pass a dingy little motel incongruously perched on a corner of land jutting out into the bay.

"What's that doing there?" I say, stopping to look at the place.

"I love that place," she tells me.

"You do? You've stayed there?"

"No. I just always wonder what it's doing there. If anyone stays in it."

"You want to?"

"Stay in it?"

"Now, yeah."

She looks up at me and grins. "Uh-huh," she says.

I feel myself getting the fiftieth hard-on of the last hour.

We walk to the hotel office. There's a small Italian woman wearing a busy hairdo and a smock. She grunts as I pay her in cash. "Make a right out the door here," she gestures, "third door on your left."

We find our way to the room. It has dark pink walls and smells of stale smoke and seawater. I pull the door shut. Turn on a bedside lamp. The bed takes up most of the room, and the mattress looks like a swaybacked mare.

"Can I smoke?" Ruby suddenly asks.

"Smoke?"

"Cigarette?" She smiles up at me, and she looks about twelve.

"Sure. I didn't know you smoked."

"I'm trying to cut down," she says sheepishly.

"Smoke your heart out, girl," I say.

I watch her reach into her jacket pocket and extract a pack of Marlboro Lights.

I go into the bathroom and remove the Smith & Wesson. Put it under the sink. I go back into the room and find Ruby sitting on the edge of the bed, smoking and staring at me. I lean down and kiss her right after she's inhaled. It tastes good.

I put my hand at the small of her back and dig my fingers into her sacrum. She moans a little, stands up abruptly, goes to the door and throws the cigarette out. She comes to stand in front of me and pulls her little black top off. She's wearing a nice red lace bra. I put my palm on her stomach and feel a pulse. She starts fiddling with the front of her pants, gets them undone, and wiggles them down to her knees. She's wearing matching red panties that break my heart. I reach around and pinch her ass. She laughs. Touches my hard-on through my pants, then starts undoing my buttons. I grab her and flip her around onto the bed, press myself into her lovely pale ass. I reach one finger inside her panties. She lets out a funny little yelping sound, then turns around to face me and pulls my head to her chest. I struggle out of the rest of my clothes, then with a hard-on so distended it looks pretty threatening, I fish through my pants pocket and produce a condom in a tired-looking wrapper. I'd have stocked up if I'd imagined things would go this way this fast.

Ruby yanks the condom out of my hand, takes it from its wrapper, and rolls it down onto my cock. Now it's her turn to shove me flat onto my back, where she promptly mounts me.

I am the luckiest man on the face of this earth.

I lay there, almost motionless, letting her have her way with me. She seems thoroughly pleased, and I'm not feeling too shabby myself. She keeps grinding into me, then periodically leans over and kisses me.

Eventually, I take my glasses off. Ruby's a little blurry now, but I've committed most of her to memory anyway.

Apparently, my taking my glasses off sends her over the edge. She comes rather fiercely, clawing into my chest as she does. Thankfully, her nails are short.

I push her off of me, onto her stomach. I threateningly put my cock between her ass cheeks, seeing what kind of reaction that one gets. I feel her tense a little but she doesn't protest. I make note of this, then enter her in a more conventional fashion. She bucks a little. I shove myself deep inside her little body. She's turning me on so much I almost want to hurt her. But not quite. I'd rather have my way with her several thousand times. Don't want her damaged.

A half hour later I'm watching her sleep. I've got claw marks up and down my torso, and though I've left Ruby pretty much unscathed, she's apparently exhausted. She's sleeping like the kitten does, curled into a tight ball, safe from the world's harms.

I envy her this abandon. I feel restless, a little nervous. I get up quietly and go into the bathroom to retrieve the Smith & Wesson before I forget it and end up extremely fucked.

I walk over to where my clothes are jumbled at the foot of the bed, put the gun in the pocket of my jacket, then go back to lie next to Ruby. She's turned over now. She is exquisite.

Ruby Murphy

23 / My Pretty Lungs

I'm curled on my side, exhausted but feeling opiated, lying half awake. I feel Ned, right behind me, sleeping. I consider turning over to look at him, but I need to run it all through my mind a few times first.

I feel him move and I turn my head slightly, see him go into the bathroom. And emerge holding a *gun*. I screw my eyes shut and feel my body go numb. When I open them again, I see Ned put the weapon into his jacket pocket. I don't know what he's doing with a gun. Maybe it's not something you mention on a first date. Maybe I've turned into a terrible judge of character and Ned is dangerous and is going to kill me.

He comes back over and I shut my eyes tightly. My heart is thumping and I start shaking. I worry that Ned is going to turn around and put the gun to my head.

I try to stop trembling and think of an escape route. How can I quickly jump from the bed? Get to the door?

Ned settles back into the bed. I sense him looking at me. Time passes. Seconds thick as lifetimes.

After a long while, when Ned's breathing sounds even, I open my eyes and carefully turn my head. He looks like he's asleep. I make note of where my pants and shirt and shoes are, where the door is, and what I can use to defend myself. The only weaponlike thing I see is the garish ceramic lamp on the dresser. I picture myself picking it up and smashing Ned over the head with it. I've never done anything to physically hurt any human or animal in my life. But then again, my life's never been threatened. Maybe it isn't being threatened now. Maybe I'm being hysterical. But then again, maybe not. I always thought my instincts were good. In the past, if a guy was trouble, I sensed it straight off and went into the fire willingly. I felt something slightly off about Ned Ward when I first met him, but I overlooked it, which makes me angry with myself. So angry it washes away some of the fear and I leap out of bed and scramble for my clothes. No sooner do I have my pants on than Ned sits bolt upright in bed.

"What's up?" he asks.

I stand frozen, idiotic. Then I grab my shoes and go to the door.

"Ruby, where are you going?" he demands, and for an answer I fumble with the dead bolt.

I make it out into the parking lot, pulling my shirt on over my head, not stopping to put my shoes on.

"Ruby, come back here!" Ned calls out.

I run down Emmons Avenue, over to Shore Avenue. I feel something jab into my foot but it's only a vague, disassociated sensation and I veer off Shore down one of the small residential streets. My breath rasps in my throat and my head is pounding.

When I reach Brighton Beach Avenue, I slow down enough to look back. I don't see Ned. I don't see anything except one stunned-looking old guy, staring after me.

I start to feel like a ridiculous ass. I'm running barefoot down the streets of Brooklyn. My fly is down and I don't have my bra. I slow down. And suddenly I think I'm a paranoid jerk. Ned's having a gun doesn't necessarily mean he'd use it on me, does it?

At that moment I see someone come running around the end of the block. I can't tell if it's Ned but I pick up my pace and hurl myself as fast as I can down the street, cutting between two houses into a small alley, running on pure instinct. I dart and cut and turn back and make circles until I'm sure I've lost Ned—or whoever it was. And then, just a couple blocks from home, my whole body gives up and I drag myself, like a wounded animal, into the parking lot of a diner where I wedge myself between a huge Dumpster and a wall.

I sit there for a long time, confused, exhausted, and scared. It's a dark, moonless night. Time passes. My mind is empty and black.

Eventually, when I can breathe normally again, I make my way home.

x

CLIMBING THE hallway stairs, I see a light on. Ramirez's door is open and I look in to see my neighbor and Elsie both sitting at the kitchen table in their underwear, staring ahead.

They don't look happy.

"You guys all right?" I ask.

"My chest hurts," Elsie says grimly. Then she looks up at me and her eyes grow round. "What the hell happened to you?" she asks.

I shake my head, not knowing how to explain. "Long story. But I'm a little worried someone's gonna come looking for me."

"What?" Ramirez is paying attention now. "What're you talking about, little girl?"

"I got into a bad spot with a guy. Maybe it's got something to do with the job."

"Job? You mean following that lady's boyfriend?" Ramirez is frowning hard. "I told you I didn't like the sound of that," he says emphatically.

"Yeah. You might have been right. It's turning into a mess," I say, sitting down, feeling my whole body turn to Jell-O now that I'm safe. "I went with this Ned guy to a motel. He had a gun. I don't know what he was going to do with it. He didn't point it at me or anything. But there's no reason I know of that this guy should have a gun. I'm a little worried he's gonna find out where I live and come get me."

Both Elsie and Ramirez are aghast and seem to think I've gone off the deep end completely. The two interrogate and chide me until Oliver, apparently having heard our voices, suddenly appears at Ramirez's door.

"What's going on?" he says, leaning his thin frame against the door. He's blinking sleep out of his eyes and his hair is sticking up, making him look like a sparrow with ruffled head feathers.

"Your girl Ruby got a little too close to a man with a gun," Elsie tells Oliver. Then, turning back to me: "You gotta call the cops, girl."

"And say what? I went to a motel with this guy and he had a gun?"

"Exactly," she says. "He had a permit for the gun?" she wants to know.

"What, was I supposed to say, 'You got a permit for that, pal?'" I fan my hands open in a helpless gesture. "I think maybe he seduced me with ulterior motives. Maybe he's in with the horse killer people."

"You don't even know if there are horse killers," Oliver says.

"There are. I know there are. I think I knew it right at the beginning. Knew there was something going on. But I didn't know I knew. Until now."

"Oh come on," Oliver rolls his eyes at me, "you're stretching it."

"No she ain't. Women know these things," Elsie counters.

Oliver shrugs, unconvinced, and all of a sudden the abject ridiculousness of the situation hits me. I'm sitting here with a moody Vietnam vet, my ex-lover—who's wasting away from cancer—and a stripper with botched implants. And I've just been to bed with a man I know very little about who carries a gun. I longingly flash on a few days ago, back when I had a simple, calm life, before everything careened wildly off course. I wish I still drank so I could just throw back a few and sit at the piano tapping out maudlin minuets and feeling sorry for myself. But I don't drink, and in lieu of extreme inebriation I have no choice but to stay up all night with my odd brood of compatriots. Elsie and Ramirez are too riled up to get any sleep, and Oliver, whose sleep patterns have been off for months, is wide-awake.

It's well after daybreak by the time Oliver and I bid Ramirez and Elsie good night and go back to my apartment. In light of all that's happened, I've decided to devote the morning to going to see Ariel to officially resign from my detective job. But first I need some sleep.

Oliver and I nestle into the bed, legs entwined.

Sleep comes quickly but I jolt awake an hour later.

I go into the kitchen to start the coffee, then collapse onto the couch, feeling like I've been dropped down a rollercoaster. Stinky is perched on the couch arm, stomach spilling over the sides. Sun is streaming across the piano. My little world looks deceptively peaceful and lovely this morning.

After I've poured two cups of coffee down my throat, I check for cell phone messages, but there aren't any. I try Ariel's various phone numbers. All I get is her voice mail.

I sit staring at the wall for ten minutes. I keep getting images of Ned. I let them come then patiently wait for them to leave.

Eventually, I wake Oliver, who has a slew of doctor appointments this morning.

As he stumbles into the shower, I try Ariel yet again, and still failing to reach her, decide that after seeing Oliver to the train, I'll try putting everything out of my mind by getting on my poor, neglected bicycle and riding into Manhattan, to go see my friend Jane, who's capable of soothing me no matter how I may have spiraled. I dial her number and she answers brightly, not only up at seven-fifteen A.M. but having already meditated, eaten fruit, and washed her yoga mat.

"You're coming to see me?" she asks, incredulous.

"I am. I have to talk at you," I tell her.

"I was considering going home after the doctors' appointments," he tells me, "but I can't leave you alone since that gun toting creep is on the loose." He goes into the bedroom to get dressed.

"It's okay. I've got Ramirez. He was in 'Nam. He can look out for me."

"He'll be home tonight?" he calls out.

"Sure," I say, though of course I have no idea if this will be true.

"You sure?"

"I am," I lie.

Oliver emerges fully clothed, studies me for a second then decides to believe me.

I stuff my yoga clothes into my backpack, throw my beloved seafoam green racing bike over my shoulder, and Oliver and I walk out onto Stillwell Avenue. We part at the subway entrance, Oliver turning back to wave and grin.

I get on the bike and head to Ocean Parkway. Fear about Oliver forms a dead weight in my chest. I start singing to myself loudly, trying to drown out the ominous thoughts in my head with a rousing rendition of a Joy Division song. When that wears thin I hum the beginning of JSB's Mass in B Minor. It's a bit too complex for my useless voice, though. I stop singing and ride.

The neighborhoods change, from Russian to Hasidic to Spanish and then black as I veer off on Flatbush, circling Prospect Park and heading into Fort Greene then finally through another blanket of Hasidim in South Williamsburg. I take the Williamsburg Bridge across into Manhattan, occasionally looking down to the murky waters of the East River.

In a few more minutes I'm at the corner of Third Street and Avenue C, once an anarchic and delirious cesspool of crime and possibility, now bordering on bourgeois with studio apartments renting for $1,600 and five star restaurants popping out of storefronts that once sold nothing fancier than crack and kitty litter. Multicolored kids from a nearby high school walk in little gangs. Black, white, Asian, Spanish, spilling out of their clothes, their lives full of big gestures and plans, which I find demoralizing. I've always found successful youths demoralizing. Particularly since I was a highly unsuccessful youth myself, barely passing from one grade to the next, lurking from one high school to another as my father and I ambled from town to town, arriving in each new place filled with hope that he'd find a moving company that treated him well and that I wouldn't stick out as the weird new kid nobody wanted to befriend.

At some point both my father and I gave up. We learned that no matter where we moved, eventually it would be exactly the same. He would take shit for being the new man on the moving crew, and I would take shit for being weird and new—a double whammy girl. I adopted a Fuck You dress code and a philosophical stance. This didn't win me any popularity contests either, but at least it afforded me the illusion that I was an outcast by choice.

I ring Jane's bell. She buzzes me in, and I hoist the bike onto my shoulder and carry it up three flights. Jane and Harry's door is open a crack. I push my way in and am greeted by two white and gray fur balls: Stewart and Blossom, the cats. They weave between my legs, trying to trip me, as all cats seem sworn to do to all humans.

"Ruby!" Harry says happily, emerging from the bedroom to greet me.

"Harry," I say, resting the bike against the hallway wall and pecking him on each cheek. "Where's the wife?"

"Where else?" he says, indicating the shower.

Jane has a bizarre compulsion; whenever a guest arrives, she gets in the shower. She's known I was coming for over an hour, ample time to shower, but as she's done several hundred times in the past, she waited until I actually rang the bell to step under the water.

"Coffee?" Harry raises his eyebrows at me.

"Great, yes, thanks." I go into the tiny living room and plant myself on the hideous black foam couch with a dent in the center.

Harry has been sitting in this same spot each day for several years, chain smoking, making notes for the true crime magazines he's constantly launching, and watching the Weather Channel, with which both Harry and Jane are obsessed.

Stewart and Blossom exaltedly sniff at my shoes as Harry comes in holding a steaming cup of coffee. I take the cup and sip from it.

"Where've you been hiding, Ruby?" Harry asks, taking a seat in the plastic lawn chair opposite the couch.

"Jane told you about my new job?" I ask, noticing Harry's peculiar getup of black socks, flip-flops, a T-shirt from a surgical museum in London, and a pair of baggy plaid boxer shorts.

"Yeah," Harry nods, lighting a cigarette, "something about the racetrack, right?"

"Right," I say, giving him the specifics, which Jane's probably already done but that Harry, in his perpetual daze of preoccupation and pot smoke, has probably long forgotten.

Eventually, Jane emerges wearing a strange pink dressing gown. "You're here," she comments, shooting a filthy look at Harry's cigarette.

"I am," I confirm.

She sits down on the hideous couch. The thing's diabolical gravity is such that she's sucked right into the center, forcing us to sit shoulder-to-shoulder.

"You look a bit worn," she tells me.

"I had a date with a man with a gun."

Neither Jane nor Harry seem particularly moved by this statement, so I detail it for them. Ned, the motel, the gun, my *Marathon Man*–style run home to Coney.

Jane's jaw actually drops. I take immense satisfaction in this. It's been a while since I've done anything that actually shocked her. Harry is frowning hard and pretty quickly launches into the now standard lecture I've gotten from both Ramirez and Oliver.

I nod my head. "Say no more, I'm quitting anyway," I tell him.

"I should hope so," Jane says indignantly. "You've gone completely insane, haven't you? I can't let you out of my sight for five minutes."

"It's just a fluke. I had no intention of getting into any of this. It's not my fault."

"Everything you do is as you intended," Jane says gravely, quoting some swami or other.

"We ought to get going," Jane adds. "It's after eleven." She gets up and goes into the bedroom to change. I give in to my compulsion and smoke one of Harry's cigarettes—even though I usually don't smoke for at least two hours before yoga practice. When Jane emerges, wearing loose yoga pants, a sweatshirt, and an odd floral scarf, she sniffs at the tobacco-scented air and shoots me a filthy look.

We bid Harry farewell then go down to the lobby, where Jane has her old brown bike chained to the iron banister. We ride over to Broadway, to the yoga center where Jane teaches and studies. A few minutes later we've rolled our mats out side by side and are lying on our backs, savoring a moment of rest before we're put through the rigors of the Ashtanga primary series. A few minutes later our teacher, Christopher, strides into the room.

"Ah," he says triumphantly, coming to stand at the head of my mat, "look what the cat dragged in." He stares down at my supine form.

I look up at him and smile. He's very easy on the eyes. Dark hair and eyes, nicely sculpted limbs, and the smile of a radiant maniac.

"Where've you been?" He cocks an eyebrow at me.

I shrug. He sniffs at me then spins on his heels and goes to the front of the room. As we all come to stand at the front of our mats, he bows his head and leads us in the Ashtanga chant.

An hour and thirty-five minutes later, after Christopher has successfully torqued all twenty of us into unspeakable poses, culminating in fifty breaths of headstand and thirty of lotus, Jane and I wring out our soaked yoga clothes, towel our hair dry, and bid Christopher good-bye.

We emerge into the brightness of lower Broadway. She flicks her cell phone on. I pull mine out too, checking to see if Ariel has called yet. She has not.

We make our obligatory stop at the Astor Place Starbucks, loathing ourselves for patronizing the place. Then, having each downed a large espresso Frappuccino, we ride our bikes to Healthy Pleasures.

We stroll the market's bulk bins, filching a dried apricot here and two cashews there. Then we make our way around to the meat counter and each buy several pounds of organic ground turkey.

"You ladies like the turkey, huh?" asks the tattooed guy manning the meat counter.

"No, we're vegetarians, but our cats eat raw meat and they love your turkey."

"Nice," Tattoo says, taping our meat packages shut, scribbling the price on them with red felt marker.

We pay for our purchases, then emerge back onto University Place.

"I've got to hurry home now or my cat meat will start stinking," I tell Jane.

"You're going to leave me?" she asks, indignant.

"Yes, and you'll be glad."

"It's true. I have lots to do. I'm teaching thirty-seven yoga classes this week. But I'd prefer it if you were forcing your company on me all day to distract me."

"I'd like to. But since I'm resigning from my private investigator job, I'd better go grovel to Bob."

"Oh," Jane says, looking sad.

"Don't worry, now that I don't have three jobs, you'll see far more of me than you'd like."

"Very good," she says, imitating Harry, who says "Very good" to virtually anything.

I get on my bike and ride away, turning back to wave to Jane, who's standing there, bike in one hand, cat meat bag in the other, looking confused.

I head east to Broadway, weaving through the thick traffic of bike-killer cabbies and lunatic investment bankers driving sport utility vehicles. I veer left on Worth Street, heading for the Brooklyn Bridge. It is hands down the nicest bridge to ride across, but it's always congested with renegade pedestrians loitering in the bike lane. As I stand on my pedals, pushing the bike to the bridge's apex, I start getting unbidden visions of Ned. I wonder if I was being paranoid, running out on what was, for all intents and purposes, extremely delicious sex—all because of a little revolver. I pull my bike over to the side of the bike lane and stare down at the water for a while.

It's nearly four now and the sun is starting to sink, enflaming the dark waters of the East River.

I take a cigarette out of my backpack pocket and light it. I smoke and stare at the water. I look over to the right, where the Twin Towers used to stand. Still gone. Every time I look at the skyline, I expect to see them, and the hole created by their absence still knots my stomach.

"You hurtin' your pretty lungs, sweetheart," comes the voice of a skinny dreadlocked black guy cruising toward me on a white track bike.

I roll my eyes at him. He grins and zips past.

I get back on my bike and tear down the other side of the bridge, narrowly avoiding a large man in khakis standing in the bike lane, taking a picture of the American flag atop the bridge.

An hour later, after having detoured to stop and sit in Prospect Park for a few minutes, I'm back on Surf Avenue.

I wave at Guillotine, who I see talking to the surly merry-go-round guy. Guillotine nods slowly. Merry-Go-Round Guy glowers.

I hop off my bike, hoist it onto my shoulder, and turn the key in my lock.

Oliver Emmerick

24 / This Body

I'm sitting in Dr. Liguori's waiting room, leafing through the bizarre assortment of magazines and wondering what's keeping him. He's usually the most punctual doctor on the face of this earth. I inspect the contents of a *Sports Illustrated*, ogling a few muscular female athletes before scanning a battered *New Yorker*, puzzling over a few incomprehensible poems and then latching on to an intriguing essay about the work of Gerhard Richter, an artist I've long admired. I get so absorbed in this that I fail to notice the good doctor standing in the doorway leading to the examining room. I suddenly realize he's been calling my name and I look up and see he's waving me in.

"Sorry, I got absorbed in the magazine," I say, still clutching the battered *New Yorker*.

"No doubt one of those stellar poems, huh?" The doc laughs his easy laugh. "Get the gown on," he says, "I'll be back in a moment."

I go through the obligatory rigmarole of donning the light blue dressing gown. When I first got sick, I'd just strip down to my boxers. Then I found the doctors were all pretty disconcerted at this, like I was some total pervert. So I learned to put the gown on.

Dr. Liguori comes back and I tell him I'm hoping I don't puke on him, having just come from another round of chemo. He smiles sympathetically. I then show him the skin around my feeding tube—

which has been a bit tender. In his inimitable fashion, he gives me approximately seventy options for dealing with this dermal distress. Options ranging from traditional prescription unguents to herbal salves I can buy in Chinatown.

The doc feels my lumps and looks at my tongue and fingernails, asking questions here and there. Then, satisfied that he's gotten a good eyeful, he tells me to get dressed and meet him in his office.

The doc's office is a pleasant chaos of books and magazines and stacks of paper. Light streams in from a northern exposure facing Fourteenth Street. He's seated in his comfortable-looking chair, staring down at some notes.

"Sit." He motions at an overstuffed chair—incongruous in an office setting.

I plunk down and look over at him. The man has a well-made face enlivened by intelligent black eyes. I know he's gay—he sometimes casually mentions his partner—but he's not one of those flamboyant vicious gay male doctors, of whom I've met plenty. They're just as bad as the disaffected Waspy hetero doctors. If not worse. Dr Liguori is just Dr. Liguori, an anomaly among doctors in that he actually converses with his patients and answers all questions, often before I've even thought of them.

"I want to know how you're doing on an emotional level," he says, coming to the point. "I talked to Dr. Blackman this morning and he gave me all his somber pronouncements, which I presume he relayed to you too."

I nod, smiling at the doc's assessment of his gloomy colleague Dr. Blackman, who is of the disaffected Waspy hetero school and seems to take sadistic pleasure in telling me he doesn't understand how I'm still alive.

"Yeah, he's a real cheerleader," I say, "but I'm used to it. You know how many doctors have told me I should have been dead weeks ago?"

Dr. Liguori nods, looking a little pained. "But how are you dealing with this?" he asks, looking genuinely bewildered, the black eyes seeming to get larger.

"I've got some pretty good friends and a lot of gorgeous ex-girlfriends keeping my mind off things. Plus, I gamble," I say, making the doc laugh as I tell him about my exploits at the track.

We go over a few more things, like him asking me again if I don't want to take up pot smoking to help deal with the nausea and me explaining it's not worth it. Weed makes me paranoid and slothful. The doc laughs again. Then, giving me a few sample packets of skin unguent and some newfangled painkillers, he sees me to the door. He squeezes my shoulder.

"Take care of yourself, Oliver," he says, his face all bunched up with concern. I have an urge to hug him but instead just tell him how much I appreciate him and bid him a good afternoon.

Outside, the Lower Manhattan sky is obscenely blue. Women are wearing short skirts and T-shirts. It's all quite radiant. And I just feel sick.

I hail a cab to take me back home, even though it's not very far. Playing house with Ruby these last few days has exhausted me.

It takes me a while to climb up the five flights to my place. I fumble with the key and finally get the door open and let myself in. I go right to my futon and collapse face first. The phone starts ringing. I put my pillow over my head and hum Saint Ludwig's Seventh to myself. Eventually, I decide to come out from under the pillow and put the real deal on the stereo. As the gorgeous first movement comes singing out of the speakers, I warily eye the blinking answering machine. I just don't feel up to well-wishers right now.

I turn the TV on to channel 71, the OTB channel, and mute the sound, not really having any idea who might be running today but having the racing bug back in me ever since Ruby and I went to Belmont.

It's fifteen minutes to post time on the eighth race, and there are some nice long odds on the board. I find myself suddenly needing to place a bet. The urge is strong enough to give me a little energy. I get up, go over to the computer and turn it on, listening to Saint Ludwig as I wait for the computer to take me to the *Daily Racing Form* online.

Saint Ludwig is on to that gorgeous second movement by the time I've glanced at the entries for the race. Trusting one particular trainer/jockey combination on the seven horse and going on pure instinct on two others, I pick a trifecta out of my hat and decide to call into the OTB phone account Ruby and I had last year, to see if the thing is still open. A surly operator asks for my account number and password then tells me I've got twenty-two dollars in the account. I drop a humble twelve on the bet, boxing my fairly arbitrary trifecta so that if by some chance the three horses I picked run first, second, and third, I will hit the jackpot no matter what the order.

It's now one minute to post time and I actually turn Saint Ludwig off and put the sound up on the TV.

My seven horse, a five-year-old bay gelding named Fluffy K, looks pretty good. Well-groomed and alert, standing quietly as the trainer gives the rider a leg up. The five and two horses don't look like much, but what the hell, it's only twelve bucks. The horses go out onto the track, meet up with their ponies and get led to the starting gate. The five horse, a gray named E Sharp, is acting up a little, not wanting to go into the gate. Two burly guys entwine their arms behind the horse's hind end and shove him into the chute. A moment later the bell goes off, the gates pop open, and they're off.

Fluffy K does me proud, shooting right to the lead, on the rail. The rest of them are bunched up in two increments of five across. Kind of a messy-looking race. I start worrying a little, not caring that deeply about my twelve bucks but alarmed at the messiness of the race, which is beginning to look like a sure recipe for disaster.

Two seconds later, though, it's all changed and the pack has thinned out. To my shock, I see the gray horse running in second. Don't know where my number two horse is, but what the hell. In the final stretch, with Fluffy K well ahead of the others and the gray holding onto second, the two horse, who I've just noticed at the back of the pack, suddenly comes around on the outside, accelerating and rapidly passing the others. The two horse reaches the gray's heels just as they pass the finish line. I hit a trifecta.

I sit there at the edge of the futon with my mouth hanging open. As I watch Fluffy K's groom lead him and the jockey to the winner's circle, the tote board lights up, announcing the payoffs. I am stupefied to see that the trifecta will pay $378. Not bad for two minutes' work.

I think to call Ruby and tell her of my good fortune, but I'm really not up to human interaction just yet, even over the phone.

I turn the TV off and put Saint Ludwig back on.

I fish one of the packets of unguent from my pocket and apply some of it to the tender skin surrounding my feeding tube. The skin becomes shiny and it all looks particularly perverse now, oily skin impaled by a clear plastic tube. It's disgusting, actually. I never expected something like this to happen to my body. To me. My body was always a wonder to me. No matter what terrible things I put it through, it retained its good musculature and strength. I used to pump savage drugs into it, starve it, mutilate it with glass shards and knives. And the body didn't really mind. It bounced back in no time. Transported and contained me. And now, after turning over a new leaf and beginning to take good care of this body, after close to ten years of feeding it well and giving it yoga classes and clean lovely women, it has succumbed to vile illness. It is diseased and punctured and has no fight left. It's only through supreme force of will that I've kept it going these last weeks. And my will is tired.

I lie down and pull the comforter over my head.

I sleep.

Ruby Murphy

25 / Ravaged

I'm midway up the stairs of my building when I sense that something is off. I reach the top of the steps and my stomach drops. The lock has been shot out. I scan around for something to defend myself. There's nothing but the stepladder Ramirez was using to go after the flying cockroaches. I pick it up and hold it in front of my body. I stand listening but hear nothing.

I knock fast and hard on Ramirez's closed door but it seems my neighbor is out.

I carefully push my own door open, half expecting to pass through the threshold and fall into a void. Ridiculously, I flash on the movie *Beetlejuice*, wherein, no sooner would the protagonists set foot outdoors than they'd fall into a hellish abyss of mutant snakes.

But all I find is my dear little apartment—in a postapocalyptic state.

"Stinky? Lulu?" My whole body is shaking as I advance through the chaos. All the things from the kitchen are smashed onto the floor. My Moroccan light fixture has somehow been yanked down from the ceiling and is lying in fractured bits. I glance over at the piano and feel a wave of nausea. Its front has been pulled off.

I hear foraging sounds coming from the hallway closet. I pull the door open and find Stinky, dazed-looking as he emerges from a cardboard box. I pick up my huge cat and cradle him in my arms, burying my face in the fur of his neck. He doesn't seem much worse for the wear.

I spend the next ten minutes searching for Lulu. Stinky follows

me from room to room, occasionally moaning balefully. Just when
I've grown convinced that Lulu is gone, she suddenly materializes in
front of me, not seeming particularly thrilled, but very much alive.

I'm so relieved I grab her and squeeze her—which makes her hiss
and squiggle out of my arms, indignantly darting under the couch.

I go over to the piano. The invader pulled off the front, baring the
old uprights' eighty-five-year-old innards, but I don't see anything
wrong. I hesitantly hit the middle C. It rings out. I put both hands on
the keyboard and run up and down it. All the keys are working.

I start looking around to see what's been taken. The TV is still
there, as is the stereo. The endless stacks of CDs seem to have been
rifled through but I don't notice any missing. I start feeling severely
spooked about the whole thing. I venture into the hall but Ramirez's
door is still closed and my knock goes unanswered.

I call my boss, Bob.

"Ah, the girl with the faraway eyes," Bob says once I've grunted a
greeting into the phone.

"What?"

"Never mind. Is something wrong?"

"Yes."

"Lovesick?"

"Someone broke into my apartment."

"Are your cats okay?"

"Seemingly. Yeah."

"But all your stuff is gone?"

"No. Nothing that I can see. But someone broke a lot of my
stuff and rifled through things."

Bob is quiet. Then: "There's something you're not telling me."

I tell him, reporting, for what feels like the thousandth time, my
activities at the track and my ill-fated date with Ned Ward.

"Christ. Call the cops, Ruby. Don't fuck with this." Bob sounds
aggravated.

"It's not my fault," I say, put out that he's getting snippy with me.

"You're so fucking naive about things that I just want to punch you."

"Thanks."

"I'll be right over," he says, "and call the cops. Now."

I hang up and do as I'm told. Though the woman at the precinct assures me that some officers will be at my door step in moments, Bob arrives long before they do.

"What have you done now, girl?" Bob asks, stepping through the door. He has his steel-gray hair pulled into a ponytail and he's wearing pink-tinged glasses that I've never seen before. He cocks his head, looking around.

"The cops are supposed to be here any minute," I tell him.

"We shouldn't touch anything," Bob says, like a man who's watched too many episodes of *Law & Order*.

"I don't think they're gonna be doing a lot of fingerprinting or conduct any kind of extensive investigation. Whoever did this didn't even take anything."

"Yeah, I can see that." Bob frowns and motions at the chaos around us. "But they were sure looking for something. What?"

"Like I know? I bet Ned is doing that creepy trainer's dirty work. Gaines probably sent him to rifle though my stuff. Or maybe Ned's on his own. I really don't know."

"You know what I think?"

"What's that?"

"You need to leave town."

"And go where exactly?"

"What about Texas? Go see your gay guy friend. The one you used to room with."

"I'm not gonna go to Texas just 'cause someone broke into my place."

"Then you're staying with me."

"No. You remember how awful that was," I say, thinking, with

horror, of the night when my ex, Sam, packed his bags and left, and
Bob, having not heard from me for a while, came by and found me
emotionally pulverized, lying on the couch. He forcibly took me and
the cats over to his place. It was a nice gesture, but he made everything infinitely worse by insisting on perpetual extended discussions
on the entangled nature of love. I didn't feel better until I went to
Oliver's a few nights later. Oliver helped me just by lying next to me,
quietly, and holding me.

"That was only because you were heartbroken and didn't want
to listen to my infinite wisdom," Bob says. "This is different. You're
coming to stay with me."

"No, Bob."

"Then I'm gonna call you every five minutes for the next
twenty-four hours," he threatens, just as the sound of police sirens
come braying up from the street. "Cops don't ever do anything quietly do they?" he says, and right on cue, the men in blue start
pounding at the downstairs door.

I go let them in. They're a Laurel and Hardy team. One tall and
skinny, the other short and fat.

"You Murphy?" Laurel barks.

I agree that I am.

They make an extreme racket trundling up the stairs behind me.
Oversized flashlights bang into walls, radios bleep, boots stomp.

"They don't seem to have taken anything," I say, showing the
cops in.

Their faces are blank. Hardy's stubby eyebrows look like aborted
crochet projects.

"You piss someone off lately?" Laurel wants to know.

"I don't think so. But maybe."

"Could you be more specific, ma'am?" Hardy whines.

Bob shoots me a look and I sigh and launch into the whole
insane story.

Neither Laurel nor Hardy shows any signs of life as I tell my tale.

Occasionally, Hardy asks for more specifics. When I give them to him, he just grunts, doesn't even bother to make more than perfunctory notes on his pad. It's not until I get to the part about Ned Ward and our tryst that both cops perk up.

"So you're saying you had relations with this Ned Ward person?" Laurel asks.

"And he threatened you?" Hardy adds greedily.

"I had, uh . . . *had relations*, yeah, but he didn't threaten me, just that I saw he had a gun."

Evidently seeing that a guy you've just screwed is armed is not something to be alarmed about. At least not as far as Laurel and Hardy are concerned. In fact, once it's clear to them that no, Ned Ward did not in fact threaten me, they lose interest in him too. Hardy gives me a card with the precinct's number. Tells me to give a call if it happens again.

Great.

The two cops clunk down the stairs, banging their flashlights and holsters into the wall as they go.

"Well, that was helpful, wasn't it?" Bob says.

I shrug.

"Got any cocoa?" my boss wants to know.

The man is a freak for cocoa. Accordingly, even though he rarely visits, I keep cocoa in the cupboard.

About twenty minutes later, sated with cocoa and reconciled to the idea that I'm going to ignore his advice to go to Texas, Bob bids me a safe evening and heads home across Surf Avenue.

I sit on the couch with one cat on my lap and the other staring at me from her perch on the couch arm. I don't feel so good. My apartment always seemed like a little fortress to me. Now it feels like a trench with a neon arrow pointing the way. Maybe I do need a trip to Texas.

I pick up the phone and dial my friend Stacy's number in Houston. He's not home.

I try Ariel. I get her voice mail, yet again.

I try Jane. The answering machine clicks on, telling me that neither Jane nor Harry can get to the phone right now.

I sit staring at the wall.

Eventually, I hear someone in the hall. I quietly get up off the couch and reach for the screwdriver in my little toolbox by the stereo. I stand shaking, waiting for whoever it is to come blowing through my door. But it's only Ramirez's door that I hear opening. I look out my peephole and see him and Elsie going into his place.

"Ramirez," I say, springing into the hall.

Ramirez and Elsie eye me warily. Elsie's face is puffy. Ramirez has a thousand years of worry in his eyes. Neither of them notices the condition of my front door.

"Are you all right?" I ask Elsie.

She shrugs. "I got pain, mama," she says. She looks so small. Her lovely wavy black hair is plastered flat against her small, acorn-shaped skull. There are dark circles under her brown eyes.

"Can I get you anything?" I ask, wanting to burst out and tell them what's happened, needing desperately to have the solace of other human beings, but trying to contain myself in the face of what they've been through.

"Oh my God, what happened?" Elsie suddenly notices my door. Her tired, puffy face comes to life.

"Someone broke into my place and fucked up all my stuff."

"The cats?" Elsie asks, knowing what a maniac I am about my cats.

"They're okay. Scared but okay. I think they must have hidden as soon as they heard whoever it was come in."

"Who did this to you, Ruby?" Ramirez is suddenly on fire. He's pushed through the door and is standing looking at the havoc beyond. The cats are now both sitting in the living room, staring ahead, as if demanding an explanation for the mess that's been made of their home. "You and your cats you come stay the night with us," he says firmly.

Though I hate being a houseguest, I'm scared enough to agree to it. I start collecting some things as Ramirez stands there bunching and unbunching his fists. It's a bit nerve-wracking when an eccentric Vietnam vet reaches the boiling point. Elsie puts a soothing hand on Ramirez's arm as I pick up the phone to tell Bob I'm staying with Ramirez and Elsie for the night.

"Oh," my boss says in a tight voice, obviously offended that I'm staying with Ramirez rather than him. I'm in no condition to smooth ruffled feelings, though. I bid him a good evening and click off.

I shoo my cats across the hall into Ramirez's place. It's pretty much the mirror image of my own but with completely different decor. Cluttered with discount furniture and velvet paintings.

Elsie goes into the kitchen to put water on for tea. Ramirez, tense as wire, withdraws into the bedroom and closes the door.

I throw some blankets I've brought over onto the hideous flower motif couch as the cats dart around, bellies to the ground, confused about the new environment. I sit down and stare at my knees.

"You need a stiff drink," Elsie says.

"I don't drink, Elsie."

"Comes a time when everybody needs a drink."

"Sure. But I'm not gonna have one. It won't help."

"Have some tea at least. The water's hot. Come," she says, reaching for my hand, pulling me up.

I stand at her side as she pours hot water into three cups then dunks in odd-looking large tea bags. The infusion starts to turn purple.

"What kind of tea is that?" I venture.

"Secret tea to help us all."

"Oh," I say.

It's not yet ten P.M., but we're all three ravaged from our collected stresses, and a half hour later as I lay stretched out on the couch, I muse that the secret tea must have contained barbiturates because my eyelids are bags of cement. Before I've had time to try to convince the cats to sleep with me on the couch, I'm out.

Pietro Ramirez

26 / American Swearing

There's not much peace to be had in this world, and lately I'm not even getting my small share of it. I wake up and find my girl curled on her side, her body all tight like she's fighting pain in her dreams. I decide right then and there I've had enough shit from the doctors, I'm taking my girl to the emergency room and that's that. I'll let her sleep for now, but then she's going in. I don't care what that shit ends up costing me.

I get up to go into the kitchen, and as I open the bedroom door, a cat comes at me and I nearly fall over. It takes me a minute to figure out why the hell there's a cat in my house, and just as I've remembered about Miss Ruby camping out on the couch, the other cat comes at my legs.

Miss Ruby herself is still passed out on the couch. I look down at her, trying to will her awake to tend to these fur-covered monsters, but she's out cold. I go into the kitchen, avoiding the animals, and put on some coffee.

I've been sitting at the kitchen table just a minute or two when my girl comes in, rubbing sleep from her eyes and tugging her T-shirt down over her pretty ass.

"Hi baby." She leans down and kisses me.

"I'm taking you to the hospital," I tell her.

My lady frowns, pulls the shirt down tighter over herself, like she's trying to completely flatten those problem titties, but doing this gives her some pain and she makes a face and sits down next to me and in a small voice says, "Okay, we'll go to the hospital just as soon as we've made sure Miss Ruby won't be needing us."

The coffee finishes brewing, and Elsie pours some in a cup with plenty of milk and sugar, then, sidestepping the cats, brings this to Ruby, waking her and urging her to drink it down and tend to her starved animals.

When Elsie comes back into the kitchen, I tell her to put some clothes on because I don't entirely trust Ruby, who I think is a bit of a dirty girl and might be getting funny girl-on-girl ideas watching my lady walk around half naked.

Elsie rolls her eyes at me. "What you think, baby?" she asks. "You think me and Ruby gonna do something?" She laughs at me, a teasing laugh that's good to hear considering there hasn't been that much laughter out of her this last week.

"What am I gonna do?" Ruby wants to know, coming into the kitchen, sipping on her coffee and working at not being tripped by her restless cats.

"Nothin'." I shrug at the girl. "Those things are hungry," I tell her, pointing at the cats.

"Apparently," she says, then goes to the refridge and pulls out some raw meat that I guess she brought over from her place.

"You sure those things ain't getting mad cat disease from eating that shit?"

"Probably are." Ruby smiles and puts the cats' bowls down.

The cats are definitely a little wilder than most cats I've seen. But, of course, I avoid spending too much time around cats in the first place.

Ruby watches the cats eating for a minute then thanks Elsie and me for letting her stay.

"And you're gonna keep on staying," Elsie tells her, putting her fists on her hips the way she does when she has a strong point to make.

I give my lady a funny look. Not that I'm opposed to Ruby being here when we're here but with going to the hospital and all, I don't want to be leaving the girl and her cats in my place.

"I'm gonna make arrangements for myself," Ruby tells us. "Gotta get Ariel on the phone, and then I may go on over to my boss's place for a day or so."

Elsie says that no, she wants Ruby staying in our place, and I'm about to pull her into the bedroom and give her a talking to but Ruby's already on her cell phone, calling the Ariel woman and talking to her.

Elsie and I go into the bedroom, and when I pull the door closed, she immediately puts her arms around me and squeezes me to her.

"Don't hurt yourself," I say, pulling back from her a little, worried she's hurting her breasts.

"Ruby won't do anything," my lady says. "You can trust her."

I frown at Elsie, then tap her lightly on the ass. "Put some clothes on. I gotta get you some help."

I watch her slip into a pair of jeans and a loose red sweatshirt. She looks good. Too good to be hospitalized.

I come out of the bedroom and find Ruby packing up her cats' meat. "You taking that somewhere?" I ask.

"I'm going to Manhattan. With the cats. Ariel's place."

"The blond lady? You're staying with her?"

"It's probably safest. She's not gonna be there anyway. She has a house on Long Island. She's going out there and I'm gonna stay at her place."

"Oh," I say, feeling a little shitty now about not wanting Ruby staying on here with us.

"Don't feel guilty, you offered to let me stay," the girl says, reading my mind.

I smile at her. "Yeah."

Elsie comes out of the bedroom looking like a million bucks, and even though I've seen her close to every day for the last five years, I sometimes still get the breath taken out of me at the sight of her.

"Close your mouth, baby," she says to me, smiling, then turning to Ruby, "Pietro's taking me to the hospital. I gotta get this shit taken care of." She motions to her chest.

Ruby looks worried, but Elsie tells her it's all gonna be okay— her chest and Ruby's break-in problem and all the rest of it too. My lady is an optimist. I guess somebody's got to be.

I go with Ruby over to her place so I can keep an eye on her while she packs up some stuff. Finally she pulls out carrying cases for her cats. The fat one goes in okay, but the little one escapes and goes under the couch. I stand there watching as Ruby gets down on her belly and sticks most of her body under the couch, pulling the little cat out and getting it into the case.

"You gonna be all right?" I ask, feeling shitty again, like I should be doing more to help the girl.

"I'll be fine, you just take care of Elsie," she says. I nod, and a few minutes later her phone rings and it's a car service there to take her into the city.

Elsie comes out into the hall and the two of them hug. They look good like that, the white girl's skin pale against the coffee of Elsie's cheek, and for a quick second I think about what it would be like if they did do some girl-on-girl shit, but the idea passes pretty fast. I carry the fat cat down the stairs for Ruby and help her get settled in the car.

The driver pulls off into traffic, and I go back upstairs. Elsie looks sad now.

"You think she's gonna be okay?" my lady wants to know.

"She'll be fine, baby," I tell her.

Elsie doesn't look convinced, but I persuade her we've got to get going. She puts some things into her big red purse and we leave.

Twenty minutes later we're waiting in the emergency room and I don't like it. Bright lights and a lot of nasty nurses and sick people. Elsie gets called in to see the screening nurse. She's in there maybe two minutes, then we're back to waiting for a damn long time before finally Elsie gets called again. A nasty white nurse shows us to a little curtained-off bed, and Elsie is told to sit on the bed and wait. I pull a chair up next to the bed and put my back against the curtain separating us from the next patient, some woman who's moaning a lot.

Finally, a good-looking black lady doctor comes in and her and Elsie seem to like each other right off. Elsie goes telling the doctor the whole story about her breasts, and I just sit there, feeling like a shithole because I can tell the lady doctor thinks this is my fault, like I wanted my lady to have huge titties and that's why all this happened. I want to tell how I liked my lady's rack just fine the way it was and how I'd be a lot happier if she wasn't dancing and showing her stuff to men, but that I also wanted to honor my lady and do what she wanted. But I don't say anything.

We're left alone again while the doctor is off having some tests run. At some point I actually fall asleep with my head resting on Elsie's bed. Next thing I know, the doctor is back, saying she's admitting Elsie into the hospital for IV antibiotics and she's explaining all kinds of things in a lot of detail but all I can think is that my girl is getting hospitalized and it's my fault.

Elsie doesn't seem to think it's my fault in any way, but that doesn't make the guilt leave. I stay at her side as we wait over an hour for an orderly to come and transfer her up to a room. I wait with her, in the room this time, while a nurse hooks up IVs to my lady's pretty arms.

"I want you to go, baby," Elsie tells me after I've been sitting holding her hand for a long time.

"I'm staying here," I tell her.

"I'm sleepy, Pietro, I need to rest. You go on. Come back tomorrow."

"I can't leave you here."

"You have to leave me here; they ain't gonna let you spend the night. I'm gonna be fine, this shit's gonna knock all that mess right out of me." She motions at the bag of drugs at the end of the IV pole.

I squeeze her hand.

"Don't look like that, baby, I'm gonna be fine. Now go on."

And eventually I leave.

I walk down Ocean Parkway, with the cars whizzing by and the night falling, and I feel bad. When I get back to Coney, I go looking for Guillotine, but the dogs aren't in the yard, which means he's gone walking them somewhere. Feeling like hell, I turn back, sort of heading to my place, but then, thankfully, I run right into Guillotine.

"Ramirez," he greets me.

"Guillotine, what's up?"

"Something the matter?"

I tell him what's the matter. He looks serious and worried. Even the dogs look worried.

"I gotta go take over at the carousel," he says. "James is home sick and the girl he's got running it's gotta go home. Wanna come with?"

I nod. Even though I should really see what' s going on over at my Inferno instead. I figure Indio's got shit under control and I'll feel better sitting with Guillotine, who won't say much.

We head over to the carousel, and the girl—a little Dominican girl named Lucy, who's got five kids at home—is relieved that Guillotine's there to take over.

Guillotine ties the dogs up in a back corner, near where all the broken-down carousel horses lie in a heap.

A bunch of white people have come over and are climbing onto some of the horses. I go around collecting $2.50 from each of them, and then Guillotine goes into the middle of the carousel and starts it up. The old fucked-up organ grinds out its song and the thing starts spinning. After telling me to keep careful count and make sure no one makes off with any of the brass rings, Guillotine sends me up to the little platform, where I feed the rings into the contraption that sticks out, just within reach of the carousel riders. They're aggressive carousel riders, each of them succeeding in getting a ring each time their horse swings by, and I'm sort of losing track of just how many rings they've got and I can see Guillotine, standing there near the organ, giving me a dirty look, like he knows I'm losing track.

Eventually, I get the big wicker basket and hold it out for the people to throw all their rings back in. When the ride's stopped and the people have gotten off, Guillotine comes over and looks in the basket, counting the rings.

"There's supposed to be eighteen," he says.

"Yeah?"

"There's only seventeen in here. One of those fucks stole one. You gotta watch those mothers," he says.

For a Frenchman, Guillotine's got a pretty good grasp on American swearing.

"Sorry," I say.

Guillotine's still frowning, but then I guess he remembers about my lady and her troubles and doesn't say anything. He pulls a flask out of one of the pockets on his army jacket and offers me a hit of whiskey. I take it. The shit burns down my throat but then pretty soon it's warming me and I feel a little better.

A nice Spanish family has come over to ride. I go collect their money, and before going to start up the organ, Guillotine gives me another hit out of the flask.

As the organ starts up with its crazy murder-movie-sounding song, I feel the whiskey's warmth working through my body. Since Elsie doesn't like drinking and I don't do much of it, the two shots have really gone to my head. I'm a little dizzy as I climb up onto the platform and start feeding brass rings into the contraption. I'm okay, though.

Ruby Murphy

27 / Man Trouble

Stinky lets out a few low groans of protest from inside his carrying case as I get myself embroiled in a discussion with the car service driver, a beefy Russian newly emigrated to the United States.

"In United States I can do anything," he tells me. "Already I have Internet business going, in five years I will be rich. I read. I listen," he presses on, "you see?" He alarms me by turning around to fix his gaze on me, making sure I'm looking at the stack of cassette tapes atop his dashboard. Financial self-help books-on-tape. *Seven Successful Ways of the Samurai, The Idiots Guide to Capitalism,* etc. The man laughs when I confess to earning less than thirty thousand dollars a year.

"Ha. If you were from Russia, you would be rich. If you had struggle as baby, like me, now you would be rich," he assures me.

He's probably right. But I'm neither Russian nor rich, I am just fucked.

I rest my head on the back of the seat as I watch Brooklyn rolling by the car windows. I'm supposed to have a piano lesson just two hours from now. Since it's too late to cancel, I'm planning to settle in at Ariel's and then traipse up to Juilliard.

I pull sheet music out of my backpack and stare at the Handel piece I haven't practiced enough. It stares back at me.

A half hour later the car pulls up in front of the Chelsea Hotel. I haul cats and backpack and a huge shopping bag of cat necessities out, hand the driver a handsome tip because I am a compulsive overtipper, and then lug my beasts up to Ariel's place. I ring the golden nipple doorbell. Ariel's small blond head pops out the door. Her face is pinched like a tight white glove.

"You okay?" I ask as she leads me inside her place.

"No. I am not okay at all," she says in a hard voice. "Frank has disappeared."

"Disappeared? Didn't you just spend two days with him?" I ask. During our earlier phone conversation, she told me she'd been shacked up with him and that was why I was unable to reach her.

"Yes, but he was supposed to call an hour ago. We had a plan we had to work out. He hasn't called. He doesn't answer his phone. No," she says vehemently, "I'm not okay. Would you be okay if you were, in spite of all your best efforts, living under the effects of a ridiculous hex passed on to you by your mother? Would you?"

I have an urge to slap her. Instead, I just let loose: "Try nearly getting murdered by a guy you go out on a date with. And then come home to find your apartment vandalized. It's not a lot of fun being with all these lunatics you put me together with. I'm just an ordinary woman, you know. It's taken me years to come to terms with that, and now, when I've finally learned to settle into myself and honor what's important to me, when things were finally okay, you know, I mean not great, but okay, then you came along, making these crazy demands on me for reasons I just can't understand."

Ariel takes a half step away from me.

"The world is full of people cut out for this sort of thing," I press on, "and I'm not one of them. I don't know why you insisted on roping me into your little drama," I say, and then abruptly run out of words.

There's a wounded, mortified, look in Ariel's eyes, and I start feeling crummy about my outburst.

"Oh listen, don't look like that, I'm sorry, I . . . Look . . ." I say, putting my hand on her arm in a conciliatory gesture.

She pulls away. "I didn't realize I was disturbing you," she says. "I'm sorry."

I look at her. I have no idea what's going on behind that pale mask of a face, its only color the violet of the scar. I suddenly find myself asking what I've wanted to know since the first moment I laid eyes on her.

"How'd you get that scar?"

Her eyes get huge and she self-consciously puts one pale elegant hand over the scar. I seem to have rendered her speechless. After a long moment, she opens her mouth, but no words come out. Then, simply: "My father."

I cringe and feel like a total piece of shit for asking.

"Indirectly," she elaborates. "He never raised a hand to me, but it was his fault this happened."

Her skin is greenish now.

"Look, I'm sorry. I was out of line."

"Yes," she says quietly, "you were."

We stare at each other. Stinky wails.

"Anyway," she says, abruptly shifting gears, "I'm going to Long Island. There are things I have to take care of. Make yourself at home," she adds, motioning at the blanched expanse of her apartment.

"Are you sure this is okay? I do have friends I could impose on."

"No, don't impose. Stay here. And, as far as our financial arrangements are concerned, I will take care of you when I return."

"Uh, when are you returning?"

"Three days at most."

"Well, I don't imagine I'm going to stay here three days. I mean, I'm not sure what I'm going to do but probably I'll go home once I've thought things through for a day or so."

"Yes. Well."

"So, uh, how about you give me a check?"

"I would be glad to, but my checkbook is in Long Island. Since you're in my apartment, you can trust that I am going to pay you."

For some reason, none of this is particularly reassuring. But I just shrug.

"Well, I'm all ready to go." Ariel indicates two overnight bags sitting near the huge white couch. "Here are keys," she says, handing me a set of keys on a horseshoe key ring.

"You like horses?" I ask, surprised.

"What?" She looks taken aback.

"The key ring," I say, dangling the good luck charm.

"Oh, someone gave me that," she says, suddenly curt. She turns her back to me, picks up her bags, and walks to the door.

And with that, Ariel DiCello is gone.

For a moment I just stand there, confused. Stinky wails. I bend over to open both carrying cases. I watch them emerge, bellies low to the ground, eyes big and round. Displaced for the second time in twelve hours.

I unpack the miniature litter box I have stuffed in a shopping bag. I scout out a spot in Ariel's immaculate bathroom where I put the box on the floor and fill it with the gallon freezer bag of litter I brought from home. Both cats come in to stare at this, neither one looking particularly approving. I leave them to it and go back to the living room, where I organize myself for my lesson.

I put out water for the cats, then, tucking Ariel's horseshoe key ring in my pocket, head out into the hall, carefully locking the place, then going downstairs and out onto Twenty-third Street.

X

MARK BAXTER is late and I'm left standing in the Juilliard lobby a good fifteen minutes. Packs of students roam. A bunch of wind instrument guys are lounging on the couches near me, occasionally looking over because, I suppose, I don't quite look like I belong. I'm too old to be a student but not sufficiently classical-looking to be a professor. I am about to give up and go back downtown when Mark Baxter appears. At his side is a tall blond woman. Mark storms over to where I'm standing.

"You're here," he says.

"Yes, Mark, I've been here for twenty minutes."

"Ah," he says. The blond woman is still standing there, at his side. She reminds me of Ariel—elegant, blond, willowy—but she's got life in her eyes.

"I'm Julia, Mark's friend," she says. "He doesn't believe in introducing me to people. Or perhaps it's just that he can't ever remember my name," she adds with a laugh.

I shake hands with her and introduce myself.

"Yes," Julia says, "he mentions you frequently."

This startles me a little. I think of what Oliver said about Mark Baxter wanting to get down my pants, but to be honest, I just can't see it.

"I'll leave you two now," Julia says. "Mark, I will see you later."

"That's entirely possible," Mark says.

The woman laughs again and walks away.

"Who's that?" I ask my cantankerous teacher as we head to the elevator.

"A friend."

"She's pretty."

"What difference does that make?" he asks indignantly, jabbing the Close Door button in the elevator.

"I see you're in a fine mood," I say, frowning at him.

"I am indeed in a fine mood," he says haughtily. "I certainly hope you've practiced."

I make no comment. The fact is, I haven't practiced much and I don't want him harassing me about it.

But harass he does.

I've gone all of two bars into the Handel when he starts yelling. "I thought you said you practiced!" he shouts, jumping up from his chair.

"I have, Mark—not enough, but some."

"What do you expect me to do?" he demands, pacing the short

length of the room. "I'm not a magician. And you're not a gifted child. You can't improve without a tremendous amount of work."

"I realize that," I say, "and it would be nice if you could calm down and listen to my excuse. It's a good one."

"I do not want excuses," he thunders, still pacing, then abruptly coming to a stop, contemplating some sort of plastic container that's sitting on top of the piano's closed lid. Suddenly, he picks up the plastic container and flings it into the trash.

"What was that?" I ask him.

"Tofu salad. I loathe tofu."

"Oh," I say, staring at my insane teacher.

Finally, after a thumbnail explanation of what I've been going through these last few days, I get Mark to calm down and actually become somewhat sympathetic. Our lesson proceeds without further outbursts for an hour, at the end of which Mark makes furious notes in my music book, scribbling down scale fingerings before sending me on my way.

It takes me a half hour to get back downtown, but the music lesson has improved my outlook and I barely notice the trip.

As I stand in front of Ariel's door, fussing with the complicated locks, I hear someone coming up the stairs. A tight-faced woman appears. She's clutching an alligator purse under one arm and a diminutive white dog under the other. She stops before the door next to Ariel's and gives me the hairy eyeball.

"Can I help you?" asks a squeaky voice. For a moment I stare from the woman's strange pulled-back face to the small dog, because it really sounded like the dog was talking.

"I'm Ariel's guest," I say, still looking from dog to woman and back.

"I see," she sniffs, and, keeping one eye on me, quickly opens her door and scoots inside. I wonder what she thought of Sid Vicious and Nancy Spungen when they roamed these halls.

I finally get Ariel's door open and slip into the long front hall. The cats don't come to greet me and there's a deep silence inside the place. I go down the dark corridor into the living room, where the afternoon sun is slanting in, bathing the many vases in ethereal yellow light.

I hear a faint rustling sound coming from the bedroom.

"Cats?" I call out, heading for the bedroom. Just then I spot both cats in the far corner of the living room, sitting side by side, staring at me with huge eyes.

I hear another sound from the bedroom and a blade of fear shoots through me.

"Ariel?" I call out tentatively, hoping against hope that she's come back for something.

"Ariel isn't here," a voice says calmly.

If there's one thing I have a bizarre aptitude for, it's recognizing voices. And this one, I know, belongs to Ned Ward. I freeze in my tracks, then slowly start backing up toward the door.

Ned comes ambling out of the bedroom, leans casually against the door frame and looks at me over the tops of his glasses. "So," he says, like we're in a thoroughly normal situation, "how's it going, Ruby?"

"How did you get in here?"

"I let myself in," Ned says, shrugging, producing a ring of pick-locks from his pocket and dangling them in front of me.

"Oh," I say, flat-line calm.

"So. That's who you're working for? This Ariel?"

"How'd you know that?" I ask, dumbfounded.

"You think I'm a jerk?"

I'm not sure what this has to do with anything.

"What are you doing here, Ned?"

"Playing with firearms," he says, lifting his pant leg and gently pulling a gun out from an ankle holster there. Probably the same one from the motel—though I'm no expert.

I stand rooted to my spot, staring at him.

Lulu sees fit to suddenly wander over and wantonly rub herself against Ned's leg. Though she is deathly afraid of most people, she occasionally warms to men. Apparently, dangerous men.

"Cute cat," Ned says. "She's a little nutty though, huh? I went to pet her last night and she hissed at me."

"Last night?"

"At your place. On Stillwell Avenue," Ned says. "What, you didn't know that was me?"

I feel myself getting light-headed. I think, ridiculously, of Balzac novels, of fainting ladies being revived with smelling salts.

"Are you all right?" I hear Ned ask.

I see boiling silver spots in front of my eyes. I blindly grope for the wall.

"You look bad, maybe you should sit down," Ned says.

"What were you looking for last night? What are you doing here now? I don't know anything, Ned, so I don't know why you're hounding me," I say, clutching the wall.

"What?" Ned squints at me and looks genuinely puzzled.

"I don't know anything. I don't have any proof of anything."

"Proof of what?" Ned asks.

"Whatever the hell Gaines is doing."

"Gaines? What's he got to do with anything?"

"What do you mean? You mean you were gonna kill me the other night just for your own amusement?"

"Kill you?"

"At the motel, Ned, I saw your gun."

"So?"

"Come on, be straight with me. Just tell me what's what. I assume you've been sent here to shut me up. Just tell me," I say.

"I don't know what you want me to tell you, Ruby." He shakes his head slowly.

"What are you doing here? Who sent you?" I press on.

"Nobody sent me. I'm here to see what the hell you're up to. You split the other night. I thought that was rude and a bit suspicious."

"Ned," I say, working to keep my voice calm, "I woke up in the middle of the night and you were standing there holding a gun. That worried me."

"What's a gun have to do with you?"

"You always carry a gun?"

"What if I do?"

"I don't make a practice of sleeping with armed men. I thought you were after me because of my suspicions about the death of Little Molly."

"What?" He squints.

"Molly. The apprentice jockey. Dead. Remember?"

He seems unsure about something now. Frowns. His glasses slide down his nose. Beyond him I notice that one of Ariel's discreet wall closets is open. Ned has evidently rifled through it. There are papers on the floor.

"What were you looking for?" I say, getting increasingly confused.

"Looking?"

"Why'd you go through Ariel's stuff?"

Ned says nothing. Reaches in his pocket and takes out his little memo pad. Reads something there. Looks at me again.

"How long have you known Ariel?" he asks me.

"Why?"

He stares down at the memo pad, says nothing.

"Ned, are you in on this horse-killing thing?" I ask, insanely, because I don't know what good it's going to do if he confesses to me. Then he probably will have to kill me. But it's all I can think of.

"What are you talking about?"

"Did you kill that horse of Gaines's last month?"

Now Ned looks completely dumbfounded.

And then the doorbell rings.

Ned points the gun at me.

"What are you doing, Ned?" I say, keeping my voice steady.

"Pointing a gun at you so you'll keep your very attractive mouth shut," he says, smiling. "Who do you suppose that is at the door there?" he asks mildly.

"I have no idea, Ned."

The doorbell rings again.

"Call the police!" I suddenly scream as loud as I can, gambling that Ned won't shoot me for doing it.

"That wasn't very nice," Ned says thoughtfully. "Now we're going to have to let this interloper in."

That said, he puts one hand on my shoulder, flips me around, and points the gun at the small of my back. "Please walk slowly to the door," he says.

I do as I'm told. He reaches in front of me and quickly flips the lock, then pulls the door open, revealing Oliver.

"I don't know who you are," Ned tells my friend, "but kindly keep your mouth shut or I'll make Swiss cheese of the lady here."

This is about the last thing on earth Oliver needs. He stands there gaping at me, his eyes huge with astonishment.

Ned pulls Oliver inside the apartment and slams the door shut behind him. "Who are you?" he asks Oliver.

"Oliver," my friend states matter-of-factly, staring at Ned's gun. And then, in a blur of motion, Oliver's leg flies up and he kicks the gun out of Ned's hand. The gun skids along the floor as Oliver, faster than light, somehow gets behind Ned and in one swift, graceful move reaches up under Ned's glasses and sticks his thumbs in Ned's eye sockets.

"Fuck!" Ned screams as Oliver does something under his jaw, sticking a finger in there, causing Ned to buckle over.

"Call 911, then find me something like a rope or a belt," Oliver tells me, seeming completely calm and poised.

I pull the cell phone from my pocket and dial with one hand

while removing my belt with the other. Oliver snatches the belt and binds Ned's hands as I tell the 911 operator what's going on.

Ned isn't exactly unconscious, but whatever Oliver did to him seems to have made him blurry. Several moments pass before he registers what's happening. By then Oliver is standing, pointing the gun at Ned.

And of all the emotions to have at a time like this, I get seized with extreme guilt. Hating myself for dragging Oliver into this mess. My avowed pacifist friend who renounced knife-fighting and karate some years ago because these made him feel too violent. Here he is brandishing a gun. And he doesn't look so good. It seems he's dropped another ten pounds from this last round of chemo.

A few moments pass and then a voice shouts the blissful phrase, *"Police, open up!"*

I let them in as Oliver maintains his gun-pointing stance.

In an instant the cops are on Ned, uttering things like, "Don't move, pal."

Though I haven't done anything illegal in a long time, cops still give me the creeps. I sit down on Ariel's white couch and stare at my knees. I feel queasy.

Reinforcements arrive and start asking me questions as Ned repeatedly states that this is all just a misunderstanding. And, if it weren't for the fact that he was armed, I think he probably could talk his way out of the whole thing. But he *was* armed.

The cops take statements from Oliver and me. Eventually, they haul a now subdued, humble-looking Ned away.

X

OLIVER AND I sit side by side on the white couch, stunned.

"You've got some questionable taste in men," Oliver says after a while.

"And you've got seriously good timing," I say. "What on earth are you doing here, though?"

"I wanted to see you. You weren't answering at home. Weren't answering the cell phone. I called Ramirez. He's listed. He told me you came here. I got a cab over and sweet-talked that little cutie at reception into telling me your former employer's apartment number. You're lucky you've got me to save you from your fits of bad judgment."

I agree with him wholeheartedly.

"I should call Ariel and tell her what's happened. Then I'm just going to go back to Coney. Now that Ned's locked up, I'm safe," I say, pulling the phone out and punching in Ariel's number.

"I'm afraid your apartment is a mess," I tell her.

"What do you mean?" Ariel asks, sounding very annoyed.

I explain.

She is very, very quiet.

"This means all my suspicions about Frank killing horses were probably unfounded," I tell her.

She still says nothing.

"Ariel?"

"Yes." Her voice is louder than usual. "I'm here," she adds. "So you'll be going back home, then?"

"Yeah. You want me to leave your keys at the front desk?"

"Yes," she says, voice icy, "that will be fine. Thank you." She hangs up in my ear.

I stare at the phone a moment, then turn to look at Oliver, who's draped himself along the couch like he's lived in this apartment his entire life.

"So?" he says.

"So that was deeply weird."

"What?"

I relay the conversation. The iciness in Ariel's voice.

"Well, it's behind you now. It's all over," Oliver says, "go home."

"And what will you do? I thought you wanted to see me."

"I've seen you. My work here is done."

"Oh."

"Go on, pack your cats up. We'll walk out together."

For the thousandth time, I'm not sure how to read Oliver. Does he want me to force my company on him? Did he really just want to get a quick gander at me?

"Stop worrying," Oliver says.

"Really?"

"Really," he affirms.

"Okay." I shrug, then go to look for the cats.

I find Stinky sprawled across Ariel's bed. As I lean over to scoop him up, I notice a handful of photos spilling out of a folder on the floor. I'm pretty sure they weren't there before I went up to my piano lesson. Ned must have unearthed them for some reason. Though what he'd want with Ariel's belongings is beyond me.

I skim through the pictures. There are a few of Frank and many of some other dark-haired man. One photo in particular catches my eyes. It shows Ariel standing next to a horse. Specifically, Ariel standing next to a horse that looks a great deal like Raging Machete. Ariel who claimed to know nothing about horses. Standing next to a lean, muscled bay racehorse with a white blaze on its face. It doesn't make any sense. And it makes me uneasy. I slip the photo in my back pocket.

I pick Stinky up and haul him into the living room, ushering him into his carrying case. I then unearth Lulu, behind the elegant toilet in the bathroom.

I empty the unused litter box, then take a quick visual survey to make sure I haven't left anything behind.

"I think I'm ready," I tell Oliver, not mentioning the photo I found or its possible implications.

"You okay?" he says, tilting his head as he looks at me.

"Yeah. You?"

"Yeah. Should I be coming with you to Coney?"

"No. I mean, not unless you want to."

"I could use a long nap. I should go home."

"That's fine," I say. I reach over and touch his cheek. He closes his eyes. Kisses my palm. Smiles a small, sad smile.

Oliver carries Stinky's case as I wrangle Lulu and the huge shopping bag and my backpack.

I lock Ariel's door and leave the keys with the receptionist—who Oliver winks at—and we go out onto Twenty-third Street, where I hail a cab.

I kiss Oliver good-bye—a lingering, almost sexy kiss—then get in the cab.

A beefy Polish-looking cabby suspiciously eyes the cats' cases.

"Cats," I say, "nice cats. I'll tip you well. I promise." His small eyes are a dull blue. I tell him my destination.

He snarls at me then jerks the car into the traffic of Twenty-third Street. I'm trying to think of something to say to try to improve his dour mood when he turns on his radio, choosing, on this fine afternoon, to blare light jazz.

From inside his cage Stinky growls at the sound.

Sebastian Ives

28 / Checking for Heat

Some mornings I get here and I just want to go home and put my head in the oven. This morning is a perfect example. I'm the only one here. Neither Arnie, Ned, Macy, Frank, or even the damned new girl has shown up. Only Domenico, little high school kid who comes to muck out stalls three mornings a week, is here. I put the kid to work and start making phone calls. No answer at Ned's and I can't reach Frank anywhere, though that one's no surprise. I try finding the new girl's phone number but don't see it anywhere and figure there's not much hope for her since this makes two mornings she hasn't shown up.

Arnie answers his phone on the fifth ring. He's none too happy about all his useless employees failing to show up. He tells me to go over to his friend John Troxler's barn, see if John can spare any help.

I hang up, make sure Domenico knows what I need him to do, and then walk over to Barn 54, where Troxler's got his string.

I find the trainer standing in front of one of his horses' stalls, looking worried, which is essentially how Troxler always looks. He's a good man. An honest trainer. He's had his ups and downs like the rest of us, and lately a few more downs than anyone's got a stomach for.

"John, how're you doing?" I say, approaching the man.

"Sebastian." He nods.

"Arnie asked me to come by and see if maybe you can spare any help this morning," I tell him, explaining how not one of Arnie's employees has materialized.

Troxler looks even more worried. Rubs his chin a little. Stares off into the horse's stall for a minute. "I can send Pedro over for an hour or two, but that's about it," he tells me.

"I'll take it," I say. "Anything will help. We ain't gonna work any today but I gotta get them all walked."

Troxler nods again, tells me to follow him around to the other side of the shedrow, where we find Pedro mucking out a stall. Pedro's a small thickset fellow, not much younger than me. Doesn't seem too upset at being farmed out to me for the morning.

I thank Troxler, wishing I could do something to make the man stop frowning. He turns back to the important business of staring down his horses. Pedro and I head back over to deal with Gaines's barn.

The morning goes by pretty fast, what with so much work to do. Pedro proves worth his weight in gold, and Domenico's doing just fine too. I wouldn't half mind getting rid of everybody, Gaines included, and running the barn with just these two. But it's not up to me.

What is up to me is making progress with the gorgeous Miss Yashpinsky. Yesterday, I told her she ought to stop by around lunchtime today and maybe we'd go over to the cafeteria together. It's getting close to eleven, though, and no sign of the girl.

I go into the tack room to start organizing what's got to be cleaned. I'm staring at yesterday's dirty bridles, which, to my deep chagrin, never got cleaned, when I feel someone behind me.

I turn around and find her there. Red hair spilling over shoulders. Wearing clean blue jeans and a pretty green top. You'd never know she'd been on a horse all morning. Looks like she just stepped out of a little farmhouse somewhere in the country.

"Good day to you, Miss Yashpinsky," I say.

She smiles. She's so pretty.

"Hungry?" I ask her.

"Yup, brought us lunch," she says, holding up a brown paper bag.

"You, dear lady, are brilliant."

I get an encore on the smile.

"I know a nice quiet place where we can eat," I tell her, the very idea of a quiet place on the backstretch making her pale eyebrows rise.

I tell Domenico to take a break and, after thanking Pedro for his contributions to the war effort, I lead the glorious Miss Yashpinsky to the far end of the backstretch. There are a few deserted barns where I go sometimes to get away from things and organize my thoughts.

We walk over there, taking little muddy paths between shedrows. On the way, we get more than a few sideways glances from various workers, and I briefly imagine what it might be like to bring Asha home to my mother, Lenora Ives, eighty-two years old and mean as a mustang. I decide to discontinue this line of thinking.

"My humble picnic spot," I say, waving my arm to take in the expanse of the two decrepit barns.

"I never even knew this was here, it's nice," Asha says, looking around. Which is when I start feeling there's some real possibility between us two, future damnations of Lenora Ives notwithstanding.

I find us two old rusted buckets and turn these over to make seats as Asha unpacks thick sandwiches, pretzels, and some Cokes.

For a little while we eat in silence. The lean roast beef sandwich she's brought me is the best thing I've tasted all year. And the view ain't bad either. The sun blistering up there in the middle of the sky is lighting up all the fire in Asha's hair. After a few minutes of silence she starts asking gentle questions about Little Molly and Gaines and all that. I tell her as much as I know, which sure ain't much. For some reason, I mention Ruby, the hotwalker girl, and how I feel there's something a little off there. Asha probes this, asking if I think the girl might have been a murderer. I tell her I can't picture that but something is off.

I watch Asha delicately wipe her mouth with one of the paper napkins she brought along, and then, abruptly, she gets up from her bucket, stands in front of me, leans down and plants one on me. The remains of my sandwich fall out of my hand as I reach up and put my arms around the girl's waist, pulling her to me so hard I fall backward off the bucket and she lands on top of me, those glorious thighs on top of mine.

The girl is a little much, though. She is so quickly in so much heat that I feel like she's gonna kill me or something, and anyway, it's not like we're in a bedroom, we're exposed to the elements and the eyes of anyone who happens to wander over.

"Hey," I say, pulling my mouth away from hers, "go easy on me, woman, I'm forty-five."

This makes her laugh. She throws back her head and grinds her hips into me and I have to start thinking of very unpleasant things indeed in order to contain myself.

"There are empty stalls over there," the wild woman says.

"Miss Yashpinsky, I am not going to make love to you in a

barn," I say, and to be truthful, I am somewhat mortified, wondering now if she's some sort of nymphomaniac.

I guess she senses all this, because no sooner have I formulated the thought than she's suddenly standing up, brushing herself off like she just fell off a horse. "I'm sorry. I didn't mean to offend you," she hisses.

Then, before I've had time to say two words, she turns and storms away.

I sit there, stupefied, calling out her name a few times until she's long out of hearing range.

Eventually, I stand up, collect the trash from our sandwiches, and walk back to Gaines's barn.

Though the office door is open, indicating Gaines has come in, I'm in no mood for him right now. I go straight to Sunrunner's stall and run my hands down the filly's legs, checking for heat.

There isn't any, though. All the heat today is apparently being contained inside Miss Asha Yashpinsky.

Women.

Ruby Murphy

29 / Horse Trouble

As the wastelands of Brooklyn slip by the car windows, I stare at my pilfered photo of Ariel and horse. I can't for the life of me figure out what this photograph means. All I know is it doesn't seem to bode well. I try moving on to more soothing thoughts as I stare out at the strange sprawl of warehouses at the edges of Bushwick and watch this give way to short buildings and throbbing bodegas. Scraggly kids hanging in packs on street corners. Exhausted young women propping children on their hips. Feral dogs scavenging the cratered streets.

I'm daydreaming so hard I'm surprised when the car comes to a halt. I look up and find we're in front of my building.

"You are here," my driver informs me, in case I had any doubts.

"Yes. Thank you," I say, fumbling for my wallet.

I give him a big tip. Being generous to surly people is perversely satisfying.

Getting out of the car, I gulp in deep breaths of Coney air. My little spot of seashore may not be the most beautiful—or cleanest—but its smell soothes me all the same.

The weight of Stinky's cage nearly pulls my arm from its socket as I slowly climb up to my apartment. I pause in the stairwell, listening. Then Stinky lets out a wail and, at the same time, Ramirez's door opens and my neighbor pops his head out.

"Where've you been, girl?" he wants to know.

"I told you. Manhattan. Hiding. Why, what's up?" I say, almost not wanting to know.

"Nothing. I was worried. That Oliver friend of yours called here looking for you, and that's the last I heard."

"He saved my ass."

Ramirez scowls. "What happened now?"

"Ned. The guy I went to the motel with. He was the one who broke into my place too. And then, somehow, followed me to my hideout in Manhattan." I relay the grim details.

His face bunches up like a fist. "You're gonna stop it now, right? You're gonna get back to your job at the museum and mind your business, right?"

"Exactly," I say, though I keep seeing Joe's big sweet horse face in the corner of my mind's eye. And I'm getting a strong urge to go to Belmont and check on him.

"Good," he says, squinting.

"Where's Elsie?" I ask, peering past Ramirez, expecting to see her there sitting in the kitchen.

"Still at the hospital. They're taking them breasts out."

"Surgery?"

"Yeah. And a lot of antibiotics. They got her on an IV."

"Oh shit, Ramirez, I'm so sorry."

He shrugs. "She's gonna get better now."

We talk a little more, until Stinky lets loose with a wail. I tell Ramirez to give Elsie my best and go across the hall.

I let the cats out of their cases and give them a snack. They both crouch before their bowls, ravenous from all the unusual activity. I watch them for a minute then go into the living room to stare at the blinking answering machine. Right now I'd like nothing more than to turn everything off. Leave my life. Leave the country. Go wander around Rome or Tangier. Instead, I hit the Play button.

"Ruby Murphy. Sebastian Ives here. I don't know where you been hidin' but I don't appreciate you not showing up yesterday and today. You're fired. But I could sure use you tomorrow. How 'bout givin' me a call." He goes on to leave me his home phone number.

I stare at the machine for a few moments. And then I dial.

"Where the hell you been?" Sebastian asks with more spark than I've ever heard out of him.

"Sorry. I got detained."

"Detained? What do you mean, detained?"

"I got hung up with something. I'm sorry."

"Your dialing finger's broken?" He's indignant. And he's right. I could have at least called, but my job wasn't foremost on my mind the past couple of mornings.

"I'm really sorry, Sebastian," I say softly.

"Apologize in person. At five. I'm gonna be shorthanded. Something came up with Ned, and Frank's off the map too. I need you."

"Okay," I say. To my own surprise, I'm actually pleased to be going back.

"Don't let me down." Sebastian, not one for pleasantries, hangs up in my ear.

I hold the receiver in my hand for a while before putting it down. I think about calling Oliver but don't want to bother him.

I go to the piano. Run through some scales. Handel. Bach. Sit loathing my useless weak fingers for several minutes. Then I just play. Next thing I know, it's nearly ten.

I make myself a protein drink, feed the cats, and then crawl into bed with *Anna Karenina*.

X

THREE-THIRTY A.M. comes about two breaths after I've put my head to the pillow. I slam down the alarm and slowly extract myself from the sheets. My apartment is cold and the night is still thick outside the windows. I stumble through the bare essentials of my morning routine.

I pull on a pair of loose black jeans, a red T-shirt, and an iridescent blue windbreaker. The cats marvel at the good fortune of being fed before they've even asked, both hesitating before sticking their faces into their bowls.

I shove cigarettes, keys, phone, and a few other items into my pockets and then head out the door.

There's just one deranged-looking teenager on the subway. As I sit down, he looks at me with huge black eyes. If I weren't so exhausted, I might worry that the kid looks like he's been up all night huffing glue and is in a murderous mood, but I'm too tired to care.

As the train pulls out of the station, I stare at the darkness and reflect that I'm in no shape for physical labor. However, the minute I let myself contemplate going back home to bed, I get a vivid image of Joe, soft bay ears pointed forward.

X

GAINES'S SHEDROW is quiet in the semidarkness. The horses have had breakfast and most of them are napping. I anxiously head to

Joe's stall. I find him with his nose buried in his bedding, getting at some oats he spilled out of his feed tub. He doesn't look up as I come in and stand at his side. I pat his neck. He's a little peeved at the interruption and puts his ears back some, letting me know this isn't a good moment to chat. I leave him to his business.

I find Sebastian leading Sunrunner out of her stall. I walk toward him, trying to look contrite.

"Morning, miss," he says.

"Hey, Sebastian. Sorry."

"Nice jacket," he comments.

I stare down at my $4.99 windbreaker. "Thanks," I say, half convinced he's being sarcastic.

"Bring this girl up to the training track," he says, indicating the filly. "Bishop's working her this morning," he adds, sounding reverent as he utters the name of Bishop Marlin, one of the most celebrated exercise riders on the backstretch.

It's very soothing to plunge right into work and have time to think of nothing but horseflesh.

As I lead Sunrunner out of the shedrow, she pricks her ears forward and whinnies fiercely at no one in particular.

"Come on, time to work," I tell her with a firm pat on the neck.

The filly has other plans, though. She freezes in her tracks and stares at a colt being led from the barn across the way. I tug at the lead shank again, to no effect.

"Whadya doin'?" a voice calls out behind me.

I turn around and see Sebastian frowning at me.

"Get a move on, you got three minutes to get that filly to the track," he says.

I tug at Sunrunner's shank and, thankfully, she decides to pay attention. We make our way up the wide, well-trod path to the training track. Ahead of us I see a woman I've come to think of as Grooming Mom, one of the few female grooms, a diminutive but tough-looking blonde who seems to go about most of her work with her small daughter strapped to her back. Right now she's leading a chestnut horse to the track, and the kid is there on her mother's back, looking around with interest.

As is Sunrunner. She's spooking at everything this morning, and as we near the track, she suddenly decides that the sight of the chestnut colt that Grooming Mom is leading is absolutely horrifying. Sunrunner leaps to one side, pulling me off balance so that I fall forward and get dragged on my stomach several feet. I'm so scared about losing the filly that I refuse to let go of the lead shank and barely notice all the crap I'm getting dragged over. As I wonder what I can do to make her stop, Sunrunner comes to an abrupt halt.

I look up and see Grooming Mom, standing there, holding her chestnut charge in one hand, Sunrunner in the other.

"Lose something down there?" she asks me, smirking.

I feel like a complete inept jerk as I stand up and brush off the front of my pants. Around us, grooms, hotwalkers, and trainers have all seen the little incident and are looking at me. At least I didn't let the filly get loose and hurt herself.

"Thanks," I say, taking Sunrunner's lead shank from Grooming Mom.

She's staring at me with manic blue eyes. She's quite pretty but there's a toughness about her, like she's packing a machine gun in her panties. "I'm Liz," she says. "And this is Georgeanne." She indicates the little girl on her back. The kid grins.

I'm surprised and sort of pleased that she's bothering to talk to me. Hotwalkers like me are the scum of the turf—with grooms definitely higher in the pecking order. Other than the various drool cases who hey baby me a few times each day, I generally don't seem to exist to most folks.

"I'm Ruby," I say.

"Nice to meet you. Stay on your feet," Liz advises, then tugs at the chestnut's lead shank and leads him away. Ahead, at the rail, I see Sebastian, who's driven up from the shedrow and is just emerging from his Buick.

"What was that all about?" I turn to find my fellow hotwalker, Macy, leading Cipullo's Honor, the promising colt Gaines is planning to try on the turf next week.

"Hi, Macy," I say flatly. "I hope Sebastian didn't see my little dance with the dirt."

"Nah, don't worry," Macy drawls.

Sebastian catches sight of us. "Come on, what are you two doing?" He waves us over.

Macy and I both lead our charges to the rail, where Sebastian, who's evidently stepping into Ned's assistant trainer shoes, is giving Bishop Marlin instructions about riding Sunrunner. As I stand holding the filly, Bishop Marlin favors me with a smile, then straps his crash helmet on, adjusts his chaps, and rests his foot in Sebastian's hands, accepting a leg up onto the filly's back.

I watch Bishop perch into the little saddle then lean forward on Sunrunner's neck, talking in her ear and patting her neck as he does so.

"He's telling her the secret of the world," Sebastian says to me.

"Yeah?"

"You know about him, right?"

"I heard he's the best," I say.

"That's why." Sebastian motions to Bishop, now on the track, briskly walking the filly the wrong way along the rail. As Bishop asks the filly for a trot, he starts singing "White Christmas" in her ear.

"Singing?"

"Singing," Sebastian concurs. "You heard the Go for Gin story?" he asks.

I shake my head. I dimly remember that a horse named Go For Gin won the Kentucky Derby in the nineties, but that's about it.

"Go for Gin won his Derby," Sebastian tells me, "seemed fine afterward, wasn't hurt, didn't bleed. But next time Zito tries taking him to the track to work, colt won't go. Just refuses to set foot on the track. Throws his regular rider. So they get him a different rider. Throws her too. Finally, Zito calls Bishop Marlin in. Bishop gets on the colt, starts singing and talking in his ear, colt goes right onto the track puts in a bullet work."

I nod and make appreciative noises as, ahead on the track, Sunrunner and Bishop pass the five-eighths pole and stretch out.

Less than a minute later they come by the finish line and Sebastian hits his stopwatch. "Fifty-eight and three," he mumbles. "Come on, miss," he adds, throwing me the filly's halter.

Bishop brings Sunrunner off the track and hands her to me. "Have a fine day," he urges me, tugging lightly on the brim of his helmet.

I thank him as I take the filly and pat her hot, veiny neck. Her eyes are big and half wild from exertion. As we make our way back to the barn, I talk to the filly, telling her more than she probably cares to know about my strange personal life. By the time I've cooled her out, she's grown mellow and sweet, periodically bumping her nose into my stomach, blowing snot onto my T-shirt.

I put Sunrunner away and I'm just thinking about sneaking off for a smoke when Sebastian sees me empty-handed and puts me to work grooming Antrim, a big nervous bay colt. This is the first time Sebastian has actually let me groom, and I suppose it means my stock is rising. Thinking about it gives me a moment of pride and I even start wondering if maybe I ought to quit my museum job and actually do this for a living. I could pack up the cats and move into the Belmont female dormitory. Though I guess I might not last very long.

This notion is confirmed when Antrim, who's apparently not too happy with my brushing his back, pivots his neck and nips me on the shoulder. It's only a halfhearted warning sort of nip but it hurts. I'm tempted to bite him back. Instead, I'm more careful about keeping clear of those teeth.

A few hours later, having rubbed half a dozen horses, cleaned tack, and done an astronomical amount of horse laundry, I'm drained, my head is pounding, and I want to go home and curl up in a fetal position on the floor. Instead, I head to Joe's stall to groom him.

The colt nickers softly as I come to stand at his side. He sniffs at my head, resting his fuzzy nose against my ear, then gently exploring my hair with his mouth, lightly nibbling but not using his teeth. I allow myself a few moments burying my nose in his neck and breathing in the warm smell of him. After a while he gets impatient and moves off to nuzzle at his bedding. I get to work currying him, finding the special spot on his withers that he seems to love having touched. I watch his eyelids droop shut and his lips twitch as I make tiny circles with the currycomb. I pause for a minute and pull the picture out of my pocket, comparing the bay horse in the picture to Joe, looking specifically at the shape of the blaze on the two horses' faces, both Joe and the picture horse. It's a match. Joe is the horse in the picture with Ariel.

My stomach churns a little.

I lean down and go over Joe's legs with a soft brush. After a few minutes of this I glance up and find Sebastian, leaning on Joe's stall guard, frowning down at me.

"You're not using a hard brush on his legs are you?" he asks.

"No, I'm not. Soft brush only." I indicate the plump brush that's the only thing—other than a rub rag—allowed to touch the horses' delicate legs.

"All right," he says. "Looks like Joe's good and clean. You can go home now."

"Oh?" I look over at him.

"You gonna be in tomorrow or what?" he asks.

"I'll be here," I tell him, meaning it.

I bid Sebastian and Macy good-bye, and then, rather than heading out to the train station, I skulk over to the deserted barn to hide out until nightfall, when I plan to sneak into Gaines's office. I'm not even sure exactly what I'll be looking for. Nor where I've gotten the sudden nerve for breaking and entering. But I'm extremely unsettled about the picture of Ariel with Joe and I've got to do something.

Of course, I don't know how far I'm gonna get with my little scheme. I've never tested my lockpicking abilities before. And they're pretty modest to begin with. I had a short-lived boyfriend, Johnny, a locksmith slash second story man, who showed me a few things, and for our four week anniversary gave me a beautiful set of picklocks. The affair ended a few days later and I never put the picks to use. But I held onto them.

I approach the empty barns, looking all around to make sure no one's spotted me. The various security guards who patrol the backstretch are just rent-a-cops but they seem like the type to get triggerhappy over a hotwalker wandering where she's not wanted.

I walk into one of the deserted stalls, check around for rats, and finding none, throw my windbreaker down on the hard dirt surface and sit. I'm afraid to light a cigarette, on the off chance someone might notice smoke wafting from the stall and send a fire crew over. Instead, I decide to do my yoga. Sort of a strange time and place to do it but it's probably the only thing that will calm and focus my mind before the insanity of breaking and entering.

Just as I strip down to my spaghetti-strapped undershirt, a pair of rats appear from a hole in the far wall of the stall. Brazen as hell. Their little muzzles twitching as they sniff me like I'm some overgrown piece of cheese. I stomp my foot to suggest they hang out elsewhere but they just stare at me. I try my best growling dog imitation. Which worries the little brown bastards enough to make them dart down through a hole in one of the walls. I'm not sure I trust them to stay down there, though. You always hear that those stories of rats attacking people are just urban folklore. They're not. At one point, right after I'd broken off with Tony—the drunken car service driver—I lived in a hovel in Tampa, right near a garbage

dump. I thought the rent was so cheap because of the fragrant proximity of garbage. As it turned out, it probably had more to do with
the proximity of rats. And these were no timid rats. They would not
only go through what few dry goods I had in the kitchen each
night, but one day, tired of eating my macaroni and cheese dinners,
one of them decided to crawl into bed with me and snack on the tip
of my nose. I moved after that.

When the rats fail to reappear after a few minutes, I decide it's
safe to start my practice. I get through my first five sun salutations
without interruption. My breathing grows deep and regular. My
head is throbbing slightly but not enough to stop me. That's the
thing with yoga—it's so addictive that once you've started your
practice, no matter what happens—pain, dizziness, loss of limb—
it's hard to stop.

By the time I get to my last pose, Kurmasana—tortoise pose—
I'm covered in a sheen of sweat despite the fact that it's not particularly hot out.

I finish up with twenty breaths in headstand, and then, folding
my legs into lotus, I lift my ass in the air and balance on my arms for
ten breaths. I disengage, shake out my limbs, and lie down to rest
for a few minutes, keeping one wary eye out for my furry
stablemates.

When my sweat has dried, I stand up and look around. The sun
has set. Foraging sounds emanate from the nearby barns. Horses
munching hay. Goats going as far as their tethers will allow, rooting
around for trash. In the distance I see grooms and hotwalkers, zipping around on bikes, drinking and riding, pretty much owning the
racetrack now, when all the others have left and it's just them, the
guards, and a whole lot of horses.

Oliver Emmerick

30 / Portable Souls

I'm lying on the futon, staring at the ceiling, and to tell the truth, I can't move. Earlier, a nurse, Simone, a lovely Haitian woman, came by to poke at me awhile. She was rubbing soothing unguent onto the raw skin near my tube when suddenly she looked right into my eyes and I saw that she knew—these tender ministrations would be her last. She was trying to make my body pass into the next world with some iota of comfort. Moments after this look of ours, I lost consciousness. When I came to, Simone was long gone. Isabelle was here, kneeling at the side of the futon, apparently talking to spirits the way she does. This is one of the things that made me fall in love with Isabelle when we first met. She was beautiful, intelligent, and a hypersensitive soul who felt the life force in all things and communicated with it. I didn't know which particular life force she was trying to speak with right then, probably what was left of mine. And that wasn't much.

I hadn't realized how close to the end I was as Ruby and I sat in Ariel's apartment. I'd been in intense pain and nauseous as hell but I thought I still had weeks in me. Then I got home and knew I'd never go outside again. It took me two hours to climb the stairs. Deedee found me that night, unconscious, and sent for Dr. Liguori and a whole team. No one had to tell me this was it. I knew. And then I passed out again.

I use all the will I've got to reach my hand over to Isabelle. I touch her hair.

"Hey, you're awake." She smiles, showing her pretty little teeth.

I nod slightly.

"There's a whole horde of babes here," Isabelle says. "You want to see them?"

I'm not sure that I do. But they've come. So I suppose I should. I nod again.

They traipse in from the kitchen, where I guess they were hanging out. Deedee and Kathleen and Rebecca. All ex-girlfriends. And all, I have to say, damn fine women. And Buddy. Not a woman. One of my closest friends. With his wife Jenny, another lovely whom I'd once thought about seducing until things with her and Buddy got serious. Actually, I still thought about seducing her. But I contained myself.

Ruby isn't here, though. Probably doesn't know.

"Bach," I say now.

"Bach?" Deedee has sprung to my side. "Which Bach?"

"D Minor Concerto," I tell her, and though there are, I think, two in D minor, I know she knows which one I mean.

The music comes on. Beautiful. I pass out.

The next thing I see is three women, draped across my futon. I can't breathe very well. I can't see all that well either, but these three are recognizable. The honey and mud of their hair. Their smell. I know each woman's smell very well. My sense of smell is still with me.

Isabelle has her head right next to mine.

"Ludwig," I say, and I see her spring up, knowing at once I mean the Seventh Symphony.

"Second movement?" I hear her say.

I manage to nod.

And then I go.

Rudy Murphy

31 / Murderous Whispers

I've put my shirt back on over my T-shirt and I'm sitting crouched in the abandoned stall, obsessing about smoking. I stick a piece of gum in my mouth and decide to turn the cell phone on—the one that I conveniently forgot to give back to Ariel—and call Jane. I might even tell her what I'm about to do. Just in case it all goes wrong and I end up in jail.

Jane and Harry's answering machine comes on, reciting the phone number I know so well.

"It's me. I guess you're otherwise engaged."

"Ruby," Jane's voice suddenly cuts in.

"You're there?"

"Yes." She sounds serious. "I've left you messages at home."

"Oh? What's up?"

"This isn't good."

"What?" I say, not liking the tone of her voice.

"Oliver," Jane says softly.

"What? He's worse?" My heart skips a few beats.

"Ruby, he's dead."

"What?"

"Your friend Kathleen called here. She's been trying to reach you all day. She finally called me, thinking I'd know how to find you. He died several hours ago."

"That's impossible," I say. "I saw him yesterday. He was doing *karate*. He was fine. He can't be dead."

"I'm sorry," Jane says. I can hear her crying.

A horse whinnies in the distance.

232

"Kathleen said three of his ex-girlfriends, herself included, were draped across his bed when he died."

I let out a sound distantly related to a laugh. My body is impossibly heavy. Tears start streaming down my face.

"Where are you?" Jane asks softly.

I'm not sure if she means it literally, but that's how I answer: "At the track."

"What? I thought that was all over with."

"I've got some things to do out here," I say in a flat voice. Because part of me has just died—and with it any reservations I might have had about what I'm about to do.

"Oh, Ruby," Jane sighs, "what are you getting into now?"

"I'm breaking into Arnold Gaines's office," I say, rushing on before she has time to say anything. "I'm not sure what I'll find. But something's very wrong."

I tell her about the photo of Ariel with Joe.

"Ruby, that's insane. Your friend has died. You're in no condition to do something like this. We'll come get you," she says.

"No, don't. I'm sorry. I have to do this. Especially now. It'll be okay. If someone catches me, I'll talk my way out of it."

"That's supposed to make me feel better?"

"I'll call you as soon as I'm done."

"Why don't you come over. You shouldn't be alone."

"Not right now. Later," I say.

"Promise?"

"Promise."

"Are you going to be okay?"

"Not really. I never thought Oliver would leave me."

"He didn't leave you, he died."

"That means he left more completely than anyone ever has."

Jane is quiet. Then: "I think you should just come over here now," she says softly.

"I can't. I've got to do this."

"And you *promise* you'll call me the moment you're done?"

"I promise."

X

IT'S A PROMISE that's hard to keep a few hours later when I suddenly find myself with a gun pointed at my head and a fair-haired sociopath whispering murderously in my ear.

"What do you think you're doing, Ruby?" Frank is saying, his mouth much closer to my ear than I am comfortable with. Though I'm surprised he knows my name, I can't say it's a great shock to find him wielding a weapon.

After leaving the deserted barn, I checked on Joe, found him in one piece, rubbed his nose, and made my way over to Gaines's office. I was just trying out my picklocks when Frank came up behind me, cupped his hand over my mouth, and nudged what was unmistakably a gun into the small of my back.

"Frank," I say, surprising myself by sounding almost calm in spite of what is clearly not a situation favorable to my well-being. "I'm not doing anything."

"You've done plenty. Too much, I'd say."

He turns me around so I'm face-to-face with him. And his gun.

"What were you gonna look for in there?" he says, indicating Gaines's office with his chin.

"I just don't want any horses dying," I say simply.

He stares at me hard, pale green eyes like ice water. Then: "Neither do I."

"Ned?" I venture.

"Ned?" He says.

"Is it him?"

"Him what?"

"Killing horses?"

He stares at me again. "We're going to take a little ride," he says,

ignoring my question. "Come," he adds, almost solicitously, indicating the office door.

He pulls a key from his pocket, opens the door, motions for me
to go in.

"Have a seat," he says.

I park myself in Gaines's office chair. Frank puts his gun down
on top of the desk, then starts furiously pulling drawers open, scavenging through various forms. I want to ask what the hell he's doing
but I keep my mouth shut. I stare at the green walls. Pictures of
horses. An equine anatomy chart. The desk strewn with condition
books, candy wrappers, and pencils. I feel curiously blank. I have
absolutely no control over anything, and in a weird way, it's a relief.

"You're going to help me," Frank says, pulling me out of my
reverie. I notice he's scribbling things onto a form, not looking at
me. "We're taking Raging Machete off the track," he says, still scribbling. "You'll help me get him in the van and you'll do exactly as I
say when we go through Security."

"Where are you taking him?" I ask.

"A place I know. I'm making a phone call now. Keep your mouth
shut," he says. He picks up a horse's leg bandage, drapes part of it over
the phone receiver, then punches in a number. He then launches into
something that might be humorous under different circumstances: a
pretty lousy job of impersonating Gaines's oil slick voice. He tells the
security office he's vanning a horse to the veterinary hospital for emergency surgery. Frank, his hotwalker, will be driving the van through
Security shortly, with a copy of the horse's papers.

Frank finishes the call and looks at me as he puts the phone
down. "Come on," he says, motioning for me to walk out of the
office ahead of him. He picks his gun back up off the desk almost
like an afterthought.

He locks the office behind him and indicates that I should walk
in front of him. I can't feel it, but I know he's got the gun at my

back. We start heading over to the eastern lot, where Gaines's horse van is parked.

It's a dark night, no moon, air thick with notions of rain. Frank keeps glancing around, nervous. We reach the vehicle, a blue six-horse van. Frank produces the keys from an immense ring in his pocket and opens the driver's side. He grunts at me to get in and move over. Quietly pulls the door shut and starts the engine. He stares ahead for a minute, like he's having some sort of inner monologue. Puts the van in drive. Slowly noses it out of the lot. A guard posted at the parking lot exit just waves us on, leaving the job of checking our business to the guards at the main gate who we'll have to pass in order to exit the track.

We park the van and Frank nudges me out. In silence we walk over to Joe's stall. A few of the other horses grow restless hearing us.

I find Joe dozing with his head just an inch over his water bucket, like he took a particularly exhausting pull of water and it put him right to sleep.

"Put his halter on," Frank says in his tight, low voice.

I walk in, talking softly to the colt, who blinks his eyes open and points his ears forward. I pat his neck and slip the halter on. Frank stands at the stall door, frowning, watching me as I lead Joe down the aisle and out to the van, where, without turning his back to me, Frank pulls the loading ramp out. I make a soft clicking sound in my throat and lead Joe into the truck's entrails. The colt loads without a fuss, probably figuring we're shipping him to another track to race.

Frank closes the back of the van and motions for me to come get in the cab.

"Where are we going, Frank?" I venture.

"It's best if you keep your mouth shut," he answers without looking at me.

I keep my mouth shut.

He drives the van to the security gate, hops out and hands some forms to the two guys in the little shed. The guards glance over the forms, then nod at Frank, apparently satisfied. Frank comes back to the van. His face is a blank mask.

I seem to be the furthest thing from his mind, just a sack of bones breathing here in the cab of the van.

I go deep inside myself, trying to dig a well to hide in. I find Oliver there. I picture his beautiful face and the way he looked the day we came here to the track together. So thin. His old suit pants barely staying up even though he'd punched new holes in his belt. The bones of his broad shoulders were poking out of his striped, button-down shirt. Our shoulders touched as we sat. The calmness of two souls understanding each other, sitting there on a spring day, playing the ponies.

I come out of my reverie when Frank veers the van off the highway and into a rest area. He parks, then slowly turns and looks at me. "We're going to handcuff you now," he says matter-of-factly.

I'm not sure who "we" is, but my heart is pounding so loudly I can't believe he doesn't hear it. He produces a set of handcuffs, reaches behind me, and roughly pulls my hands together. I feel him snap the cuffs on. Tight. I don't know where he got handcuffs. I suppose I don't want to speculate.

He pulls a horse bandage—maybe the same one he draped over the phone when impersonating Gaines—from one of his jacket pockets. He starts wrapping the bandage around the back of my head and over my eyes. I sit mute and limp.

I feel Frank steering the van back onto the highway. I sink into myself, into a black molasses of adrenaline and sweat. Time stands still. Then passes.

Eventually, the van slows and comes to a stop.

"I'm going to unload the horse," Frank says, speaking for the first time in a long while. "Don't move."

I hear him open the door and jump out. There's a chorus of

barking dogs and then Frank's voice threatens the animals in a harsh whisper. The dogs quiet down. I hear his footsteps on gravel. A door creaking open. Moments later there's noise from the back of the van and the sound of Joe's hooves going down the loading ramp.

Though I try not to, I keep getting an image of myself mutilated. Hog-tied in the back of the horse van. I try thinking of something else. Of Jane. Of Oliver. Minutes pass. Frank eventually pulls me out of the van and guides me forward.

There's a strong smell of manure. Then I feel a closeness. We're inside. Sounds of horses. Another creaking door.

He pulls the bandage off my face. I blink a number of times in what seems like impossible brightness, but after my eyes adjust a bit, it turns out to be very dim light. I am in a stall. With Joe. Who pricks his ears forward, looks at me with curiosity, and then gently nuzzles me.

We're in a small dank stable with a very low, cobwebbed ceiling. Five other box stalls contain natty-looking horses.

"Frank," I say as calmly as possible, "what's going on? Where are we?"

"Where no one will find you," Frank says. "Trust me, what I'm doing is in your best interest."

"Why?" I say, searching his hard face.

"Hello?" a deep voice calls out. A black man in a cowboy hat comes in through the low front door.

"Coleman, what are you doing here?" Frank asks, frowning.

"That's a fine-looking horse," the cowboy says, feasting his eyes on Joe and ignoring both the question and the situation. "How are you, little lady?" he asks, smiling at me, like it's the most normal thing in the world to find a strange woman with her hands cuffed behind her and a guy with a gun standing in a horse's stall.

"Isn't it a little early for you, Coleman?" Frank asks as the cowboy comes into the stall and pats Joe on the rump.

"You get to be my age, sleep don't last that long," Coleman says, "so I thought I'd come in and get an early start around here. What with the new guest and whatnot." He indicates Joe with his chin.

I start to feel hopeful because, although I don't know where the hell we are, the place is evidently the province of this Coleman fellow—and he doesn't seem like the kind to stand around watching a woman get murdered.

"How long you leaving this guy here?" Coleman asks, still looking at Joe.

"I don't know yet. And there's her too," Frank says, pointing at me, "but she won't cause any trouble."

"Ladies are trouble no matter which way you look at it," Coleman decrees. "No offense, miss," he adds, tipping his hat at me and smiling, revealing a row of big tobacco-stained teeth. He looks like any other cowboy you'd see. Worn-out cowboy hat, leather vest, tired blue jeans, and beat-up boots.

"I've got her restrained," Frank says, motioning at the handcuffs behind my back.

"Aw, she don't look like she'd do no harm, why you got her cuffed, Frank?"

"It's better this way," he tells Coleman. "I've got something for you," he adds, reaching into the pocket of his jacket. He forages around and fails to find what he's looking for. "Where is it?" he says to no one in particular, patting himself down all over.

"What's that, Frank?" Coleman asks politely, though he really doesn't seem to care.

"My organizer," Frank says, looking around, leveling his gaze at me. "You take it out of my pocket?"

"No." I shrug. "How could I?" I raise my handcuffed hands.

"Where the fuck is it?" he spits through clenched teeth, alarming Joe by getting down on all fours and searching through the stall bedding. To no avail.

As Joe and Coleman and I look on with matching baffled expressions, Frank storms out—presumably to search the van. Moments later he's back. And not happy.

"I must have set it down in the tack room. At the track," he says, looking daggers at me, like I made him do this.

I say nothing. Frank turns and goes over to talk to Coleman.

"Well," I hear Coleman say, "you do what you gotta do, Frank. I got horses to look after."

The cowboy shuffles off down the aisle, bangs some buckets around, and goes outside. I hear horses whinnying in an adjacent barn. Joe pricks his ears forward with interest.

Frank's looking at me with poison in his eyes: "I've got to go back and get my organizer. I'm leaving you here. Don't try pulling any stunts with Coleman. I'm making it worth his while to make sure you stay where you belong."

I just look at him, then watch him walk out through the low barn door.

I slump against the stall wall and breathe and try to think.

Joe comes over and starts grooming my head, getting a little rough, taking a nip at the back of my skull. I let him.

As Joe loses interest in my head, I look around at the other horses in the barn. They all have shaggy coats, round bellies, and skinny necks. They're what you'd call backyard horses—only they don't have a yard. They're all four standing with their heads poking over the tops of their stall guards, looking at the barn door and waiting for Coleman to come back and feed them breakfast.

Eventually, the cowboy appears, clanging buckets and coughing.

"You need some help?" I call out to him.

Coleman just chuckles. "Your friend Frank told me you'd be trying some clever tricks to get me to take your cuffs off."

"It's not a trick. I was just asking if you needed help."

"That's mighty nice of you, miss, but I been doing this forty-seven years, I don't think one more morning's gonna break me."

"These all your horses or you boarding some for people?" I probe, trying to keep things alive between us.

Coleman moves his hat back on his head and scratches at his hairline. "The bay mare and the chestnut are mine. The gray's a boarder. And the other bay. Got another six across the way there too." He motions outside.

"You own the land here?"

"Yeah. It's ours. Me and a few other cowboys. Grandfather land. The city can't take it from us," he says, then frowns, like he's already said too much, which I suppose he has since he's given me the important though startling information that we're within city limits. Must be Queens or maybe the far reaches of Brooklyn. Which is somehow immensely reassuring.

Coleman frowns. "Why don't you just be quiet in there now. I won't be but a half hour, then I'm going on home for a spell. You mind your own business, I mind mine, and everything's gonna be just fine."

I say nothing. But Joe pipes in, whinnying at the sound of Coleman rattling feed tubs. The colt starts pacing the stall, narrowly avoiding pinning me to the wall.

"Can you please feed this horse before he kills me?" I call out to Coleman, who's got his back to me as he dumps feed in the chestnut horse's stall.

"Frank didn't say nothing about feeding," the cowboy grumbles.

"It probably wasn't foremost on his mind. Please. Joe's hungry."

"Joe?"

"The colt."

"Oh yeah? I used to have an Appaloosa named Joe," Coleman reflects, turning back to look at Joe and me. "That is one hungry-looking horse," he concedes.

After a few more moments Coleman comes into the stall and unceremoniously dumps a scoop of grain onto the floor under Joe's water bucket. Joe, who's not accustomed to eating off the floor, actually pauses and looks confused for a minute before finally putting his nose to the ground and eating.

"Thank you," I tell the cowboy, who just grunts, then shuffles down the aisle and goes back outside.

I watch Joe eat, which makes me wonder if my cats have eaten. I've still got my phone in my pocket but I can't reach it with the handcuffs. I start picturing the cats, starving, scared. I obsess on this image. Maybe because it beats wondering what's gonna happen to me.

Before I've had time to go too far into my dark thoughts, Coleman returns and, ignoring me, starts halfheartedly raking the dank narrow aisle—though to what end I'm not sure, it's a hopeless murk down there.

I feel like a zoo animal as I stand looking over the top of the stall door, watching Coleman, who seems completely unfazed by this, like I really am just another animal, and not a particularly noteworthy one at that.

"So where do you ride around here?" I ask conversationally, figuring I ought to shoot some questions at him, try to make him warm to me.

He looks up from his raking. "Everywhere," he says.

"Oh yeah? Trails?"

"Trails?" He looks at me like I just fell out of the sky. "I guess you could call it that. You know. Over in the flatlands. Along Jamaica Bay some."

"Oh yeah?"

"Sunday, though, we ride to the projects."

"What do you mean?"

"I mean me and ten or fifteen of the others spend the whole of the day Sunday riding through the projects, so the kids in there can get a look at the horses."

"What others?"

"Other fellas from the Federation of Black Cowboys, what'd you think?"

"Oh," is all I say, but my mind starts racing. Sebastian is a member of the Federation of Black Cowboys. What does this mean? Sebastian is in with Frank and Coleman? What? My head starts spinning.

"You mighty curious," Coleman says now. "You thinking you gonna get out of that stall and ride away on Joe there and leave me in a pile of shit with Frank?"

"Oh no. Nothing like that." I smile.

"That's good, 'cause that ain't happening. I owe that man, and he's waited a long time to call in the favor."

"Oh yeah?"

"That ain't none of your business, nosy lady, now you just be quiet in there. I'll be out of here soon. You'll have the place to yourself awhile."

"You're going to leave me here like this?" I say imploringly.

"I'm gonna leave you here exactly like that, 'cause that's the way Frank wants you. He'll be back for you soon enough."

I look at Coleman, and whatever tiny blossom of hope I'd felt shrivels up and dies. Though he doesn't seem like the kind of guy who goes around doing a lot of favors for white male sociopaths, neither does he seem like someone who'd welsh on a promise.

"All right, miss, you and that horse be good now. Frank'll be back for you soon," Coleman says, then waves and walks out of the dank little barn, leaving me there, cold and damn scared.

Sebastian Ives

32 / Extra Heat

It's taken some serious dedication on my part, but I've finally got Asha giving me the time of day again. After our disastrous picnic, I couldn't find her anywhere. Then, this morning, she was riding a few for John Troxler so I saw my chance. I got the girl hotwalker, Ruby, to do a little extra work so I could take time to hang on the rail with Troxler, on the pretense of thanking him for Pedro's help the previous day. Of course, I was really putting myself where Asha couldn't ignore me when she hopped down off that crazy filly Troxler had her working. It was already ten-thirty, so I knew this had to be Asha's last mount of the morning. Sure enough, she handed the filly to the groom and came over to have a word with Troxler. She did a little double take when she saw me, nodded at me curtly, then talked with Troxler about the filly's problems. I pretended to be intensely interested in the conversation, and I think it made Troxler suspicious. He was probably wondering if I was spying for Arnie, trying to find out if we should claim the filly if ever Troxler ran her for a tag.

As soon as Asha finished talking with the trainer, I wished Troxler a good day and followed the lady down the way, calling after her.

She turned around but didn't look happy. "I'm in no mood for insults," she hissed like a beautiful tiger.

"You would be the last person in the world I'd ever insult, Asha. I think very highly of you."

"Then what was all that about yesterday? Huh?"

She was speaking very loudly and I don't like attracting attention, but hey, if I had to do it, it might as well be because a good-looking woman was yelling at me in public.

"Can we talk about this?" I asked in a calm voice.

"That's what we're doing, mister," she said, her voice still pitched pretty damn loud.

"Asha, please, can we go somewhere and speak privately?"

"Why? So you can shove me off you again? I've had enough of that."

"Please?" I said softly, trying to look handsome.

She pouted, then shrugged. "Okay."

I took her back to Gaines's office, offered her a seat, and laid it all on the line. I told her I liked her a lot but that she came on a little strong and it made me wonder if I was just one in a string of half a million innocent men.

And then I thought she was going to kill me.

She hissed and spat that I was accusing her of being a sex maniac when in fact she simply liked me.

After that I believed her and willingly put my head on her chopping block.

When I'd finished up work for the day, I drove right to her place in Floral Park—a cute little one bedroom above an electrolysis shop. I half expected to find her lounging naked on a bearskin rug, but I was off the mark. She was dressed in pretty velvet pants and a nice white top. She'd brushed her hair out so it was almost tame.

"Hi," she said, voice gentle, seeming nothing like the hissing firecat she'd been earlier.

She showed me in. Her place was a little cluttered but clean. Two large furry cats rubbed against my legs and I saw approval on Asha's face as I bent down to pet them.

Standing up, I looked around and complimented the apartment. "Who's that?" I said, pointing to an enormous photograph of a racehorse that hung above the fireplace.

"That's Xtra Heat, of course," Asha said, and I remembered her mentioning she'd worked the champion mare a few times down at Laurel Park, in Maryland.

"You remind me of her," I said then, not sure what I meant by it.

"Thank you." She gulped in the compliment, which could have been interpreted the wrong way since Xtra Heat, for all her heart and speed, wasn't the prettiest mare in the world.

We stood looking at each other for a while, then Asha made us some food. I'm not sure what it was exactly—no meat involved—but it tasted okay.

Afterward I helped her with the dishes, and for a moment I felt like we were an old married couple. It wasn't a bad feeling. When the dishes were done, Asha took my hand and led me to the couch. I could sense she was a little afraid to make a move, so I did the work. I pulled her underneath me and kissed her hair and her neck and her cheeks and her mouth. She purred.

Eventually, I got up from the couch, pulled Asha to her feet, and led her toward what I presumed was the bedroom.

It was a tiny room, mostly taken up by a big soft bed with lots of white bedding on it. We stood there, wedged between the bed and the wall, looking at each other. Again I tried to look handsome.

I started pulling her pretty shirt over her head. It got stuck in her mane and she laughed a little as she extracted herself from it. She wasn't wearing a bra and had a lovely little chest. It was startling, though, to see how white the skin of her breasts was. Nice, but startling. Pretty soon I was pulling her velvet pants down over her splendid hind end and at last I had those gorgeous muscular thighs under my hands. I kneaded them. This made her laugh a little, like maybe I was touching them like I would a sore horse.

She pushed me backward on the bed and removed every stitch of my clothing. She inspected me from head to toe, kissing her way south. I think she was liking what she found. Her body was moving in what seemed like sort of involuntary spasms, and pretty soon she'd put a condom on me and was climbing on top of me. Her thighs were wrapped around my hips. White on brown. It was very beautiful. I sighed.

We stayed in the bed a long time. Slept some. Woke up and made love again. At one point Asha got up and made us some toast with jam.

Around eleven at night I was feeling guilty over not having tended to Prince. Neil had fed him, but I was guessing my horse was mad at being in his stall all day. When I tentatively proposed driving out to the Hole, Asha literally jumped up and down with happiness, like all her life she'd been waiting to get up in the middle of the night and go driving to the end of Queens to see a horse. Like she didn't see enough horses as it was.

In no time we both had our clothes on and we were in my car, driving.

"We won't stay long," I told her. "I've gotta be back at the track at four-thirty."

"Sleep is overrated," Asha informed me, squeezing my thigh.

"Not at my age," I told her. She laughed.

We pulled into the Hole about twenty minutes later. It was a dark night with a lot of moisture in the air. I nosed the car down the dirt road and noticed lights on in Coleman's barn. I thought about going in to make sure everything was okay, but Coleman's a strange man and strange men keep strange hours. I figured he just had insomnia and was checking on those natty horses of his.

I parked a few feet away from the big manure pile, just in front of Neil's barn. Nunu let out a low growl at the strange smell of Asha, but I quickly reminded the rottweiler that she was A-okay. Nunu didn't seem that convinced but she let the lady pass unmolested.

Prince, hearing my voice, was practically kicking his stall door down, and as I turned on a light, I saw him shaking his head like some kind of half-wild stallion.

"Wow. He's glad to see you," Asha commented as she went right to Hanover's stall and let herself in. I saw her drape her arms around the huge horse's neck. Hanover didn't look unhappy about any of this.

"I think I'll put him in the paddock out back, let him stretch his legs a little," I said. "Neil probably thought I was gonna come by, so Prince probably hasn't been out of his stall."

I might as well have been talking to the sky, though, for all the attention Asha was paying.

I put my horse's halter on and led him out the back of the barn and down a little path to the small paddock. The moment I let go of his halter, Prince lay down on the ground and rolled, delighting in dirtying himself up. The horse had no dignity whatsoever; he kept rolling, kicking his legs up, squealing like a foal. I stood there, watching Prince carry on, thinking about the sweet redheaded woman inside the barn. My luck was definitely on an upswing.

Ruby Murphy

33 / Panic in a Haystack

The one thought that's kept me from completely losing it is that, for the first time, my yogic talents are going to pay off: I'm not actually handcuffed *to* anything, and I can probably jump through the cuffs.

As Joe finishes nuzzling at the now bald spot of dirt where his feed was, I bend forward to start warming up. I feel my hamstrings burn as I flatten my torso against my thighs and dig my chin into my shins. I slowly lift my arms up behind me, rotating them over my head as I do almost every day at the beginning of my yoga practice. I bring my arms to touch the ground. The handcuffs are actually an effective tool for keeping my hands joined the way they're supposed to be in a perfect rendition of Prasarita Padottanasana C. As I swing my arms back up and stand, I manage to spook Joe, who lets out two short snorts and looks at me with huge eyes. I start talking to him as I go through a few more standing poses, moving slowly so as to not spook him again. I work up a light sweat, then kneel, lower my butt to the ground and, stretching my arms as long as possible behind me, crunch my torso up and start scooting my ass backward through my arms. In a few seconds I have my hands back in front of me, where they belong. I stand up, then reach both arms over the top of the stall and feel for the door latch. Which is not within reach. I spook Joe again by jumping up and draping my torso over the top of the stall door. I lean forward and unlatch the handle. The door creaks open.

I shut it behind me then make my way to the front door of the barn and think for a moment. I don't imagine I'll get far through the wastelands of outer Brooklyn at dawn in handcuffs. I pull my phone out, feeling a bath of relief wash over me now that help is imminent. I try turning the phone on. Only it's not working. I push the On button several times to no avail.

Panic comes back.

I push the stable door open and look out into the weedy yard between barns. Two very serious pitbulls are chained to the stable yard fence. The beasts just stare at me, knowing that's all they've got to do to keep me rooted to my spot. One of them, a honey-colored dog with a deceptively sweet face, licks her chops at the sight of me. There's no growling. The dogs' bodies don't even tense up as they stare with hard marble eyes.

I look from the dogs to the road beyond the fence. The sky is starting to fill with light, wan bits of pink streaking through masses of gray. An airplane passes overhead, flying so low it seems like it's going to land right there on the little nameless road in front of the stable. The air smells of seawater, and there are gulls arching low in the sky, just below the airplane that now dips into the horizon.

I try calculating the exact length of the pitbulls' chains, wondering if I can make it to the opposite side of the yard and inside the other barn to look for an alternate escape route. Then there's a flood of headlights on the dirt road and I see a compact white car nose into view. It's probably Frank. In a borrowed car. Coming back to do what he's going to do to me. I retreat back inside the stable and look for a hiding place.

Just above Joe's stall is a small hayloft with two sickly bales of straw protruding over its edge. I shove a ladder against the edge of the loft and climb up clumsily, cuffed hands in front of me. Outside, I can hear a car door slamming, then the pitbulls growling a warning. I settle flat on my stomach, reach down and push the ladder away. This probably isn't a terribly effective hiding place and will just further infuriate Frank when he finds me. But I refuse to be a sitting duck.

I hear the dogs growling out there. There's an ominous thudding sound followed by silence.

Another plane passes overhead.

Dawn filters in through holes in the stable walls and roof.

After a time, the barn door creaks open. I lie as still as possible, peering over the edge of the loft, working hard at repressing a sneeze. The bales of straw are practically pure dust and I've breathed in a lot of it.

I see someone enter the barn. He's wearing a wide-brimmed rain hat and has his head bowed down toward his chest. It's not Frank, though. Nor Coleman. This person is very slight and moves swiftly.

He peers in a few stalls then comes to stand in front of Joe's. He goes into the stall, takes hold of Joe's halter, and lifts the colt's upper lip to look at the identifying tattoo there. I can now see the person in profile and I see the scar. The long pink scar marking an otherwise flawless face.

Joe doesn't look too pleased with the way Ariel is manhandling him. The colt pins his ears back, shakes his head, and takes a nip at Ariel's sleeve. This doesn't go over well. Ariel hisses at the colt and, to my horror, whacks him on the side of the head. I feel sick. Ariel is now out of my line of sight but I hear her foraging, and a few seconds later she comes back into the stall, holding what looks like a heavy-duty extension cord. The thing is split down the middle and she's attached metal clips to its ends. I watch her approach Joe again. The colt pins his ears. Ariel roughly takes hold of his halter and talks to him, attempting a soothing whisper. She pulls Joe's head down and starts trying to stick one end of the extension cord into his nostril. Joe backs up. Undaunted, Ariel produces a twitch, a frightening gizmo that looks like a billyclub with a loop of thick chain at one end. She doesn't have much success putting the twitch on Joe's lip, though, and Joe is getting increasingly agitated. So, for that matter, is Ariel. I can't figure out what the hell she's trying to do but I know it's not in the horse's best interest. My heartbeat is coming so fast and loud I feel like Ariel is going to hear it. My hands are shaking. I try to calm myself, to think.

By now Ariel has managed to get the twitch on Joe's lip. She twists it fiercely so that if the colt jerks to either side, it'll hurt him. I watch her lift the colt's tail and insert one end of the extension cord in the horse's anus. With a wave of nausea, I realize she's going to plug the extension cord in and electrocute Joe. Easy to pass off as a heart attack.

There's a pitchfork just outside Joe's stall, and I get onto my knees and get ready to jump down, grab the pitchfork, and slam it over Ariel's head. Then several things happen at once. I jump down, landing very painfully on hands and knees, and at the same time I hear a crashing sound inside the stall.

I get to my feet in time to see Joe rear and then come down, smashing into Ariel, who lets out an inhuman scream and keels forward. The colt darts to the other side of the stall. I look in and see Ariel lying on the straw with a crescent-shaped gash in her forehead. Blood drips into her eyes as she stares at me.

I pick the pitchfork up. "Come out of there, Ariel," I say.

"You're dead," she hisses, her face a tight mask as she unsteadily gets to her feet.

"What are you doing? Why?" I ask her.

"I've had enough of this," she says evenly.

"Enough of what?" I stare at her, my mouth open.

"This is what my father left me," she says, indicating Joe, "this and twenty-six others."

"You own Joe?"

252 / MAGGIE ESTEP

"Who's Joe?"

"Joe. Raging Machete. Him." I motion at the colt with my chin.

"Yes. I own Joe, then, or most of him," she says, voice graveyard calm.

"And you're going to kill him?"

"Kill is a strong word," she says thoughtfully. For a moment she stares at me, dinner-plate eyes big and blue. Suddenly, she turns and reaches into a bag she has there in the straw. I bring the pitchfork down over the back of her head and there's a thudding sound. She collapses forward—but she's not out. I lift the pitchfork again and bring it down harder, spooking the poor horse, who rears again as Ariel lands face first in the straw.

"Joe, it's okay," I say to the colt numbly as I stare from my hands clasping the pitchfork to Ariel's prone form.

I want to touch her, feel for a pulse, but I can't. I can't do anything but stand there, whispering to soothe the horse. Time freezes.

Eventually, I hear someone screaming outside the barn. A few seconds later the barn door is torn open and, in a blur of movement and blasphemy, Coleman appears.

He's speaking gibberish and cradling one of the pitbulls in his arms. "How could you do this to Honey?" he says, coming toward me, his voice a low moan. He extends his arms, showing me the lifeless mass of honey-colored muscle, the head lolling unnaturally back.

I shake my own head and point at Ariel on the ground. "She must have done that. She's a terrible woman. She tried to kill Joe," I say, "and me."

"Both my dogs," Coleman says, oblivious. "Pokey too. He's lying out there." Coleman's voice is acid with pain, "My dogs," he says.

"I'm so sorry, Coleman." I force myself to look at the inert dog, who at that instant twitches.

Coleman twitches in response. Feels for the dog's pulse. "She's alive," he says triumphantly.

Illustrating just how alive she is, the dog lets out a small growl and stirs again. Coleman puts her down.

"Pokey!" he calls out, hopeful. He looks to the door, but he clearly doesn't want to leave the barely revived Honey.

"I'll go see," I say, and still holding the pitchfork between my bound hands, come out of the stall.

"Put that down," Coleman thunders.

I drop the makeshift weapon then go out to the yard, where I find a very much alive Pokey, leveling his murderous gaze at me. "He's alive too," I call back to Coleman.

I hear Coleman's choked cry of relief.

I go back into the barn. I'm numb. I've never even hit anybody, much less snuffed out a life. I come back to where Coleman is standing. Honey has gotten to her feet now and is busy truffling around Ariel's head, familiarizing herself with the scent of her would-be assassin. Who, as it happens, is also alive.

"The bitch has a pulse," Coleman says, disappointed. "Let's get her out of the horse's stall before she tries any more stupid shit."

It's hard with my hands bound, but while Coleman lifts her under the shoulders, I grab Ariel's feet, clad in elegant taupe sandals. We lay her body in the aisle. Coleman goes back into the stall to retrieve Ariel's bag and the gun she'd been reaching for when I beat her over the head with my pitchfork.

"Who is this female anyway?" Coleman asks, gingerly holding the gun.

"Ariel," I tell him, "your friend Frank's girlfriend. And one of Joe's owners."

"Huh?" Coleman blinks at me.

"She owns a big percentage of Joe. And some other horses. And I think Frank was supposed to off Joe—and maybe me too, but he didn't, so she was gonna do her own dirty work."

I am nauseated as I look down at Ariel's face, hating myself for having been duped by her.

"Apparently her father left her a string of horses," I explain. "She's got a few loose screws, so I guess she got into financial trouble and hired Frank to kill her own horse for the insurance."

Coleman frowns. "That's a big accusation you making, miss."

"He didn't do it, though. I think maybe he's killed some horses before but then he took up with this apprentice jockey, and I guess she was pressuring him to stop."

"Tiny blond woman?" Coleman interjects.

"Yeah, Molly. Why, you know her?"

"He brought her by here once."

"I think she talked him out of the horse killing. And then she got killed."

"Huh?" Coleman says again, looking at me like I'm truly insane.

"I think our friend here is an accomplished murderess." I point at Ariel's prone form.

"Yeah?" Coleman doesn't look convinced.

"Yeah," I tell him. Then I tell him all I know. And it doesn't make him happy.

"This lady is going to jail," he says evenly. "Ain't nobody gonna fuck with my dogs and not do time." He's evidently not fazed that she very possibly killed Little Molly and nearly killed Joe. And me. It's the attempt on his dogs that has him riled.

"We ought to let the dogs at her for what she did," Coleman adds. "Wake the bitch up and send her into the yard, let Pokey and Honey do their thing."

I say nothing. I tend to agree.

"I gotta call the cops," Coleman says now. "You got a phone?"

"Yeah, but it's not working."

"Then I'm leaving you here while I go across the way to use the phone."

"You think you might take these handcuffs off first?"

Coleman shrugs. "I don't have the key."

"What if Ariel wakes up?"

"Shoot her," Coleman says matter-of-factly, wedging her gun between my two bound hands.

"I need a smoke," I say as I stare at the weapon.

"You need what?" Coleman scowls.

"A smoke."

"I thought that's what you said," the cowboy grumbles. "No smoking in the barn."

"I'm having a nicotine fit."

"Builds character. Stay here. I'll be back." He walks off, Honey and Pokey at his heels. The dogs don't seem much the worse for the wear. They calmly go back to their posts near the gate, ignoring me now that Coleman's told them I'm okay.

I walk to the door and, wedging the gun under my arm, fish with my bound unihand for my pack of smokes. It takes some doing but I manage to extract one from the pack and light it, careful to exhale out into the yard. I glance around at my surroundings. I feel like I've walked into some remote corner of the Appalachians. To my left is a gargantuan manure pile. To my right, two trailers stacked on top of each other. Across the dirt road are a number of ramshackle constructions that look like chicken coops but are evidently stables. A tired purple school bus with the legend FEDERATION OF BLACK COWBOYS emblazoned on its side sits with its front end poking out of a driveway.

I stare up at a sky of uniform slate gray. A plane is flying low. I pull smoke deep into my lungs. And nearly jump out of my skin when someone comes up behind me and puts their hand on my shoulder.

The cigarette flies out of my mouth and I flip around, fumbling to get the gun from under my arm and into my hands and aim it at Ariel. Only it's not Ariel. It's Ned.

"What the fuck?" is all that comes out of my mouth.

"Hi," he says, gently taking the gun from under my arm and pointing it down at the ground. "What's up?" he asks conversationally.

"Ned," I say numbly.

"Ruby," he says. "I guess that would be our horse assassin?" He motions toward Ariel.

"What are you doing here?" I say.

"Oh, nothing. Guess you're just doing my job for me," he says, reaching into his pocket. I shrink away from him, expecting him to whip out a can of mace.

"I think it's time for you to know who I am," he says, flipping open a little protective case revealing an ID card with a picture of Ned, or Special Agent Edward Burke, according to the FBI badge. "Hey," he says, noticing that my smoldering cigarette has fallen to the ground, "no smoking near the barn." He smiles.

"What the fuck is this?"

"I'm sorry." Ned shrugs, turning serious again, "I thought you were in on it."

"You're a cop?" I spit.

"FBI. I thought you knew that."

"How the hell would I know that?"

"I thought that's why you were avoiding me. Until I saw you at her apartment." He motions at Ariel again. "Then I couldn't afford to risk you blowing my cover. I'm sorry if I misled you. I feel badly."

"You mean all this time you were an FBI guy?"

"Since 1993, yes."

"What the hell were you doing at the racetrack?"

"Trying to catch horse assassins."

"But you know all about horses."

"Sure. What I told you was true. Started walking hots before school when I was a kid. Got out of high school and spent a summer at Belmont and Saratoga rubbing for Will Lott. Even got to be foreman. I could've been a lifer at the track. But then I ended up in the FBI."

"Jesus." I shake my head.

"You want to tell me what happened here?"

I don't really feel like *looking* at the guy, much less speaking to him, but of course I end up telling him all I know.

"We got her now," Ned says eventually. "Attempted murder, never mind contracting to have her horses killed. I imagine we're going to find she's responsible for Molly Pedersen's death as well. Murder and attempted murder."

"Attempted murder? Me?"

"Frank."

"Frank? When?"

"He showed up at the barn about an hour ago. She shot him. He's in ICU as we speak."

My jaw hangs open.

Ned reaches over and shuts it. I recoil. He looks wounded.

A cop car pulls up. Two uniformed black guys emerge from the cruiser. They're both exceptionally tall and have to struggle to get out of the car.

"You're the Ruby person?" asks Cop One, a light-skinned mustached man with a narrow face.

"Yeah," I say, wondering at the turn of phrase.

Coleman comes to stand next to me and indicates the barn door to the cops. "The female inside the barn there tried to murder my dogs, Eric. And this lady here. And her horse."

"He's not my horse," I clarify.

"Right. Tried to murder her own horse. She's in there." Coleman continues motioning at the barn door as Ned introduces himself to the officers. After a few exchanges they all go into the barn. I follow.

The cops both have to duck to get in.

"Oh yeah," Coleman says, casually indicating Ariel's supine form in the aisle. "Ruby hit her on the head with a pitchfork. You might need an ambulance."

Both cops stop in their tracks and look at me like I'm dangerous.

"Call the lieutenant," says Cop Two, the darker-skinned one, who has huge eyes that seem to be threatening to pop out of their sockets.

Cop One nods, then takes my elbow. "I need you to step outside with me, ma'am," he tells me.

I look over at Ned for help, but he's on his cell phone and paying no attention.

What had seemed surreal for the last fifteen or so minutes abruptly becomes reality.

"So this was self-defense?" Cop One asks.

"She was trying to electrocute the horse," I say, "and possibly me too."

"And what were you doing here? And whose horse is this, if it's not yours?"

"I already told you, it's her horse. She was trying to kill her own horse."

I can see from the look on the cop's face that he thinks I'm a total raving lunatic.

I go back, explaining the whole story from the beginning, slowly. By the time I get to the part where I smash Ariel over the head with the pitchfork, Ned comes to rescue me.

"It's okay," he tells the cop, "I've got a handle on this." The cop glowers as Ned/Edward takes my elbow and guides me away. He's gotten hold of some sort of handcuff skeleton key and he unlocks the cuffs. I rub my wrists.

Meanwhile, an ambulance has pulled up in front of the stable. Ned and I watch the cop direct the two paramedics—a stocky Latin woman and a chunky white guy—to Ariel.

A few moments later the Latin woman emerges. "Unconscious," she tells us, in case we hadn't noticed.

Cop One grunts. The Latin woman goes over to the ambulance and pulls out a stretcher and some gear. Soon, she and her partner are wheeling Ariel over to the ambulance.

After a quick tête-à-tête with his partner, Cop Two gets in the back of the ambulance, leaving Cop One behind.

The ambulance pulls out of the little yard, siren wailing away even though they're not likely to encounter traffic in the short journey to Baptist Medical Center. Driving fast and making noise are probably the lone pleasures of paramedic life.

Cop One turns to Coleman and starts interrogating him as Ned leads me a little ways down the muddy path in front of the stable.

"You okay?" he asks as we take seats on two overturned milk crates.

"No," I say, still not used to the idea of Ned's new identity.

"Do you hate me?"

"I don't know. I'm not thinking about it. My friend died."

"What do you mean?"

"My friend. Oliver. The one who disabled you at Ariel's place. He's dead. Yesterday morning. Cancer. I didn't get to say good-bye."

"Dead? But he just kicked my ass."

"He won't be kicking anyone's ass now."

Ned looks at me gravely. He reaches over to put an arm around my shoulder. I pull away. Then look at him. His eyes are the same bright green they were when we first got each other's clothes off. This gives me the creeps.

"Is the thought of me going to make you nervous forever?"

"I don't know."

We fall silent and watch a sleek dark car pull up. Two men in suits emerge. A short red-haired man and a tall gangly guy who looks like Lurch from the Addams Family. Ned introduces them as his FBI cronies.

"This is Agent Storace," Ned indicates the redheaded man, "and his partner, Agent Osterberg." Ned motions at Lurch, who nods.

"You're Ruby Murphy?" Agent Storace fastens his small brown eyes on me. He looks suspicious and leering at once.

I nod. He takes my elbow—evidently a preferred contact point for law enforcement officers—and steers me to the far side of the stable yard. Ned quickly follows, relaying a few key facts to his associates.

Once they've sucked me dry—and told me I'm going to have to go to the police precinct and give a statement—they turn their attention to Coleman and leave me standing there.

I take my phone out and punch the On switch. Nothing. I shake it. Nothing. I bang it against the edge of the stable yard fence. It comes to life.

I call Jane.

"You're out of your mind," she says when I finally let her get a word in. "I don't know how you could have gotten into something like this. This is it now, yes? You're going to calm down. Come over. We'll talk about Oliver."

"I'm not ready to talk."

"Then you'll come over and be silent."

"I have to go to the police station. Then go home. I'll call from home. It might be a while."

Jane doesn't sound terribly thrilled but eventually we hang up.

I call Ramirez and ask him to feed my cats. He's got a lot of questions for me but I cut him short, promising that a full explanation is forthcoming.

I stare at the manure pile. At a horse with his nose over his stall door. At Pokey and Honey, both standing guard again, excited by the goings on. I realize I'm hungry. Or at least, I think I am. I think that's what the unpleasant boiling sensation in my stomach is about.

More cops have arrived. Uniforms and homicide detectives. A pair of them fences off Coleman's stable with ominous yellow crime scene tape.

Eventually, Cop One comes and takes my elbow again. Puts me and Coleman in the back of his car. Ned comes to poke his head in the window and assure me this will be a brief adventure. I shrug.

Coleman and I sit in silence as we're driven to the cop shop.

Mark Baxter

34 / Movements of the Gods

I take a moment to stare up at the pockmarked drop ceiling of my room. I still fail to see gods there, though I sense they are hovering. Mind you, I am not schizophrenic. Lately, pop culture has made much of the alleged charms of schizophrenics. But I know the truth of this illness. My mother wanes in and out of it, as well as a multitude of other diseases carefully detailed in the *Diagnostic and Statistical Manual of Mental Disorders*, a copy of which I keep at my bedside. I myself do not hear the gods speaking to me. Though sometimes they move through my hands. And I'm certain most psychiatrists would consider my speaking to the spirit of JSB to be a strong indication that I'll follow in my lovely mother's footsteps. But they would be wrong.

"What are you looking at, Mark Baxter?"

"Oh," I say, turning my attention from the ceiling to the cellist, "not much."

"I've noticed this alarming predilection for ceiling gazing a number of times," Julia says.

"Congratulations, my dear."

"I suspect it's time to eat," she says, unfazed by sarcasm.

"You spend far too much time thinking of food. You will grow fat in your dotage."

"What a terrible thing to say. Most people tell me I'm too thin."

"No. You are not. You are fine."

"I'm fine?"

"Don't fish for compliments, it's an unpleasant tendency."

"In me?"

"In cellists."

This makes her blink. I've genuinely stumped her this time.

"Mark Baxter, it's possible that my attraction to you is waning," she says after a long pause.

Now it is she who has stumped me. Do I care? I might.

"All right then, let us go eat," I finally concede.

She sniffs a little then elegantly rises from the floor in one fluid motion. She is a slender lioness. Or maybe an antelope. Though frankly, I loathe animals.

As we amble to the bank of elevators, more than a few of our fellow students look at us. I'd like to think they're considering Julia fortunate to have gained access to me, but in truth they are probably wondering at her sanity and pitying her. But that is fine. People thought Glenn Gould—to whom some have compared me— unbearably eccentric. I begin to steer us toward the trusted hideous diner we frequented recently, but Julia is taking it upon herself to turn our luncheon into a major event. She insists we must go else-where. I've had little sleep in these last days and my resistance is low. I go along with her plan.

We end up at what appears to be a dismal hole in the wall. A man with large horrible earrings seats us at a tiny table and foists menus upon us.

"This is the best meal you'll have all week," Julia informs me. She's in a strange haughty mood now and I'm slightly frightened. Though I hadn't realized it, I do not want her to abhor me.

I order some sort of deranged braised tofu product that proves to be edible. I take care not to dwell on Julia's plate, which is smoth-ered in seaweed, a thing I have difficulty even looking at. Before my mother was put away, we went to the ocean several times. My mother loved water. She taught me to swim, and I wasn't opposed to this activity until seaweed became entangled in my hair. I have a

keen sense of smell, and long after my mother had carefully sham-
pooed me, I could still smell the lingering grotesque odor. I do not
like seaweed at all.

Julia is uncharacteristically quiet throughout the meal. Attempting to entertain her, I tell her an anecdote about young JSB, who, in
his quest to hear great musicians, undertook the long journey from
Luneburg, where he was living, to Hamburg, to hear the great
organist and scholar Reinken. After staying longer than planned,
Bach found himself with almost no money as he journeyed home.
He was quite starved and stood outside an inn, taking in great
breaths of the cooking smells emanating from that establishment.
As he stood, forlorn and hungry, someone threw two herring heads
out the window into the rubbish pile. As JSB proceeded to feast
upon the fish heads, he found a Danish ducat hidden in each head.
With these newfound riches, he was able to buy himself a fine meal
and travel several more times to Hamburg.

The anecdote earns a small smile from Julia. She then sighs
deeply and says, "Oh, Mark."

I'm not sure how to interpret this, so I ask for the check and pay
the bill.

We proceed back to Juilliard.

"You will come help me?" I say as we head to the elevators.

"I thought surely you'd be delighted if I left you alone," Julia says.

"No," I say simply.

She looks at her watch. A small delicate gold watch. She frowns.

"Please, Julia," I say, surprising myself.

"For a short while," she agrees.

I feel relief wash over me. Julia has, remarkably, helped my concentration immensely. With her curled on the dirty carpet of my
room, I am able to make the gods fly through my hands in an aston-
ishing way.

We return to my room, which, at Julia's insistence, I've taken to leaving unlocked. I am feeling lighthearted but anxious to get back to work as I throw open the door and find Wanda there, lying on top of the piano.

"Please get down, that is not a strong instrument," I say, alarmed.

Julia is standing in the doorway, looking confused.

"Hello, I'm Wanda," the vixen says, extending her hand in Julia's direction while remaining prone on the piano.

"Wanda, please, get down now," I say, trying to sound authoritative.

Wanda shoots me a hurt look. Julia continues to stand in the doorway with her mouth slightly open. Wanda slowly slinks off the piano. She is wearing a red dress and a strange yellow coat. Her hair is pulled on top of her head, with strands of it spilling down over her shoulders. She is wearing high-heeled sandals. She is a beautiful woman but I loathe her.

"Julia," I say, turning to the cellist, "this is Wanda. I'm not sure what she's doing here but she'll be leaving soon. Please don't be disturbed."

To her vast credit, although Julia clearly is disturbed, she nods slightly then walks into the room, removes her light jacket, and sits down cross-legged on the befouled carpet.

Wanda is very confused by this.

"I have work to do, Wanda," I say, relishing the opportunity to turn the tables on her.

Wanda is apparently at a loss.

I loved her once. But that emotion left abruptly the other night.

"I don't have time to be toyed with anymore," I tell her, surprising myself.

Wanda actually blushes. She looks on the verge of saying something, then suddenly walks to the door.

I follow her into the hall. "You were cruel to me," I tell her.

"I was just playing with you, Mark. I never thought you minded," she says, shimmying closer to me.

"I minded, Wanda. I told you I minded."

"Oh," she says, dejected.

"Well I don't care," she says petulantly.

"That's nice," I say.

She is perplexed.

"You should go now," I say gently.

"Apparently," she says, shooting a dirty look toward my practice room, "I can see now why you don't have time for me."

"The cellist is helping me work."

"I'm sure."

"I realize it's difficult for you to believe."

"Oh fuck you," she says then. She turns and walks down the hall. She has a lovely rear end.

I go back into my room. Julia is now curled into a ball on the floor.

"Are you okay?" I ask.

She looks up and smiles. "I'm fine. You'd better get to work. You have seventy-one hours before the competition."

I stare down at my watch. She's right.

I sit on the piano bench and am just clearing my mind when the phone chirps in my pocket. I hadn't realized I'd left it on. I hesitate. I do not recognize the number on the caller ID. It is probably Wanda. All the same, I risk it.

"Yes," I say into the phone.

"Mark, this is Ruby. I need to know when we can have another lesson. I can't wait a week."

"Oh?" I say, reflecting that the gods are certainly toying with me now. All three of my women in the space of but a few minutes. "I'm sorry, Ruby, but as I mentioned to you, I have a competition in three days. I'm afraid our lesson will have to wait. Besides, you can't possibly have practiced much in the space of two days."

The Wench launches into some crazy story that I'm at a loss to fully understand. It appears that her friend has died and she has been arrested. How exactly our lesson is meant to fit into all this, I'm not sure, but the fact remains I haven't the time for it now.

I humor Her Royal Stubby Fingeredness for several more minutes, and finally, after promising her a lesson four days hence, I bid her a good afternoon and turn the phone off.

Julia is still curled on the floor.

I look to the ceiling and then to the girl. I get up from the bench and then crouch down at Julia's side and stare at her. I touch her cheek.

She smiles.

Ruby Murphy

35 / The Bends

They've got me in one of those narrow interrogation rooms one sees depicted on TV. A desk. Two homicide detectives: a sinewy black woman and a nasty Dominican guy. They're not even pretending to understand how I got planted down in the middle of all this. And I'm getting more than a little worried. My stomach is churning and only the surrealness of it all keeps me from completely losing my mind.

It's getting grimmer and grimmer—until Ned appears.

"Our perp is regaining consciousness at the hospital," he tells the detectives. "I need this witness over there." He motions at me.

As I get up to follow Ned out of the wretched little room, the detectives look embittered over Ned snatching me from their jaws.

Out in the hall I see Coleman sitting on a bench. He seems exhausted and defeated. He looks at me with a hangdog expression. "Lady," he says, reaching to touch my arm, "you know, don't you, that I didn't know none of this about Frank, right?"

I shrug at him.

"What am I going to do with that horse of yours?" the cowboy asks, fanning his hands out in a helpless gesture.

"He's not my horse," I say regretfully. "I'm sure he'll get taken from Ariel and sold off. Seized by the government," I say, looking at Ned, who nods.

"Somebody gonna have to pay me a boarding fee, though," the cowboy grumbles.

"You'll be taken care of," Ned says in a clipped voice.

Coleman shoves his hands in his pockets and looks down at his feet.

I follow Ned outside to his car. He tells me to put my seat belt on. I do as I'm told.

"I didn't rescue you just because you needed rescuing," Ned tells me as he noses the car into traffic. "I'd like to see how our friend Miss DiCello responds to you. Sort of use you as bait."

He looks over at me for a second. "Of course, now you'll truly hate me."

"Not hate," I say. "What do you want me to do?"

"Nothing, really. Just stand there while I ask her some questions."

"That's it? Stand there?"

"That's it."

"I can do that," I tell him.

I sense he's got more to say, but he keeps it under his hat.

x

IT'S STRANGE to find the previously always poised Ariel DiCello in a pastel hospital gown. She is strapped down to her bed and a cop is standing guard nearby. There's a bandage over her forehead. She's propped up on a bunch of pillows, her hands folded into her lap, and she is staring at them as if they surprise her, like, while she was unconscious, a team of renegade surgeons cut off her own hands and put these in their place.

Ned pulls a chair up. I stand behind him.

"So. Miss DiCello. Can you tell me what happened?" Ned starts out, innocuously enough.

Ariel stares. Then, after a moment, puts a hand to the bandage on her head. Eventually, leveling her pale marble gaze at me: "You did this."

Both Ned and I look at her, expecting more. But that's it.

"She did what, Miss DiCello?"

"*She* brought it on." Ariel points at me accusatorily. "Another scar. From a horse." She pauses. Then: "*This* was a horse," she points at her existing scar, "threw me and stepped on me when I was nine. I nearly died. And of course, I was scarred for life," she says bitterly. "Now, because of you, it's happened all over again."

"You were trying to kill your own horse," I say, barely containing my rage.

"That doesn't matter," Ariel says, at which I hear Ned turn to ask the cop if she's been Mirandized. She has.

Evidence of this appears right on cue: A suave-looking guy in a pricey suit introduces himself as Ariel's lawyer. Asks for a few minutes alone with his client.

We oblige and go out into the hallway with it's Band-Aid-colored walls.

Ned confers with the cop. I sit down in an orange plastic chair attached to three others just like it. I have fallen into some sort of time hole reverie when Ned comes to sit in the chair next to mine.

"She's cracked," he says in a soft voice.

"What?" I say, snapping to.

"Ariel has cracked. Against her attorney's advice. Admitted pretty much everything we suspected."

"Little Molly."

"Right. Injected her with a lethal dose of methamphetamine."

"Because of what I told her?" I ask, feeling sick. "She hired me to confirm her suspicions about Frank and Molly and then she *killed* that poor woman."

"Basically, yes."

I stare at Ned.

"She met Frank when she hired him to electrocute one of her horses. A gray gelding. Horse was crazy and never lived up to his breeding. Ariel is apparently some sort of horticulture nut. Pumped pretty much all her assets into the development of some kind of flower."

"The hybrid orchid," I say numbly.

"Right. And she got into a financial hole. All she had left were these horses her father willed her. Evidently, she's got issues with horses in the first place. So she didn't have any qualms about hiring someone to whack a horse. She hired Frank. Then dated him. Then started losing it when he took up with Molly."

I just keep staring ahead. Stunned. Sick. Sad as hell.

"You okay?" Ned asks, tentative.

"No." I shake my head.

"Can I help?"

"No. Can I go home now?"

"Can I give you a ride?"

"I'd prefer if you didn't. I'll see about a car service," I say, standing to walk over to the nurse's station.

A stiff, gray-haired nurse directs me to a phone booth. I make the call.

Ned is still sitting there in the orange chair. His hair is hanging in unruly strands and his glasses are all the way at the tip of his nose.

"I'm gonna go," I tell him, motioning vaguely, feeling as weird as he looks.

He nods his head. "Right," he says. "I'll probably have to be in touch with you about things, you know." He looks up at me.

"Yeah." I stare at him for a long second, then turn and walk down the hall to the elevator. The elevator doors whoosh open and an orderly wheels an empty stretcher off. I want to hop on the stretcher and get wheeled into oblivion.

I push through the revolving door and find a small Sikh guy standing on the sidewalk, in front of a navy sedan. "Car service?" he queries.

I get in the car.

The driver turns around to look at me. "Why sad, lady?"

I shrug. This seems to trouble my driver. Who nonetheless turns back around and pulls ahead into traffic.

Eventually, he pulls onto Stillwell Avenue. I pay him. Get out. Walk into my building.

"Finally," a voice calls from the top of the stairs, and I crane my neck and find Elsie there, wagging a finger at me.

"Hey," I greet the small woman.

"You're alive?" She squints at me, almost seeming disappointed.

"I am," I confirm. "And you're out of the hospital."

"Yes," she says, indicating her chest, which looks considerably smaller. "You come in here." She motions me inside the bright yellow kitchen.

Ramirez is enthroned at the table, bedecked in his traditional wife beater and boxers. "What the hell you been doin', lady?" He scowls at me.

"Nothing," I say.

Elsie pulls a chair in next to Ramirez's, sits down and looks me over head to toe.

"Are you all right?" I ask Elsie, hoping to distract her from interrogating me.

"I'm gonna be okay. And I'm suing," she adds, delighted. "What I want to know is what the hell you been doin' with yourself," she says, making it clear I've got to give a thorough accounting.

I give her a thumbnail sketch of the last twelve hours, starting with Oliver. My two friends bow their heads in sadness. I tell them the rest of it too. The unbelievable rest of it.

Ramirez makes disgruntled clucking sounds in his throat. Elsie's eyes are big and full of wonder.

"So the blonde was crazy." Elsie seems thrilled. I think that, as a species, small, dark-haired women like Elsie and me are always happy to find confirmation that elegant willowy blondes are socio-pathic basket cases.

"The blonde was more than crazy, she was a murderer."

"She'll plead insanity," Elsie muses.

"I'm sure," I agree. "And she might not be lying. Listen, I've got to go look in on my cats," I tell my neighbors.

"You don't trust me?" Ramirez scowls.

"I trust that you fed them, yes," I counter.

"Baby, come back over in a while. You shouldn't be alone." Elsie touches my arm.

I try to smile at her, then retreat to my place, where both cats are planted at the door, indignant as hell at my prolonged absence. I immediately lie down on the floor and let them bump their heads against my hands and hair. I stay like this for a long time.

The phone rings. I let the machine get it, but when Jane's voice comes on, I pick up. I tell her the latest.

"Are you finished now?" she says, sounding angry.

"Finished what?"

"Attempting to change yourself by having life-threatening adven-tures?" Jane says, doing her best impression of a shrink.

"I didn't deliberately get into this mess, you know."

"You think you can erase everything by putting yourself in danger."

"I do?"

"Sure."

"What do I want to erase?"

"Well, Oliver's illness and now his death. Before that your heartbreak from Sam moving out. There's no eradicating those experiences. They mark you. You can't remove them."

"Are you done?" I ask her.

"Quite," she says.

Stinky chooses this moment to let out a wail of complaint, signaling I should get off the phone and pay attention to him.

"I've gotta tend to my cats."

"Come over later? We'll go to yoga? Four o'clock class?"

"I dunno," I say. "Maybe. Probably. Oh, hell, okay. I'll see you at three-thirty."

Jane coos her approval.

I hang up.

Eventually, I go to the piano and practice scales with a vengeance. It helps.

X

A FEW HOURS later, feeling better than I have any right to, I hoist my beloved 1980 Peugeot onto my shoulder and carry it down to the street, where I hop on and veer into the light traffic of Surf Avenue.

The bright morning has turned into a blistering afternoon. Within a few minutes I'm soaked in sweat, the salt of it getting in my eyes and half blinding me. Which I don't mind that much.

Forty-five minutes later I've picked Jane up outside her place and she's riding next to me on her clanky brown bike, jabbering away about the particulars of tortoise pose as if this were just an ordinary day. I'm grateful for this.

We chain our bikes outside the yoga studio on lower Broadway and then make our way to the end of the long line of aggressive go-getters, rabid in their desire to hurry up and *relax*.

Jane and I unfurl our mats side by side in the huge pink and green studio. The room slowly fills with all sorts of humans, mostly females with expensive haircuts, lovely pedicures, and delicate yoga togs. Ruth, the teacher, a lanky woman who favors strange pink unitards and huge, bordering-on-garish necklaces, comes in toting a harmonium. She sets this down, gazes out at the sea of students, greets a few by name, offers Jane and me a huge grin, then sits cross-legged behind the instrument, hits a low G, and intones a long vibrating chant of *Om* that gets taken up by the forty some people in the room.

We launch into our first series of sun salutations, followed by a completely merciless sequence of standing poses. As I balance on my left leg, right leg extended in front of me, Ruth, who doesn't know me well but seems to have an uncanny knack for peering into my soul, comes over and tilts her head like a curious puppy would.

"Are you okay?" she asks softly.

I shrug.

She looks worried for a moment then commands, "Leg higher," willing my extended leg up several inches.

An hour and a half later, as the lot of us take headstands and breathe twenty-five long breaths, Ruth comes over again. I see her upside down, her long feet and legs, the crazy unitard, the amber necklace, the calm, lovely oval face. She's peering down at me, as if contemplating some strange act of faith healing where maybe she'll reach into my chest cavity, extract my heart, massage it a little, then return it to its nest of arteries. But all she does is move my feet slightly forward, then gently pat each foot with her fingertips.

The class ends and Jane and I go to the packed changing room. We fight for a tiny corner in which to peel off our wet clothes and towel ourselves down. It's a veritable flesh mart in here, wall-to-wall naked women in all shapes and sizes.

We emerge from the yoga studio, get back on our bikes, and ride east to Jane's place, where Harry has threatened to cook for us.

Though a devout carnivore, twenty years of being married to a vegetarian has made Harry fairly adept at cranking out the bland nutritious cuisine his wife craves.

"Ruby, I'm sorry," Harry says as I come in the front door and set my backpack down. He puts one hand on my shoulder. I'm not sure how much more sympathy I can take. I ask what's for dinner. Then feign surprise and delight at his answer: yams and tofu.

Jane has busied herself hanging wet yoga clothes in the bathroom, putting unguent on her battered feet, and generally neglecting me, which reassures me. I might lose it completely if she went against character and actually paid attention to me.

Harry is in the kitchen, poking at the yams as I settle into the fur-covered couch and light a cigarette. The cats, Blossom and Stewart, come bump their heads against my legs as I blow smoke rings and think of nothing.

We eat our yams and tofu and I watch Jane feed tiny chunks of yam to Blossom. Harry and I both invoke Jane's wrath by lighting up after-dinner cigarettes, but by the time I stub mine out, Jane, exhibiting her incredible ability to fall asleep at the drop of a hat, has unceremoniously nodded out right there on the couch. I realize it's time to go.

I get up and put my backpack on.

"You're leaving?" Jane wakes up enough to notice.

"I am."

I kiss Harry on both cheeks and thank him for the feast. Jane walks me the short distance to the door, Stewart and Blossom weaving between her legs. I head down the stairs, turning back to wave at my friend. She urges me to ride safely. She looks worried.

I don't ride particularly safely. I take the Brooklyn Bridge back over and tear up the incline toward the bridge's apex, narrowly avoiding a collision with a tourist who's straggled into the bike lane to take photos of the nighttime skyline. I fly through downtown Brooklyn and on into Prospect Heights, past the park and onto

Ocean Parkway, where I ride like a maniac, reaching Surf Avenue a mere twenty-five minutes after leaving Jane's.

I hoist the Peugeot onto my shoulder and haul it inside. Ramirez's door is, thankfully, closed. I need silence and solitude right now.

I feed the cats, then put on my favorite Einsturzende Neubauten CD at full volume and lie on the floor for a very long time, feeling the wide wood planks of the floor vibrate and hum with the deranged beautiful music.

I go to bed around one A.M.

I sleep until noon. Feed the cats. Note that the answering machine is blinking fiercely. Decide against listening to messages. Sleep some more.

When I absolutely can't sleep anymore, I get up and sit at the piano. In my nightgown. I play. Until night comes.

Then, when the sky turns dark blue and all the lights of Coney turn on, I go outside.

It's a sweltering Friday night and Astroland is in full bloom. I weave between packs of people. Huge black women in tight, color-coordinated outfits balancing precariously on spike heels. Spanish girls with silky ponytails tapping rhythms down their backs. Sexy black boys with gold teeth leering into the neon night. I get ensnared in a human traffic jam and bump right into Rite of Spring Man. He stands there looking pleased, his boom box blaring out the second movement of Stravinsky's opus.

I nod at him. He grins. "God bless you, baby," he says.

I walk forward into the bright night that knows nothing of all the strange things that have happened to me. I start losing myself in the glowing anonymity of the place I call home.

I weave my way to the Eldorado Arcade and go to the change machine for five bucks worth of quarters. I plant myself in front of one of the Skee Ball shoots and start rolling the big wooden balls up the little metal ramp. For some reason, my body is particularly fluid and I'm consistently shooting balls into the fifty point slot, generating a long green snake of prize tickets. I start feeling pleased with myself, even letting myself pause to glance around and see if there are any kids looking on enviously. That's when I notice Ned, standing by the horse-racing game, catty-corner to my Skee Ball shoot.

My heart falls into my shoes and my legs go soft. I clutch hard at the big wooden ball I'm holding. Ned slowly takes his left hand out of his pocket and waves. A weird, shy-seeming wave just like Oliver's. For a minute I feel like I'm going to pass out. Ned takes one step toward me, then stops. A little girl bumps into him. I watch him mumble "Sorry" at her.

"What are you doing here, Ned, or Ed, or whoever the fuck you are?" I say.

He takes a few more steps toward me. "Sorry," he says.

"What are you doing here?" I repeat.

"I wanted to play Skee Ball." He puts his hands back into the pockets of his jeans. "I swear, I wasn't trying to find you, just thought . . . well, I just wanted to come out here."

One of the longest moments of my life comes, stays, and then passes. I hand Ned the wooden ball I'm holding. "Play, then," I say.

He takes it from me. Rolls it up the little metal ramp and right into the fifty-point slot. Two green tickets shoot out of the ticket dispenser.

"Can I buy you an ice cream?" Ned asks.

His glasses have fallen down to the edge of his nose.

"Sure," I say.

Ned Ward / Edward Burke

36 / The Mercy Seat

By now I've come to expect everything to go wrong. It doesn't come as a great shock when I get home and find my front door wide open and the kitten missing. When Lena the émigré failed to let herself into my place for a couple of days, I did away with the booby traps. And, apparently picking this up on her sociopathic radar, Lena has gone and done the deed. The kitten is gone. The door wide open. It's a miracle none of the neighbors have taken the occasion to rob me of what's in the place. All my paperwork has been gone through and the laptop is slightly askew on the desk, indicating Lena probably went through my files. The only thing missing, though, is my kitten. And I don't like people bringing innocent creatures into their personal affairs.

I look around, half expecting a ransom note, but I don't see one. I go back out down the hall and pound on Lena's door, but, of course, no response. I feel myself growing light-headed and have to lean against the wall for a minute and close my eyes. I'm standing like this, against the wall, eyes closed, panting slightly, when I hear something. I open my eyes and see Mrs. Small doddering toward me with her walker.

"Neddie," she squeaks, "everything okay?"

"Fine, Mrs. Small, thank you. I was just feeling light-headed."

"At your age? You should be out running marathons, Neddie." She wags a crooked old finger at me.

"You're right, Mrs. Small. I guess I'm not as strong as you." I smile down at her.

"Damn straight, Neddie," she says, and proving her mettle, quickens her pace as she shuffles down the hall to the elevator.

I return to my apartment and sit on the couch for a minute to breathe and get my head together. It's been the worst week of my life. What with meeting a girl I like but suspecting her of nefarious activities, having her run out on me within mere moments of physical intimacy, then thinking I was going to have to arrest the girl—who now can't stand the sight of me, and who can really blame her? Not to mention that my role in the Ariel DiCello investigation is over and I'll probably have to go on to some less than exciting assignment, and to be honest, I'm beginning to wonder if I shouldn't just hang up my bureau badge and work with horses.

And now, to add insult to injury, a Russian psycho has kidnapped my kitten.

This is what sends me over the edge.

I get my tools and walk down the hall and let myself into Lena's place.

In keeping with the disturbed slutty theme of her psyche, her apartment is bordello-like. Red satin sheets for curtains and two cheap chairs covered in fake leopard fur. It's so predictable I want to laugh, but I don't have much laughing inside me just now. There's no sign of the kitten or where Lena may have gone. I begin to panic, wondering if Lena's done something truly terrible to my kitten. Visions of bunny boiling à la *Fatal Attraction* float through my mind.

It's more than I can take. I return to my apartment for more tools and then go back again into Lena's, where, in spite of it being extremely illegal, I install a few strategically located bugging devices.

I spend the next twenty-four hours at home in the apartment, fielding calls from the bureau and waiting for activity inside Lena's place. Sadly, there isn't any. When it becomes clear that I'm going off the deep end, I pull myself together as best I can and take a long succession of subways to Coney Island.

When I arrive there at the tip of Brooklyn, I dial Ruby's number. Her answering machine picks up. I do not leave a message.

I go over to the beautiful old Cyclone rollercoaster and stare at it for a while. I don't think my body is up for the kind of beating a ride on it would give me, so I content myself with looking at the thing, listening to the chorus of screams rising up above each dip in the contraption's tracks. All around me, people seem purposeful and happy. I drift over toward one of the horse-racing games that involves rolling little plastic balls up a wooden surface and into various holes, this action sending a corresponding automated horse forward in its course along a platform ahead. I stare at this for a long while, reliving actual horse races in my mind's eye.

The game operator is a youngish guy who barks into a microphone, entreating the players to hold onto *his* balls until the bell rings. I watch the guy, imagining that anytime Ruby walks by, he probably entreats *her* to hold onto his balls. With this unpleasant thought clouding me, I walk on toward the Eldorado Arcade, where there are dozens of Skee Ball chutes. It's there that, at last, my luck seems to turn a little. I spot Ruby, resolutely playing Skee Ball.

She's intently focused on her game, feet planted hip distance apart, arm curled as she stares ahead, taking aim, then rolling the ball up and right into a fifty-point slot.

I look around to see if anyone else is watching her, but apparently not. I linger as she plays several games, obsessively pumping quarters into the thing. As I stand there, pondering what to do or say, Ruby suddenly stretches and looks around. She does an almost comical double take at the sight of me. I feel my heart skid to a halt. I offer a tentative smile. She's asking what I'm doing here. She clearly thinks I'm stalking her. I can't blame her.

I speak to her softly. Trying not to look like a buffoon as I gaze at her and feel warm things.

She lets me play, handing me a ball. A moment later I ask if I can buy her an ice cream, and after a few seconds' hesitation, she agrees.

We walk in silence to Denny's Soft Serve on Surf Avenue. Ruby deliberates a long while over the flavors, then settles on pistachio. I try not to be lewd as I watch her lick the stuff, her tongue a violent pink against the green of the ice cream.

"Aren't you getting one?" she asks me in a friendly tone.

"Nah, don't have the stomach for it right now."

Ruby shrugs. We walk slowly down the avenue.

I want to tell Ruby about the kitten but it's too complicated. Instead, I pick the innocuous subject of Xtra Heat, the great racing mare that everyone—and women in particular—loves. Her owners bought her for five thousand dollars. A plain bay filly barely bigger than a pony. Nonspectacular breeding and really not that much to recommend her. Until they raced her. She proceeded to win race after race. They put her in bigger and bigger stakes races. Against champion fillies. Against world-class colts that were practically twice her size. And she won. Running mostly on heart. At last count, she had earned over two million dollars.

By the end of the Xtra Heat conversation, Ruby is finally animated. She insists that we ride the Cyclone. What can I do? I agree.

After our third ride on the damn thing, I realize I'm going to rethink my previously negative stance on chiropractors. I tell Ruby this. She actually laughs, showing me her pretty, even teeth.

I walk Ruby to her door. I don't try to kiss or touch her or ask anything of her. Thankfully, she offers.

I go upstairs with her. Her neighbor—a Spanish guy who's got his front door open—is sitting at his kitchen table, shameless in his boxers and a stained white undershirt. The guy gives me the once-over, asks Ruby if everything is all right. She tells him that everything is fine. The two exchange a few more words and then Ruby and I go into her apartment.

She's cleaned up since my escapade of searching through her

stuff, and I so strongly wish I hadn't had to do it, hadn't seen the private things of a woman I really like. Not that I found some vast reserve of sex toys or incriminating photos, but I saw her little home without her in it. I violated a woman I like.

I sit on the couch as Ruby goes into the kitchen to do something with her cats. Eventually, she finishes up with the animals and comes to stand a few inches in front of me. It almost looks like she's going to hit me. I wouldn't mind. Not that I'm some S&M guy, just that it might break the ice. She doesn't hit me, though. Instead, she laces her hands around my neck and pulls my face to hers. She kisses me violently. Biting my lips. Drawing blood.

She pulls me into the bedroom and ferociously tears at my clothes. She's angry. She pushes me back on the bed.

She strips down to her white T-shirt and red panties. She puts her hand down the front of her panties. I feel certain I am going to die of lust.

"Come here, please," I say, reaching for her. She shakes her head no and stands there, touching herself, staring at me in a distinctly unfriendly fashion.

I am naked, with a raging hard-on, at her mercy.

When she finally peels off her panties and climbs on top of me, it's the biggest relief I've ever experienced in my life.

I struggle to hold back but I can't. Like a pimply boy, I come in two seconds flat.

She laughs. I go down on her, but this makes her restless, she pushes me off. "Just wait a few minutes, then you can fuck me again," she says in a weird, harsh voice.

I shrug.

We lie side by side, still.

And then I tell her about the damn kitten.

She frowns as I tell the story. "Did you fuck her?" she asks unceremoniously.

"Nope."

"Then what the hell?"

"Exactly. The woman is nuts. And I want my fucking cat back."

"Well," Ruby says, mercifully taking my cock into her hand, "I don't know how I can help with that."

She puts her mouth on me.

I wake up in the middle of the night and, after staring around, remember I'm at Ruby's. Only she's not in the bed.

I get up, put my boxers on, and walk into the living room.

Ruby is sitting in front of her piano, apparently just staring at it.

I go up to her and ask if everything's okay.

She shrugs. "I don't know. I can't trust you, Ned/Ed."

This is a valid point.

"You can just call me Ned," I say.

She blinks.

I offer to leave. She says no, I can stay until morning.

She's not communicative when we wake up, and not wanting to push my luck, I kiss her on each cheek and leave without having coffee. She looks so sad as she sees me to the door.

A number of days pass. There's follow-up work on the DiCello case but it doesn't keep my mind off Ruby or my kitten.

Eventually, after calling in favors with a few detectives I know, I manage to find out that Lena is out at her aunt's place on Long Island. I show up unannounced, pound on the front door of the ugly little two-story house. Lena herself comes to the door, and seeing me, immediately retreats.

I pound and threaten and she finally relents and lets me in. She looks awful. Her face is puffy and she's wearing baggy sweatpants. Her hair hangs lank at her shoulders.

My kitten is asleep on the couch.

"This is all I wanted," I say, walking over to the couch, scooping up my kitten, and then heading right back to the door.

Lena says not a word. Which, I admit, piques my curiosity.

"What's the matter with you, Lena?" I ask, standing at the door, holding the purring ball of kitten.

"You do not care," she says limply.

"You kidnapped my fucking cat."

"That is all you care about."

"Damn straight," I say.

"I am going back to Russia. I am beautiful in Russia," she says.

And I'm sure she is.

I take the kitten back to my car, where I've got a little carrying case waiting. I inspect her, half expecting to find new trauma, but there isn't any. Her wounds have actually healed and she's in fine form. I put her in the case and place this on the passenger seat. I stop every few blocks to peer into the case and make sure the kitten is all right. She seems to be fine. About halfway home to Queens, I call Ruby, figuring she won't pick up but I'll leave a message.

I start talking into the machine.

"Yeah?" She surprises me by picking up.

"I got my kitten back," I tell her.

She laughs a little. "That's good, Ned, I'm glad."

"Can I take you to dinner?" I ask.

There's a long pause. And then she says yes.

Ruby Murphy

37 / Raging Machete

I wake up to the sound of rain drumming at the windows. For a second this soothes me, until I remember that today's the day of Oliver's memorial. I turn my head on the pillow, wanting to bury my face back in sleep. The cats are both there, though, staring at me, willing me out of bed.

I slowly sit up. My eyes are swollen the size of golf balls. I've cried more in the last ten days than in the collected thirty-three years of my life.

I swing my legs over the side of the bed and hobble into the bathroom to throw water on my face. I look like someone threw a Buick at my head.

I feed the cats, drink down my coffee, and read a dozen pages of *Anna Karenina*. I unroll my yoga mat and stand there uttering the Sanskrit prayer that claims I am bowing to the lotus feet of the jungle physician who eliminates delusions brought on by poisoned snakes. Why not?

I fold over into my first standing forward bend and then spring back into crocodile pose. The confusion is going around in my head, but eventually, as my body gets warmer, it wanes—or at least gets more evenly distributed throughout me.

An hour later, as I lay flat on my mat, breathing and drying, I feel better. Not completely restored, but better.

I find myself putting on a vibrant blue halter top, slinky blue pants, and a pair of tacky but sexy pink pumps. Oliver always liked me best at my sleaziest. I pull my mess of hair up in a knot on top of my head, licks of it spilling out and trailing down my neck. I stuff wallet, cigarettes, and hairbrush into my red tote bag then go to the door. I turn back and stare at my apartment. I let myself see Oliver again, as he was the last time he was here. Skinny but ebullient. Face lit up from within.

I turn around and go into the hall, pulling the door shut behind me. Just as I slip my key in the lock, I hear the phone ringing inside.

I go back in, stand listening to the machine informing callers that I'm out.

"Miss Murphy, this is Sebastian. You're needed."

This is startling enough to warrant picking up the phone. "Hello?"

"Ruby."

"Sebastian?"

"Absolutely."

"What's up?" My heartbeat accelerates.

There haven't been any drastic developments in the last week. Ariel is in a nut ward and will, as Elsie predicted, plead insanity. Probably serve time on a flight deck. Frank has recovered from what could have been a fatal gunshot wound. He's out on bail. Gaines and Sebastian are continuing on with their lives, as are the rest of the horses in their care. Except Joe, who is now officially government property and still at the Hole, awaiting transport to Versailles, Kentucky, where he's to stand at stud.

"You just gonna leave us hanging over here?" Sebastian chides. "We need you walking hots."

"But Sebastian, I was just . . . you know . . . I'm not a real hot-walker."

"You looked real to me."

"I liked it, Sebastian, but I can't get up that early in the morning. And I live a million miles away from the track."

Silence.

"Sebastian?"

"I liked having you around."

This just about floors me. I've seen Sebastian once since this whole mess came unraveled. And it's not like he made any great show of affection.

"The horses liked you," he amends.

"Sebastian, I'm honored that you've asked, but I don't think I can do it."

"But you'll think about it. Yes?"

"I'll do that."

"Have a nice day," he says, hanging up in my ear.

I put the phone down, stare at it a second, and then proceed back into the hall and out to the subway.

I get on the train and burrow deep into my thoughts.

I'm emotionally seesawing between thinking about Oliver and dwelling on Ned. Yesterday morning, as he was getting ready to leave my place, he got a phone call from the bureau. He's to go down to Tampa for yet another horse-racing investigation. He was somber as he told me this. And I had mixed feelings at hearing about it. I like the guy, but I have reservations. Maybe Tampa is the best place for him.

Moments after Ned left my place, Mark Baxter, who I hadn't been able to reach in days, finally called. He didn't sound happy.

"What's the matter, Mark?" I asked, not daring to inquire about the piano competition.

"I lost," he said gloomily.

"I'm so sorry," I said.

"They placed me *second*," he fumed.

"Second? That's hardly losing, Mark. What, weren't there like six hundred pianists in the competition?"

"Five hundred and sixty-three."

"And you were *second*?"

"It's just not good enough. It's the end of my career," he announced.

"Mark, even Secretariat was second once or twice. Doesn't take away from his greatness, though."

"I have no interest in historical facts about the equine species right now, Ruby."

"Okay, then give me a lesson."

"I must recover my strength first."

I sighed. I humored my eccentric teacher a while longer and then, having extracted a promise of a lesson sometime soon, I hung up and sat on the couch ruminating for a long time.

And I'm ruminating once more. So much so that in what feels like seconds, the subway is pulling into the Second Avenue stop.

When I was a kid, coming out at this subway stop was always an adventure. The neighborhood was unruly, mildly dangerous, and endlessly interesting. Now it's like Seattle down here, only not as pretty. Mean-spirited bankers and dot com moguls mingle with fashion victims and Ivy League artistes. Most of the poor Spanish and Jewish families are gone and a neighborhood I used to love has been homogenized beyond recognition.

I make my way down Eldridge Street, to the huge community center where the memorial is being held.

On the steps outside, packs of Oliver's friends are lingering. Carpenters, musicians, sculptors, and yoga people. And of course, droves of ex-girlfriends, each one sexier than the next. I go inside, up a wide marble staircase to the auditorium.

Bright flowers are strewn everywhere and Arvo Part's *Tabula Rasa* comes insistently throbbing from a portable CD player. Photos of Oliver have been tacked to the walls. Oliver in his band, baretorsoed and insane-looking. Oliver in a dance performance. Oliver smoking a cigarette. Oliver sitting in lotus.

I take a seat in the back. I'm not feeling social. I don't even know why I came.

I get up halfway through the service and leave.

I don't know how to say good-bye to my friend.

I walk, heading south on Allen Street and right on East Broadway, under the overpass leading to the Manhattan Bridge. A train thunders above, making the whole structure groan in metallic misery. The sound makes me feel like killing myself. Instead, I decide to call Jane. Of course, there's not a pay phone in sight and I've long since turned Ariel's cell phone over to the cops.

I find a pay phone on the corner of Market Street, but a Chinese guy is barking into it. I stand behind him, waiting. He turns around and levels a murderous gaze at me. He's kind of cute. I stare at his ass. He finally slams the phone down and storms away.

I put a quarter in and dial Jane. I get right to the point: "I feel like killing myself, do you mind if I come over?"

"Of course, come over, but weren't you at Oliver's memorial?"

"Yeah. But I didn't feel right. I left."

"Yes. That's why I stopped going to memorials years ago. Harry and I were going to take a ride, do you want to come?"

"Where to?"

"I don't know. You know Harry. He just wants to drive."

"I'll be there in ten minutes," I tell my friend.

I walk north, weaving through Chinatown and then up through the Lower East Side.

Harry and Jane are waiting on their stoop, just standing there, looking pleased to be alive. Harry immediately offers me a cigarette, which I accept and fire up as Jane makes disapproving sounds. We head up Avenue C to where Harry's blue Honda is parked.

"Where to, madame?" Harry asks when we've settled into the car. "Your choice," he says benevolently.

"Can we go see Joe? He's leaving tomorrow."

"Who's Joe?" Harry asks, baffled.

"The racehorse," Jane clarifies, "the one she saved. He's at the Hole."

"Ah . . . the Hole," Harry says dreamily. "I'm very curious about this place."

Harry grew up in East New York, on Dumont Avenue, which is in fact the very road leading into the cul-de-sac that is the Hole. But he never knew of the place's existence.

"It's hard to imagine I spent twenty years of my life a few blocks from it but never noticed this Hole." Harry shakes his head in disbelief. "Let's do it," he decrees, pulling the car into traffic.

He weaves the Honda through the streets of Alphabet City, over to the FDR and then onto the bridge, into Brooklyn.

On Atlantic Avenue, we pull over near an Arabic grocery store where Jane wants to buy strange Arabic candy. Jane is fanatical about candy. She doesn't even eat much herself but she always likes to have a few pieces in her pocket to dole out, like some sort of demented sweets fairy.

Harry and I sit and smoke as she pops into the store, emerging a few minutes later toting two brown paper bags stuffed with odd bonbons.

Jane feeds me strange candy as we drive deep into Brooklyn, through the grand decay of Crown Heights, on into bleak Brownsville, then through East New York, Harry's childhood stomping grounds. We ride past the building he once lived in, a little two-story brick now ramshackled and blaring ominous hip hop from its entrails. We drive to what Harry had always thought was the end of Dumont Avenue, where it forks into a huge garish housing project.

"Now go to your left, Dumont picks back up on the other side of the projects here," I tell Harry, who is disbelieving but follows my instructions.

Coming to the other side, we find the big dip in the road that leads down into the Hole. Junk cars and weeds share the swampy terrain with packs of wild dogs. Shooting off the sides of the central dirt road are the various stables, horse noses poking out of stall doors.

A rotund Puerto Rican lady riding an equally rotund chestnut mare lopes down the road just ahead of us as Harry noses the Honda in front of Coleman's stable.

Coleman himself is sitting there on an overturned milk crate, feeding raw meat to Honey and Pokey. The cowboy looks relaxed, completely at ease in his world, as he should be considering no charges were brought against him.

Coleman looks up, frowning at our car.

"Hey, Coleman," I say, sticking my head out the window.

"Well if it ain't Miss Troublemaker," Coleman says, slitting his eyes at me.

I introduce the cowboy to Harry and Jane. Coleman nods at them.

As I get out of the car, the pitbulls emit low threatening growls. "Shush up," Coleman says, turning the dogs mute.

"I came to say good-bye to Joe," I tell the cowboy.

"Get in there and throw some tack on him." Coleman motions toward the barn behind him.

"Tack? I'm not gonna ride him, Coleman."

"What you doin' here, then?"

"Saying good-bye to him."

"Ain't no better way to do that than have a little lope through the dunes," Coleman says. "I'll come with you. Gotta get Rusty out. Been in his stall two days."

I stare from Coleman to Harry's car, where he and Jane are still sitting, looking around them at the strange vision that is the Hole.

"What's the matter, girl?" Coleman asks me.

"What?"

"You gonna get on your horse or what?"

"I can't ride Joe," I say, a little dejected.

"Why not?"

"He's a racehorse."

"So what? You know how to ride, right?"

"A little. But not a racehorse."

"He's just a horse. Likes to go fast. Hang on tight and let him do his thing. You'll be fine," Coleman says, seeming irritated that I'd even think twice about it.

It probably isn't the wisest idea in the world, but it does appeal to me. Coleman suggests we put a halter on under Joe's bridle. That way Coleman can keep him on a lead rope and, essentially, pony us along on the ride, tugging Joe in if he tries to take off with me.

Eventually, my desire to get on the horse outweighs any notions of caution. I walk over to Harry's car. "You guys can get out and walk around, you know. Coleman put the pitbulls away," I tell them.

"We will, we will," Harry says, nodding slowly.

It's as if they're afraid to get out and walk around, afraid the whole thing will evaporate like a strange dream.

"I'm gonna go put some tack on Joe," I say, expecting protests from Jane, who is obsessively protective of me, but she just nods pleasantly.

"Can I borrow your shoes?" I ask, eyeing Jane's brown oxfords.

"What?" She frowns.

"I can't ride in these," I say, motioning down at my pink pumps.

"Oh," Jane says. She dutifully removes her shoes. I slip them on. They're a bit big but a vast improvement.

"Thanks," I say, handing her my pumps.

I go into the barn and find Coleman foraging through a dusty trunk. "I got an English saddle in here somewhere," he tells me.

I help him sort through the heap of ancient tack. Toxic clouds of dust and mold rise up and make me sneeze. We finally unearth a small jumping saddle buried under some moldy blankets. It's got a crusty girth still attached to it, and Coleman locates a bridle that will fit Joe.

I find Joe hanging his head out of his stall, ears pricked forward. He whinnies gently as I come in to stand at his side.

"And how is Your Equine Highness today?" I say, draping my arm over his muscular neck. He stands perfectly still, taking in the worship. I immediately feel better than I've felt in days.

I put a halter on the colt and lead him into the aisle. He hasn't been getting out much since moving into the Hole. Coleman hand-walks him every day and lets him trot around the small paddock out back but it's not like he's been putting in any serious workouts. He's visibly excited as I give him a perfunctory brushing then start putting the tack on. He doesn't even pin his ears back as I tighten the girth. The other horses look on with interest, sensing Joe's excitement, probably flabbergasted at this strange thoroughbred stablemate who's so anxious to go out and work.

Harry and Jane both make appreciative noises as I bring Joe out onto the dirt road in front of the barn and present the colt to my friends.

"He's beautiful." Jane's eyes milk over and she stands there, looking absurd in her green socks.

"That's the biggest horse I've ever seen," Harry decrees.

"He's a big guy," I concur, taking a moment to panic over the fact that I'm about to climb aboard a seventeen-hand stallion who assumes that anytime someone gets on his back, he's supposed to run as fast as his slender legs will take him.

"Ruby, is this a good idea?" Jane's face pinches with worry.

"Joe will take care of me," I tell her, though I'm not sure I believe it.

"She'll be fine, miss." Coleman beams a reassuring smile at Jane as he snaps a lead rope onto the halter I've left on under Joe's bridle.

I lengthen the ancient saddle's left stirrup, stick my foot in, and hoist myself onto the colt's back.

It's a long way up.

Joe points his ears forward and takes a few steps to the side as I settle into the saddle. I shorten the reins, gently taking his mouth into my hands. I look to my left and squeeze with my outside leg, asking Joe to walk forward and left. I feel his body tensing with anticipation as he takes a few quick steps.

Coleman steers Rusty to Joe's side and, keeping a short hold on the lead rope he's snapped to Joe's halter, takes us past the other stables, out toward the road we have to cross in order to get to a makeshift bridle path leading to the dunes.

In the distance, a horse, probably a mare, whinnies hotly. Joe pricks his ears and looks over in the direction of the call but remains calm. He settles in, arching his neck and focusing, playing with the bit a little.

We reach the busy road where cars whiz by at remarkable speeds. Joe looks surprised but not particularly frightened. I guess this is nothing compared to roaring racetrack crowds.

Coleman holds the colt's head closer to Rusty's neck now, effectively blocking most of Joe's view of the traffic.

We make it across the road then weave through sleepy backstreets, toward the dunes. Weeds, stunted trees, and trash line the path. To our right is an immense empty lot, to our left, bumpy barren land. Coleman loosens the lead rope and Joe takes big relaxed strides, looking around, intrigued, and probably expecting a racetrack to appear at any second.

"You're doing fine. Let's trot," Coleman tells me, asking his mount for a slow trot.

I feel Joe's muscles bunch up as he tucks his head in. We trot over a small hill. Just ahead is Jamaica Bay, deceptively pure looking. There's not a soul in sight and the afternoon sun is mirrored in the placid blue-gray water.

"Okay," Coleman says, "let's lope."

Rusty and Joe both transition into fluid canters. I take a stronger hold on Joe's mouth. The two horses are cantering side by side and I can feel Joe gathering himself, preparing for his job. He doesn't realize that I'm not going to ask him for a full gallop.

"Wanna race?" Coleman flashes a grin at me.

"No!" I say, but Coleman's got other plans. The cowboy makes a sound in his throat and unceremoniously shakes Rusty's reins. The little quarter horse gets excited, throws a buck, and picks up speed.

Joe points his ears forward with interest and then does what he was born to do: takes off with me.

"Hey!" I hear Coleman shout behind me.

"Joe!" I yell at the horse, to no avail. The tenuous hold I had on his mouth is history now. He's pinned his ears back and transformed himself into a running machine.

I grab hold of his mane and bunch my body up tightly in order to stay out of the way and not throw him off balance. I feel him stretch out, lower to the ground. I'm terrified but completely exhilarated.

The world whizzes by in an incomprehensible blur. I hear the music of hooves against hard sand. I melt myself into the colt, trying to become part of his immense body. I look ahead through slit eyes, attempting to see what's in front of us, but it's all fuzzy and the wind is making my eyes tear. Thankfully, Joe seems to know exactly what he's doing, knows where each foot is falling, and I have no choice but to trust the colt.

As my heartbeat pounds in my ears, keeping time with the sound of the colt's hooves, the fear suddenly leaves. Fear about Joe taking a wrong step and sending me flying out of the saddle. Fear about the rest of this day. Fear about whatever it is I've spent most of my life fearing. It's gone. Torn off me by the colt's blinding speed.

I'm not sure how many seconds or minutes go by. What we're doing defies time itself, but just when my whole body starts to ache with the effort of staying balanced, I feel Joe slow down, at first almost imperceptibly, then downshifting to a canter. I scramble to regain my seat as he falls into a brisk trot. We've reached the end of the beach. Just ahead, a bouquet of rocks juts up from the sand. Joe drops to a walk just short of the rocks. He's breathing heavily as he points his ears and looks ahead. I lean forward, resting my torso against his neck, breathing in the smell of his sweat.

"Thanks, Joe," I whisper to the colt. He flicks his ears.

We turn back toward the stable, looking for Coleman and Rusty. Ahead of us the sun is starting to fall out of the sky.

Gargantuan, the next Ruby Murphy mystery, will be published in April 2004.

Look for Maggie Estep's *The Love Dance of the Mechanical Animals,* a collection of essays that work together to further illustrate her edgy talent, her appealing voice, and her insightful take on the stranger aspects of life. Turn the page to find an early taste of what will be in bookstores in September 2003 from Three Rivers Press.

The Love Dance of the Mechanical Animals

Are We Sluts?

I've been on a lustful rampage lately, having my way with all sorts of unsuspecting individuals, and most of them are sick. I don't mean emotionally disturbed. They have the flu and now, predictably, I'm sick, too. I haven't even slept with most of these people, have just been having high school–like make-out sessions because ever since breaking up with my longest-term boyfriend to date, I've been psy-chically—and physically—flailing all over the place. I've got naked with one guy, then suddenly freaked out, threw all my clothes back on, and went running off into the blistering sunset. I actually had sex with another guy but then felt compelled to get up and leave the moment I'd gotten what I came for. For a few weeks, I did pause on Extremely Young Guy, even letting him spend the night once. But he was old school Dominican, and I kept imagining that one day, as we walked around arm in arm, we'd run into his mother—who's only five years my senior—and she would probably kill me. Because, although Extremely Young Guy is of age, I don't think the average Dominican mother has tremendous tolerance for chain-smoking white writer chicks corrupting their soft-skinned sons.

So Extremely Young Guy and I called it quits. And I moved on. To making out with sick people. The incredibly delightful Man with the Glass Eye, a guy who, as you probably guessed, has a glass eye and is intensely smart and sexy in a sort of demented gentleman way but who won't actually give me any because he knows I'm on the rampage and, in the immortal words of Bartleby the Scrivener, would *prefer not to* be another notch in my sociopathic belt of love. Though, finally, a few nights ago, weakened from a bout of flu, he did let me kiss him. And, evidently, I'm now playing hostess to his germs. Or maybe it was Wonder Boy, another contender, who's beautiful but tends to smoke an extraordinary amount of weed—which causes him to sigh a lot. Wonder Boy was sick, too. And no sooner had he managed to get unstoned enough to shove me forward on the bed and hike up my skirt than he started sneezing. All over my ass. We fucked and sneezed and sneezed and fucked.

Fucking and sneezing. This is all starting to make me feel like an episode of *Sex in the City*. Specifically the one where the ladies start wondering if they're A) Women in search of interesting relationships or B) Unmitigated sluts. I always refused to watch *Sex in the City*, because its author, Candace Bushnell, was the most favored of my former literary agent's authors, and this agent, if and when she returned my calls, would always tell me she was too busy to see about my foreign rights, she had to have dinner with Candace. I started holding Candace responsible for my lack of sales in France. And refused to watch *Sex in the City*. Then they snuck it into *The Sopranos* time slot—*The Sopranos* being the whole reason I got cable in the first place. And I found myself watching it, and, with mounting horror, relating to it. Particularly to the "Are We Sluts?" episode.

I don't know if the *Sex in the City* ladies figured out whether or not they're sluts, and I guess the verdict is still out on me. But at least I mean well. I really am fond of each and every person I swap germs with. I don't bring home people I hate. In fact, on some level, I even love them. Each and every one of them. And there are a lot of them right now. And they're making me sick.

Between the Man with the Glass Eye and Wonder Boy, I was probably already infected two times over but I didn't have any symptoms. Enter my gambling partner, Liz, and her two-year-old daughter, Georgeanne. We three get together biweekly and either go to the track or watch live racing on cable and call bets in to our OTB phone account. We're pretty serious about this stuff, and Liz and I are cultivating young Georgeanne's statistics abilities now so she'll be supporting us all with her winnings by age five. She can already say *long shot* quite well.

Both Liz and Georgeanne were recovering from the flu but I cavalierly told Liz that thanks to my diligent vegetarianism and daily yoga practice, I could doubtless withstand any germs she and her daughter might inadvertently spray my way. So the two of them bundled up and traipsed out to Brooklyn, where we three sat transfixed in front of my TV, rolling around on the floor, cheering on our horses, stuffing ourselves with the batch of cornbread I'd just cooked up, and coughing and sneezing. Or at least they were coughing and sneezing. I didn't start feeling sick 'til a few days later. I was with the Man with the Glass Eye. We were over in Chelsea seeing the artist Damien Hirst's latest show, which I liked because it features a great many garishly gorgeous medical tableaux and surgical tools. I love surgical tools. I'm obsessed by alterations to the human body. Probably because I have a bionic hip. I got into a fluke boating accident when I was a barbiturate-abusing adolescent. My hip joint was smashed to bits and they had to put in a metal hip. I sometimes set off airport metal detectors. I even have a little card certifying that I am not a terrorist but rather possess a fake, metal hip. In any case, I'm fascinated by medicine. And was immensely taken with the Damien Hirst show.

As the Man with the Glass Eye and I stood peering into one of the immense fish tanks filled with gynecological tools, I found myself so moved by the piece's combination of brilliance and stupidity that I leaned over to try kissing the Man with the Glass Eye for the second time. And sneezed in his face. Within a few hours, I was oozing snot, coughing, sneezing, and shaking with chills. I retreated back to Brooklyn, ingested juice, covered myself in seventy blankets, and have spent the last few days coughing like a late-stage consumption victim, hallucinating, and pondering the eternal question: Are we sluts?

Bad Day at the Beauty Salon

I was a twenty-year-old unemployed receptionist with dyed orange dreadlocks sprouting out of my skull. I needed a job, but first, I needed a haircut.

So I head for this beauty salon on Avenue B.

I'm gonna get a hairdo.

I'm gonna look just like those hot Spanish haircut models.

I'll be brown and bodacious, grow some seven-inch fingernails painted bitch red, and rake them down the chalkboard of the job market's soul.

So I go in the beauty salon.

A beautiful Puerto Rican girl in tight white spandex and a push-up bra sits me down and starts chopping my hair.

"Girlfriend," she says, "what the hell you got growing outta your head there, what is that? Hair implants? Yuck, you want me to touch that shit? Whadya got in there, *sandwiches?*"

I just say, "I'm sorry."

She starts snipping my carefully cultivated Johnny Lydon post-Pistols hairdo. My foul little dreadlocks are flying around all over the place, but I'm not looking in the mirror because I just don't want to know.

"So what's your name, anyway?" my stylist demands then.

"Uh, Maggie."

"Maggie? Well, that's an okay name, but my name is Suzy."

"Yeah, so?"

"Yeah, so it ain't just Suzy, S.U.Z.Y., I spell it S.U.Z.E.E.; the extra 'e' is for extra Suzee."

I nod emphatically.

Suzee tells me when she's not busy chopping hair, she works as an exotic dancer at night to support her boyfriend named Rocco. Suzee loves Rocco, she loves him so much she's got her eyes closed as she describes him: "6 foot 2, 193 pounds, and, girlfriend, his arms so big and long they wrap around me twice like I'm a little Suzee sandwich."

Little Suzee Sandwich is rapt, she blindly snips and clips at my poor punk head. She snips and clips and snips and clips, she pauses, and I look in the mirror: "Holy shit, I'm bald."

"Holy shit, baby, you're bald," Suzee says, finally opening her eyes.

All I've got left are little post-nuke clumps of orange fuzz. I'll never get a receptionist job now.

But Suzee waves her manicured finger in my face. "Don't you worry, baby, I'm gonna help get you a job at the dancing club."

"What?"

"Baby, let me tell you, the boys are gonna like a bald go-go dancer."

That said, Suzee whips out some clippers, shaves my head smooth, and assures me I will love getting naked for a living.

None of this sounds like my idea of a good time, but I'm broke and I'm bald, so I go home and get my best panties. Suzee lends me some five-inch pumps, paints my lips bright red, and gives me several shots of Jack Daniels to relax me.

Eight o'clock that night I take the stage.

I'm bald, I'm drunk, and by god, I'm naked.

Holy shit, I'm naked in a room full of strangers. This is not one of those recurring nightmares we all have about being butt naked in public. I am naked. I don't know these people. This really sucks.

A few guys feel sorry for me and risk getting their hands bitten off by sticking dollars in my garter belt. My disheveled pubic hairs stand at full attention, ready to poke the guys' eyes out if they get too close.

Then I notice a bald guy in the audience. I've got a new empathy for bald people; I figure maybe it works both ways, maybe this guy will stick ten bucks in my garter.

I saunter over.

I'm teetering around unrhythmically; I'm the surliest, unsexiest dancer that ever go-go'd across this hemisphere. The bald guy looks down into his beer; he'd much rather look at that than at my pubic mound that has now formed into one vicious spike so it looks like I've got a *unicorn* in my crotch.

I stand there weaving through the air.

The strobe light is illuminating my pubic unicorn. Madonna's song "Borderline" is pumping through the club's speaker system for the fifth time tonight: "Borderline borderline borderline. Love me till I just can't see."

And suddenly, I start to wonder: What does that mean anyway?

Love me till I just can't see.

What?

Screw me so much my eyes pop out, I go blind, end up walking down Second Avenue crazy, horny, naked, and blind? What?

There's a glitch in the tape and it starts to skip.

"Borderl . . . ooop . . . Borderl . . . ooop . . . Borderlin . . . ooop."

The Jack Daniels is catching up with me. I stumble and twist my ankle. My g-string rides between my buttcheeks, making me twitch with pain. My head starts spinning, my knees wobble, I go down on all fours and vomit. In the poor bald guy's lap.

I'm now butt naked on all fours. But before I have time to regain my composure, the strip club manager comes over, points his smarmy strip club manager finger at me.

"You're drunk, you can't dance, and you're fired."

I stand up.

"Oh yeah, well you stink like a sneaker, pal," I say, thrusting out my bottom lip.

I hobble off the stage, into the dressing room, and then, out of the club.

A few days later I run into Suzee on Avenue A. Turns out she got fired for getting me a job there in the first place. But she was completely undaunted; she dragged me up to a wig store on Fourteenth Street, bought me a brown shag wig, and then got us both telemarketing jobs on Wall Street.

And I never went to a beauty salon again.